Prentiss Ingraham

Land of Legendary Lore

Vol. 1

Prentiss Ingraham

Land of Legendary Lore
Vol. 1

ISBN/EAN: 9783337347468

Printed in Europe, USA, Canada, Australia, Japan

Cover: Foto ©Andreas Hilbeck / pixelio.de

More available books at **www.hansebooks.com**

Land of Legendary Lore

SKETCHES OF ROMANCE AND REALITY ON THE

EASTERN SHORE OF THE CHESAPEAKE

BY

PRENTISS INGRAHAM
::

ILLUSTRATED

THE GAZETTE PUBLISHING HOUSE,
EASTON, MARYLAND.
1898.

THE MOTIVE.

The "Poet Priest of the South," the Reverend Father Ryan, has beautifully and pathetically expressed the sentiment that

> "A land without ruins
> Is a land without memories,"

and the words find a chord to vibrate in the heart of each one who holds a love for one's country, his birth-place and the soil that rests lightly upon the ashes of his dead.

Go where one will, become what one may, remembrance wil turn longingly to the dead past, and

> "Be it ever so humble"

the heart treasures the recollections of home and with tenderest feelings recalls the "days of Auld Lang Syne."

In all this broad country of ours, its mountains, valleys and prairies, dotted with cities, villages and homes, there is no single spot more filled with memories of the earlier history of America than is the favored spot of which I write—this "LAND OF LEGENDARY LORE."

Settled afar back in American history, a century and a half before the United States sprung into existence as a nation, under the touch of the magic wand of Freedom, the country washed by the deep blue waters of the ever restless Chesapeake, the Eastern Shore of Maryland, once the favored dwelling place of the Indians, whose graves and war implements alone remain to mark the passing away of an aboriginal people, was the Mecca of early settlers, the haven of mariners from the wide world over, as well as the ideal haunt of buccaneers, and from them all, in the passing panorama of life, have sprung the legends, romance and reality of this story told of old times in Maryland.

From the ashes of the past has sprung up a Land of Promise, as it were, and Talbot, the Garden Spot of the Eastern Shore of Maryland, today inhabited by a hospitable, progressive people, will never forget its past as long as there are graves, legends and fireside tales to keep memory alive.

ACKNOWLEDGMENTS DUE.

In preparing a work of the kind now placed before the public, it has been my desire to make it as exact as possible, historically and biographically, yet I am fully aware that errors occur in its pages, and for all such I ask the generous consideration of the reader.

Fully conscious of my inability to get at all the facts, having to rely upon hearsay and tradition, as well as the freely given aid of others, I hereby acknowledge assistance willingly given me by records furnished, letters and data from the published sketches of Dr. Saml. A. Harrison, extracts from Scharp's History of Maryland, Jenning's History of Friends, Talbot County Court Records, Books of the Society of Friends, *Century Magazine*, *Lippincott's Magazine*, New York *Sun*, Baltimore *Sun*, Baltimore *American*, Washington (D. C.) *Star*, Easton *Gazette*, Easton *Star-Democrat*, Easton *Ledger*, and personally from Col. Oswald Tilghman, Mr. Robert B. Dixon, Mr. Wilson M. Tylor, Mr. S. Elliott Shannahan, Miss Clara Earle, Mr. Samuel Patchett, of Easton, Prof. C. W. Chancellor, M. D., of Baltimore, Mr. T. H. Sewall, of St. Michaels, Mr. Howard Mullikin of Baltimore and to one and all of whom I express my grateful appreciation.

PRENTISS INGRAHAM.

"Ah! what pleasant memories haunt me
As I gaze upon the sea,
All the old romantic legends,
All my dreams come back to me."

CHAPTER I.

THE WHITE-WINGED CANOE.

 ITH faces turned toward the past, we look upon a scene two and a-half centuries ago, the beginning of the incidents that planted the corner stone of civilization in the midst of savagery, and the rising of the Star of Empire, which was to shine upon a new world, lighting the retreat of one people to despair and death, and guiding another people to advancement and to power. Our eyes turned thus backward fall upon a *terra incognita*, a wholly unknown wilderness to those of our race; but then the abiding place of a mighty tribe of red men, the Indian Nation of the Nanticokes,* whose villages and hunting grounds occupied the beautiful peninsula formed by the Chesapeake Bay and the Atlantic Ocean; today known as an Eden Land—for such it has become under the magic wand of the white man.

Other landings of Europeans had been made years before upon the coast of the now United States, on the Gulf and Atlantic shores of Florida, in Virginia, in Delaware and in New England, and an occasional ship had sailed up the Chesapeake, but the canoes alone of the Indian had broken the blue waters now known as the Choptank, Avon and Miles Rivers, that wash the white sands of this Land of Legendary Lore of which I write, a land of traditions indeed, of beauty and of promise.

Upon the peninsula where the pretty town of Oxford now stands, looking backward through the mists of over two centuries, we picture there the village of a race in no way akin to us, save through the kinship of humanity.

The lodges of these people dotted the woodland, women and children were gathered about the primitive homes, warriors, in

---

[* The Nanticokes were a tribe of the Algonquian (Algonkin) Nation, and their tribal grounds were east of the Chesapeake. They are now extinct.

all the glory of barbarous war paint and trappings, stood on the shore, or skimmed over the waters in their light canoes.

It was a scene of wild life, the home of a savage people.

Suddenly, around a point of land, now known as Benoni's Point, came a large canoe, urged on by a dozen paddles and fairly flying over the waters. Its prow was turned toward the Indian village, and a white wall of foam parting on either side told with what speed the red crew were urging their frail craft.

At once a cry of alarm rang through the village, for a foe must surely be in pursuit of the canoe to cause it to come on as it did. Men, women and children flocked to the shore to know the cause. What could it be? Was there to be an attack on the village by another tribe?

There had been strange stories told of a people, whose skins were white, having come across the mighty waters and settled upon the land to the south and far to the north, but those on the Avon had not seen these pale faces. They had not yet learned to dread them, to find out that man's inhumanity to man dwelt in the white heart as in the red. They had only to fear foes of their own race, and these they could meet, as they often had before. They were yet to learn the bitter lesson that civilization advances into new lands with the Bible in one hand, and the sword in the other.

They were upon the threshold of a mighty discovery, the beginning of the end of their race.

Loud sounded the tom-toms in warning, for surely the large canoe must be pursued by many foes. Nearer and nearer it came and every eye was upon it, while the warriors of the village had armed for battle. Suddenly a cry arose, a wail as it were of alarm and horror commingled. A woman's lips had uttered it, and all eyes had turned upon her.

There she stood, both arms outstretched before her, and her hands pointing to the wooded shore that shut out from the village the sight of the majestic Chesapeake. All beheld now why her cry, why her outstretched, pointing hands.

Was it a low sweeping cloud, flying from behind the heavy woodland into view? In speechless amazement all gazed, and the reason was before them, why the large canoe was urged on so desperately in flight. They saw not the canoe now, for their eyes were upon the flying cloud. On it swept, over the land it seemed, until suddenly it shot out from behind the sandy point and cries broke from all lips as there appeared a large dark mass like a giant canoe, beneath the clouds of white that rose far above it.

Never before had such a sight been seen by those who stood awestruck gazing upon it. Full into view it came, flying along before a stiff ten knot breeze, holding its course as though to glide on up the Choptank, and sighs of relief fell from every lip to think that the strange, mystic thing of apparent life was not coming toward their village.

But afar off the sound of voices was heard, human forms were seen moving about, there were strange cries coming from the mysterious black and white cloud, and then the course was changed and it came rushing straight on toward the Indian village. There was no outcry now. All those untutored beings were too dazed for utterance. They could but stand and gaze in awed silence.

The canoe that had been flying from this strange cloud was now close to the landing and from it arose a cry of alarm followed by the words:

"Behold the Winged Canoe!"

Yes, it was a "winged canoe" of the pale faces, for the first time entering those unknown waters.

It was a beautiful brig, spreading canvas from deck to truck, speeding along into the waters of the Avon, and come upon a mission good or bad.

Was her coming to bring light to a people struggling in the darkness of barbarism, or were despair and death to follow in her wake? A short half hour told the story, for the sails were taken in one by one as the brig came on, and sweeping up into the wind when near the shore, a heavy plunge was heard as the anchor was let fall and the "winged canoe," stripped of her white wings, lay motionless upon the waters.

Then from her black sides burst flashes of red lightning, the roar of thunder such as the poor Indians had heard from the black storm clouds when the Great Spirit was angry, and through their village tore a hail of iron dealing death and destruction. The roar of the guns was the death-knell of the Nanticokes!

Such was the coming of the first vessel and its pale face crew into this beautiful Land of Legends.

CHAPTER II

F it is really true, for we have only tradition for it, that the Norsemen, those rugged sea kings of centuries past, ever visited the shores of North America eight hundred years ago, nothing tangible, nothing of good for the advance of progress, ever came of it; and though the great captain of captains, Columbus, never actually set foot upon the mainland of our country, his voyage and discovery of the islands of the West Indies was the opening wedge that began American history.

Amerigo Vespucci, by his latter discoveries, and ignoring Columbus, managed to give his name to this grand continent; and Cabot and other adventurers, rather than explorers, followed and thus begun the peopling of our shores with Europeans—their motive being solely to find gold.

What the treatment of those adventurers and their cruel followers was to the natives of the New World, those who came after deemed it the right course to pursue, and the Indians' extermination even then begun, has been religiously adhered to down to the present day, when they remain but a mere handful of the once mighty race that roamed from the Atlantic to the Pacific, from the frozen north to the shores of the Mexican Gulf.

The "Passing of the Indian" forms a unique but bitter story told in the settlement of our country, for, from the first, they seemed marked for doom.

A few more years and the passing of the red man of North America will have been completed ; the prairies, mountains and valleys where he buried the ashes of his dead will know him no more ; only the ruins of that race of Americans alone remaining, for the last remnant will have gone truly beyond the Land of the Setting Sun. It will be the irony of fate, indeed, that the real

American will have passed away forever, while the descendant of races of other lands far across the sea will occupy his country.

So went from the shores of the Chesapeake the mighty tribe of the Nanticokes whose villages, hunting grounds and graves of their fathers were here in our very midst.

Traces of these people who have gone, in their rude implements of war and home utensils, are yet to be found, while hardly a white man of today whose age is fourscore years and ten can point out a single Indian grave.

What a sad commentary this upon the so-called Christian land of America, that even the graves of a mighty people are unmarked and unknown!

Homes have been built, churches erected ; school-houses dot the land ; villages and towns where walk the busy throngs are everywhere, perhaps, and beyond doubt, occupying the very sites of Indian burying-grounds, and still no one of us can point to the last resting place of a Nanticoke, a Delaware or those who lived, loved and went to rest on the shores of the Chesapeake only a century ago.

As the white invaders swept up the Chesapeake Bay in their mighty "winged canoe," dropped anchor in the depths of the Choptank and turned their iron guns upon the peaceful hamlet where the thriving town of Oxford now stands, so has the mailed hand of the conqueror since fallen, in his greed for a new world and the yellow metal for which men risk life to gain possession.

Coming in a vessel of war, if a lawless one, against a people who had no flag to protect them, the armed invaders beat back from their onward path those whose superstitious fears and teachings led them to look upon the white men as warriors from another world, or as braves sent by the Great Spirit to drive them into the Happy Hunting Grounds.

Was it a wonder that these untutored savages looked upon the palefaces as foes to the death, and, after their first superstitious dread was over, finding them flesh and blood, sought to protect their homes and their kindred ?

Was it a wonder that, beaten back into the forests, they sought new homes ? Still hounded by their white enemies, they could not believe in the claimed friendly intention of those who came with a sword in one hand, a torch in the other, to kill and to burn.

They were born warriors; but they could not successfully resist the iron heel and mailed hand of oppression with only their crude weapons of warfare.

And so, back from the shores of the majestic Choptank, the beautiful Avon and picturesque Wye now a garden spot of loveliness, passed the red race before the march of the white; it being the same old story here in our midst, as it was else where, that the Star of Empire, though rising from a red and deadly horizon, must guide onward and upward in the advance of civilization.

With the passing away of a mighty race from this favored land there came hither to find new homes and associations those whom we call our ancestors, and the tales told of early days in Talbot cannot but be of interest to many of her citizens here, as well as to those who have gone far away who cling to this country as their Fatherland.

CHAPTER III.

 WO centuries and a-half ago there was civilization in Talbot and its environs only *in embryo*. Towns and villages were not dreamed of; those who came here then were intent upon finding gold in this New World, for the yellow metal was then as now an idol and had its abject worshippers. When the newcomers did not find this country of the Chesapeake a gold field, but instead, a land of milk and honey, of fair promise for getting riches, many of them were content to settle here and begin the good work of rescuing from the Indians, as well as building out of a wilderness, the beautiful surroundings we now call home and of which we are so proud.

The natural cruelties of the Indian, and to which they were trained from infancy, were more than matched by the barbarianism of the English settlers who, in their early days, knew only war, prosecuted along any lines to end in favor of the Englishman.

Going back to the seventeenth century, it is very true that along our coastlands the Indian had his innings most of the time, after he had learned the ways of the settlers, but there was more or less drifting this way of other comers to the New World who thus gained a firm footing, which no human red tidal wave could wash loose to be swept back across the Atlantic.

In this generation of the practical, even in poetry and fiction, what does it matter to our generation who was at fault, the untutored redskins or the gold-seeking palefaces?

Might is right in many empiric creeds and the red blot, on the page of history in the settlement of America, time can never blot out; but the fact remains that the white man is here to stay, the red man has crossed the Great Divide and conscience has long since been buried in the grave of forgetfulness.

But though the red sovereigns of the soil have gone, we are reminded that he was a stern reality when we come across the relics of his war implements, turned up by the peaceful plough in many a field, or listen to the tales of the fireside of those days of the long ago.

It has been truthfully said that one does not wish to trace his ancestry too far back, as he will surely find them barbarians, buccaneers or perhaps worse.

It does not, therefore, become us to turn the sunlight into the dark recesses of the past, whether our ancestors came hither by the grace of God and the King's command, or left the old country for its good, else we might be horrified to know just what deeds were then done with the sword, or under the protection of the Cross, to lay the foundation for future progress.

Not that our ancestors cared a rap for the future of generations yet unborn, for they didn't; the almighty present and fight for self and spoils being the governing incentive, with gold their beacon. That the pure deviltry, as developed in the red man, was finally overcome by the wanton cruelty and inate wickedness of the white man stands to our advantage today. Hence those early days ended with our race in the ascendency.

Those in authority then did not stop to consider that Poor Lo had a grievance; that, if any inheritance comes by "Divine Right," he inherited these streams and forests and hills and vales to dwell in, fish, hunt enjoy life as best he could in his crude way until the Gitche Manito called him hence.

They simply wanted the land and sea, the brooks and fertile meadowlands, and *took them*.

If they traded with the Indian the latter came out at the small end of the horn.

If they taught the Indian the white man's ways those ways were crooked and evil.

Not going too closely into history it will yet be well to trace Talbot back to its early settlers, and who established here many landmarks that time has almost entirely obliterated—yes, even from the memory of the "oldest inhabitant."

Of course Talbot is, or rather was, English in its inception. Then there were, too, as the names of today show, Irish, Scotch, and a few French, while, with its shores open to the world, there drifted hither a number of Hollanders ; and all, as has been proven, when they became *Americanized* by renewed generations, made a race that has mastered the world in all that goes to add to enlightenment.

So much for the early settlers of Talbot and their descendants, many of whom now can look back over half a score of generations and point with pride to their "family tree."

To those whose ancestry may cause them to suffer qualms of conscience instead of to swell with pride from traditionary lore, by discovering deeds in the misty past, or a few closet skeletons and other things not conducive to fond recollections, let them find consolation in the lines of Moore, slightly transposed:

> "When cold in the earth lie the friends thou hast loved
> Be their faults and their follies forgot by thee then."

CHAPTER IV

OW many localities in our broad land, where high cliffs and picturesque scenery lend color to the legend, boast of possessing a "Lover's Leap?" All have about the same old romance of an Indian girl and her lover, driven, from some mischance, to go separate ways thus severing heart-strings, and despair driving the dusky maiden to end her unhappiness by taking the fatal leap from some lofty cliff designated by nature for just such a contretemps. Sometime the legends have it that both lovers took the leap together, and this makes the story doubly interesting and pathetic.

Now Talbot has no "Lover's Leap" within its borders, and is thus, in this respect, behind the other localities that have; but Talbot has no spot to so designate, Nature not having built this particular country in that way, as it lacks high cliffs for despairing red skins, or even paleface lovers, to throw themselves off of as a means of getting rapid transit to the Happy Hunting Grounds.

Yet let it not be for a moment believed that because lacking in Lover's Leaps, Talbot has not Indian legends equally as sad, if not thrillingly dramatic. One legend runs of how a band of brave Algonquins, driven by their foes to the point of land now known as Bachelor's Point, where stands the home of Dr. Councell, and where their wives and kindred awaited them in their village, calmly determined to die before the faces of the victors.

Quickly they weighted themselves, their wives and children down with heavy war implements, and chanting their weird death song, waded boldly out into the Choptank that stretched its blue waters away for miles before them. Deeper and deeper they went into the waters that were to be their grave, while their foes, crowded upon the shore amid the deserted tepees,

witnessed their splendid courage as they disappeared beneath
the waves while the echo of their song of death still floated in
the air.

Another point of interest in Talbot is what is known as "Evergreen," the home of Mr. McKenny Willis on Island Creek, for
there it is said the first white child was born in a settler's cabin.
The first grave dug for a white woman in Talbot county was on
the little island at Oxford, and there are old people still living
who remember hearing their grandparents tell of the little burying ground a woman's form first consecrated, and which in time
grew apace until another site was chosen as the last resting
place of the dead.

It was in those first days in Talbot that a young Englishman
landed here, having come over before the mast in a vessel that
was driven into the Chesapeake and found a haven of refuge in
the mouth of the beautiful Avon River, as now known. A man
whose lot in life had been cast above that of his fellows, but
who seemed to carry a shadow in his heart, and separating from
his shipmates he cast his fortunes among the Indians.

How long he dwelt with them is not told, but he quickly learned to speak their language and taught them much of the white
man's mode of life until the great Chief was glad to honor him
in many ways. It has been said that the influence of this young
man made peace between the Nanticokes and the white invaders;
giving the latter a stronger foothold upon the Maryland Peninsula. Be that as it may, the mysterious stranger was made a
chief among the Indians, and the beautiful daughter of the red-
skin king was offered to him as a wife, for the maiden had learned
to dearly love the handsome paleface brave from beyond the big
waters.

Realizing this fact, and a man of honor, the stranger told the
pretty Indian girl how he already loved a fair maiden of his own
race in England, but she was the daughter of a great and rich
man, while he was poor and unknown. It was because she had
promised to be true to him that he had come to the new world to
seek a fortune in the yellow gold he had heard was to be found
here ; but alas ! he had found nothing and dare not return a poor
man to claim the hand of her he loved. Lalaree, the Indian girl,
listened to his story, and gazed with awe upon the gold-mounted
miniature of her fair rival.

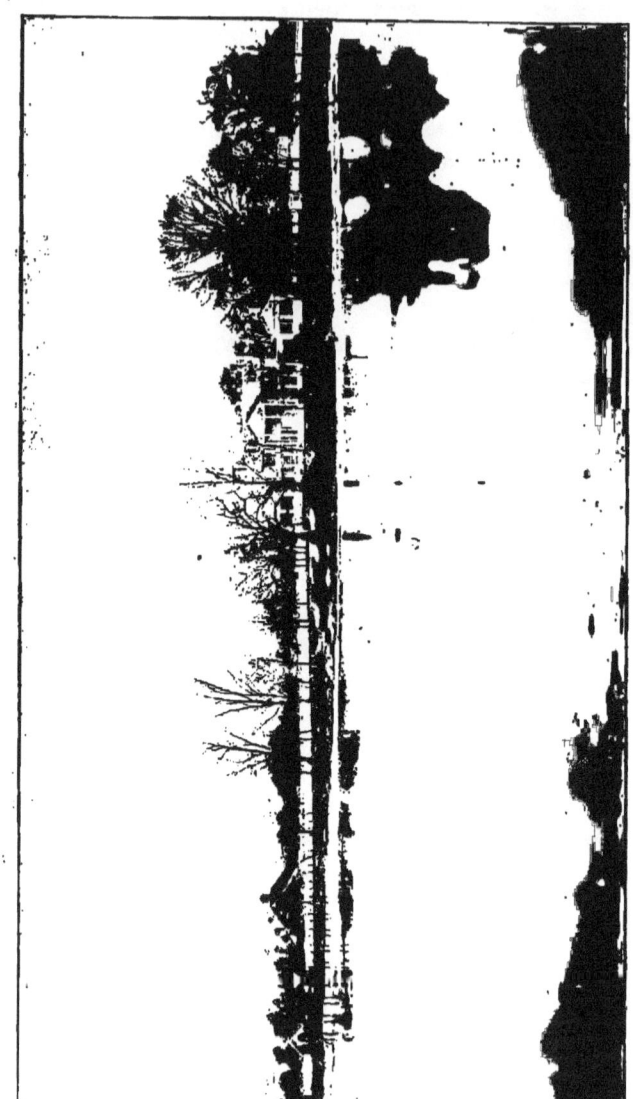

"THE ANCHORAGE," COUNTRY SEAT OF COL. CHARLES A. CHIPLEY.

Then she seemed to realize that the man she loved was not of
her people, and her heart was prompted to a noble deed instead
of mad jealousy, and she told how there was an Indian tradition
handed down for generations, that a large winged canoe had, one
terrible night of storm, been driven upon the shore of the big waters, three sleeps* from where they then were, and all the white
braves had perished, for their bones rested in the wreck. The
eyes of the young man glistened with hope at this story, and he
asked the Indian maiden for all the information she could give
him, and was surprised to hear her reply :

"Lalaree will guide the paleface chief to the wrecked winged
canoe, and there he will find that she has not spoken with a
crooked tongue, for there is the yellow metal to make him rich,
so that he can return beyond the big water and marry the beautiful white maiden he loves."

True to her word, the good Lalaree guided the young Englishman to the eastward by a well-beaten Indian trail leading to the
ocean, and after several days came to the point where now stands
the summer resort of Ocean City. There, driven upon the shore,
by some mighty tidal wave, it would seem, was the wreck of a
vessel, which the young man's sailor eye told him at a glance
was of Spanish build. And there, in decaying cabin and fore-
castle, were found the skeleton forms of a score of seamen, their
bones bleached white by the waters. And more, in the cabin
were chests of Spanish gold and silver, with precious stones and
massive plate and other valuables half covered with sand.

"There is indeed a fortune here, and this ship was surely a
Spanish pirate," cried the young Englishman, and, with those
who had accompanied Lalaree and himself, he gathered up the
treasure, packed all in the iron-bound chests and hid them in the
sand beyond the reach of the waters. †

It was just two months after that a homeward bound English
brig anchored off the Sinepuxent shore, and two boats landed
through the surf their crews, led by the Englishman, to get the
buried treasure.

Homeward, with his fortune went the young Englishman and

---

*Indians count journeys by nights that pass, calling a journey of days so many
"sleeps."

† Until a few years ago there were still signs of the treasure wreck to be seen at Ocean
City.

matching the riches of the father of the maiden he loved, he claimed and was given her hand.

Lured by the beauties, adventure and possibilities of the Chesapeake country, at his own expense he fitted out a ship and with a number of good people, set sail for the new world once more, and where he and his bride were to make their home. In the waters of the Avon River the vessel dropped anchor and on the picturesque shores of that stream was erected their comfortable home and where dwell their descendants today, for their name is woven deep into Maryland history past and present.

But the Indian maiden who sacrificed her love for another, what of her? With her love she gave up her life, for with the going of her lover across the sea to claim another for his bride, she faded away as an unnourished flower, and when the English vessel dropped anchor in the Avon the wild myrtle was growing upon her grave.

For a long time her grave was marked by a stone that bore the simple name :

"LA-LA-REE."

But Time, the merciless iconoclast, crumbled it away and no trace remains of where rest the ashes of the Indian girl, though the story goes that she was buried on the point of land formed by Trippe's Creek and the Avon, and now the home of Mr. J. L. Banning.

CHAPTER V

NCE the loveliness of the landscape, the climatic advantages of this part of the country, with its marine advantages, wealth of woodland, richness of soil, and munificence of natural food in its waters and its game were known, it became an attractive region for people of the better classes, with ordinary means in which to seek a home. Attractive indeed must be the scene that will allure a man from his Fatherland. With the authority of King James I. of England, issuing patents to colonize all the coast from Cape Fear River in North Carolina to Passamaquoddy Bay in Maine, and thence across to the Pacific, this narrative of our Eastern Shore country has nothing to do, for it is the work of the historian who details events in a groove of dates.

It was through a severe storm on the Atlantic that three ships under Wingfield and Smith—the latter better known as "Pocahontas Smith"—intending to land further south, were driven into the Chesapeake, and the country at once attracted them, thus causing the first settlement on the James River, and where the landmarks of those early days still remain. This was a hundred and ten years after the discovery of America by the early Cabot and over forty years after the founding of St. Augustine, Florida by the Spaniards.

After founding the Jamestown settlement Captain John Smith returned to England and came out with other vessel loads of people, while he surveyed the coast from the Penobscot downward, to discover if he had selected the best locality for his colony. This survey convinced him that the storm had accidentally driven him to the most delightful of all places, for the Chesapeake and its tributaries, the James, Rappahannock, Potomac, Patapsco, Choptank, Wye and Avon added to the climate and grandeur of scenery rendered it all that heart could desire and eye delight in. Thus it was that early in the seventeenth century the Chesa-

peake Bay and its environs became the Mecca of the adventurous pioneers of the Old World.

Lord Baltimore's first colonization was in New Foundland,
but the climate and barren country made the venture a failure,
and he then turned the prows of his ships to the sunny land of
the Chesapeake. From the King he received a domain that
gave to him all of the Maryland and Delaware of today, with
parts of Pennsylvania and New Jersey. Here was established
an asylum for Catholics, and the name of Maryland was bestowed on the new province.

Lord Calvert had founded meanwhile a colony, the St. Mary's,
in 1633. Thus it was that this favored land adjacent 'to the
Chesapeake begun to grow in white population and prosperity,
until Oxford, in Talbot, recognized as a splendid harbor and surrounded by navigable waters and fertile lands, formed the nucleus of what has been builded into the garden spot it is today;
in fact, a number of citizens of the ancient regime still strongly
maintain that here was the original site of the Garden of Eden.

That nothing is said of the Choptank and Avon in the Bible
does not disturb their equanimity in the least, they simply know
that no other place can be so beautiful as Talbot, and I know
several who know just where that fateful apple tree of Eden
stood, though I dare not point out the locality—the farm is not
for sale.

Bringing their different creeds, orthodox or otherwise, over
with them along with their goods and chattels, there was of
course more or lesss friction engendered among these new-com-
ers to America; for man is not content to serve God in his own
way without discussing the gigantic mote that is in the eye of
his neighbor who selects a different method; and though "Peace
and Goodness" and "Do unto others as you would have others
do unto you" are diamond-studded golden rules with silver lin-
ing they appear to suit well enough for "others" but not for
ourselves, as witness the Religious wars of the world, the carrying of the cross in one hand the sword in the other.

Envy, hatred and malice therefore found a footing here with
the coming of the paleface settlers; and jealousy, rivalry and
bickerings—from the settlements of the Pilgrims and Puritans
on the cold New England shores to those of the Hollanders of
New York, the Protestants and Catholics of Virginia and Mary-

land, Huguenots of the Carolinas and Spaniards and French of the Gulf shores—were the regular routine, man's inhumanity to man, looming up in striking contrast to Christ's teachings.

In the midst of these troublous times in settling the New World with the people of varied lands of the Old World, there came hither one whose name is indelibly linked with all that is good in those old times. He followed those of his race and simple creed, who had already founded several flourishing settlements in New Jersey and was thus encouraged to establish another on the banks of the broad and majestic Delaware.

A free state, builded upon the principles of universal brotherhood was the noble aim of this man, whose people had long been persecuted, buffeted about and shamefully abused, while imprisonment and exile had been their lot. With his hopes for the future not quenched by proscription and cruel treatment, William Penn's philanthropic and lofty purpose was to establish for his people, the Friends* an asylum of refuge and rest.

From King Charles, Penn received a charter that made him proprietor of the vast domain bounded in the east by the Delaware and running northward and southward over three degrees of latitude while it extended westward through five degrees of longitude. This domain received in part his name—Pennsylvania, and there he established a grand commonwealth without respect to religion, race or color, and though the red man was then very much in evidence in the village of brotherly love, as it was at that time, the black man is even more in evidence there today.

Brotherly love, justice and the right hand of hospitality were the weapons used by Penn against all people, and there was a hearty response to his desire to build up a great nation in this land of promise.

Penn's father, Sir William, having been a Vice Admiral in the British Navy, gave his son a fine education, though he was expelled from Oxford on account of his religious opinion. He studied law, had been a soldier, and was well equipped mentally, physically and by training for the leadership of a persecuted people in this "holy experiment" in the New World.

By his simplicity, truth and love of fair play he conquered

---

*The term Quaker was bestowed upon the sect of Friends in derision by Gervas Bennet, a prosecuting and persecuting Judge, because George Fox bade them *quake* at the name of the Lord.

Indians, Swedes, Dutch and English and dug the foundation for his people to build upon to the grand success they today maintain and upon whom is indelibly imprinted the stamp of this remarkable man.

Expelled from Virginia, by Act of Assembly, the Friends sought a refuge in Maryland and were granted lands on the Eastern Shore in 1649. Upon Maryland therefore falls the honor of granting freedom in their religion and justice to the Friends.

In a short time therefore a settlement was established in Talbot county and a Meeting house erected on Miles River* followed by another on the Wye. About each there was land for a school house and graveyard, both most necessary adjuncts in any community.

With English Protestants and Catholics, Friends, and a minority of other nationalities, Talbot county begun to become populated and prosper and this of course meant the establishment of a seaport within its bounderies, Oxford being the site chosen, and named after the old University town of England.

*On the site of the present country seat of Mr. Robert B. Dixon on the inlet known as "Betty's Cove."

CHAPTER VI

TALBOT'S FIRST TOWN.

ROM all the data, facts, fancy and fiction, with due allowance for time's elapse, treacherous memories and other drawbacks, all that can be learned of its ancient history, Oxford could add sixty more years to its age and be correct in its figures, it having been first settled in 1635. I have been to some pains to glean the real facts about the earlier life of this old-young town, and but little remains now amid the new, but the legendary "oldest inhabitant" "just doesn't remember" what his grandfather told him about this and that person and place that had existence a century or two ago. Thus, it is that truth and fiction will be mingled with history, and the historian is right or wrong, according to his lights and prejudice.

Oxford, as I can get at the facts, was first known as Thread Haven, being settled by English merchants. This recalls the fact that the river, now practically called the Tred Avon, was then known as the Thread Haven, as here was the port to which numerous merchant vessels came loaded with thread, cordage, ropes, hemp, etc., to find ready trade with the outlying country for tobacco. From Thread Haven it was merged in time into the The Third Haven—it is so called upon many old maps—and gradually by the mysteries of nomenclature drifted into Tred Avon. Oxford was the site first chosen for the future metropolis of Maryland, before Baltimore was thought of. It was originally laid out by a woman, Mrs. Margaret Lowe.

She it was who left in her will the "Strand," along the Avon, for "commercial purposes only," "Vancouver's Island," for "bonded warehouses," and Jack's Point, on Town Creek, really a river—as most Maryland creeks are, to use a paradox—as a common.

Mrs. Lowe was a philanthropist, from all said of her, a woman of unbounded charity ; and when she died, so highly was she regarded that she was "buried with military honors," as the records show. Her burial place is near Oxford, "unmarked, unhonored and unknown."

'In 1695 Oxford was surveyed by a King's officer, and named Williamstadt. Just how and when it merged into Oxford is lost in the mist of years, but it is said to have been named by an English gentleman, who came over just fresh from the halls of learning by that name in old England. With a view, perhaps, of keeping up the old scholastic dignity of the name, a large academy, Eastford Hall, was established here, but was burned. Rebuilt under the same name and on a grander scale, it became a "Maryland Naval Academy," which, prospering for a while, at length failed through mismanagement and merged into a summer hotel. In 1888 it burned down, fortunately in the day time, so that it did not prove a holocaust, as would have been the case had it occurred at night. Today it is not even a picturesque ruin, so complete was its destruction.

Properly speaking, Oxford is on an island, for at a very high tide it is cut off, the narrow neck of land connecting it with the mainland being overflowed. Town Creek, the considerable stream referred to, runs to the north ; to the westward is the Tred Avon, and southward is what is also called the Tred Avon river, but in reality is an arm of the Chesapeake, the mouth of the Choptank river likewise being a part of the bay.

The old settlers who hunted out this lovely spot of the Eastern Shore builded better than they knew; for, though other counties may appear as beautiful as Talbot, they have not the healthfulness, nor can they boast of the almost total freedom from those irritating insects known as mosquitoes. Some years ago the U. S. Government sent out officers for statistics of healthfulness of the entire country, and, with Royal Oak, four miles from Oxford, as the centre, and ten miles around as the circle, statistics showed that this part of Talbot county held the palm.

There is no undertaker in Oxford and but two doctors, and, in spite of its age, the little "village of the dead" close by has not many graves. It is true that in olden times "family burying grounds" were the correct thing, but there are a few of them scattered about, and I regret to say that these have gone to

GOLDSBOROUGH STREET, EASTON'S FAVORED RESIDENCE SECTION.

EASTON'S COURT HOUSE GREEN ON ELECTION DAY.

decay, and the descendants of those who sleep in the sacred spots appear to think more of other comforts than those derived from weeding out old graves.

While upon this subject, it may be well to speak of the old Episcopal Church near here—a hundred years ago the only place of worship in the vicinity. It was in this church yard that Robert Morris was buried in 1750. Said Morris was the father of the great financier of the Revolution, the friend of General Washington. His home was in Oxford, and he was a shipping merchant of large means. When visiting his vessels that came into port, he was always saluted by their guns, for those were the days of piracy upon the high seas, and all ships went armed. Going on board of one of his ships one day, he asked the captain not to salute him ; but not caring to be guilty of such a breach of marine etiquette, the skipper told his mate that he would accompany Mr. Morris ashore and when the boat left the ship he would give the signal and the salute must be fired. The mate mistook the captain's taking out his handkerchief for the signal, the salute was fired, and a wad from a gun struck Mr. Morris on the shoulder, causing a wound that proved fatal some days later.

Some attest that Robert Morris his son, was born here, and the honor of being his birthplace is given to a part of what is now an old wing of the Tred Avon Hotel, the Morris homestead having stood there. Other houses here are just as old, but no one seems to have heard which one can be claimed as the birth-place of the great Revolutionary financier, the man who came so promptly to the aid of Washington in the time of his great need.

A Philadelphian remarked to me that it was wrong for the people here to allow the grave of the father of Robert Morris to remain in such neglect, and I could not but agree with him, and add : "As it is for Philadelphians to allow the grave of Benjamin Franklin to remain in a like condition."

History has it that Robert Morris, delegate to the Continental Congress, organizer of the Bank of North America, one of the framers of the United States Constitution and United States Senator, was born in England in 1734, yet his father came to Oxford years before the birth of his illustrious son, dying here, as stated, July 12th, 1750. If I question the oldest inhabitants here, they fall back upon their grandfathers, who lie around

Old White Marsh Church, and I am not yet in the ethereal condition to interview them upon the subject, so *quien sabe*?

In the Oxford burying ground is the tomb erected to Colonel Tench Tilghman, of Revolutionary fame. The cemetery is on Town Creek, and is built, if I may so speak of the narrow house of the dead, around what was once the family burying ground of the Tilghmans, the old seat, "Plimhimmon," still standing a few hundred yards away. In those early days the Tilghmans, Goldsboroughs, Chamberlaines, Matthews and other noted Maryland families, whose descendants live in Talbot county, dwelt on lordly estates for miles around Oxford, and a number of their mansions still stand to connect the present with the past, and each family, like the man in Texas, had its "own private burying ground."

So much for a few of the old memories that cluster about Oxford, whose citizens celebrated in 1895 its bi-centennial from the resurvey by Captain Phillip Hemsley, British army, in 1695. Today it is a pretty village, numbering some sixteen hundred souls, and still such a seafaring place that besides the three clergymen, two physicians, several storekeepers and the principal of the public school, it is perfectly safe to call every other man you meet "Captain," and not go far wrong, for if not skippers of a vessel, they have been, or own an interest in one.

The people are well-to-do, intelligent, charitable and stick to the Golden Rule as closely as any like community. All are patriotic, talk boat, discuss the affairs of the nation, and are pretty equally divided in politics, and religion.

There is a fine public school, there are three churches, one shipyard, half a dozen dry goods stores, twice as many groceries, a couple of hardware houses, a drug store, all excellent in their way, and a tomato cannery, wheelwright and four large oyster packing houses, sending tons of the delicious bivalves as far West as Denver.

A branch of the Pennsylvania Railroad runs there direct, four hours from Philadelphia, and railway and boat communication across the bay from Baltimore and via Claiborne and Easton, besides two steamer lines direct daily. It is a local option town, and a "wink" at the soda fountain in the drug store does no good. Even hard cider is frowned down.

Oxford is the haven of a couple of hundred vessels in the

oyster and coasting trade, and it has a record for building fast
schooners, buckeyes and canoes. In the fall, when the busy
season opens, it is a beautiful sight to see the fleet of vessels
sailing to and fro, and in the storms of winter it has had to
mourn its gallant sailors lost. In the summer season it has a
number of visitors to fill its three hotels, which may keep open in
the winter as well, as the town is beginning to grow into an all-
the-year-round resort. And why not? for a more delightful spot
for outing cannot be found, and its waters are the yachtsman's
paradise.

Near Oxford is a "Lover's Spring," so called from the fact that
those who drink of the waters will love the one who gives the
potent draught; this must be kept a secret as those suffering the
pangs of "unrequited affection" would flock there like locusts,
and prove an equal plague.

 ITHOUT going particularly into the geography of this part of Maryland, it may be expedient to speak of the attractions of the Chesapeake as an inland sea connecting with the ocean, and whose waterways form such a vast shore line of this "middle land," as it may be called, between the cold north and warm south. It is the situation of the Eastern Shore which renders it so delightful as a home, neither too hot in summer nor too cold in winter, and thus its climatic advantages are unsurpassed anywhere.

To the early settlers the Chesapeake Bay constituted both their strength and their weakness, where today it strengthens this locality alone and with its many navigable waters, rivers, inlets and creeks, bringing three-fourths of the farms in Talbot upon waters that freight and pleasure craft can go to the head of, it thus enables the farms, as well as the villages on the streams to have the means of transportation at their very doors. In those days, that tried men's souls so thoroughly, these same waterways brought the war vessels of foes to the hamlets and farms, thus being a drawback.

But the wealth of these waters then, in oysters, fish, terrapin, crabs and wild fowl were a source of vast pecuniary revenue, though today they are far more so and yield supplies that go to the Gulf, to Maine and the Pacific. Being so favorably situated, the Eastern Shore residents are within the world, with their easy access to Baltimore, Washington, New York and it is not to be wondered at that those who dwell in the very heart of this favored district, Talbot county, are clannish, devoted to home and care not to leave the old family hearthstones.

The Bay and its adjacent waters rival the canals of Venice in their facility for social intercourse, the pleasure craft being a means of communications as frequently seen as the carriage and saddlehorse. The roads were not to be boasted of in those days, as they are now, and the waters were mostly the means of transportation, and were as much to the colonists as the railroads of today are to the people. They traded and traveled on the waters, fought on them, sported on them and in them, and the homes then settled were within sight of the shores, few being inland.

The Indians had found the Chesapeake waters all that their hearts could desire, and the colonists were only too willing to follow the lead of the untutored natives—where it was to their advantage and pleasure, not otherwise. The tide with a good flow and ebb, and with the true sea-brine in taste, does not retard sailing and rowing, and as the Indians, guided by Nature, had built the very best craft in which to sail these waters, the whites adopted their methods, the result being the canoe and pungy, skiff and buckeye, of today.*

By means of these boats, the coasting buckeye, the farmers of St. Michaels, Royal Oak, Tilghman's Island, Tunis Mills, Oxford, Trappe and Easton get their grain and other produce to Baltimore markets at about one fourth the cost of freight and half the time that producers away from the Chesapeake can.

The ships from London and Bristol two hundred years ago brought supplies to the doors of the people, anchoring in the rivers, and went back with a return freight of tobacco and other products grown in this country. In those days too the Chesapeake abounded in wild geese, brant, and ducks of many varieties and the "canvas back" still holds the palm among epicures as the most delicate of wild fowls.

Venison was accounted a "tiresome meat," so plentiful were deer in those days; squirrels were so numerous that rewards were given for their pelts, wild turkeys were found in the forests, a few bears now and then, with pheasants, ortolans, quail snipe, woodcock, pigeons, hares, raccoons and opossums. The waters rivaled the forests in producing all sorts of edibles, the pompano, bonito, perch, shad, bass, bluefish and many other varieties of fish and crustaceans.

Nealy all the cultivated berries known in this country today then grew wild, with many indigenous wild fruits, while the flora was remarkable, the soil encouraging the growth of hard

---

* The canoe is built of four hollowed logs, from twenty to forty feet long; it is from three to seven feet wide, and carries three sails, a jib and two leg of mutton sails. The buckeye, also called bugeye, is of the cano: style of build, sharp at both ends, decked over and a staunch and fleet craft. These vessels are the fleetest that can be found in any land, and the Chesapeake people handle them with the greatest of skill. The craft of one hundred years ago is the craft of today.

and soft woods side by side, and fine grasses grew luxuriantly.
Within a score of years only, after the coming of the Colonists
to Talbot, orchards of apples, peaches, quinces and plums became a noticeable feature of the country, the exigences of tobacco culture having caused the clearing away of heavy timber-
lands. Sheep raising was not profitable in those days, on account of the many wolves, but the fecundity of cattle, hogs and
other domestic animals was remarkable, wild horses were a nui-
sance to the farmers.†

Was it a wonder then that a land so favored as this particular part of the Chesapeake country two hundred years ago became the haven of people of all lands, who eagerly sought homes
here, where climate, health and advantages were unsurpassed?
The men who came here were of many nationalities, but the
English predominated.

The clearing of new lands, and want of proper drainage and
sanitary arrangements naturally caused much sickness then,
fever and ague, with small-pox as a steady thing, for all had
the small-pox or expected to have it next time it came round,
and womanly beauty was often marred by the indelible pits.
As for other ailments of the colonists the neighborhood Doctor,
or "Medicine Man," could regulate them while the superstitious were given to "spells" to cure disease.

People physicked themselves sick, then sent for a doctor and
that meant in many cases a funeral, for medicine as then practiced was not the science it is today, and "powders," "castor-
oil," "rhubarb," "sagetea," "bloodroot" and "poultices" about
comprised the Materia Medica of the itinerant practitioner.

Cupping and leaching were frequent, while wounds were filled with gunpowder or turpentine and most crudely dressed.
Tobacco was then served as a purchasing medicine, a pound of the
weed buying three pounds of meat, two pounds of tobacco were
given in exchange for a fat chicken, while a hogshead of the
staple weed secured all the table luxuries that the gun and rod
did not. Thus was it a couple of centuries past, the beginning
of colonist life in Talbot. To look upon that primitive picture,
then upon the one of today, forms a striking contrast indeed,
and sharply drawn is the line between the old and the new.

---

† Wild horses are still quite numerous on Chincoteague Island.

CHAPTER VIII.

ERHAPS, to interest the reader who does not personally know this favored part of "God's terrestrial football," I could not better acquaint him with the land of which I write than to quote from Mr. Calvin Dill Wilson in Lippincott's Magazine of January, 1898. Mr. Wilson has so thoroughly painted his subject that no words of mine could in any way add to his description of the "Eastern Shore of Maryland." He says : "That division of Maryland which is known as "The Eastern Shore" contains no vast extent of territory, and it is peopled by no immense multitudes; no great historical event has occurred there; * it has not had the fierce light of publicity turned upon every happening within its borders ; it is not a state ; it is not an empire ; it has no gold or silver or coal-mines, no oil or gas-wells ; and it has no imperial possibilities. It is not the centre of the world ; no large metropolis exists upon it, and none ever will exist there."

"Nevertheless it is a famous region ; its local name is known to most of the intelligent citizens of the United States, and the place indicated by the title is at once understood. It has a greatness of its own, and has claims upon public attention. Its situation is interesting ; its population has a marked character ; its products are valuable, and are in demand everywhere in this land, and in many places outside America ; and its fame is great because of the sensations it provides for the palates of men. The grapes of Ephraim or the onions and garlic of Egypt were not more famous among the Jews, or the wheat-fields of Egypt among the Romans, or the eel- and mullet-ponds of Lucullus, or

* Yet Mr. Wilson might have added that it has been a land of history in America for nearly three centuries.

the wines of Falernia, among the same people, than some of the products of this region are among moderns."

"The Eastern Shore" lies, like an arm thrust up by the ocean between the Atlantic and the Chesapeake Bay ; around it break the surge and thunder of the sea ; and ocean's breezes sweep perpetually over it; It is a sand-bar, but it is something more ; it is a garden, and an orchard. Nature seemed unkind when she strewed this sand upon clay without stones ; but she repented, clothed it all in verdure, made it yield almost every fruit, vegetable, and berry in profusion and of finest quality, filled even the swamps with cypress, cedar, and pine, stored the streams with fishes, filled the waters along the coasts with shell. fish, and valuable funny creatures, sent flocks of birds into the fields and woods, and flights of wild fowl upon all the waters. But, despite the fame of its products, the Eastern Shore is one of the less well-known portions of our country. Few persons have any accurate conception of it or knowledge of its characteristics ; they have only a vague impression that it is a noted place from which many table delicacies come.

"Yet it is an interesting region. It is a part of the Chesapeake and Delaware peninsula, which contains an area of six thousand square miles, bounded on the north by the State of Pennsylvania, on the east by the Delaware Bay and Atlantic Ocean, and on the west by the Chesapeake. Its length is about two hundred miles, and its greatest breadth seventy, while its narrowest part is fifteen. Of this territory the Eastern Shore of Maryland comprises four-ninths, Delaware three-ninths, and the Eastern Shore of Virginia two-ninths.

"Its local name is no recent invention; it was baptized so long ago as to give its title, as things go in America, a quite venerable antiquity. In a letter written by Lord Baltimore, dated October 23, 1656, he says "his lordship requires his said lieutenant and Council to cause the bounds thereof to be kept in memory, and notoriously known, especially the bounds between Maryland and Virginia, on that part of the country known there by the name of the Eastern Shore."

Some persons have an impression that this region is a confusion of swamps and sandy deserts ; but in fact a large part of it is in many respects an earthly paradise. To a certain extent isolated by its geographical position, it is nevertheless connected with the outer world by first-class railways and daily lines of boats. Its relative seclusion is the explanation of the development of marked characteristics among many of its people ; there the breath of modernism has heretofore only begun to modify long established customs and habits. This is therefore an excellent place to study fixed types of character, and to examine survivals from the past.

"The population was originally almost entirely English, and the settlers belonged largely to the class of gentry ; the estates are still called "manors" and "houses," and the customs are largely English. The language of the better classes is quite Elizabethan, and the libraries contain chiefly English classics ; the proverbs on the lips of the people are those of the days of Shakespeare. The superior homes are large and spacious, surrounded by trees, and the inhabitants bear marks of culture and refinement.

"The most picturesque estates are to be found on the smaller islands, chiefly on the Chesapeake side. There is something fascinating about islands ; to own one, to have a stately mansion upon it, to be surrounded by a lovely family and numerous servants, to have one's rich fields yield abundant food, and his woodland material for fires, to have the surrounding waters supply fish, oysters, clams, crabs, terrapin, ducks, and wild fowl, to have one's own quail, rabbits, grouse, and woodcock, to have one's own boats for sailing and for reaching the mainland when desired, is indeed to realize a dream.

"The railway accommodations on the Eastern Shore are now of an excellent kind ; the necessity for rapid transit in shipping fruits and vegetables from this garden spot, which adds so large a contribution to the markets of several great cities, has developed this industry. The peninsula is netted with railways branching from the main line, which bisects it from north to south. Six millions of consumers, within twenty hours' distance from the lowest point of the peninsula, await the products of this fertile territory. Railways and steamers put the farmers and fruit-raisers and fishermen in quick contact with the markets. There is scarcely a region in the United States of equal extent that possesses so large a proportion of cultivable land. The upper portion of the peninsula possesses a heavy and gently rolling soil, which is covered with fine farms, superior forests of oak and chestnuts, and is admirably adapted to growing the cereals. Other portions have a lighter soil, especially suited to fruits and vegetables.

"One-half of the counties of the Eastern Shore have heavy crops of wheat, corn of superior quality is grown in nearly every section, while oats, rye and barley flourish. Peas, tomatoes, white and sweet potatoes, turnips, asparagus, beans, in fact, all the principal vegetables, there reach their highest perfection. Fruits of a superior quality are raised in endless variety; the fig and the pomegranate ripen in the open air in the extreme southern counties, while in other sections peaches, pears, apples, plums, cherries, apricots, and quinces flourish wonderfully. Watermelons, strawberries, raspberries, blackberries, currants, cranberries, and whortleberries are also shipped to the cities in immense quantities. Grape culture has recently become a leading pursuit.

"In this region the peach is cultivated to a larger extent and with greater success, both as to quality and as to quantity, than anywhere else in the world. In 1875 the peach crop was the largest known on the peninsula, and there were then carried over one railroad and its connections nine thousand and seventy-two car-loads of peaches. These figures represent millions of baskets of peaches, and a great many millions of quarts of strawberries, raspberries, blackberries, whortleberries, cherries, currants, and gooseberries. At the same time we are to remember that at least an equal amount of peaches and other fruits was shipped by boat, or used in the canneries or evaporating establishments.

"The waters of both shores abound with life in various and useful forms. Shad and herring-fisheries are numerous. In nearly all the waters are to be found in great abundance rock-fish, sturgeon, sheep's head, trout, and so forth. The extent of the oyster-beds in the peninsula is about five thousand three hundred and seventy-three square miles, giving occupation to more than ten thousand hands afloat. Besides six hundred dredging vessels, averaging twenty-three tons each, there are two thousand canoes, which take about five bushels each daily by tongs during seven months of the year. The product is not less than ten million bushels, worth in first hands five million dollars. Hard and soft crabs, turtles, and terrapin are plenti-

ful nearly everywhere. Wild fowl are found in wonderful variety of numbers and quality on the Atlantic shores. The choicest game-birds in the world are here. Inland, woodcocks, par-
tridges, snipe, wild pigeons, rabbits, and squirrels abound. The
climate is a happy mean between the tropical and the temperate.
The soil seldom freezes to a greater depth than six inches;
ploughing in December and January is quite common. The
planting and ripening seasons of the lower parts of the peninsula are two weeks in advance of those of New Jersey, and four
or five weeks earlier than those of Pennsylvania.

"To the angler this region offers great attractions. For the
gunners there are the canvas-back duck, the redhead, the mal-
lard, the summer duck, the green-winged teal, the long-tailed
duck, the black duck, the buffel-head, the tufted duck, the
golden eye, the shoveller, the pin-tail, the blue-winged teal, the
snow goose, the Canada goose, the sheldrake, the brant, the
dusky duck, the scaup duck, and the bald pate. Here are to
be had the long-billed curlew, the short-billed curlew, the
red-backed snipe, the willet, the red-breasted snipe, the long-
shanked snipe, the yellow-shanked snipe, the tell-tale godwit,
the turn stone, the ash-colored sandpiper, the purre, the black-
bellied plover, the red-breasted sandpiper, the woodcock, the
quail, the English snipe, the clapper rail, and the reed-bird.

"Any account of the Eastern Shore would be incomplete without some mention of the diamond-backed terrapin, which has
been awarded the palm for delicacy and general excellence, and
which, when averaging over six inches across his under-shell, is
worth up to seventy dollars per dozen, when in season. Forty
years ago these terrapins were wonderfully abundant, but they
had not then come into general appreciation. The first really
large catch was credited to John Ethridge, of Body Island, who,
in ten days' fishing, caught over two thousand terrapin, and
sold them in Norfolk for about four hundred dollars. This was
the birth of the terrapin industry. He at once returned to the
spot and dug out two thousand more, which he sold in Baltimore for three hundred and fifty dollars. These sales became
known, and the extermination of the wild terrapin commenced,
so many being obtained that for some winters they were sold at
Southern points for two dollars a dozen. Eventually artificial
propagation came into vogue as a staple industry. The largest

LLANDAFF BRIDGE OVER THE PEACHBLOSSOM.

PEACHBLOSSOM CREEK—A TYPICAL TALBOT LANDSCAPE.

and most important farm is on the Patuxent, and consists of a
salt-water lake which has been surrounded by a high fence to
keep out the musk-rats and foxes, these being the chief enemies
of the terrapin.

"The wild terrapin are difficult to catch. The hunting of
them is done in the summer and fall; the hunters dig long shallow ditches on the marshes and flats, and when the tide gets
low they scratch the bottom with rakes until it is covered with
a muddy paste. When the tide comes in it brings a few terrapin, who find the soft bottom and realize that they have discov-
ed a good place to burrow and spend the winter; each tide
brings more, and the mud is kept soft betweentimes. When
winter comes the hunter goes down to his preserve with a huge
pitchfork, and pushes it into the mud till he strikes something,
and in case he judges it to be a terrapin and not a stone, he digs
it out and puts it in his basket   All through Maryland and
Virginia the darkies are to be seen day and night on the marshes, armed with long, light iron rods, probing for terrapin. As
the weather becomes cooler, the hunter takes large quantities of
brush and makes a fire over the place where he knows the terrapin are buried. The terrapin imagine that spring has come, and
crawl out to be captured.

"The Eastern Shore produces more table delicacies than any
other region of equal area; and it is claimed that a family may
there enjoy the luxuries of life cheaper than elsewhere, and
that the really poor man can live on the peninsula for less than
anywhere else, save perhaps in parts of Asia. The poorest inhabitants of the peninsula are colored people. The rural negro
there probably averages annually for his work less than two
hundred dollars in cash, and many earn less than one hundred
and fifty dollars a year, while others do not make one hundred
dollars in cash. Nevertheless the negro of the peninsula is
seldom without the means of appeasing his hunger and of clothing himself comfortably. The winter is always short and usually mild, while fuel is extremely cheap and in many parts to be
had for the gathering.

"There yet remain a goodly number of the old-time slaves,
some of them of extreme age.

"Here and there are to be found men who bear on face, form,
and manner the stamp of the old Eastern Shore aristocrat.

These are well fed, prosperous, with an air of good breeding, of command, and of conscious superiority. They still wear the slouch hat, keep the coat open, and show a wide expanse of fine linen shirt-front They are genial, hearty, hospitable, and proud. The Eastern Shore has its own share, of bright-eyed, fresh-complexioned, cheery, spirited girls, who outrival their peaches in color and perfection.

"The homes of the aristocrats are filled with old things, old silver, old china, old pictures; the lawns have old boxwood hedges and old trees. The villages are chiefly of a very old-fashioned kind; one seems to have stepped out of the present into a remote past, when he visits portions of the Eastern Shore.

"One can get some idea of the influences that have been at work there from the names of places. Here are the names of the counties; Worcester, Somerset, Dorchester, Talbot, Caroline, Queen Anne, Kent, Cecil, names great in English history, and Wicomico, recalling the aborigines. Its rivers are Chester. Wye, Elk, Sassafras, Nanticoke, Choptank, Pocomoke, Wicomico, Manokin, and the bay on the ocean side is called Sinepuxent; most of these also recall the aborigines. These aborigines had permanent settlements or villages near the waterside, where they cultivated the soil and raised corn, beans, tobacco, and other crops; it is evident that they appreciated their advantages in the way of vegetable produce. All down the bay there are shellheaps, often from six to fifteen feet deep, relics of the Indian oysterfeasts.

"A leisurely pilgrimage over the Eastern Shore will well repay the observer of things American. Endless numbers of coves and estuaries indent the shores. The sleepy, old-fashioned villages invite to dreams, by their quietness and quaintness. The ocean lashes one beach, and the gentle tides of the Chesapeake lap the other.

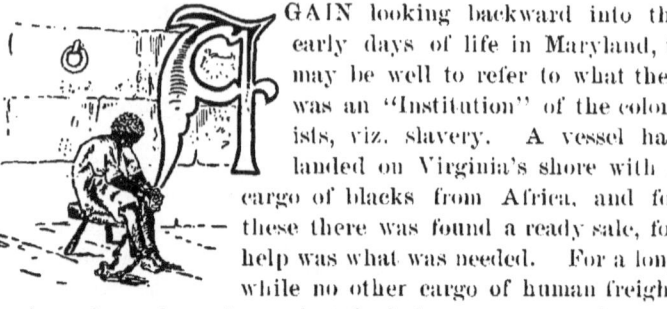

CHAPTER IX

GAIN looking backward into the early days of life in Maryland, it may be well to refer to what then was an "Institution" of the colonists, viz. slavery. A vessel had landed on Virginia's shore with a cargo of blacks from Africa, and for these there was found a ready sale, for help was what was needed. For a long while no other cargo of human freight was brought to these shores, but the bait was too tempting not to be seized upon by bold mariners as a means of making a fortune quickly, and other adventurous mariners seized the opportunity to capture Africans and bring them over.

Remember those were the days of lawlessness afloat and ashore, buccaneers infested the coast of America and other lands, Captain Kid, Morgan and other pirate chiefs were skimming the seas for treasure, and king's officers and adventurers on land were making what capital they could in any manner that promised large returns of gold.

Therefore the slave trade began to prosper and even correct New England, with her Puritans and Pilgrims, were glad to shift the heavy labor upon broad black shoulders and own plantations and slaves, only the poor Africans could not stand the severe winters of that region, and hence, in a spasm of virtue they relegated slavery to the more genial clime of the further south, Delaware, Maryland and Virginia, and it extended thence into the Carolinas and the Gulf coast.

Without a word in favor of enslaving a fellow being, with only a feeling that the institution of slavery was wrong, I can only say that "the times" allowed it, and the laws of the land made it a legal feature of this country, and only the advance of civilization has wiped it out.

"As the twig is bent the tree inclines," and so Southerners, born to consider slavery right, it was hard indeed to teach them that their ancestors were all wrong in upholding it, especially as its doing away with struck a hard blow at the pocket.

Admitting the wrong of slavery, with no wish to argue that many poor whites who work in factories throughout the north, are in even worse slavery today than were the blacks of the south, there is certainly one thing it accomplished, and that is it took out of densest barbarism in Africa those who were brought from there by lawless acts, and civilized their descendants who dwell in this country. It did more in the civilizing of Africans than all the missionaries have done, and can ever accomplish, and the American negro of today, through the slavery of generations of his ancestors, is fortunately a distinct race from those whence he sprung, ninety-nine one hundredths of whom are living in densest barbarism in the Dark Continent's jungles, clothed only in a smile, possessing only a cheap edition of a Bible as an amulet, and narrowly escaping being Darwin's "Missing Link."

But to early slavery in Maryland, not forgetting for an instant that Talbot is Maryland, for on the western shore all was then St. Mary's, and on this shore all was Talbot, there were not only black slaves in those days but white ones, "redemptioners" and indentured servants.

The Indians, not born to slavery, receded before the white man, their hunting grounds becoming tobacco fields, for then it was "King Tobacco" as later it became in the South "King Cotton" though just now wheat and sugar are rivals for the royal titles. Of course there can be found no one today whose ancestors came over as "English convicts," but the fact remains that such were sent to the colonists as "white slaves" to work out their term of sentence, and having so done they were glad to remain here and build up a new character with their home. In my research after facts I have found no one who traced his family tree back to a convict—but let that pass, for two centuries of time wipe out a legion

WASHINGTON STREET, EASTON.

of memory it were well to forget, and one who has nothing pleasant to remember can well pass his leisure hours in trying to forget.

"Redemptioners" were invited to Maryland and the laws scrupulously protected them while in service and made provision for their well-being after they had finished their term of service. Many of these people won fortune and influence and built up wealth for their descendants, who now enjoy their thrift and the saving of a penny to leave to posterity. Others are not so fortunate as far as the inheritance is concerned.

So valuable was tobacco culture here then that many persons were kidnapped in London—an old English game often played—and sent here to be sold into slavery. The landlords were granted lands in proportion to the number of their servitors, and and the aristocratic "lord of a manor" was required to have a large following. If land was rented it was paid for in the commodities of the country, and the landlord could take up a hundred acres for each slave, then he could import as many servants as his means would allow. When labor was high, land and living were cheap. It was not until negro slavery became a fixed fact that white slavery ceased. When white labor was disfranchised, then began the lording over the black slave by those who were cruel taskmasters.

There were many and good laws to protect the slave, and often these were rigidly enforced, though quite as often not. The slaves were acknowledged as citizens, forced to do military service as well, and the severest penalties were put upon them to prevent their running away from their masters, to whom they were so much property. The person who harbored a runaway slave was fined 500 pounds of tobacco for each twenty-four hours he kept him in hiding, and, if unable to pay the fine, he could be publicly whipped, so it was a rule that worked both ways. If severe, the law was just for both master and slave. It gave servants the right to appear in court. If master or overseer or mistress illfed them, gave them insufficient clothing and bedding, overworked or abused them, or in punishment gave them over ten lashes, there was a heavy penalty for each offence. If greater punishment was needed than ten lashes, the slave had to be brought before a magistrate.

So just were the laws to govern slavery, even among the blacks, there is little doubt there were among the lawmakers those who

had been "redemptioners," or indentured servants, and knew
from sad experience what it was, thus acting upon the adage that
"a fellow feeling makes us wondrous kind." It was indeed an
atrocious law, however, that allowed the selling of a debtor into
slavery. The following advertisement in the Maryland *Gazette* of
March 16th, 1769, may be of interest, the runaway being an
Irishman :

"FORTY SHILLINGS REWARD.

Last Wednesday morn, at break of day,
From Philadelphia ran away
An Irishman named John McKeoghn,
To fraud and imposition prone,
About five feet five inches high,
Can curse and swear, as well as lie,——
How old he is I can't engage,
But forty-five is near his age.——
He came, as all reports agree,
From Belfast town, in Sixty-three.
He stole, and from my house conveyed,
A man's greatcoat, of bearskin made,
Besides a pair of blue-ribbed hose,
Which he has on, as I suppose.
He oft in conversation chatters
Of scripture and religious matters :
But take the rogue from stem to stern
The hypocrit you'll soon discern.
Whoe'er secures said John McKeoghn——
As soon as I shall get my own——
Shall have from me, in cash paid down,
Five dollar bills and half a crown.
                                    MARY NELSON."

There are Nelsons in Talbot, but I have found no one who
owns descent from said John McKeoghn.

If the truth must be told, the people of Talbot then did not regard slaves as they later did under the pressure of civilization,
as part and parcel of their homes and families. The people were
more fond of cock-fighting, horse-racing, entertainments and the
minuet than of books, though they were withal cultivated, hospitable, honest and brave. Today slavery is a thing of the past,
and never again will there be trading in human lives ; but that
slave time knew its virtues as well as its sins is proven by the
noble conduct of the slaves of the South during the civil war,
where no act of hostility and inhumanity was committed by them
when the women and children were at their mercy, and today
there are connecting links between the white man and the negro,
the old-time "uncle" and "auntie", which show how strong
were the ties of affection between the two races, and which nev-

MILES RIVER—THE YACHTSMAN'S MECCA.

CHOPTANK RIVER AND DOVER BRIGDE.

er could have been so had the master been the tyrant many would have you believe him. The old time negro is fast disappearing, and soon the places that knew him will know him no more. Like others he served well his part in making the history of this mighty new world, his descendants have stepped into his place, and he is slowly passing into the Beyond to be remembered only as a strong type of "Slavery Days in Dixie."

CHAPTER X

OLD TIME CUSTOMS AND PEOPLE.

 HUNDRED and fifty years ago there was on the Chesapeake shores a distinctive aristocratic class, and Talbot may be said to have been the social head-centre of the, even then, large, well educated and wealthy clique who were considered "to the manor born." Their associations were with the English-born merchants, officers of the Crown and professional men, of course including military and naval dignitaries, and these alone were the recipients of lavish hospitality of the wealthy planters of the Eastern Shore.

In places the clergy founded fairly good schools, and served as tutors for the children of the rich, landed class of aristocrats, who, themselves, were content with their own limited education, for it was limited then to a marked degree. So very meagre was the education of even the aristocrats then that the clergy and lawyers were alone up in books, while but few could boast of an intimate acquaintance with the three R's.

Not for a moment let it be thought that the clergy neglected their spiritual duties in teaching the A B C's—for a consideration—to the children of the wealthy, for they did not, any more than they allowed religion and teaching to interfere with their sports, for in those days, fox hunting, cock-fighting and horse-racing parsons were very frequently found. They could preach as long and pray as earnestly as they could ride and chase a fox.

Dress distinctions bespoke the man in those days, as did also his seat in the Church, for the old English customs even now cling to the people of this part of Maryland, and yet the seed of hostility was then taking root against the Motherland, a seed that later sprung into a mighty harvest, for the reaping was a Nation. It is unfortunate that more praise cannot be bestowed upon the clergy of the English Church of that day, but it cannot, for they brought ill repute upon their religion and thus enabled an opening wedge of other creeds to enter, take root and prosper. The Methodists gained a firm hold upon the community, as did also the Presbyterians, while the Friends, pursuing the even tenor of their way, took good care of their people, mentally, bodily and spiritually. Perhaps it were just as well not to delve too deep into the creeds and lives of our ancestors, who were making a new world for themselves—and their posterity—but let the veil of forgetfulness drop between the then and now, or, as it can be better put:

"Let the dead past bury its dead."

Had we lived in those days we would have done as they did, so we can only claim better morals and behavior in the broad glare of public opinion of to-day. One thing is assured, and that is, that the present generation owe far more than posterity alone to the brave pioneers of long ago, for we inherited from them at least the mighty nation that now is ours, and which was bought with their blood and heroism. Running one's eye down the long roll of names that helped to build up Maryland, and which are linked with the Eastern Shore, particularly with Talbot county, we find many engraven on the pages of history, and which the withering touch of time can never erase.

It may justly be said that Kent county has the honor of being the oldest foothold of a government in Maryland, for a settlement was established on Kent Island by William Claiborne, a man upon whom much censure and abuse has fallen, yet who, in the light of recent years, is not regarded as black by far as he was then painted, and whose descendants to-day are among the most prominent of Maryland's families. Talbot was taken from Kent county, which then embraced the whole Eastern Shore, in 1661, and in 1695 Kent Island, called the "Gem of the Chesapeake," was added to Talbot. In 1706 Kent Island was detached from Talbot and given to Queen Anne; but Talbot is now a very large domain of land and water in itself.

To call the roll of ancient names in Maryland is almost to read over the present directories of its numerous towns and villages. Referring to those most prominent, and which are a transcript from Revolutionary War annals, we find the Andersons, Adkins,

Bartletts, Bartons, Bayards, Biddles, Bowies, Brents, Buchan-
ans, Brownings, Batemans, Calverts, Cabells, Calhouns, Carrolls,
Caulks, Cecils, Chamberlains, Chews, Clays, Claibornes, Carl-
tons, Comegys, Coutees, Courseys, Dandridges, DeCourseys,
Dennys, Dixons, Downs, Dickinsons, Duvalls, Eagers, Earles,
Edmondsons, Edens, Emorys, Everetts, Gibsons, Gilmores,
Goldsboroughs, Gordons, Grangers, Greys, Hammonds, Handys,
Hansons, Haywards, Hollydays, Howards, Hynsons, Hughletts,
Henrys, Hughes, Jenkins, Jenifers, Kerrs, Kemps, Latrobes,
Lees, Lloyds, Lowes, Lowndes, Leonards, Mullikins, Magruders,
Marshalls, Martins, Masons, Mays, McHenry, Morris, Nichols,
Morris, Ogles, Pacas, Palmers, Pascaults,|Peales, Penns, Pick-
etts, Pinckneys, Polks, Prestons, Pues, Rasins, Ringgolds, Roes,
Rutledges, Scharps, Schleys, Slaters, Skipwiths, Smiths, Shan-
nahaus, Stewarts, Spragues, Stones, Taylors, Teackles, Tildens,
Tilghmans, Trippes, Tharps, Vaughans, Veaseys, Vickers, War-
fields, Wetherills, Wilmers, Whittinghams, Wirts, Wroths, and
so on, *ad finitum.*

CHAPTER XI.

UST why family graveyards were almost invariably placed in full sight of, and close to the dwelling house of the living is not easily explained. Some assert that it was a desire of the living to have their loved dead near them, while others say that in the olden time it was to protect the graves from Indian despoilation, or the bodies being unearthed by the wild animals. Whatever the motive, family burying grounds of the South are strangely near the habitation of the living. In many cases here in Talbot the dead are inearthed close up to the mansion, or quite within a stone's throw of the broad piazzas upon which the families are wont to gather on summer evenings. These resting places of those who have gone before, under the eye of the living, seem a constant reminder that man's span of life was of short duration, and he, too, must soon go into the shadows of the Great Beyond.

In New England, and the Middle States the early settlers lived close together, the farms were not large, and a community had one burial place, there seldom being family burying grounds on a home estate. But in the South it was ever different and every plantation and farm, with rare exceptions, had its graveyard.

In Maryland, on the Eastern Shore and particularly in Talbot, these family burying grounds were a feature of every country home. Though there have been perhaps fewer changes here in Talbot of proprietorship of estates, so many remaining in the hands of descendants of the first American ancestors, yet quite a number have changed ownership, and the bones of the dead went with the land, so to speak.

The change of owners meant also neglect of the burying ground on the estate; for new comers, unconnected by kindred ties with the dead, cared little, if anything, to keep the sacred spot in good condition; for death is sacred, and human ashes sanctify earth if anything does.

Talbot is dotted far and wide with these old family graveyards, a few in a fair state of preservation and well kept, yet most of them crumbling to decay, the brick walls a ruin, the gravestones time-worn, broken, moss-grown and even the inscriptions almost obliterated by the storms of many and many years. A few of these once respected sanctuaries of human ashes have even their history unwritten, while in places there are graves that are unknown entirely.

By a strange coincidence, however, one grave, standing alone and unmarked by a stone, many know of and recall its history. It is, however, marked by two trees, a large and small holly tree growing at the head and foot, and, *en passant*, I may remark that the holly grows to greater perfection and beauty in Talbot than any other place I ever knew. Many of them grow to the size of forest trees.

But to return to that lone grave. The one whose ashes rest there was a character, from all reports handed down of him. He was a hard drinker, or perhaps it would be as well to say an easy drinker, as he was fond of his glass at all times. He was also very fond of tobacco, smoking and chewing.

Dying, he did not wish to be deprived of either his rum or his tobacco, and doubtless having a respect for the Indian belief that one starting for the Happy Hunting Grounds should be well supplied, he left instructions that his coffin should be made extra long, and be left open at each end, while at the head should be placed a jug of liquor, the very best of spirits, and ten pounds of tobacco, smoking and plug.

His idea for having the ends of the coffin left open was, that should the Devil come after him his spirit could play hide-and-seek with his Infernal Majesty, by slipping in and out at will.

Whatever his real motive, he was buried as described; and there, in full sight of the passerby is his grave, marked by the holly trees, while the corn and the rye, the juice of which he loved so well, grow in the surrounding fields, fields which now, however, know the cultivation of tobacco no longer. It may be said with truth that this lonely grave really is haunted by *spirits*, and many an old toper longs to know just what age has done in the way of improving the contents of that jug.

The most remarkable of all family burying grounds in Talbot, and in fact without its equal as such elsewhere in the United States, is the one of Wye House, the home of Colonel Edward Lloyd. This graveyard is across a beautiful old garden running to the rear piazza of Wye House, and filled with a most luxuriant growth of box hedges, trees and flowers, with arbors and many picturesque nooks. The graveyard has the proportions and imposing appearance of an English village cemetery, and is encircled with a high brick wall, massive and well preserved still.

There are tombs that show wealth and loving regard from their designs, especially so when one recalls that they were placed there over two centuries ago.

A striking feature of this remarkable burying-ground is that seven of the tombs bear the name of Edward Lloyd, revealing the fact that seven generations of that name lie there and have been buried from Wye House.

And more: there are now living three generations of the same name, Colonel Edward Lloyd, the present courtly master of Wye House, a true gentleman of the Old School, a man who has lived his three score years and ten in the full knowledge that he bears a great and honorable name.*

Then comes Edward Lloyd, Jr., the Colonel's son, whose home is near Wye House on a beautiful island in the Wye river, and his son, Edward, making ten generations of the one name.

It is within this quaint old cemetery of the Lloyds that Admiral Franklin Buchanan, who married Colonel Lloyd's sister, lies buried, while near his grave is that of Commodore Lowndes of the U. S. Navy. Also here are the graves of Captain Winder, U. S. Army, and of General Charles Sidney Winder, U. S. A., and later a gallant officer of the Confederacy; so there side by side, connected in life by kindred ties, rest those who wore the blue and those who wore the gray. In addition to these graves there are many more of note, among the Lloyds and their kindred, in the Wye House cemetery.

Another famous burying-ground is the Tilghman's, at the Hermitage, and branches of the same distinguished name have

---

* The wife of Col. Edward Lloyd is the granddaughter of Francis Scott Key, author of the "Star Spangled Banner."

their graveyards at Rich Neck Farm on Tilghman's Point, and
on several other estates which have passed out of the possession
of the family. In these there are grave stones recording dates
of the death of those whose ashes lie beneath, over two hundred
years ago.† In sight of the Tilghman's old time mansion of
Rich· Neck is the burying ground, only a short distance from
the mansion, the foundation of which was laid over two centuries ago. The little cemetery shows that the monuments were
crowded most closely, considering the vast amount of land to
draw upon; but then, perhaps, the old timers, knowing the
healthfulness of the spot, did not expect many to die. It is
walled in with stone, and ruin, desolation and death are indelibly stamped upon all. The oldest tomb there is in a fair state
of preservation, and bears the name of one "who departed this
life May, 1696," just 202 years ago.

It is stated of this old burying ground that when a party
was given at the mansion years past, a young man, fond of his
cups, hid there a bottle of whiskey upon his arrival, for future
reference. Later he returned to the spot with a few congenial
spirits to indulge in a drink, but did not know that meanwhile
a stray hog had been caught by the negroes and thrown over
into the sacred spot for safe keeping until the morrow. The
hog had followed the example of those about him and had gone
to sleep when the party, returning for the spirits, found, as they
supposed ; other than ardent spirits, for up sprung the animal
with a wild rush, The bottle fell on a tomb and scattered the
contents, while the terrified youths fled like deer to the mansion,
swearing off as they ran.

A strange feature of the Oxford Cemetery is that, while it is
Talbot's oldest town, there are no very old gravestones in it, as
White Marsh and family burying-grounds received the dead of
that early age.

The burying-place of the Goldsboroughs at Ottwell was another of the very old ones of Talbot, but some years ago the Goldsborough family had the ashes of their ancestors removed to Easton and entombed in the Spring Hill Cemetery. The Chamberlain burying-grounds, both on the Plaindealing and Bonfield

---

† The Rich Neck farm has been bought by a syndicate of Easton capitalists, and the
intention is to make of it an all-the-year-round resort, being an ideal spot for one.

estates, are very ancient, as Maryland history goes, and there are others scattered throughout the county that all trace of has been lost.

Of the burying-grounds about the old churches, mention has been already made in these pages, but the present age dwells more upon the living of today, rather than the dead of long ago.

CHAPTER XII

MARYLANDERS "to the manor born" are natural genealogists. They learn at their mother's knee, along with their prayers and A B C's, who they are and who was their father and grandfather before them. Many of them also learn to go back six, and even to the ninth generations as Americans, while upon the Eastern Shore, and particularly in Talbot, a number of them to-day dwell upon lands granted to their ancestors away back in the days of Governor William Claiborne and Lord Baltimore. This is particularly true of those who were Church of England people, Roman Catholics and the Society of Friends. Ancestors that could be regarded with pride by their descendants were constantly spoken of to the children of those days, and they were made to realize that they, too, had perhaps been born to greatness. If there had been any "black sheep" in the family flock, they were simply passed over in silence.

But those same children never realized and enjoyed the true pleasures of childhood as known later, when stereotyped customs no longer kept them in stocks. Joys they had, but with all the pomp and circumstance that their elders could awe them with. They learned their lessons well, of kinship even to the fourth and fifth cousins, and when they grew up had the genealogy of by-gone generations at their tongues' end.

Thus the custom came down to the present day, and Eastern Shore people not only know who their families are for generations, but the history of generations of their neighbors' kindred, with the added fact that where they ignore the frailties in their own blood, they can unearth for you at any time the skeletons in other closets not sheltered by their rooftree. But this has been human nature since time immemorial, to see the mote in the other fellow's eye, and to bring a microscope to bear upon it, too, in the observance.

A look at the life in the plantation homes of those days is of interest, viewed from our lives of to-day. The large and crumbling manor-houses cannot be said to have been most comfortable, compared with modern comforts. They were too draughty, and wood fires, even in enormous hearthstones, did not give a genial and steady warmth, while the furniture was too precise and stately for comfort. The plantation, from the mansion to the slave quarters, was a settlement in itself. There were picturesque windmills to be seen, a necessary appointment for the grinding of flour and cornmeal. The hominy was beaten for use, and the bacon and hams all cured on the place. If there were fifty "hands"—slaves—on the plantation, this meant over 10,000 pounds of bacon and 4000 pounds of meal to be stored away for the annual consumption, not to speak of other edibles that were a necessity.

Then there had to be homes for these fifty laborers and their families, homes for themselves apart from the "Great Home," as the planter's mansion was called. The stables, granaries and storehouses were locked each night, but the mansion never, for it would have been regarded as inhospitable to turn the key against a friend or traveler. Large as their houses often were, they were not large enough for the hospitality of their inmates. Spacious rooms and halls and broad piazzas were the features of these homes, with armchairs, rocking chairs and settees that to-day would be stiff and devoid of all ease.

The dining rooms were of most generous proportions, and the sideboard, with its decanters, was a most important piece of furniture, while there was brandy from France, rum from the West Indies, wine from the Madeiras and gin from Holland ever there to be served. You were well waited on, your wants were anticipated, a helping arm aided you to bed after a late flow of spirits, and, as surely as the morning came, your mint julep was brought to your room by a servant as an eye-opener. The tables were bountiful, and with every delicacy land, water and importation could provide, while the cooking was such as to make the name of Maryland cooks famous the world over; and just here I may add, the lessons taught then are handed down to the present age.

Terrapin, oysters and canvasback ducks, as also venison, all *luxuries* now and high priced, were then so common that hired laborers of the planters had it put in their contracts that they

TRINITY CATHEDRAL, SEE CHURCH OF DIOCESE OF EASTON.

were not to be fed on these edibles "more than once each week."
And think, too, of fine brandy selling at $2 per gallon, Antique
Rum 50 cents per gallon and best wines at $1 per gallon. These,
too, were drunk out of solid silver tankards and the finest cut
glass. When invited to drink, and not to extend an invitation
would be strange indeed, few ever refused, and even the clergy
were always ready to drink the very good health of his host, and
his own in particular.

Two marked features of a well equipped planter's home were
the family burying ground and a coach-in-four, the latter often
having negro postillions. These old-time carriages have all gone
into the misty past; not a trace of them, with their swinging
bodies, on huge leather springs, being found. They were used
then for formal calls, state affairs and to go to church in, the latter often distant many miles, while to-day the coach-in-four is
not known here, but is the pleasure vehicle of wealthy northern
people. Those who dwelt north of that invisible line—Mason
and Dixon's—that marked the division of the north and south
so thoroughly in the bygone, often wondered at the wealth, ex-
travagance and luxurious lives of southern people, and perhaps
there was engendered a feeling which the good people are urged
to pray against being led into—*id est,* "envy, hatred and malice."
But the war has changed all that now, and it is oftener the
northern folk who ride in their coach-and-four, have a full retinue of servants and live luxuriously, while the southerner accepts the iconoclastic situation with true philosophy and makes
the best of it. To do this shows true grit in the blood, and this
the southern people, from mountaineer to fisherman, statesman
to planter, certainly has to an abnormal degree.

The family burying-ground of an estate was not one to be hidden away in a remote corner, for it was often within full view of
the front piazza, as though to be put where the living could keep
vigil over the dead. Often it was in the garden, and the well
trodden paths leading to it showed that the dead were not forgotten lying off there in the gloom of the grave and eternal
night-shades. I remember one burying-ground where not one
of the graves, and there were a score or more of several generations, was marked by slab or tomb, only upon the little mound,
so strangely unlike all other things on earth, grew ivy, violets,
forget-me-nots, roses, jassamine, geranium and other flowers.

A visitor to the house, an English nobleman, asked with surprise of the lady of the house: "Why, how do you know the graves apart?" "How do I know my dead apart? Why, you might as well ask me how I knew my living loved ones apart, for the going out of life of those who rest here each broke a heart-string which no other love can unite."

The genuine "Old Maryland way" was most cordial in its friendships and hospitalities, the homes always keeping "open house" and being constantly crowded, while with convivial meetings, visitings and the utmost scope of hospitality, the ladies even were busy, while horse-races, fox-hunts and other sports kept the men on the go, bringing into use all the horses and vehicles as well as the yachts and barges afloat. Such was the Old Maryland way in the last century, yes, and down to within the life-time of many who have not yet passed their allotted space of three-score years and ten.

CHAPTER XIII.

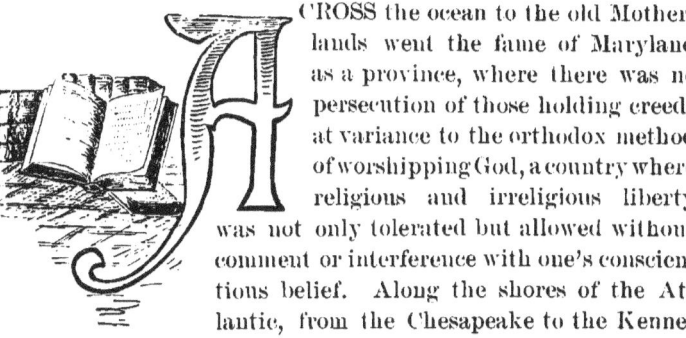

CROSS the ocean to the old Mother-lands went the fame of Maryland as a province, where there was no persecution of those holding creeds at variance to the orthodox method of worshipping God, a country where religious and irreligious liberty was not only tolerated but allowed without comment or interference with one's conscientious belief. Along the shores of the Atlantic, from the Chesapeake to the Kennebec, the same fame of religious liberty in Maryland went, and thus those persecuted for holding conflicting creeds were glad to find a haven of refuge in this much favored land.

The result of this liberal allowance of thought in a man was the coming to the Eastern Shore of Maryland of that sadly persecuted sect, the Quakers. They came from across the sea, from Virginia, from New England and elsewhere, to see this Eldorado which would be an asylum to them. Especially did the Friends settle in Talbot county, and an unswervingly honest, temperate, generous, yet clannish people, they left their impress ineffaceably upon this country. At that time, 1650, be it recalled, Talbot county embraced territory now included in Queen Anne's and part of Kent and Caroline counties, as well as its own extensive domain. In New England, Boston in particular, where only a century ago alleged "witches" were burned at the stake, the Friends were terribly persecuted, for the Eastern States were not then traveling upon the broad gauge of advancement and true liberty that now distinguish their citizens This persecution in New England gained for Talbot many of what are among its best people of to-day, the Friends. They came hither to find an asylum and found it, while the beautiful country

---

*Meaning those whose are unjustly, though not with intentional injustice, called Quakers.

delighted them.   They came to work hard, to found new homes, new associations and to lay the corner stones of future greatness and fortunes.

The log cabin homes erected, and in this each gave to the other a helping hand, their fields planted, they began to turn their attention to the building of their Meeting Houses, where they could worship in their own silent way.   To me, there is nothing so effective as silent prayer—it leaves one wholly alone with his conscience, often afar from pleasant companions; and to think of one's sins is the sure way to reform himself.

But this is wandering off into unforbidden ground--Religion —and there are so many devious and distinct ecclesiastical toes to tread upon, one is not safe in diverging from the beaten path which means, in the immortal words of Abraham Lincoln "with malice toward none and charity toward all."

But to those Meeting Houses of our "Friends, the Quakers:"* It was three years after the establishment of Talbot county that the Friends came here to settle, in 1657, the first coming from Virginia, and the Meeting Houses, primitive in the extreme, for they do not believe in "an outward, visible show of an inward spiritual grace," were erected at Wye, Little Choptank, Island Creek and one, which was doubtless the first, on "Betty's Cove," Miles River.

This one on Betty's Cove was built of clapboards and stood on the boundary line between the homes of R. B. Dixon and Dr. Cherbonnier, while it covered ten acres of land and faced the river, from which it was distant but a few rods.   The records show that here also was a graveyard, and that the little building was repaired in 1676, but in 1693 it was abandoned, left alone with its encircling dead, while a larger and more pretentious Meeting House had been erected in a more central location at the head of the Third Haven, on Avon River.   This last building was so placed as to be convenient to every part of the country, even by vehicles on the highways, the bridle paths or water, for, from the Avon, vessels have cleared, and come from every part of the world.

The locality of this greater Meeting House, great still in the memories that cluster around it, could not have been better

---

*The name of Friends was adopted by this sect from the words of Jesus Christ to his Disciples: "Ye are my *friends*, if ye do whatsoever I command you."

chosen, for it is just south of Easton, in its suburbs now, and
hence the site of sites, showing how well chose they who located the county town just where they did. The Friends' Meeting
House at the head of the Avon was also not a long walk across
for those who came by boat to Betty's Cove on Miles River,
while as all roads lead to Rome, it is said, so all highways and
streams in Talbot lead to Easton. This house was a frame
building with massive timbers, boarded and shingled, and to-
day stands as a monument of the old time style of building.

As the records have it: "Our joint Quarterly Meeting for
both Shores, held at ye home of Ralph Fishbourne ye 27th day
of ye First Month 1683, the meeting decided upon this greater
House, it being unanimously agreed that Betty's Cove Meeting
be removed to ye great Meeting House." Hence the greater
House was built, the lesser one, about which still rests the
ashes of the Talbot Friends' ancestry being left to crumble to
decay, if not into forgetfulness, for

> "So the multitude goes, like the flower or the weed,
> That withers away to let others succeed
> So the multitude comes, even those we behold,
> To repeat the old tales so often retold."

Among the Friends who attended the old Meeting House was
Wenlock Christison, who fell a victim to his creed and was sentenced to be hanged in Boston, yet was later released from
prison, not because of humanity, but because the English government ordered a mitigation of his punishment. Many are the
names in Talbot to day of the ancestors of those who attended
that old Meeting House, and whose ashes there repose, and
among them can be named John Edmonson, William Southbee,
Howell Powell, Thomas Taylor, John Pemberton, William Cole,
John Dickinson, William Dixon, and Gorsuch, Johns, Berry,
Pitt, Kemp, Bartlett, Sharp, Williams, Webb, Sparrow, Bork-
head and many more too numerous to mention here.

It is stated as an indisputable fact that George Fox, the
founder of the Society of Friends, attended the meeting at
Betty's Cove that originated the building of the old Meeting
House near Easton, and later also attended what Eastonians
now speak of as the "William Penn Meeting House." It was
in 1684 the meeting was held, and George Fox describes
the greater house in his journal as being located upon the Avon

River (old style Tredhaven). This meeting lasted five days, the first three attended by all of the Society of Friends, the last two only a men and women's assemblage for discipline. The Friends were not alone in attending their meetings, for Romanists, Protestants, Indians and Negroes were often present, in fact this new house had to be enlarged to hold the people.

To John Edmondson fell the honor of entertaining George Fox, his farm at the time being the one known as Cedar Point, owned by Mrs. Edward B. Hardcastle of Easton, but leased to Charles H. Leonard. In his journal Fox says that he attended the meetings each day, going by boat, and the boats were so numerous in the river the scene reminded him of the Thames of London. He also spoke of "seeing both rivers"—the Avon and the Miles—from the Meeting House, and this shows to what an extent the heads of the two streams have filled up in the past two hundred years. George Fox also at that time had interviews with the chiefs of the Algonquins, Susquehannahs and Iroquois, whose villages he visited.

At that time the Friends in Talbot kept a boat—the "Good Will"—and horses, expressly for the use of their ministers in traveling through the country. Upon his return to England George Fox sent to the Meeting House a number of books, some of which are still held by the Society, and this was the first library known in Talbot. This greater Meeting House was built in no slipshod manner, as its fine state of preservation to-day shows, after having withstood the storms of over two hundred years. The builders did not slight their contract, as is too often the case with them in this hurrying age.

There was a committee of Friends appointed, as the old record reads: "To agree with ye carpenters for ye building of ye said house * * * 60 foote long, 44 foote wide, and to be strong, substantial framed work, with good white oak sills and small joyst, and ye upper floors to be laid with plank and ye roof to be double raftered, and good principal rafters every 10 foote, and to be double studded below, and to be well braced and windows convenient, and shutters, and good, large stairs into ye chambers, which chambers are to be 40 foote square at each end of ye house, and 20 foote vacant space between them : and for other conveniencys to be left to the discretion of ye aforesaid Friends."

Now there was no going behind this contract, only 1 fail to see, with my limited knowledge as a builder, how in a house "60 foote long by 44 foote wide," two chambers on second floor could be made at each end 40 foote square, "with 20 foote vacant betwixt them." Still there stands the old Meeting House to-day, stout, staunch and with wondrous staying powers to resist the ravages of Old Father Time, and any one, Friend, Protestant, Romanist, can go out and measure the dimensions and then figure on those "40 foote square rooms with 20 foote vacant space betwixt them," and see how it was done in "ye long time ago."

CHAPTER XIV.

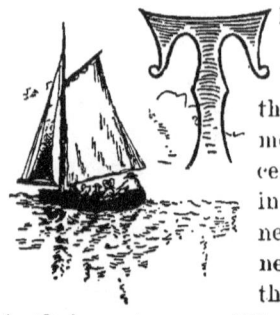HE records show that this old Friends' Meeting House, built so long ago, a connecting link still strongly uniting the present with the past, had the first meeting beneath its roof the 5th of December, 1684. Dwelling near it today in a little cot lives "the old sexton," a negro. Struck by the strangeness of a negro for grave digger, in a late visit to the old Meeting House, for the negro race in their acute superstitions are wont to "see things" not visible to mortal eyes, and hence give graves a wide berth, especially at night, I asked him if the ghost ever troubled him.

"I never seen none, sah ; but I does hear warnings in the old church jist before any one dies who is to be buried here."

"What are the warnings ?"

"Well, sah, they is crackings of the timbers in the old house, and knockings, telling me to git ready ter dig a grave, for some one is coming soon to fill one, and they know, sah, for them warnings never fails."

I heard "knockings" too; but set them down to the creaking of the timbers under the influence of the wind, but then I had not the faith of the old sexton in things spiritual.

From a minute dated 6th of 12th month, 1690, a house was erected on these grounds, near the river side, for the accommodation of visitors from a distance (the two chambers over the meeting rooms probably being insufficient). The statement is, "That Friends on this shore are to pay to Ralph Fishbourne 2041 ℔s. of tobacco ; It being ye one-half of what he disbursed for building ye house for conveniency of Friends from a distance, at the creek side, near our Great Meeting-house." As late as the early part of this century some persons now living can remember when they went to and from this meeting in row or sail boats (in preference to carriages), and had only to walk a very short distance, this tributary of Third Haven River, which is merely a ditch now, being navigable then.

It is evident that provisions were furnished these Friends by the members here, if they were not already supplied. The minute in regard to it reads : "This meeting considering ye great distance yt many Friends have to come both by land and water, yt may repair to our Yearly Meeting, whereby they may want necessarys, therefore this Monthly Meeting appoints Joseph Rogers to inquire into ye same, and to give Friends account, yt so they may be supplied if any want to be." Thus proving that it was not a spirit of inhospitality that prevented all visitors from being entertained at private houses, but doubtless an inability to accommodate the large number who came, or to find means of transportation for them.

For several years monthly meetings were held two days in succession. The reports varied but little in expression, but it is evident, from their length, that considerable business was accomplished. As the smaller meetings declined, others were established elsewhere. Some resigned, or suffered themselves to be disowned on account of the slavery question, which agitated the minds of Friends at an early date; and many were disowned for marrying those not in membership with the Society, in consequence of the ceremonies being performed by a minister or priest (for they styled *all* by that appellation), because tortures had so frequently been inflicted through their instrumentality; therefore a breach of the discipline in that respect was deemed almost an *unpardonable* offense; but from a decrease of members and a more charitable spirit toward all Christian denominations rules of discipline in this particular have relaxed greatly.

Marriage intentions in those days were announced in the meeting by the parties themselves, in both the men's and women's meetings, on two separate occasions, and thirdly, in a written form, together with the written consent of the parents of both, consequently it embraced three months before the ceremony was accomplished. At the present epoch the "passing," as it is termed, is settled in writing. The first marriage on the meeting records bears the date of 1668,* and reads as follows : "William

---

*These records began at the first Meeting House on Betty's Cove.

Southbee, of Talbot Co., in the province of Maryland, the 29th day of the First Month (O. S.) and in the year 1668, in an Assembly of the people of God, called Quakers, at their meeting, at the house of Isaac Abrahams, solemnly in the fear of God, took Elizabeth Read of the aforesaid county and province, spinster, to be his wife ; and she, the said Elizabeth Read, did then and there, in like manner, take the said William Southbee to be her husband, each of them promising to be faithful to each other. To which the meeting now witnesseth, by signature.'' A regular record of marriages, births and deaths has been kept since 1668, and it appears even earlier than that.

Settlements of estates, contracts (either legal or otherwise), all disagreements, also consent asked for certificates of removal, and for traveling Friends and ministers, as well as for *approval* of marriages, were submitted to the meeting, and committees appointed to investigate the clearness of the cases. Tobacco being the currency for many years, all collections and business transactions of the church were made in that way except in occasional donations of grain, produce, furniture and cattle. The first collection in money was made in 1713. In that era tobacco seems to be the staple crop. The Indians considered it a *sacred* herb, a precious gift of the Great Spirit to his children, and the act of smoking, with them, has always something of a ceremonial or even religious character.

Friends were conscientiously opposed to paying tithes; but their personal effects and slaves were often seized to the amount equivalent to the assessment, though they were compensated out of the meeting's fund for their loss. The records show that care has been exercised in providing for indigent members when afflicted or unable to support themselves, and assistance rendered to fit others for business. The subject of education claimed their early attention, and several schools were established under their superintendence. A school-house was built on a portion of these old Meeting House grounds in 1782, but was removed to Easton in 1791. A proposition was made in 1816 to move this Meeting House there ; a lot of ground was purchased and bricks burned for the purpose, but the matter was reconsidered and thought inadvisable.

Friends were much exercised in regard to taking oaths. This meeting applied for an act of the English Parliament on the sub-

ject; and in 1681 Richard Johns and William Berry were requested by the Meeting to appeal to the Maryland Assembly to
exempt the Society from taking oaths,—which was favorably received by the Lower House but not by the Upper ; but in 1688
Lord Baltimore published a proclamation resolving to dispense
with oaths in testamentary cases. Thenceforth those who had
any scruples in the matter were permitted to affirm. The spirit
of war has always been denounced by Friends as inconsistent
with a Christian life, believing that arbitration is a much more
peaceable and satisfactory mode of settling disagreements. Min-
utes state that collections were made several times for the benefit of their members suffering from the Revolutionary War in
this country, and from the effects of the Rebellion in England
and Ireland.

We are informed that it was a usual custom with Friends,
after attending the sessions of West River Yearly Meeting, to go
on board of the slave-ships and select their slaves. In 1759
the Yearly Meeting of Maryland advised care in importing and
buying negroes ; in 1760 condemned importation ; in 1762 condemned importing, buying or selling slaves without the consent
of the meeting; but in 1777 slave-holding was made a disownable
offense. The first William Dixon freed and provided for a number of his slaves long before the consciences of others had been
moved in the matter. Some voluntarily manumitted theirs.
Isaac Dixon, James and Benjamin Berry, Sarah Powell, Benjamin Parvin, John and Sarah Register, John and Magdaline
Kemp and James Turner were a few of the number. Schools
were afterwards provided for the benefit of these colored people;
and their efforts were unceasing until the general manumission
occurred in 1863.

The following account is given of William Penn's visit here,
in 1700. "We were at a Yearly Meeting at Treadhaven, in Maryland, upon the Eastern Shore, to which meeting for worship
came Wm. Penn, Lord and Lady Baltimore, with their retinue;
but it was late when they came, and the strength and glory of
the heavenly power of the Lord was going off from the meeting;
so the lady was much disappointed, as I understand from Wm.
Penn, for she told him she did not want to hear him, and such
as he, for he was a scholar and a wise man, and she did not

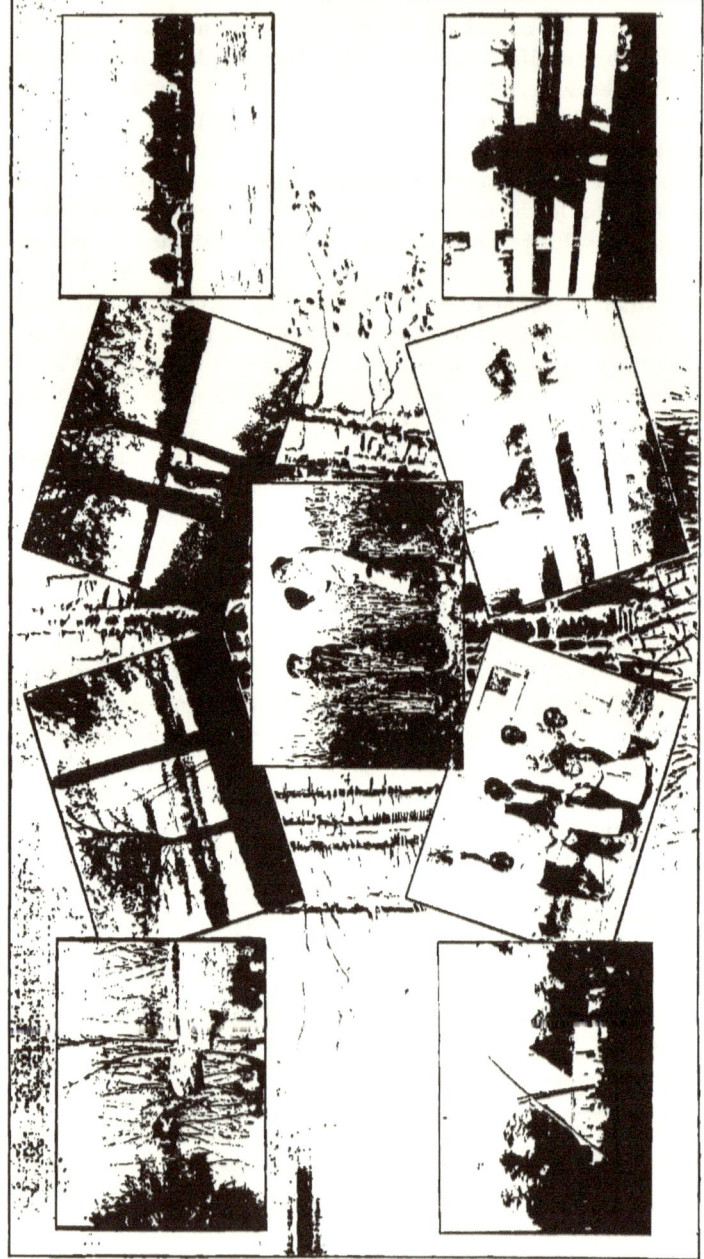

question but he could preach ; but she wanted to hear some of
our mechanics preach, as husbandmen, shoemakers and such
like rustics, for she thought they could not preach to any purpose. William Penn told her 'some of these were rather the best
preachers we had among us.' " Letters and epistles were received and read at this meeting from William Penn as well as
George Whitehead, Daniel Gould and other prominent Friends.

An interest has always been manifested in the welfare of the
Indian race. The mild and persuasive treatment of George Fox,
William Penn and others seemed to insure their respect and confidence through succeeding generations. Therefore credit is due
the society for the primary step towards their promotion.

So little did our early predecessors appreciate one of the comforts of life (as well as health) that for almost a century they
had no means of heating this building (foot-stoves, filled with
hot embers, were sometimes used by woman Friends). Some
opposition was offered when a stove was proposed, and afterwards bought (in 1781), declaring that their religious zeal ought
to be sufficient warmth. It is authentic that one of the members
was so unyielding that, to show his disapproval, he called it a
"dumb idol," and made it a receptacle for his overcoat, but as
there was no fire, no damage was done ; the following Sabbath
he repeated the act without noticing the fire, and the odor aris-
ing from the smoking garment attracted his attention (much
to the amusement of the witnesses, especially the children),
and Friend Parvin had the humiliation of going to its rescue
—convinced of his error as to a stove being a "dumb idol."

This house was saved twice from being destroyed by fire; once
by a Friend whose name was Sarah Berry (about the year 1810);
she extinguished the flame by rubbing it with a stick, not having time to obtain water or give the alarm. This ancient building brings many memories. Since its erection great progress has
been made in the arts and sciences—nations have been formed
and fallen asunder ; and now this house is following the course
of all terrestrial things—decay.

What memories crowd upon us as we stand in the presence of the Past ! How great is the mind of man, and how
wonderful ! It grapples with complex subjects but to reduce
them to comprehensive simplicity. It measures the length and
breadth of our land and knows the coming of the seasons. It

VIEWS IN EASTON TWENTY YEARS AGO.

Washington Street in 1878. Same scene after the fire.
Market Space before the fire of 1878. Thompson & Kersey's 20 years ago.

"ARISTON," ON THE AVON, OWNED BY MRS. K. J. ROBINSON.

brings into action latent forces—commands them, and they obey.
Yet how insignificant when it attempts to comprehend the dura
tion of time, and to measure the untold length of the past! Two
hundred years! what is it but a drop in the ocean, but a thought
in the history of ages? Yet, short as it is, generations have
come and gone, the young have become old and passed away.
Sturdy oaks, that withstood the storms of winters, and among
whose inviting branches carolled birds for scores of summers,
have flourished and fallen.

In the silent yard of the old Meeting House lie entombed the
ashes of those whose presence once made glad the heart, whose
buoyant steps delighted the ears of loving friends, around whose
board echoed the voices of happy children, and from whose gates
the stranger turned not away. The moss-covered stones and
sodded mounds remind us of loved ones whose hearts no longer
pulsate with the quickened fire of youth, whose hoary heads no
longer bow in humble reverence to the Author of Light. The
young and the fair are there ; in the morn of life, Death waved
his wand, and they are not. The middle-aged are there ;
he pointed his pallid finger to the strong man, and his proud
form lies prostrate. The aged are there ; he beckoned, and they
obeyed his summons. Those lie there whose welcome voices
once sounded within these walls, calling the attentive ones to a
higher and better life. Here *they* were led in childhood by the
hands of faithful parents.

On the face of those rough-hewn timbers are written, "Passing away, passing away." The plain, undecorated walls seem
to echo the voices of long ago, and humbly call the weary soul
to rest. The unpainted benches remind us of the untarnished
lives of true Christians. The unassuming door-ways, low ceilings and unsteepled roof are typical of the meek and lowly who
adorn not the exterior, to be seen of men, but who worship God
with an humble and contrite heart. No organ peal is heard ; but
beyond the solemn silence break the heavenly words, "Peace, be
still." Countless changes have been wrought since those foun-
dations were laid. Cities have sprung into existence ; millions
of acres, on whose surface civilization had never trod, have become fruitful ; foreign lands have been visited and peopled; new
nations have flourished, and old ones perished.

Then the forest still resounded with the axe of the settler, and the voice of the engine was unknown; now iron wheels thunder through the cleared and fertile valleys. Then small craft wandered over the trackless sea, subject to the whims of the wind; now iron steamers can stretch their foamy wake from shore to shore, regardless of the weather. Then months were occupied in communicating with foreign countries; now electric cables pulsate with the heart-throbs of continents. Then persecutions on account of religion were not infrequent; now the glorious liberty of conscience extends throughout our land. When the Tred Avon Meeting House was erected, the author of Pilgrim's Progress was still preaching the gospel in England; Dryden, the father of modern English prose, was in his glory, and the name of Alexander Pope had not been heard. In that house the parents of George Washington could have worshipped in childhood, and Peter the Great could have heard the teachings of Jesus.

In reviewing the changes wrought by the works of man, the thoughtful mind marvels with astonishment; but in contemplating the unchangeable laws of the Deity, we are dumb with admiration. During these twenty decades, man's works have crumbled into dust; but the sun, undimmed in glory, still moves in his mighty course, the King of Day; while the moon, the faithful watcher of the night, reflects his splendor as in the beginning. The unwearied stars still march to heavenly music, without deviation from their fixed course.

We are passing away; our lives, like the waves, last but a moment; our voices, like the sigh of the wind, are forgotten; our forms are but clouds on the blue vault of life, changing and disappearing. In the impenetrable future, endless generations will follow to take the place of those gone before.

CHAPTER XV.

 CITY often springs into existence from a cross-roads where a store and a blacksmith's shop alone are to be seen. Then comes a dwelling or two, a school-house and a church. With the school-house and the church as a firm foundation, the cross-roads pushes ahead more rapidly, grows into a village, buds forth into a town and then spreads into a city. Many a pretty town and prosperous city in our land has been built up around a church, once placed off to itself in a location convenient to the surrounding country. There people gathered on the Sabbath Day to hear the Gospel preached in the good old way, and not "as it is preached to day" in many cases. There they also gathered on a more serious duty still than religion, to lay away in the little churchyard some loved one who had gone into sleep eternal.

As time passed on, the neighbors grew closer together, a home for the parson was built, and soon the lone church became the center of a flourishing city, though many of the older people loved to remember it, and loved it best, when it stood a silent sentinel alone, save its dead, over whom it kept watch and ward. How stirring are the lines of Alexander Smith, who, in a poem put into the mouth of a man crossing a lone moor after midnight, the words :

> "I heard a distant spire
> Start in its sleep
> And murmur of the hour."

The country church holds an attraction for nearly everyone, and in village, town or city the places of worship are generally the most attractive feature, save to travelling men, and they are hunting "the best hotel." There were no "drummers" at that time in Talbot, for they came into particular and favorable use with the steamer, the telegraph, rapid transit and electricity. Nothing is too swift for the drummer, and they deserve all they

get. The first Methodist Church of which there is any record
in Talbot was erected in 1774 on a site now in Kent County, and
no trace of it remains, though one now stands in St. Michaels on
the site of one erected prior to 1800. To-day the Methodists are
a power in Talbot, but when they first gained a foothold here
they had a hard row to hoe, and it was sometime before they
could gain converts.

The Rev. Francis Asbury was sent over by Wesley from England, and he at once begun earnest work in preaching Method-
ism wherever he could find a sinner, and sinners were by no
means rare then, as now. He and his fellow Methodists met
with persecution, as had the Catholics, Church of England people and Friends; but he was unswerving in duty and came to
Talbot as a bonanza of wickedness and a soil in which to sow the
seed of salvation. He preached one sermon, and the people of
Talbot promptly jailed him, and in Easton. This was no damper
to his ardor, for he begun to preach through the iron grating of
the jail windows. This drew a crowd, and he kept it up, with
prayer and psalm singing, telling the people all about a beautiful Heaven and a terrible Hell, until ribald laughter ceased; he
was allowed to go and "Those who had come to scoff remained
to pray." Those who had ordered his arrest at once saw that
they had made a mistake, for he drew crowds like a circus, and
he was promptly turned out, as it was said that if he was kept
in jail he would convert every man, woman and child in Talbot.

It is asserted of this indefatigable worker in the vineyard of
sinful souls that he preached *eighteen thousand* sermons, prayers
not counted, and rode *one hundred and fifty thousand miles* preaching the Gospel. There is a befitting monument to his memory
(1854) in the Mount Olivet Cemetery, Baltimore. James Hur-
ley, another Methodist preacher, was arrested and fined for
preaching, so he "whipped the devil 'round the stump" by getting down upon his knees and *praying an exhorting sermon*.
Freeborn Garretson, a third itinerant Methodist minister, was
arrested in Cambridge and put in jail, but his cell had no window facing the street, and the jail keys were hidden to prevent
his friends from aiding. But persecution arouses sympathy and
destroys bigotry, and when he was released from jail he found
the seed he had sown taking root, and then came the hard struggle to keep out the tares.

More than a century before the Methodists gained a Church
footing in Talbot, and some years prior to the building of the
Betty's Cove Meeting House of the Friends, there was a Church
of England house of worship erected in Talbot, and more, it was
by no means an ordinary structure, but one quite imposing in
those crude times. I refer to what is known to-day as the "Old
White Marsh Church," or rather its ruins, for it was accidentally partially destroyed by fire only a short time since, the victim of carelessness after it had stood for nearly two centuries and
two-score years a monument indeed to the ancestors of many of
the oldest and most prominent families in Talbot. Deserted
long ago for the new Parish Churches in the town of Easton and
villages of Trappe and Oxford, the old White Marsh had been
left to its silence, gloom and neglect. The sacred ashes of the
dead that sleep under the shadow of its walls did not guard it
from ruin, for their tongues were forever silent, their voices no
longer echoed within the old sanctuary, and memory alone could
appeal to the busy throng of their descendants.

The silent pleading of the old church, of the dead about it,
was not heard, at least not heeded, and so the ashes of the
quaint old edifice and the ashes of generations tenfold who worshipped beneath its roof were mingled together. If there is sa-
credness in the consecration of a church to the worship of God,
there should certainly be reverence in the hearts of its members
—united to it by ties so binding as their religious roof-tree,
where they have been brought to attend divine worship since
childhood, as their parents and generations of grandparents
were before them—I say there should have been reverence
enough in their hearts to have preserved that old edifice and its
tombstones, kept it from destruction, and honored it as a connecting link with the long ago.

At least, now that fire has made it but a ruin, those who are
connected to it by the sacred ties of other years should, at least
for the sake of the mouldering tombs still there, make of the ruined walls a monument to revere and point to as ages pass away.
Who will undertake the task to train ivy over those massive old
walls, clean up the burying ground, place tablets with the obliterated inscriptions on the stones and encircle all with an iron
fence? Will not the good women of Talbot move in this matter,
for where woman wills the thing is done.

WASHINGTON STREET, EASTON.

MORELAND BUILDING, EASTON.

The bricks of old White Marsh were all brought from England, in the clipper ships that traded with Oxford over two hundred years ago, and those same bricks were paid for in tobacco. When the parishioners of the old White Marsh began to desert it for more conveniently situated churches, other houses of worship of their creed were erected in St. Michaels, Trappe and other villages in Talbot. General Tilghman began at his own expense a stone church at Oxford, back in the forties. The death of the General at his home of Plimhimmon, near Oxford, caused the work on the church to cease just as the walls had been raised a few feet high.

The wild myrtle and the ivy now found an abiding place there, and in a score of years had made of the walls a most picturesque ruin of what appeared to have been a very ancient structure. Several years ago the ruin was taken in hand and completed, it now being a very handsome church.

Many years ago, when the town of St. Michaels had but three hundred people, yet with the surrounding country to draw from was of some importance, there stood an old Methodist Episcopal Church, about which many recollections are still treasured by the oldest citizens. In the burying ground hard by stands a monument bearing the following inscription:

"Erected by numerous friends
in memory of
Garretson West.
Born in Talbot county in 1800,
Born again in 1818,
Died in 1853.

Now, this second birth doubtless refers to his conversion, for he was a noted Methodist preacher, unlearned, yet earnest and a "burning and shining light as an exhorter." Of this good old man many stories are told, of how he never used Psalm book or Bible in giving out his hymns or teaching the Scriptures, astonishing those not in the secret of his marvellous learning of the Holy Book, when the truth was *he could not read.* Blessed with a wonderfully retentive memory, he had the Bible and hymns read to him and committed all to memory at a few readings, while, with a mind fixed upon all in Sacred Writ as *fact,* he argued from that standpoint against all "cisms." On one occasion he gave out as a text: "Rest! My text is found between the first and last pages of this sacred Book," and then he went on to preach a most powerful sermon that must have made sin-sick sinners in the rear pews terribly uncomfortable. Knowing that he was not up on Scriptural quotations, he would not say where just such a verse could be found, but would aptly put it: "You'll find it in Scripture."

There was another quaint character in St. Michaels, who was driven to conversion through fright. He believed in "signs," was very superstitious but a hard customer. To the people he was known as "Uncle Isaac", and one night a man went to his little home and called out in a sepulchral voice :

"Isaac, prepare !"

"For what ?" called out Isaac.

"*For death !*"

"*Who is that ?*"

"*The Lord !*"

A scuffling was heard within, soon the door opened and Uncle Isaac darted out, making a bee line for the old Methodist Church, at a speed that was wonderful. There was a revival meeting going on at the church, and in rushed old Isaac, up the aisle to the "mourners' bench," when down upon his knees he went, beginning to pray and sing vigorously. Of course he was more than welcomed as a "brand snatched from the burning ;" but the story was too good to keep, leaked out, and when it reached the convert's ears he "blackslided" in a manner most forcible, while his expressions were of a carmine hue.

In tearing down the walls of old Christ (Episcopal) Church in St. Michaels to give place to a new one, under the church were found, in a good state of preservation, several tombs of ministers long since called to their rest. The present church was erected in 1812, but is the third built upon this spot. The first record-ed baptism is in 1682.

St. Joseph's Church at Wye in the long ago now remains only as a memory in the hearts of good Catholics. Various are the traditions told of this ancient chapel as to its age and history, but if it went back into two centuries ago, the records do not re-veal the fact. It is said that there was a small mission on the site where St. Joseph's was later erected, and years ago inscrip-tions on surrounding stones revealed dates as far back as 1640 ; but no proof of this exists, and it is believed to-day that the St.

Joseph's Chapel was the first one built there. To prove this, old records show that the Rev. Joseph Morely built the chapel, and in 1764. From a list of the principal Jesuit Rectors in Maryland now before me, I find that they date back to 1633 and up to 1773, and Father Morely's name is among them and the date 1758, so if he founded the chapel it could not have existed in the sixteen hundreds.

From 1773 until 1806, for thirty-three years, the Jesuits as a priestly body were unknown, for those who remained in Maryland attached themselves to the secular or Bishop's clergy, for they did not care to relinquish their active missionary work here. Father Morely was one of those who remained, and he toiled faithfully for his people until his death June 3d, 1787. For some reason the records of St. Joseph's were not kept or were destroyed, hence very little, save in the way of tradition, can be learned of the mission chapel and its pastors ; but Rev. Joseph Morely certainly left a saintly legacy to his successors.

A few extracts from Father Morely's day-book may be of interest and also fix the date his mission was founded. He says : "March 18th, 1765, I took possession of a tract of land I bought of Parson Miller and his wife and Sarah Wellington, on which I put eight negroes which I bought from Rev. Mr. Lewis in White Marsh, Prince George County, viz., Nancy, Zun, Frank, Paul, Lucy, Davy, Nancy and Henry. Their expenses in transporting them came to £10—$50.00. May 11th, 1765.—I received from Rev. Matthias Manners, to pay for our land in Talbot County, £260, 10s. [This was not the land upon which the Chapel of St. Joseph's at Wye was built, according to the following : "May 30th, 1765.—To Mr. John Miller for land, £272, 11s, 9d. The deed of our land at St. Joseph's, Talbot County, was signed, sealed and acknowledged before Col. Richard Tilghman, Provincial Justice, &c. May 31st, 1765.—The deed was entered in Talbot Court."]

These entries in Father Morely's daybook would indicate that St. Joseph's was built in 1765, and that is looking a long way back into the past for the existence of a church, while many are the traditions that cluster about it and its dead. The church that was started there is another one of the bonds that are so frequently found in Talbot connecting the old with the new.

CHAPTER XVI

ROM things spiritual, the Old Churches, it may be *apropos* to turn to things ghostly, tell weird tales that are told even to-day and have been handed down from fireside to fireside. Some are true, known to be, yet those that are founded upon superstition are, by many, just as firmly believed. There is a cross-roads village a few miles from Easton which is known as "Hole-in-the-Wall." As to just how it got its name accounts differ, according to the narrator, but it is more often called by that old time appellation than by the one it bears on Uncle Sam's Post Office records, Hambleton.

One of the tales told of how it got its queer cognomen is that the sailors of ships, crossing the ocean to the then flourishing and busy seaport of Oxford, were wont to slip ashore with their smuggled goods and pass them through a hole in the foundation wall of an old building. There the secret agent, never seen by them, counted the cost of the articles and handed back the money in payment. Thus neither the sailor nor the agent saw the the other and hence could not be recognized before a court on trial for breaking the law.

Another version is that a man dwelt in the old home who had a very pretty daughter, whom he did not allow to receive company, and when a young man did his courting, it was to his interest to discover if the "old man was about;" hence a hole in the wall had been made for the gallants to peep through and reconnoitre.

Still another story is that a suitor for the girl's hand went there one night and, through the hole in the wall discovered his hated rival in the house and saw enough to prove to him that he was the successful one, and, in his jealous rage he determined to kill the one who had made him miserable. He had fired upon his rival, killing him, had made his escape, was not suspected of the crime, later married the girl, and only on his death bed confessed that he had done the deed. Whichever the true story, or if all of them were more or less correct, the place is to this day called Hole-in-the-Wall.

It is within a quarter of a mile of this spot, the quaint little cross-roads village, that the ruins of White Marsh Church stand, with its moss-grown graves surrounding. As there is no marsh near, Talbot county being strangely free from even sea-marshes, it is not known why it was called the White Marsh Church, but such is the name handed down. Of this ancient church a strange and weird story is told, yet a true one. It was in 1711 that the Reverend Mr. Maynadier, a Huguenot, was the Rector of White Marsh. The rectory was an old brick mansion on a farm, a mile distant from the church, and the house still stands in excellent repair, the property of Dr. Johns. The story is that the rector's wife died, and her last wish was that she should be buried with a valuable family ring upon her finger, for it was customary in those days to bury a body without removing jewelry they had most worn in life.

Two strangers who had attended the funeral had observed this valuable ring and determined to secure it that night, so they went to the old church yard, for it was then over half a century old, and digging into the grave, removed the coffin, broke it open and attempted to take the ring off the woman's finger. It would not come off, and so a knife was used to sever the joint, and this was the means, with the restoration to fresh, cool air, that revived the woman, who, not being dead, suddenly uttered a cry and sat up in her coffin. Tradition does not say what became of those two grave ghouls, but it is to be hoped that the fright they received turned them from their evil ways.

As for Mrs. Maynadier, she realized the situation, and though alarmed and ill, she was possessed of great nerve, so drew her shroud about her form and started upon her homeward way. What must have been her feelings, as she trudged through the night to the home she had been taken from in her coffin a few hours before! And what *would* have been the feelings of a benighted being who had met her on that lone highway? Verily he could have taken oath with truth to having *seen one from the grave*. In the rectory the old clergyman was seated before his hearth

alone, doubtless recalling the wife he had won in the long ago,
far across the sea, and whom he had just buried in their adopted
land.   Sad must have been his memories, deep must have been
his sorrow, as he sat there looking into the past and thinking of
the loved one in the White Marsh burying-ground.

Suddenly he was startled by a fall against the door, followed
by a low moan.   A fearless man, he sprung to the door and beheld the fainting, shrouded form of his wife.   The sight nerved
him to action and drove away fear.   He raised her in his arms,
bore her to her bed, gave her stimulants, chafed her hands, one
still bleeding from the cruel cut of the ghoul, and soon restored
her to consciousness.   Then he called his servants, told them the
weird story and sent to Oxford for a physician.

Such is the story, and more, Mrs. Maynadier recovered from
her illness and lived for many years.   She and her brave old
husband now lie side by side in the old White Marsh church-
yard.   It is alleged that the blood stain from Mrs. Maynadier's
hand still remains upon the door against which she fell.   The
Jenkins family of Easton are descendants of Mrs. Maynadier,
the heroine of this true story.

That there are old houses in Talbot county visited by "wandering spirits from the grave" there are some who really believe,
and the negroes are particularly careful to avoid places where
they may see what in the further south they call "hants."   Of
one of the old houses on Peach Blossom, now owned by Mr. Chas.
S. Carrington of Easton, stories are told of its being "haunted,"
and with all due allowance for the noises made by prowling rats
and sighing winds.   The story goes that, away back beyond the
memory of the present generation, a mother in the ancient house
was wont to watch for the coming of her son by boat to Easton
between midnight and dawn twice a month.

To keep his mother from waiting up for him, as often the boat
was very late, not arriving until after daylight at times, the du-
tiful son told his mother he would not come at specified times,
so she would not know when to expect him, and thus obtained
her promise to retire and allow him to go to his room unwel-
comed, for houses were seldom locked at night in those days.
But the good woman knew that her son would come as before,
and though she did not wait up, she retired one night but did
not sleep.   Often her son would bring a friend, his particular

chum in Baltimore, and so the mother always prepared supper enough for two and left it on the table, so they could slip into the house and, going to the dining room, have their meal and retire to sleep until late the next morning.

One night, when the moon shone like day, the mother lay awake listening for her son. She knew the time the boat should arrive with a fair wind, and waited to hear her son enter the house. Time passed, ample for him to have gotten a horse and wagon at Easton to drive home. But he did not come, and the mother was growing anxious, when she heard the sound of coming wheels. Some distance from the house the sound ceased, and soon after a step was heard ; creeping to the window, the mother saw her son had come, but alone. She heard him enter the house, and, not going to the dining room, as was his wont, go directly to his room.

Not wishing to let him think she was awake, she did not go to his room, and was dropping off to sleep when she heard a deep groan. Instantly she arose and, lamp in hand, went to her son's room, for surely he must be ill, she thought. She knocked at the door and again heard a low moan but no response. Entering the room quickly in alarm, she found the lamp burning as she had left it and the bed undisturbed, but *no one was there!* She went downstairs to the dining room and parlor but found no one ; her son's coat and hat were not in their accustomed place. "Surely I heard him come home, saw him approach the house," she cried : "My God, what does this mean?" At once she aroused the other inmates of the house, and a thorough search was made—but the young man was not there ! Nor was the horse in the stable, the negro man who slept there not having been disturbed. "Some harm has befallen my poor boy !" cried the mother, and in vain did those about her try to comfort her, for she repeated over and over again, "He is dead ! I feel it ! I know it, for *I saw his ghost!*"

Those were not the days of telegraph and rapid mails, and when the next packet came it brought the dead body of the young master. He had been found slain in his room, robbed, and no clue to his assassin. His particular friend was away from Baltimore at the time ; and, strange to say, months after, word came that he had been shot in New Orleans in a gambling den. When the son's strong box in his room at home was opened, it was found that the family jewels and much gold were gone, and there were a few practical minds who said that the mother had not seen her son's ghost, but his *friend*, who had murdered him, had gone to his room in his Talbot home, got the contents of the box and escaped.

That is the way of looking at it in the broad glare of day, but at night, it is said, the ghost of the murdered master, who was buried near the old home, can be seen and heard by those whose sight and hearing admit of their "seeing things." As for Mr. Carrington, ghosts do not disturb him, though he is fond of telling weird stories, and tells them in a way that nearly inclines one to a belief in the supernatural.

Upon the "Perry Hall" estate, the home of Mrs. Mary H. P. Cox, on Miles River, there stands a massive old oak tree, the interior of which is hollow. The story goes that in the days of the Revolution a young French officer who came over with Lafayette to aid in fighting our battles, fell in love with a Talbot maiden; and, unable to get leave of absence to visit her, deserted and came to her home. He was found out and proclaimed a deserter and, to escape the death penalty, fled; but his rival for the maiden's love got on his track and, tracing him to the old oak tree, found him concealed in its hollow. Instantly he was taken out, and the death sentence was read to him, his rival saying that he would immediately carry it out.

"I did not leave my command from fear, but because love made me a fool. I am no coward, but appear so in the eyes of the one I loved; hence, am ready to die; and to you, Monsieur, I leave the one I so madly loved. I am ready." With these words, he took his stand against the old oak. The soldiers were drawn up before him, the word to fire was given by his rival, and the unfortunate Frenchman fell dead. He was buried where he fell, and the tree is called "The Frenchman's Oak." At the head of his grave some one placed a stone bearing his name, but it has long since disappeared. The Frenchman's rival did not marry the maiden, however, for she would never again see him; and rumor has it that she died of a broken heart within a year after her lover's death, and was buried by his side.

With such a *real* ghost story as the one of old White Marsh church-yard, which is looked upon to-day as being haunted, or as the negroes say, "the land of hants," Talbot naturally has

other tales of the supernatural and superstitious. One is that
in the dim past a rich old man of Talbot, whose home still
stands, left his fortune to his three sons in equal shares ; but the
eldest, in the absence of his younger brothers, so changed the
will that he was to get the lion's share, and also to hold the estate in his keeping. His plan went well with him until one
night, a year after his father's death to the day, he was returning on foot with some friends from a long hunt after birds, and,
to save time, being tired, decided to cut across a field and over a
fence where his father had lost his life. The old man had died
from the effects of a fall in getting over a fence, which the party
of hunters would have to scale at the fatal spot.

The family burying-ground was right at this very place, and
the son did not care to pass where his father lay buried, after
his act against his brothers. But with friends to accompany
him he pushed on, and the three were suddenly brought to a
halt when within a rod of the fence and old burying-ground.
And no wonder, for there stood in their path a shrouded, misty
form. The face was indistinctly visible, but the erring son knew
it and stood in horror, trembling violently. Suddenly a voice
was heard, cold, sepulchral, yet distinct : "My son, do not wrong
your brothers, but do right by them as you hope for mercy when
you die !" Then the white form turned, placed one hand upon
the top rail of the fence and leaped over—a flash of fire and sul-
phurous smoke bursting forth from where the fingers touched it.

Another moment and the form leaped the wall of the burying-
ground and disappeared among the trees that surrounded the
old man's grave. The three men had seen the form, as also the
flash of the burning rail, though the latter felt sure that the
ghost of the old man had come from a very hot place, and from
the advice he gave his son about hoping for mercy could realize
how it was himself. Whether it was a real ghost or one of the
brothers, the next day the imprint of a hand was found burned
on the rail. The ghost served its purpose, too, for the eldest
brother hastened to the county Court-house the next day and
"did the right thing by his brothers," so that he might "hope
surely for mercy when he came to die."

There is a well authenticated ghost story, which has the nov-
elty of being more than the mere spirit of a human being returned to earth, for a horse and two-wheeled chaise are also seen.

"NORTH BEND," RESIDENCE OF R. B. DIXON.

ANOTHER VIEW OF "NORTH BEND."

This treble ghostly alliance is of an old doctor who practiced here in Talbot many years and drove about in a two-wheeled vehicle of peculiar pattern drawn by an old white horse that suited the man and the trap. All knew the old doctor, his horse and chaise, and his calls took him far and wide through the country. But the doctor loved his toddy and was wont at times to get very merry, in other words, very drunk. But as long as he could stand up he would go, and he was considered a better physician in his cups than others who were perfectly sober.

One night the doctor was sent for in haste to see his best friend, who had accidentally shot himself. The doctor was drinking heavily at the time, it was a wretched night of storm, and he was in no hurry to go, at least until he had fortified himself with more drinks. It was a long drive, the roads were not the best, and in his semi-intoxication he went to sleep, lost his way, and the next day was found far off the highway in vain trying to find himself and the home of his wounded friend.

"Oh! show me the way," he pleaded piteously of the neighbor who had found him.

"No need now, doctor, for it is too late," was the answer.

"Too late? Too late?"

"Yes, doctor, for I just came from there, and he died two hours ago, bled to death. You could have saved him had you arrived last night," was the stern response.

"I could have saved him?"

"Yes."

"Show me the way."

"No need now, doctor, but that path will take you to your own house, if you will give your horse his head," and the man rode on.

That was the last ever seen of the old doctor alive, for he was found later in the day dead in the wreck of his old chaise, and with his horse also dead, for a bridge across a creek had gone down with them. The doctor and horse had been killed and the vehicle wrecked. The ashes of the old man of medicine lie in the old White Marsh burying-ground, surrounded by the graves of those whose bodies he cured of aches and fevers, and yet the inscription, "Rest his soul," does not appear to have had its effect. Tradition has it that belated people who travel the highway where he met his death, on each anniversary of the night on which he was killed, hear the hoofs of the old horse coming rapidly up behind them, hear the rattle of the old sulky, and can see the misty outline as the spectres come close, but never pause, while also a pleading voice is heard, crying: "Show me the way! Show me the way!" I have never seen the phantom nor heard the appealing entreaty, but I know where the highway is, and have stood by the old doctor's grave, whom I found to all intents and purposes resting well.

There is still another weird legend known as "the ghost of Plaindealing." Now, "Plaindealing" is the name of an ancient estate and also an arm of the Avon River, called here a creek, though it is wide and deep enough for steamers to ascend. It is very broad, and its head is near the village of Royal Oak. The name was given the creek by the Indians, who met on its banks a party of Friends to trade with them pelts, deer skins and things of their manufacture for those that the white men had brought from the Old World. As the Friends in trade always dealt honestly with the Indians, the latter gave to the spot the name of Plaindealing.*

A part of the old homestead of Plaindealing still remains, though a fine brick building, that also dates far back, has replaced the greater part of the mansion first built. Here, in the legendary part, the owner kept up a stately and hospitable style that was famed far and wide, for he lived as he had in the old country, being "to the manor born." Through some tragic chance, for a dark mystery hangs over the affair, the owner of the mansion fell, it is said, from the upper story over the carved railing in the hall, breaking his neck and leaving a stain of blood on the floor which ages have never erased.

After his death, the house, through neglect, began to go to wreck. Its handsome panelling and carving begun to decay, its walls to become moss-grown, its spreading roof to show its age, The old furniture became covered with dust, the old portraits of well-born men and women in powdered wigs and cue were stained and mouldy, while from the wet cellar came the air as from a tomb. The family burying-ground, just across the lawn upon the banks of the creek, grew up dense and dank with weeds and

---

*A stone now marks the spot, and stands at the very edge of the water of the creek, just where the Indians in their canoes landed to trade with the white men.

trees, while the vaults cracked open and revealed their ghostly occupants to the inquisitive one who ventured near.

It was the ideal spot for spooks to haunt, while to enhance the dismalness of the old abode, it became the dwelling place of an old woman known as "Katie Coburn, the Witch." This "witch," the last of her kind known in Talbot, was old, deformed, hideous, and was guilty of diabolical ways and impish incantations to make herself feared. That she was dreaded by all, especially the children and negroes, there was no doubt, for the former were kept out of mischief by being threatened with her, and the latter felt that the sight of her was a *hoodoo* upon them. The negroes accordingly gave Witch Katie a very wide margin of room when they met her, and wore charms to counteract her spells, the "left hind foot of a rabbit, killed at the dark of the moon," doubtless being in great demand after a meeting with the "Witch of Plaindealing."

Not far from Plaindealing there lived a farmer whose cows pastured near the old burying-ground. One afternoon the boy whose duty it was to drive the cows home had to go near the lonely spot, and beheld to his amazement a stranger there ;—a man tall, stately, in the ancient garb like that worn by those whose portraits were in the deserted mansion. The man spoke to the boy, but the latter fled for home, told his story, and it was not believed. Again he saw the same man, and again, until at last he spoke to him, and for response saw him walk to a certain spot in the burying-ground and point downward, at the same time stamping his foot. This same performance was gone through with several evenings after, between the boy and the silent spectre in quaint old time costume.

On one occasion the spectre led the boy, now no longer afraid of him, into the old home and pointed to a portrait on the wall. The boy saw that the "ghost" was strangely like the portrait, dress and all. Then he was led back to the grave-yard and the spectre pointed downward and stamped his foot, as before. As it was growing dark, and the cows had gone on ahead, the boy suddenly decided to go home, and he lost no time in doing so, his parents again laughing at his story. But then came the rumor that "Witch Katie" had not only disappeared from Plaindealing, but also from the country. The boy had not seen her since the coming of the quaint man of the grave-yard. At last

so impressed were the parents of the boy with his story of his
ancient ghost, seen in the gloaming each day, and now become
the talk of the neighborhood, that the father went one evening
at sunset to have a look at the spectre.

"There he is, father, see, he has gone to the same spot and is
pointing to the ground !" cried the boy. But what the boy saw
the man could not, yet was impressed by the look and manner of
his son, and said, "Well, my son, we will see what your ghost
is pointing out to us." That this intention was carried out, and
more, that digging there, a treasure of some kind was found,
there is not the slightest doubt, for curious neighbors, visiting
the grave-yard some days later, found a deep hole there, freshly
dug, and in it the imprint of a box that had been buried.

Of the quaint ghost that appeared in the gloaming nothing
more was heard, and the family of the boy to whom the spectre
had revealed himself certainly grew suddenly rich. The legend goes that they belonged to a noble family in England, had
been defrauded of their inheritance, and so came to America to
seek a home, and this ghost of one of their ancestors had enriched
them by pointing out the buried treasure, making his presence
visible alone to the boy.

Such are a few of Talbot's ghost stories, all bearing the imprint of truth ; while there are others, *ad infinitum*, not quite so
well vouched for as those I have retold, but which I will not
relate, for be it known that this is a narrative of legendary real-
ities, not of fiction.

HE seed of Quakerism and Wesleyanism certainly fell upon and took firm root in genial and kindly soil in these old counties of the Eastern Shore of Maryland, softening society from its aristocratic harshness and too much pride of ancestry, and bringing it in consonance with the beautiful scenery that is to be found here on every hand. The towns are more characteristic of the dim past than are those upon the other shore of the Chesapeake, and elsewhere in the early settlements of the northern parts of the United States. The sun-set and twi-light of to-day seem of the misty by-gone, in their exquisite softness and splendor, and the people are, many of them, in keeping with their old homes, though just now, they are awakening to the possibilities of what a land of promise they possess.

The people generally retain also a purity of English blood, and their language at times partakes much of "old English." There are dwellers upon the Choptank, Avon, Miles, Wye and Chesapeake shores of Talbot, that have their old homes, come down to them from generation after generation for over two hundred years; and who can trace their families as far back in England before their American ancestor came to this country.

Indelibly written in the pages of the history of the Eastern Shore of Maryland, and particularly of Talbot county, we find names that we greet each day as the descendants of worthy ancestry. Men and women of these names we meet every day in business life and society, and to the people of Talbot, the names of any one tells the story of who and what their ancestors were, and how well they are upholding the honored reputation of their forefathers. If there are closet skeletons in the past history of any one of their ancestry, the mantle of charity is kindly drawn

Residence of J. Harry Ratcliffe, St. Michaels,
site and part of the building where meetings
were held by Methodists as early as 1778.

House in St. Michaels struck by cannon ball
from British fleet in 1813.

PASTORAL VIEW ON THE AVON.

over the remembrance; while if there are any good stories to tell of any of the ancient *regime*, they are told with great gusto, even if against themselves. And more, they are generally good story tellers; and if of English descent, even, can see a joke at a flash, not having to wait until it is moss-grown before they can catch the point.

Referring to some of these old families, it will be well to see just how far back they can go in tracing their American lineage. In the past more than now they were wont to intermarry among their particular set, the result being that there is a blood kinship and connection by marriage among a legion of good folks, some young men of to-day being so fortunate as to count their pretty cousins by the score ; and, be it known, that cousins count here, even unto the fourth and fifth remove. It is interesting to note from the name of the Eastern Shore people, their lineage from English, Irish, Scotch, Dutch, German, Welsh, Swedes and Danes, and an old timer can tell to just what nationality one originally belonged, by hearing him named. Some of these names have been metamorphosed, a few dropping a consonant or two, or a syllable even, while there have been those of one country merged into another or blended together, just as have the descendants of the several nationalities intermarried. All this may be owing to the meagre education in the earlier days, when even some of the clergy could read and write but fairly well, and not unfrequently the Justices appointed made their mark instead of their name, for the simple reason that they could make a cross mark but not a letter. Perhaps after all it was often better to know too little than too much, as is now the case when learning penetrates all barriers, shatters all idols, tramples all traditions under foot, often crushing our happiness under the iron heel of adamantine investigation and destroying our fondest illusions.

From whatever race they sprung, those early settlers of Maryland—whatever their creed or condition in life, whether descended from aristocrat or redemptioner—the brave soldiers from the shores of the Chesapeake won immortal renown in their patriotic and military record during the long struggle of the Revolutionary War. It was the daring Maryland Regiment of Four Hundred that saved the American army in the retreat from Long Island, and glad they were to throw themselves into the breach as a sacrifice, if need be, to check the British advance, while Wash-

ington's army crossed to the mainland. Washington knew the
material of which the Marylanders were made, and with the
American army on the very verge of a panic and rout, he called
upon the men from the Chesapeake's shores to come to the rescue, and he called not in vain. Nobly the gallant Four Hundred
responded, and they were hurled upon the advance of Cornwallis with irresistible fury and *esprit*. What mattered it that their
ranks were torn with iron hail, that they fell by scores to rise
no more, for they were of the stuff of which heroes are made,
and with "do or die" as their motto, their thinned ranks closed
up shoulder to shoulder as the iron storm swept them, and they
beat back the British and thus enabled the American army to
make good its retreat. Yet at what a sacrifice! The death call
numbered twelve officers and 260 men of the Four Hundred
Marylanders.*

Pursuing the even tenor of its way since its early settlement,
Talbot County has had citizens whose names have become known
throughout the country; in fact, Maryland may be called the
cradle of men born to greatness. At the head of these famous
sons can be said to come the name of Colonel Tench Tilghman, a
man who won his spurs in the Revolutionary War, and whose
character throughout was that of a hero. A book about Talbot
would be incomplete without a just tribute to those of her sons
who brought honor to their State, and hence short sketches of
some of them I place before the reader. It is true that the people of the present age do not delve much into the story of worthy
citizens of the past, and but for the Civil War that brought heroes to the front, and won from the country just recognition,
thereby recalling other great men in our other wars, and in
statesmanship, many of those of the dim bygone would sleep now
in graves unmarked—yes, "unmarked, unhonored and unknown."
The grave of Franklin in Philadelphia has but a simple slab,
and is unknown to the thousands of people who pass it daily in
their going to and fro. Sentiment appears to be relegated to the
past in the busy whirl of life in this age, though certainly it
should not be so.

*In 1895 a monumental pillar was erected in Prospect Park, Brooklyn, in honor of the
Marylanders who made this magnificent charge. It may be well to state here that in the
late Civil War upon any field, whether they wore the Blue or the Gray uniform, Marylanders made a glorious record as soldiers.

But to return to the worthy citizens whose memory is still green in Talbot, and who may be set down as Maryland's notable men. Tench Tilghman was born on December 25th, 1744, at "Fausley", his father's plantation, situated upon a branch of St. Michaels River, near Easton. He was one of a family of twelve—six sons and six daughters—for there were generous old families in those days, even among the rich ; and to a certain extent Talbot keeps up with her record as productive of prolific families. Tench Tilghman was the eldest of six sons, and of his early education little is known further than that he attended school in Easton, and was also under the charge, with his brothers and sisters, of a private tutor. Later his maternal grandfather, Tench Francis, for whom he was named, obtained for him the advantages of the best schools, and also influenced him to enter upon a business career in Philadelphia.

He was thus engaged at the breaking out of the War of the Revolution, and at once sacrificed his business interests for love of country, entering the army as a Lieutenant of Light Infantry. He was Lieutenant of the Military Commission appointed to treat with the "Six Nations" ; Mohawks, Oneidas and other tribes, and his report is published in the American Army Records. Recognizing his ability as an able ally, a man of quick perceptions and nerve, Washington appointed Tench Tilghman one of his military family; and later, in addition to being his *aide-de-camp*, he became the Commander-in-Chief's confidential secretary. The military record of Col. Tilghman is a matter of history, and his brilliant services gained for him the honor of carrying to Philadelphia, to Congress, the report of the surrender of Cornwallis at Yorktown. He made the long ride in four days, arrived at midnight and told the glad tidings, and by dawn the town was wild with joy. Congress later voted him a fully equipped charger and a sword, the latter now being in the possession of his great-grandson, Col. Oswald Tilghman, of Easton, with many other souvenirs and important letters and documents. In 1779 Col. Tilghman visited his uncle, Hon. Matthew Tilghman, of Rich Neck Farm in Talbot, and there met his cousin, Miss Anna Maria Tilghman, who became his wife several years later. At the close of the war Col. Tilghman entered into a business partnership with Robert Morris, known as the Financier of the Revolution, and assumed control of the firm's bus iness in Baltimore, where he died (when still a young man) in 1786, his wife surviving him a great many years.

Hon. Edward Lloyd, a distinguished leader in the Puritan Colony from Virginia to Maryland, 1649, was born on Wye River, Wales. He was a Land Surveyor, and was made First Commander of Anne Arundel County in 1668. With many others he moved to Talbot, patented a large land estate on the Wye, and returning to London in 1668, died there, leaving his son the property known now as Wye House. Edward Lloyd was born in 1697 at "Wye House," Talbot, and was descended from Edward Lloyd the first of his name in America. Edward Lloyd married Sarah Covington. His grandson married Elizabeth Tayloe, and their son is the subject of this memoir. He was a member of the Ninth and Tenth Congress of the United States, Governor of Maryland 1809 to 1811, and served as United States Senator 1819 to 1826. He married, 1797, Sally Scott Murray. He died in 1834.

Hon. Matthew Tilghman was born at "The Hermitage," the first seat of his family in Maryland. He inherited large estates in Bayside. He was a member of the Maryland Legislature from 1751 to the breaking out of the War of the Revolution. His public career was so constant and exalted for many years, he became known as the "Patriarch of Maryland". In 1783 he retired to private life on his estate at Tilghman's Point, where he died and is buried.

CHAPTER XVIII.

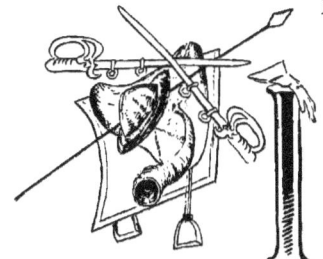

N REVIEWING the history of Talbot's people, we find among them many who are historically linked with this land of yesterday and to-day. It would be my wish to dwell with considerable length upon the biographical sketches of those men of the past, but it is impossible in a work of this kind to write down of them other than data in a most condensed form. There is one of those men of long ago who deserves more than passing notice, for Talbot owes much to him as its chronicler, and who became far-famed as the "Historian of Maryland," John Leeds Bozman. He was born in 1757 at "Belleville," near Oxford, and came from a distinguished family. After obtaining his majority he was sent to England to study law, and returning home, was admitted to the bar, but eventually turned to a literary career; yet his pen fame does not depend upon his sketches, poems or newspaper articles, but upon his "History of Maryland," a work which is a monument to his memory. Mr. Bozman's life-work was broken in upon by ill-health, and he died at his home "Belleville," where his remains lie buried unmarked by epitaph.

The grandfather of Hon. William Hindman came to America, sent by the Bishop of London to a parish in Talbot, for he was a clergyman of the Church of England. He died several years after his arrival, leaving a family, the son, Jacob, being the father of William, his mother being a Miss Trippe, daughter of a prominent Dorchester county family It was at "Kirkham," the home on Miles River, that William Hindman was born, as were also his brothers and sisters, heirs to the estate of their father, which is now known as "Perry Hall." James, one son, was a gallant officer in the Revolution, and lived till 1830. Jacob became a clergyman, and was at one time Rector of St.

Peter's, better known as the old White Marsh Church. John entered the American army and reached a Colonel's rank. From him descended Col. James Hindman, a prominent officer of the regular army in the war of 1812.

William Hindman was educated under the care of a tutor at home, then sent to London to study law. Returning, he was admitted to the bar in 1765. Though a lawyer, he was also a planter, and begun to enter into the public life of the Eastern Shore, his ability soon making him a leader. He became a State Senator in 1777, and after years of service was elected delegate to Congress in 1784. Later he held other more important offices and in all won distinction for himself. At his death he set his slaves free, an act that did not benefit them much, as they became a worthless lot, and "Hindman's negroes" were known and dreaded, while land in their neighborhood depreciated greatly.

Hon. John Dickinson was a wise statesman and Revoluionary patriot of Talbot, and deserves to be ranked among the most distinguished men of the age in which he lived. The importance of ancestral trees is not overlooked in Talbot, and hence we can trace back even the humble members of a family, and especially those who have written their names upon the scroll of fame. In 1653 about, the Dickinson brothers, three in number, of a prominent English family, came to America, Walter Dickinson settling in Talbot. William Dickinson, son of Walter, married the daughter of Howell Powell, a wealthy member of the Society of Friends, and their son, Samuel, married Judith North, a Quakeress, but it was his second wife, Mary, of Philadelphia, that was the mother of the subject of this sketch. The fame of Hon. John Dickinson is too well known to need further comment here, for his record has been inscribed most faithfully upon the pages of the history of his times.

Col. Jeremiah Banning was a sailor, who also bore a military title. A native of Talbot, he was the son of James Banning, who died, leaving a widow and several children. The widow later married Mr. Nicholas Goldsborough, who, having no children, made those of his wife legal heirs, and they, Jeremiah, Anthony and Henry, all rose to prominence. Anthony removed to Chestertown ; Henry became a Judge of the Talbot Court, and was a captain in the war of the Revolution ; while Jeremiah became a merchant sailor, making many voyages to foreign ports. After a long voyage he entered upon a mercantile life in Oxford. In 1752 he sailed for London. It was upon his return from the Barbadoes that Mr. Banning learned of the defeat and death of Braddock by the French and Indians. A voyage was then made to Lisbon, with Sir Harry Franklin, and Mr. Banning arrived there to find the place almost destroyed by an earthquake, and that thousands of lives had been lost. In 1760 he sailed again for Barbadoes on the ship Friendship, with others, convoyed by two sloops of war. Caught in a hurricane, one of the sloops went down under the stern of the Friendship with all hands, and next day a French privateer attacked the fleet and a desperate battle was fought, the Frenchman escaping. In 1761 Mr. Banning was made captain of the Friendship, and was afterward captured by a French vessel of war. After imprisonment, exchange and many adventures, Captain Banning again reached home, but to sail soon after for London, to be captured again by the French. He was soon recaptured by a British cruiser just before reaching port, where prison awaited him and his crew. Narrowly escaping in Lisbon from becoming a victim of the Inquisition, Captain Banning sailed in the British ship of war Portland and reached London in safety, sailing thence to New York and back again to London, then in 1766 to the Chesapeake, arriving home once more and saluting the port of Oxford with seven guns.

He brought on the same ship Hood, the "Stamp Master," from London commissioned to enforce the Stamp Act in Maryland. Hood barely escaped from Oxford with his life to Annapolis, thence to New York and then back to England. It was unknown to Captain Banning that the passenger bore such an odious reputation. In 1768 Captain Banning took command of the ship Pearl and made several long voyages, but was in 1773 made agent of a London house for the Eastern Shore. When the war with England began, Captain Banning was made an officer of a regiment of militia and was also appointed assessor, and it is of interest here to say that James Denny of Talbot was the first man assessed in Maryland. In 1776 Mr. Banning was appointed major of a battalion and also became a magistrate, holding the latter position until 1778. In 1777 he was selected colonel of a militia regiment and also naval officer of the port of Oxford, and next received the appointment of collector from

George Washington, then President of the United States. In April, 1788, he was elected chairman of a delegation of four chosen to represent Talbot County in a general convention to be held at Annapolis "to ratify and confirm the Federal Government as now established of the United States." This proof of his country's confidence and approbation was (to use his own words) "perhaps the most pleasing circumstance in his life." The other deputies from Talbot County referred to were Hon. Robert Goldsborough, Hon. Edward Lloyd and Mr. John Stevens. In 1785 he laid out the town of Easton and named its streets. He died in 1798, full of honors and years, at his country home, "The Isthmus," now the Easter property, and there he is buried, though no stone marks his grave. Mr. Banning's second son, Freeborn, born 1777, entered the British Navy, later that of the United States as a lieutenant, served under Captain Henry Geddes, whose daughter he married, and his home on the Avon is now occupied by his grandson, James Latimer Banning.

Robert Morris, of Oxford, and who lies buried at the old White Marsh Church, was the merchant prince of his time. Born in England, he made Maryland his home and built up in Oxford an enormous business, owning a fleet of merchant ships that sailed the world over. As a mercantile genius Robert Morris was a marvel, as a friend true as steel, as a *bon vivant* incomparable, while he was generous to a fault. He was the first to introduce the keeping of accounts in money instead of in tobacco, powder, etc. The manner of his sad taking off in the very prime of life has already been told, but a touching incident of his death is that his favorite spaniel would not leave his master's side in his last illness, and when he died, lay beneath his coffin. When the body was to be borne to the grave, it was found that the faithful animal was also dead. The great Financier of the Revolution, his namesake and heir, was the son of Robert Morris of Oxford.

Mr. John Goldsborough was the son of the first Robert Goldsborough of "Ashby," on the Miles ; born Oct. 12th, 1711, died 1783, was a member of the General Assembly, High Sheriff and Justice of the Peace.

William Perry was born Aug. 24th, 1746, of well-known English ancestry, was educated in England, married Elizabeth, daughter of Jacob Hindman of "Kirkham," now known as Perry

CHRIST P. E. CHURCH AND EASTON PRIMARY SCHOOL.

EASTON HIGH AND MANUAL TRAINING SCHOOL.

Hall and still in the possession of a descendant, Mrs. Mary H. P. Cox. Perry Hall became the home of William Perry, taking his name, and is one of the finest mansions of the olden time. A planter of wealth, Mr. Perry also held exalted positions of trust under the Government, was an active and devoted patriot through the war of the Revolution, and at its close was chosen State Senator, then Judge. While President of the Senate he died in 1799, and was buried with great pomp at Annapolis, in St. Anne's church-yard, where his grave is unmarked.

General James Lloyd Chamberlaine dwelt at "Peach Blossom," an estate he got through his marriage with Miss Robins, at that time Talbot's richest heiress. He espoused the cause of the Colonies against England and was made a brigadier general of the Maryland line, serving with great honor to himself and his state.

Away back in 1669 there settled upon Poplar Island, Talbot County, a man and his wife whose name is written down in the old records in the Easton Court House as Alexander D'Hyniossa, Hinojosa, De Onisissa, Inniosa, Lujossa, D'Hinojosa. But what's in a name, especially when the old-time scribes were not as particular about spelling as have to be those of the present. Margaretta was the name of this man's wife, and there were born to them on Poplar Island children, seven in number. The master and his wife humbly petitioned the Province of Maryland in 1671 for "naturalization papers," and they were granted. This man, Alexander D'Hinojosa, often appears on the Court Records, spell his name as they might, and to the general public of that day he was known only as the tobacco planter of Poplar Island, but he was a man with a history, as will be shown. Though living a life of quiet ease with his family upon a lonely island for years, Alexander D'Hinojosa had enjoyed a most eventful career as a soldier, statesman, Governor of a Province and political exile. It was in defence of Delaware that he sacrificed his home, fortune and position, and that State may yet erect a monument to its last Dutch Governor, when it was a province of the New Netherlands, as all the settlements of the Hollanders in America were then called. It was in 1656 that Alexander D'Hinojosa was chosen to command the military of the new Dutch colony in Delaware, he having distinguished himself as an officer in Holland, and later been under service in Brazil. The worthy therefore bore the following commission :

"The * * * * * regents of the city of Amsterdam having resolved to send a company of soldiers to their colonies in New
Netherlands, the name of Alexander D'Hinojosa was proposed
to them ; and they, on the good report rendered them of the fit-
ness and fidelity of said D'Hinojosa, have appointed and commissioned him as their lieutenant, to command in good corre-
spondence and unity, and wherefore we order all officers and
soldiers to obey him, for such is their Worship's pleasure. In
witness whereof the seal of the said city is affixed hereunto tenth
of December 1656. Having besides a seal impressed in green
wax   (Signed) J. PARVER."

    The expedition set out for New York, and Lieutenant D'Hin-
ojosa marched by land to a fort now the site of the town of New
Castle, Del., arriving May 1st, 1657. From the first D'Hinojosa
took an active part, for in 1658 he was sent to New York to represent the Council, in 1659 was made First Councillor, then Captain Lieutenant, and the same year was selected to visit the Fatherland to represent the needs of the Colony. In 1660 he was
made Governor of the Delaware Province. In 1664, as the Duke
of York was given by Charles II., whose brother he was, territory
that did not belong to England, viz., all lands between the Hudson and Delaware Bay, Col. Nichols with a fleet was sent to take
possession. Governor D'Hinojosa hastened to place at the dis-
posal of Peter Stuyvesant, in New York, "5000 lbs. of powder
and all necessaries and all his people." His offer was declined.
Peter Stuyvesant surrendered. The English fleet then visited
the Delaware, and D'Hinojosa, deserted by his people, refused
to surrender the fort, and it was stormed and taken by the British, the Duke of York getting his share of the plunder, which
was very large. D'Hinojosa was the only Dutch commander
who made a stout resistance to the English, and he surrendered
only after half his garrison had fallen. D'Hinojosa was banished, and it was then he found refuge in Maryland, for his estates had been taken, his property given to his enemies, his
negroes traded off and his faithful soldiers even sold into slavery.
Seeking a home on Poplar Island, D'Hinojosa lived there for
many years, but returning to Holland, died there, and what became of his family is not known, no mention being made of them
after 1698.

    Wenlock Christison, the "Quaker Confessor," as he was

called, lived in the hard reckoning days of long ago, among
those who did not agree in religion. There was bitter persecution in foreign lands of men of differing creeds, and when that
feeling of hate toward those who thought they had the power to
force a man along the highway to Heaven or Hades, alluding to
their mode of worship, was transplanted to the new world, it became even more vindictive than it had been across the water.
These persecutions were particularly bitter in New England
against the Quakers, for the Puritans, serving God by rules, not
ordained by the Almighty but by rules they themselves had
made, allowed no man to think differently or worship according
to the dictates of his conscience. Thinking, or pretending to
think, that they enlarged the bounds of their own creed by
damning that of others, the Puritans were determined that those
who called themselves Friends would not abide among them,
even claiming that they were no more than heretics. In Vir
ginia, too, the laws against the Puritans were severe, and it was
a Godsend to the Society of Friends when Maryland was thrown
open to them as a home of refuge. Among those who sought an
abiding place here was Wenlock Christison.

The records of the Talbot Court and those of the Friends
themselves show not a single case of persecution visited upon
these people here, and hence Wenlock Christison found his lines
cast in pleasant places when he came, an exile from Massachusetts after he had narrowly escaped execution there and did receive a public whipping. Such a man, one of influence, ability
and whose persecutions had made him a martyr, naturally became a leader of his sect in Talbot, and his name often appears
upon the old records of the Friends' Meetings here. The records
of the Avon River Meeting-house of Friends are the earliest,
most complete and exact of any relating to this county, and in
going over them carefully, (through the courtesy of Mr. Robert
B. Dixon I had access to them) I was struck with the thorough-
ness of every detail from the first to the last record. The first
record begins: "At our men's meeting at Wenlock Christison's,
the 24th of the First month, 1676,he, undaunted by threats of
death and the hanging of his fellow Friends, Wenlock Christison
defied his persecutors, and was therefore brought to trial for his
religion and sentenced to death, where he uttered the remarkable words:

"The God doth justify me! Who art *thou* that condemnest?" So near death did Wenlock approach that "his grave clothes were made for him." At the last moment he was pardoned by the King, who sent a messenger over in a special ship for the purpose; and with twenty-seven others of his Society, was set free, but not until Wenlock and several of the leaders were stripped to the waist and whipped through the town of Boston. Thus it was that Wenlock Cristison came to Talbot, and became a farmer, his home being the land upon which now stands "Woodstock." There, in the old brick house, still standing, he lived and died; and his ashes rest in an unmarked grave, though until his death, he was as a "shining light unto his people."

Hon. John Bozman Kerr was of Scotch descent, his grandfather settling in Talbot, in 1769. John Bozman Kerr was born in Easton in 1809. Was educated at Easton Academy; was matriculated at Harvard College. Studied law and was admitted to the Bar in 1833; and later entered upon a literary career, delving into history and becoming a noted authority upon historical research in Maryland. He also took a leading part in politics, and did much for the advancement of the schools. In 1849, he was sent to the United States Congress, where he became a most useful representative of his District; but was later appointed *Charge d'affaires* at Bogota, New Grenada, by President Fillmore, but declining the appointment, he was made resident Minister to Nicaragua, and the Central American States. After a brilliant record as a Minister, he entered upon the practice of law at St. Michaels. In '62, he was appointed a solicitor to the Court of Claims, and in '69 made Sixth Auditor of the United States Treasury. He died in 1878.

General Perry Benson was one of Talbot's great men of long ago, having won the titles of Captain in the regular Continental Army and Major-General of Volunteers in the Maryland State troops, while the services he rendered are remembered with pride and gratitude by the people of the Eastern Shore.

General Benson descended from a family that settled in Talbot two hundred years ago, taking up land on the St. Michaels river near Royal Oak, and the Benson property became known as "Wheatlands." There the ancestors of Gen. Benson are buried, and he also lies among them. Born in 1757, Perry Benson passed his youth at Wheatlands; he early became a "Minute

"FOLLY," HOME OF MR. ZENUS BURNS, MILES RIVER.

THRESHING SCENE NEAR SKIPTON ON MR. JACOB GANNON'S FARM.

Man," as they called the Maryland soldiers who were organized to protect their homes. Of the Talbot company organized in 1776, Greenbury Goldsborough was Captain; Woolman Gibson, First Lieutenant; John Thomas, Second Lieutenant; Perry Benson, Ensign. Later he joined Washington's Army and became an officer in what was known as the "Flying Camp." His command was in the battles about New York and Philadelphia and in Jersey, and for his gallantry he was made a Captain. At the battle of Brandywine, he was wounded while assisting General Lafayette from the field.

The Maryland troops being dispatched South in 1780, Captain Benson saw hard service and his command won an enviable reputation, and the subject of this sketch greatly distinguished himself at the battle of the Cowpens, and in leading a charge on Fort Ninety Six in South Carolina. Here he fell terribly wounded, and was borne from the field under a heavy fire, on the shoulders of a colored man, Thomas Carney, of Maryland. For negroes had been enlisted in the army, and brave soldiers they made, too, as the records show. Thomas Carney was a man of herculean size and not only carried Captain Benson off the field, but his own musket as well, fainting from the heat as he placed his wounded officer down before the surgeon. Quickly recovering, the gallant colored soldier returned to the field to aid other wounded men.

After the war, Perry Benson was appointed a Lieutenant Colonel of State troops, in Talbot county, in 1794, and in 1798, when war with France was threatening, he did much to stimulate the military ardor of the citizens. When war with England came in 1812, Perry Benson was made a Brigadier General of Maryland State troops, later a Major General, and all through those stirring times on the Chesapeake Shores, he rendered most valuable services to his State, and in the attack on St Michaels, near his home, was the ruling spirit.

At the close of the war, he retired to his home full of honors, bravely won, and died at "Wheatlands" in October, 1827, leaving many connected with him by kindred ties. His grave is at "Wheatlands," and is marked as it certainly should be, by a monument worthy of the man and his record as a brave soldier.

Dr. Ennals Martin belonged to a family that came to Talbot about the middle of the seventeenth century. Thomas Martin,

RAILROAD BRIDGE OVER THE CHOPTANK RIVER AND MARSHES.

STRANDED ON THE BAY SHORE.

the grandfather of the subject of this sketch, having settled at "Hampton," on Island Creek. Dr. Ennals was born at "Hampton" in 1758. He was sent north to get his education, studied medicine in Philadelphia, and through his medical preceptor Dr. Shippen, was appointed director of the medical corps at Washington. He entered the army as Surgeon's Mate, receiving his commission in 1777.

Later, a hard student and devoted to his profession, he was made an Assistant Surgeon though still very young. After the surrender of Yorktown, he resigned, and for his services, Maryland voted him about $2500. Offered many inducements to settle at Philadelphia, he declined and took up his residence in Easton, and actively began the practice of medicine. Tradition says that his methods were heroic, even drastic, but his ability was great and inspired confidence ; his bluntness also caused his patients to fear him and his doses. Dr. Martin's practice was wide-spread, his fame went beyond the confines of his State, and many were the honors he received. Dr. Martin was the first to introduce vaccination in Talbot county as a preventive to small pox ; and it took just such a bold man as he to overcome prejudice against its use. Dr. Martin was also a writer of prominence upon medical subjects, and his whole life was wrapped up in his profession, but his brusqueness gained for him the name of the "Abernethy of Talbot." He was a devoted farmer as well as physician, and made the science of agriculture a study. At the death of a favorite son, not wishing him to be placed in a private burying-ground that might fall into other hands, he gave to the vestry of Christ Church at Easton the lot of ground in which his son was buried. Dr. Martin married Miss Sarah Hayward of Dorchester and had a large family. He died in 1834.

Dr. Tristram Thomas was born at "Roodly," the family home in Bolingbroke Neck, near Trappe, in 1769. He was educated in Wilmington, Del., studying medicine, and graduated in Philadelphia, and began to practice in Trappe, but moved to Easton, and his name became known throughout the State before many years, as one who stood at the head of his profession. Dr. Thomas was three times married, and left a large family, one of his sons Philip Francis Thomas, having been Governor of Maryland, and Captain Charles Thomas, a distinguished officer of the United States Navy. Dr. Thomas is buried in Easton, in that part of

Spring Hill Cemetery, which was once the burying-ground of the Episcopal Church.

In connection with the Bannings whose family figures prominently in the archives of this county, and whose interesting manuscripts are in the possession of Mr. James L. Banning, who has kindly furnished much data, it will be interesting to note some details relating to the famous Royal Oak, after which the present village is named.

In the war of 1812, a British fleet anchored in the river opposite St. Michaels, and opened fire on the town, whose people are said to have replied with two cannon furnished them by one Jacob Gibson. What this small battery was unable to effect in the way of defense, a ruse supplied as a means for their protection. Lanterns were hung in the tops of tall trees and succeeded in misleading the British gunners, who gave their pieces such elevation that the balls passed over instead of into the town. A few miles from St. Michaels stood the famous oak, that from this engagement was called Royal, a veritable monarch of the forest, huge and wide spreading, and from whose limbs above the roadway hung two cannon balls of local fame. It was a white oak, doubtless identical with "Bartlett's" Oak of Revolutionary times, and from its huge size probably stood there before America was discovered. The tree had a diameter of nine feet just above the flare of the roots.

Under its spreading branches was formed and drilled a company of militiamen that fought in the war of the Independence, but now naught of them remains, but memories associated with those troublous times, and its name perpetuated in the village of Royal Oak. Near the site of the famous tree, has been planted a locust post that holds aloft the cannon balls. Of these the larger was fired into the town of St. Michaels from a British vessel in 1812, and passed through a house, entered a chicken coop, killing the chicken, the only blood it shed. The ball was obtained by Robert Banning of the Isthmus (1776-1845,) and with the smaller one was hung from the famous oak above the roadway.

When the tree fell in 1864, the balls with their iron straps and ring struck the fancy of a Miles River boatman as an excellent device for a "kelick" or anchor. In this capacity they served until secured by Henry G. Banning, who had them hung in his lawn at Wilmington, Delaware.   In 1880 Dr. Robinson and others of Royal Oak who knew of them, and who were interested in the preservation of relics, erected the locust post, which now holds them, so the balls are again where they belong on the site of the Royal Oak.   May they long hang there, one of the mementos of the legendary lore of Talbot.

This chapter cannot well be closed without venturing somewhat beyond the confines of the present limits of Talbot, for, be it remembered, in Colonial days her borders were wider than now, and so interwoven were her prominent people with historical events between the bays that the song and story writer might find this territory as replete with material as many another locality around which has been woven a halo of romance in poetry and prose.

If the peninsula of which Talbot county forms a part was not fated to be the birth place of the immortal Washington, he was assigned a locality not far away; and if the land was not immortalized by the battles of Brandywine and Yorktown, and if the sight of its shores did not prompt the patriotic strains of the Star Spangled Banner, such events and others occurred so near that this section must be included in the theatre of action.   There is that notable Captain Lambert Wickes, a collateral ancestor of the Kent county family of that name, whose career as an English commerce destroyer in 1776 and 1777 is a history in itself, and almost without a parallel.   His short and successful naval career of only fourteen months was spent mostly in cruising around England, and ended in his untimely death off Newfoundland at the early age of thirty-one.   During those fourteen months he terrorized the English merchant service, on one occasion capturing no less than fourteen merchantmen in five days.

A counterpart of Paul Revere is easily found in Rodney's furious ride from Dover to Philadelphia, July 30, 1776.

Later in the war of 1812 we read of the battle of Caulk's or Cork's field in Kent county.   Here the British bound for Chestertown to burn it, were turned back to their ships with heavy loss, carrying their mortally wounded leader, Sir Peter Parker, "that he might not die on the d— Yankee ground."

Many an old historic event of the Peninsula is of similar tenor, and needs but the pen of some Cooper or Irving to weave it into a narrative of absorbing interest.   Men from this section fought in almost every battle of note in the Revolution except perhaps Bunker Hill. These would include Kirkwood, that brave and meritorious and unrewarded soldier who fell in his thirty-third engagement. Caldwell, whose blue game-cocks gave the nom-de-plume to the Delaware boys. Rodney the signer, Haslett, McDonough, Hunn, Patton, Bennett, Jacquett, Lambert Wickes. and Geddes.

"That vile rebel" George Latimer, also his father. James Latimer, the President of the Delaware Assembly of 1787, that was first of all the states to ratify the Constitution of the United States. and Jeremiah Banning of Talbot county. Chairman of the Talbot county delegation sent to Annapolis for the same purpose in 1788.

Among the early settlers of this region there were many factional contentions and troubles with the Indians. Notably on Kent Island was this the case, where it became necessary for an Assembly, meeting near the Chester River, to pass an ordinance, legalizing the act to kill an Indian at sight at any time or place. Thus in a thousand ways is our shore dotted with those spots of historic lore, each fact a thread in the fabric of our mighty nation.

CHAPTER XIX

TOLD BY GRAVESTONES.

EFORE dismissing wholly the old burying grounds of Talbot, and obeying the injunction to "Let the dead past bury its dead," it will not be amiss to write down a few of the quaint old legends told by gravestones, as often seen here. The fact must be borne in mind that in those days of an almost forgotten age, the story of the dead expressed a full belief in the worth of the dear departed. Those good old souls told the stone cutter to chisel just what they believed was the right thing, and they would have been horrified could they have looked far enough into the future to read the sign a wag put over a certain cemetery:

"Here lie the dead,
And here the living *lie*."

There is doubtless more truth than poetry in many of the inscriptions, for gravestones, like obituaries, often lie. But then the good old Roman way was best perhaps:

"*De mortuis nil nisi bonum*,
When men from earth have passed away ;
If they had vices do not own 'em.
Such was the kindly Roman way."

Yet what does it matter after all what may be said of us when dead, for, be it good or evil, it falls upon ears that hear it not.

"Wealth and glory and place and power,
What are they worth to me or you ?
For the lease of life runs out in an hour,
And death stands ready to claim his due ;
Sounding honors or heaps of gold,
What are they all when all is told ?

A pain or a pleasure, a smile or a tear—
What does it matter which we claim ?
For we step from the cradle unto the bier,
And a careless world goes on the same.
Hours of gladness or hours of sorrow,
What does it matter to us to-morrow ?

Truth of love or vow of friend--
    Tender caresses or cruel sneers—
What do matter to us in the end ?
    For the brief day dies, and the long night nears.
Passionate kisses, or tears of gall,
    The grave will open and cover them all.

Homeless vagrant, or honored guest,
    Poor and humble, rich and great,
All are racked with the world's unrest,
    All must meet with the common fate.
Life from childhood till we are old,
    What is it all when all is told ?"

In the burying-ground of Wye House, on a battered shield supported by mortuary emblems, one may read this notable inscription:

Henrietta Maria Lloyd.
She now takes her Rest within this Tomb
Had Rachel's Face and Leah's fruitful womb,
Abigail's Wisdom, Lydia's faithful Heart,
With Martha's Care and Mary's Better part.
Who died the 21st day of May,
(Anno) Dom. 1667, aged 50 years, — months, 23 days.
To whose Memory Richard Bennet dedicates this Tomb.

In Oxford Neck, at "Belleville," on lands held by the Bozmans and Kerrs, on a marble monument, we find the following :

This memorial of
A beloved child, with sure
Tokens of Manliness of Soul,
Has been set at the foot of his Grandmother's Grave,
And it will suggest, after 38 years,
Hopes too soon blighted,
With womanly Virtues, Well tested,
In the character of
Sarah Hollyday Kerr,
Born at Boon's Creek Plantation
March 31st, 1781.
Died at Easton, Maryland
April 1st, 1820.

On another :

"Chamberlaine of Oxford, Maryland, from 1714. and of Saughall Magna Shatrick Parish. Chelshire, England, from 1334, 7th of Edward III., and from Little Barrow, Chelshire."

Other stones in the Wye House graveyard have the following, just as they are thereon inscribed :

"Here lies interred the body of Col. Philemon Lloyd, the son of E
Lloyd & Alice his wife, who died the 22nd of June, 1685, in the 39th
year of his age, leaving 3 sons & 7 daughters, all by his beloved wife
Henrietta Maria.

No more than this the Father says,
But leaves his life to speak his praise."

"Here lieth the body of Col. Edward Lloyd, eldest son of Col. Philemon Lloyd, and Henrietta Maria, his wife, born Feb. 1670, died Mar.
20th 1718. He had by his wife Sarah, 5 sons and one daughter. He
served his country in several honorable stations, both civil & militery,
and was of the council many years."

"Here lie interred the remains of the Hon. Col. Edward Lloyd, who
departed this life the 27th of January, 1770. Aged 59 years."

"Here lieth interred the body of Philemon Lloyd son of Col. Philemon Lloyd and Henriette his wife, who departed this life 19th March,
1732, in the 60th year of his age. He was one of the council and secretary of this province."

"Here lie interred the remains of Mrs. Ann Lloyd, wife of Hon. Col.
Edward Lloyd, who departed this life the first day of May 1789, aged
48 years."

A rather peculiar inscription on an old tomb, but not in the
Wye Cemetery follows, and its composer seemed to be struggling
after rhyme rather than a tribute to the dead. After the nearly
effaced name comes this verse:

This world is a city of crooked streets—
Death is a Market-place where all men meets—
If life were a merchandise which all could buy,
The Rich would live, and the poor would die."

Scattered here, there, everywhere, in Talbot are gravestones,
and the inscriptions are as quaint as the people were of those old
days, when the skull and cross bones were put on a slab as em-
blematic of death.

"Here are placed the remains of John Bozman Kerr, Jr.,
2nd Child of John Bozman and Lucy Hamilton (Stevens)
Kerr; Born without loss of Citizenship At Home of United
States Legation, Leon, de Nicaragua, Central America, On
Palm Sunday, March 20th, 1853, and died at Baltimore
Maryland January 28th 1857.
Quis desiderio sit pudor, aut modus tam chari capitis."

The following on a tomb in Christ Church, St. Michaels, is in
Latin, but the translation is given, and it will be read with interest by all in any way connected with the Reverend Nichols,
who wrote the modest lines he wished inscribed to his memory.

"Here lie the remains of H. Nichos, Master of Arts, Fellow of
Jesus' College, the unworthy Pastor of this Church for 41
years. 'Trample upon the salt that has lost its savor.' "
Born Apr. 1st, 1678.
Died Feb. 12th, 1748.
Aged 70 years.

Upon another are the sympathetic and hopeful lines :

"Asleep in Jesus ! far from thee
Thy kindred and their graves may be !
Yet there is still a beloved sleep,
From which none ever wake to weep."

In the old White Marsh burying-ground there are many quaint
inscriptions. At the right hand corner of the ancient church, is
a tomb, the slab now broken, which records that there lies the
body of Robert Morris. In this fact a glance into the history of
the past, reveals that this Robert Morris of Oxford, Md., was
the father of Robert Morris the great Financier of Revolutionary
times, and whose loan of a large sum of money to General Washington, saved, it may be truthfully asserted, the American Army
from starvation and destruction during the memorable winter at
Valley Forge. It was the fortune left to the son Robert Morris,
that was the foundation of his State's great wealth and enabled
him to aid his country with the golden sinews of war. And
there lies Robert Morris, Sr., "Unhonored and unknown." Then
he was a wealthy shipping merchant of Oxford, Md., and was
accidentally killed by a shot fired in his honor from one of his
own ships. Upon the tomb the inscription reads :

"In memory of
Robert Morris, native of Liverpool in Great Britain.
Late merchant at Oxford. Punctuality and
Fidelity influenced his dealings.
Principle and honesty governed his actions.
With an uncommon degree of sincerity,
He despised art and dissimulation.
His friendship was Firm, Candid and Valuable,
His Charity Free, Discreet, and well Adapted. His zeal for
the Public was active and useful.
His hospitality was enhanced by his Conversation, seasoned
with cheerful wit and sound judgment :
A salute from the cannon of a ship, the wad fracturing his arm
was the means by which he departed On the 12th day of July
M. D. C. C. L."

) 7 5)

The burying-ground on the estate of the late General Tilgh-man, known as Plimhimmon, was later merged into what is now the Oxford Cemetery. It is situated upon the banks of a pretty stream on whose opposite shore in full view arises a grove of fine trees, where stands Plimhimmon Mansion.* In this cemetery stands a cenotaph to Colonel Tench Tilghman, the aide-de-camp of Genl. Washington and his Confidential Secretary throughout the war of the Revolution. There beneath its shadow rests Col. Tilghman's wife, born July 17th 1755, died January 13th. 1843. Other of the Tilghmans are also buried there. On the monu-ment, which is a pedestal and obelisk, the following is inscribed to the memory of the gallant Revolutionary officer :

"In memory
of
Tench Tilghman, Lt. Col. in the Continental
Army, and Aide-de-camp of Washington, who spoke of
him thus .
He was in every action in which the Main Army was concerned. A great part of the time, he refused to receive pay.
While living, no man could be more esteemed, and since
dead none more lamented. No one had imbibed sentiments
of greater friendship for him than I had done. He left as fair
a reputation as ever belonged to human character."
Died April 18th, 1785.
Aged 42 years.

Probably about the first land survey on the Eastern Shore ex-cept Kent Island, was a tract of one thousand acres on the Bay Shore about five miles from St. Michaels called Rich Neck or Mitchell's Point. It was surveyed 20th Oct. 1651, and sold about 1688 to James Murphy who is buried on the place. A large flat stone marks his grave, on which surmounted by a skull and cross bones is inscribed :

"Here is interred the body of Capt. James Murphy, who departed this life on the 6th day of May 1698 aged 58 years."

The grave yard is enclosed by a stone wall, and in it with many others is also interred Col. Matthew Tilghman Ward, who died in 1748. Lightning struck and badly damaged several of the stones in 1893. Another grave in Bayside is that of Thomas Impey, bearing the date 1658. One of the earliest tombs is that of Elizabeth Martin buried at "Hampton," Island Creek Neck,

*Now the estate of Mr. W. H. Myers of Oxford.

"RATCLIFFE," A TYPICAL SOUTHERN MANOR—NEAR EASTON.

RESIDENCE OF WILSON M. TYLOR, EASTON.

near Trappe. The stone has been removed to Easton and is
dated 1676. In the Methodist Episcopal Cemetery, a stone says:

"Col. Joseph Kemp died Sept. 24th, 1835, aged 55.
"He lived a Christian soldier and ended his warfare in peace."

In the same cemetery is found

"Lucretia Auld. Died July 6th, 1827, aged 22 years."

It was Lucretia Auld who owned the celebrated Fred Douglass.
On the Talbot shore of Wye river, about half a mile above
its mouth, may be found by careful search mid tangled vines,
weeds and marsh grass, a grave stone, now nearly submerged in
the oozy soil in which it lies, bearing this inscription : *

"Here lyeth immured ye bodye
of Francis Butler, Gent, son of
Rhoderick Butler, Gent, who was
unfortunately drowned in St. Michaels River, the 3rd Mar.
1689, aged 42 years or thereabot.—
Memento Mori."—

There is common tradition among those in the immediate
vicinity and among the oystermen, who ply their trade on Miles
and Wye rivers, that "He was an English sailor washed ashore,"
which fails to explain how his name was ascertained, or who
was good enough to mark his grave with a slab—a rather costly
article in those days.

It is not surprising that all knowledge of him was lost, when
it is known that he was without kinship in a land where his
sojourn was a bare two years. Yet few of our early settlers
came into the province with brighter prospects of contributing
a name to history. Having the advantage of powerful friends,
whose influence was promptly felt upon his arrival, his success
was practically assured. It is to be regretted that his untimely
end robbed him of a promising career.

His earliest record locates him in London, September, 1687,
when he was favored with a letter from Lord Baltimore, directed
to the members of his Lordship's council in Maryland. He
doubtless left for Maryland on receipt of the letter, as he,
"Mr —— Butler," was present at a council meeting held at St.
Mary's on the 5th of April following, and "presented the fol:
Lre from his Lop in his favour, viz.—

'Gentl :
The bearer is so powerfully recommended to me that I cannot re-

---

*Contributed by Mr. Howard Mullikin, of Baltimore.

fuse giving you these Lines, which are to assure you that the Countess of Tyrconnell has laid her comands on me by the hands of Sir Wm. Talbot to desire you to afford him all the favor and civility you can in Maryland where he is resolved to trye his fortune. You must therefore receive him very kindly and in anything that may be for his advantage there assist him what you can that soe he may find some good effects from these comands sent by Sir Wm. Talbot from my Lady Tyrconnell to the Gentl. Your Lo: Friend C. BALTI-MORE. London 7 bar the 5th 1687.

To the Honble Coll. Vincent Lowe

Coll, Henry Darnall, Coll Wm. Digges and the rest of the Deptyes of the Province of Maryland.'"

To this letter the Council "expressed their readiness and willingness to give all due obedience, according to the purport thereof," and on the 10th of April, five days later, they appointed "Mr. Butler" sheriff of Talbot county, as the following will show.

"Major Peter Sayer, present Sheriff of Talbot county being intended for England, as he himself gives out, whereby there will be a vacancy of the Sher: Place of that county their honors in consideration of the great favour his Lop has signified in behalf of Mr.—— Butler recommended to his Lop by the Countess of Tyrconnell were pleased to offer the Sheriff's Place of said county to the said Mr. Butler, which he accepted, giving good security, as usual in such cases.

In the foregoing, Francis Butler is referred to as "Mr Butler" and "Mr. —— Butler." One would not therefore be justified in asserting it to be Francis Butler, who was appointed to the Sheriff's place, &c., did we not know from Administration account of "Francis Butler, of Talbot Co., Gent. decd." dated 3d Aug., 1664, that it was really he who was High Sheriff. This account allows tobacco to Henry Williams for "taking up the Bodie &c,"—and to the "Coroner of Kent Co. for viewing the body, &c."—and finally, several parcels of tobacco are referred to as being due "Mr. Francis Butler, late High Sheriff of Talbot Co., decd."

Taking the statement on the gravestone that he was drowned in St. Michaels river, with that of the admin. acc't that Kent County's Coroner viewed the body, it is safe to say the body floated out of the river and across the Eastern Bay to Kent Island, which then belonged to Kent county. The question naturally arises, why was he brought to this lonely spot on the Wye for burial?

A glance at the old county maps of Talbot will show it to be the locality of the "Ancient town of Doncaster" and here lived Major Peter Sayer, whom Francis Butler succeeded as Sheriff. It is fairly reasonable to suppose he took up quarters with him, his predecessor in office, thereby gaining benefit of his knowledge of the office, as well as the comforts of a home.

The union of Trippe's Creek with the Tred Avon, forms a strip of land, whose terminus is but a few yards wide ending in Ship Point, and which is also the extreme end of Bailey's Neck. Not long ago, some farm hands at work on the Tred Avon shore, about fifty yards from Ship Point, discovered human teeth and bones in the sand, and further investigation soon revealed as many as nine skulls, which were clearly identified as Indian remains.

These bodies must have been buried origianlly about three feet deep, and in one hole, body upon body. A confused mass of bones was presented, ribs and vertebrae, arm, and leg bones, so that the identification could hardly have been made, had it not been for the decidedly characteristic skulls. These were so close together that a large tub might have covered the lot. The bones were so friable from age, that a knife passing through the soil would have cut the bones and clay alike, which made it no easy matter to rescue an entire skull, or large bone even from the surrounding clay. Such as were removed entire soon became dry and strong enough to bear handling. Some jaw bones had teeth worn down, indicating middle life to their owner, others showed the perfect and unworn teeth of youth. What those remains could tell of prehistoric Talbot is left to imagination.

The land there about is somewhat prolific of relics of the Stone Age, arrow and spear heads, hatchets, celts, hammer stones, etc., while beds of shell show that oysters were appreciated then as now. Judging by the stone relics already found, it takes but a little stretch of imagination to picture the dusky hunters pressing the game onward, to the slaughter at this point. And but a little more to see a band of human game, similarly pressed on until retreat ended with a final stand, hemmed in by the river, whose surface may have been cut by swiftly paddling canoemen eagerly alert for a swimming refuge from a desperate conflict. To some such scene, these remains, now in possession

of Mr. James L. Banning, are probably the silent witnesses.
In years long passed human bones were found in close proximity to these, if stories handed down are to be accredited. Their
history, as mythical then as now, probably antedates a period
of two centuries The Indians were troublesome to the early
white settlers, and it may be that these fell in some encounter
with that race, which suggests a tragedy here, to which wind and
wave have long sung their requiem. These bones are the mementos of love and hate, hopes and fears of a by-gone race, a race
capable of the same feelings and impulses which dominate us,
before a steamboat whistle ever sounded over these beautiful
waters, or a ploughman ever swore in encounter with a shell
heap. Now these bones are perhaps as little thought of by us as
the sound of the whistle after its echoes have ceased, or as little
as others will think of us a few years hence, when we have no
more to show than that which the Indian grave disclosed, for.
                    "All is Vanity."

HOLY TRINITY CHURCH, OXFORD.

MONUMENT AT GRAVE OF LIEUTENANT-COLONEL TENCH TILGHMAN
AT OXFORD.

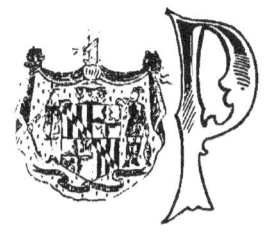ERHAPS there is hardly another lo-cality in America where the descen-dants of the first settlers can be found in greater force, still clinging to the original soil and roof tree of their fore-fathers, than in Talbot. This, in a manner, is owing to love of family tra-ditions; and perhaps, more to their having here a comfortable living for the generations as they come into existence, the young men not being forced to go among strangers and fight the hard battle of life. For this reason many of the young men have remained here as inheri-tors of old estates. Finding congeniality in distant kinship, they made their marriages in related families, thus causing much commingling of kindred blood.

If time had not effaced the stories, oftentimes the stones them-selves above these graves of the far by-gone, what a remarkable record could be read from them, if gathered in a book of Epi-taphs. What a history those old stones tell, and how many, whatever might have been the shortcomings of the departed,

"Made a saint of them when dead."

Still another reason for Talbot's sons and daughters clinging to their homes, is that, until recently, the Eastern Shore has been almost a *terra incognita* to the world at large. Only with-in the last score of years, have railroads traversed its plains. This alone has prevented outsiders from finding the favored spot. and likewise held the young at home.

In looking over the list of old families whose names will ever be among the historic records of Talbot. we find that where many might be mentioned, the limits of this book prevent other than a few insertions here. These few are so identified with the his-toric and earliest annals of this county, that my book would be incomplete without giving a genesis of some of them at least. Most of their ancestors came to Talbot as men of position in Eng-

land, connected with prominent English families, and served
as the King's officers in this new land. From the time of their
arrival to the present day, those of their name have been a
power in the land, and are justly proud of their ancestry, and
that, for many generations. They are truly Americans.

Edward Lloyd, the first of the name in Maryland, came from
Virginia with Leonard Strong, William Durand and others,
about 1650, and settled at Greenbury Point near Annapolis. He
was a Puritan, and compelled to leave Virginia because of his
non-conformity. Leonard Strong says in his "Babylon's Fall,"
"they were not invited into Maryland, only received and protected." Mr. Lloyd returned to England in 1668, and died
there. In his will, dated May 11th, 1695, he styled himself
"Edward Lloyd of the Parish of St. Mary, Whitechappel, in the
county of Middlesex, merchant, and late planter of Maryland."
He devised "Wye House" to his grand-son, Edward, son of his
son Philemon. Philemon Lloyd married Mrs. Henrietta Maria
Neale Bennet, daughter of Captain James Neale and his wife,
name-sake and grand-daughter (by proxy) of the Queen of England, wife of the unfortunate Charles I. (Tradition says Anne
Neale was maid of honor to that unhappy Queen.) Certain it is
that Captain Neale was sent by the King and Duke of York on a
secret mission to Spain.

After the martyrdom of Charles I., 1648, Captain Neale brought
his family to Maryland. His eldest daughter, Henrietta Maria,
first married Richard Bennett, who was drowned in early man-
hood. Her second husband was Philemon Lloyd. Edward, son
of Philemon and Henrietta Maria Lloyd, married the beautiful
Sarah Covington, after a romantic courtship, and resided at
"Wye House." This old homestead has been held by eight
generations of Lloyds, and there are three generations now living, the present head of the family, Col. Edward Lloyd, being the
sixth Edward Lloyd in direct succession. All with two exceptions have been members of the Maryland Legislature, and the
grandfather of the present owner was Governor of Maryland
1809-1811, and United States Senator 1819-1826.

One of Governor Lloyd's daughters married Admiral Franklin
Buchanan, and had a beautiful home, "The Rest," on Miles
river; her sister having married Commodore Charles Lowndes,
United States Navy, lived on the opposite shore of the river at

the "Anchorage." After the death of Mr. Lloyd, Mrs Sarah
Covington Lloyd married Mr. James Hollyday, the son of Col.
Thomas Hollyday of consanguinity with Sir Leonard Hollyday,
who was Lord Mayor of London in 1605. He was descended
from Walter Hollyday, Minstrel Master of the court of Edward
IV. After living at "Wye House" some years, Mr. and Mrs.
James Hollyday left that place to her eldest son Edward Lloyd, and
went to reside at "Readbourne," his plantation, about 1733.
There they built a spacious brick mansion, planned, it is said,
by Mrs. Hollyday, after consulting with Lord Baltimore. It is
a fine specimen of Colonial architecture. Their eldest son,
James, inherited that place; his brother, Henry, coming to Talbot, married Anna Maria Robins, and settled at "Ratcliffe
Manor," a part of the estate. This was one of the handsomest
places in Talbot county. As they were married in 1749, the
house was probably built about that time.

The Tilghmans of Queen Anne's and Talbot counties, trace
their descent from Richard Tilghman of Hollyway Court in the
Parish of Snodland, Kent county, England, who lived about
1400. Dr. Richard Tilghman, a surgeon in the British Navy,
came to this country 1660, and, with his wife, Maria Foxley,
settled at the "Hermitage," on land granted to him by Lord
Baltimore. Their son Richard, one of the Lord Proprietor's
Council, maried Anna Maria Neale Lloyd, daughter of Philemon
and Henrietta Maria Neale Lloyd, and had several children.
Richard inherited "The Hermitage." James married the beautiful Anne Francis, daughter of Tench Francis and cousin of Sir
Philip Francis, the reputed author of "Junius' Letters," and
lived at "Fausley" near Easton, where their son Tench Tilghman (a Lt.-Col. in the Revolutionary War, aid-de-camp and
confidential secretary to Gen. Washington) was born. They
afterwards moved to Philadelphia, where James Tilghman became a member of Penn's Council, attorney to the Lord Proprietor, and Secretary of the Proprietary Land Office of Pennsylvania.

Matthew Tilghman, youngest son of Richard second of the
"Hermitage," inherited large estates from his uncle, Matthew
Tilghman Ward, and lived at Rich Neck, on the bay-side, near
Claiborne. He was a member of the Continental Congress,
Chairman of the Committee of Safety for the Eastern Shore of

Maryland, President of the Constitutional Congress assembled to prepare a form of government for this state, and filled so many public offices, that he was called by the historian McMahon, "the Patriarch of the Colony." "Plimhimmon," near Oxford, the beautiful home of his daughter, Mrs. Col. Tench Tilghman, has passed out of the family, as has also "Hope" on Miles River, property which one branch of the Tilghman's received from the Lloyds, with one of the daughters of that house.

Samuel Chamberlaine of "Plaindealing" was born at Saughall on the Dee, England, 1697. His father, Thomas Chamberlaine, and eldest brother John, had for many years engaged in trade with the Colonies in America, and owned many ships plying between Liverpool and Oxford, Maryland. Coming over in one of these vessels, he decided to settle at Oxford in 1714.

This family derived its name from John, Count de Tankerville, who was Lord Chamberlain to Henry I. of England, 1125. Richard, son of John de Tankerville, succeeding to that position in the royal household, assumed the patronymic of Chamberlain, retaining the Tankerville arms.

In 1735 Samuel Chamberlaine, having married Henrietta Maria Lloyd, moved to Plaindealing on the Tred Avon. At that time, he was one of the richest men in the county, owning thousands of acres on the Tred Avon and Choptank rivers. He was for years a member of the Lord Proprietor's Council, Deputy Naval Officer of Pocomoke and Oxford, and Collector of the Port of Oxford, in which position he was succeeded by his eldest son, Thomas. Samuel Chamberlaine, Jr., married Henrietta Maria Hollyday, and they built the second homestead of the family in this country, "Bonfield" on Boon's Creek near Oxford. It is a large frame building with wainscoted walls and lofty ceilings, on a lovely creek so shut in by an island at its mouth as to appear like a lake. This property is now owned by Dr. J. E. M. Chamberlaine, of Easton. Plaindealing long ago fell into the hands of others.

James Earle, the progenitor of that family in this country, came from Craglethorp, Lincolnshire, England, with his wife and children in 1683, and settled on Chester river. He died the following year. One of his descendants, Richard Tilghman Earle of "Needwood," Queen Anne's county, was a member of the convention, which met in Annapolis, June 22d, 1774. He married

Anne Chamberlaine. Their son Samuel was a captain in the Revolutionary Army. A second son, Richard Tilghman, was Chief Judge of the second Judicial District of Maryland, and one of the Judges of the Court of Appeals. James Earle, a great-grandson of James Earle, the emigrant, was appointed after the Revolution, Clerk of the General Court for the Eastern Shore of Maryland, and resided in Easton, until his death in 1810. His son James succeeded his father, and at the time of his death, was Clerk of the Court of Appeals on the Eastern Shore, and cashier of the bank at Easton.

Nicholas Goldsborough, the first of the name in this country, was born in 1640, at "Malcolm Regis," near Weymouth, Dorset county, England. He married Margaret Howes, daughter of Abram Howes of Newbury, county of Berks. He left England in 1669, and went to Barbadoes, thence to New England, and finally settled on Kent Island, Maryland. His wife and three children came over a little later. Nicholas Goldsborough died soon after, and his widow married George Robins.

From his two sons, Robert and Nicholas, all the Goldsboroughs of Maryland are descended. Robert married Elizabeth Greenbury, settled at "Ashby," and became the ancestor of the "Myrtle Grove," "Shoal Creek," "Horn's Point," and "Yerbury" Goldsboroughs, many of whom are conspicuous in the history of the State of Maryland, while from Nicholas sprung the "Otwell" branch, the eldest son for six generations bearing that name. In the seventh, the rule was departed from, and the name Nicholas was bestowed upon the youngest son.

A highly venerated name, but one no longer heard except in those families who claim descent from, and are proud to perpetuate it by giving it to their children as Christian or middle names, is that of Robins. The first George Robins came to America in 1670, and settled in Talbot county on a tract of land known as "Job's Content." His grand-son called it "Peach Blossom," from the number of peach trees he imported through his friend Peter Collinson, the great botanist. These trees were imported from Persia, and introduced into Talbot, with many other trees and flowers, by Mr. George Robins.

The name died with his only son. His daughters married into the Chamberlaine, Hollyday, Nicols and Hayward families, and left many descendants. Mrs. George Robins married a

YACHTING PARTY ON MILES RIVER.

BOUND FOR THE EASTERN SHORE.

second time Mr. William Goldsborough, one of the Lord Proprietor's Council, and a Judge of the Provincial Court. The records of the Robins family have been carefully preserved, and date back to 1574. The present generation knows but little of this old place near Easton, for over a century one of the homes of the county, and the name "Peach Blossom" is associated only with the creek near the head of which it is situated. In the family burying ground may be found the names of many distinguished in their day.

The Rev. John Barclay, rector of St. Peter's Parish, son of David and Christiana Barclay, of Kincaird, Scotland, married Rachel Goldsborough, and left one daughter, who became the wife of Mr. Joseph Haskins, son of Captain Wm. Haskins and Sarah, daughter of Rev. Thomas and Elizabeth Airey. Mr. Haskins was the father of the late Mr. Barclay Haskins. Both of these names are now extinct ; but their descendants are to be found in the Hayward and Trippe families of Talbot. The last two names do not properly belong to this county, for the Haywards settled in Somerset in 1722, on land still held by one of the line. One son coming to Talbot, married Miss Robins of "Peach Blossom," and made his home at "Locust Grove." The Trippes were a Dorchester family. We find Henry Trippe of that county a member of the Maryland Legislature, as early as 1671. Dr. Edward R. Trippe and others of the name in Easton, are direct descendants of the Dorchester Trippes.

David Kerr, who came from Scotland and settled in Talbot county, held many prominent positions in Maryland, and was a member of the Legislature in 1793. He married Rachel Leeds Bozman, a sister of John Leeds Bozman, the historian of Maryland. Their son, the Hon. John Leeds Kerr, represented Talbot county in the House of Delegates and Senate of this state, was three times in the House of Representatives, and a member of the Senate from 1841 to 1843. Mr. Kerr married Sarah Hollyday Chamberlaine, and resided on Aurora street, Easton, in the house now occupied by his grandson, Col. Oswald Tilghman. None of the name are left in Talbot, and Col. Tilghman is the only descendant of this old family on the Eastern Shore, the sons and their families having settled in Baltimore and Washington.

At "Belleville," near Oxford, on land held for many years by the Bozmans and Kerrs, there is a monument to the Hon. John

Leeds Kerr, and there also lies buried Col. Thomas Bozman, grandson of William Bozman (the last named among the early Protestant settlers on the Chesapeake, 1627-29, before the charter of Lord Baltimore,) Lucretia Leeds Bozman wife of Thomas, their son John Bozman and his children, Rachel Leeds Bozman Kerr and John Leeds Bozman.

The Lowes settled in Maryland about 1675. Col. Vincent Lowe was a prominent man in colonial times, being appointed by his brother-in-law, Lord Baltimore, to many positions of trust. His sister Jane Lowe, married Charles Calvert, fourth Lord Baltimore; and while staying with her nephew, Colonel Nicholas Lowe at "Anderton," near Oxford. Lady Jane Calvert visited the Friends Meeting House, Easton, the day William Penn preached there. Col. Nicholas Lowe was the son of Henry Lowe of "Park Hall," Derby, England, a brother of Lady Jane and Col. Vincent Lowe.

It may be also said of several families of Friends, that they trace their Talbot lineage back for a quarter of a thousand years, and their descendants still gather around the hearthstone, that is upon land first settled by those of their name. In the days of extreme bigotry in creeds, a bigotry not yet eradicated wholly, it is sad to relate, it was with grateful hearts indeed that the Friends, of the Church of God, found a refuge in Maryland, and sought the Eastern Shore as a Mecca of hope for them.

From Wales came one family, prominent in the land of their birth, and settled here in Talbot, the Dixons, the ancestors of the present house of that name, so well and prominently known far beyond the state line of Maryland. The first of the Dixons obtained a patent of land from the King, still in existence, which embraced a large scope of territory. Though considerable of it has passed into other hands, there are large tracts of the original grant still held by those of the name, the handsome country seat of Mr. Robert B. Dixon, of Easton, a man of wealth and influence in both county and state. The fine country homes of Mr. Isaac H. Dixon, Mr. William T. Dixon and Mrs. John B. Dixon, are situated upon the Avon near Easton, and also upon the original patent of land.

Another family of Friends among the first settlers of Talbot were the Bartletts, and their family is among the distinguished ones of this section. Their American ancestor came from Eng-

TALBOT COUNTY RACE TRACK.

THE PAPER MILL POND NEAR EASTON.

land, and he too was granted a patent of land by the King,
much of which territory is still dwelt upon by those of the Bartlett name. Between the Dixons and the Bartletts there are
kindred and marriage ties ; and thus the inter-marriage goes on
until many families of Friends are allied, as are the Tilghmans,
Goldsboroughs, Lloyds, Earles and others. In those old days,
the Friends clung more tenaciously to the tenets of their creed,
and one then marrying out of their fold was well disciplined. It
is not so now, as time works wonders, and love not only laughs
at locksmiths, but creeds as well.

The Friends were, strange to say, large slave owners, as well as
land owners, and it is told that when a slave ship from the
coast of Africa anchored in the Avon in full view of the Great
Meeting House, the whole congregation would adjourn to the
shore from meeting, and the men going on board the craft,
would pick out from the living cargo of blacks, those they wished
for hands upon their plantations. Later the Friends became
abolitionists, as far as the abolishing of slavery among their sect
went, and it was not permitted that they should own or traffic
in human beings.

Though differing from others as they might, the Friends of
Talbot never forced upon them their views, nor found fault with
the actions of others, when those actions were based upon pure
motives. They were not bigots, never have been so considered,
and have allowed fully all rights of personal liberty and actions,
as long as they did not conflict with the privileges of others.
They were hospitable in the extreme, so much so that there
was a committee appointed at their meetings to see that "all
traveling ministers were fully supplied with liquor on their journeys". Those were the days when the parsons were wont to im-
bibe the 'spirits' to aid them in downing the Evil Spirit, that
got into the hearts of many of their flocks.

As a proof of how the Friends of Talbot have kept their
records of meetings, births, marriages and deaths, to-day their
books are relied upon by the courts as proofs of legal questions,
and in the vault of the Easton Court House their ancient books
are kept and treasured as beyond price. In those same books too
can be found the genealogy of every family of Friends in Talbot,
no matter how humble or poor they may have been or are. As
Friends have married, barriers being down now between them

and those not of their sect, these marriages connect them with
the other old families of Talbot in many cases; and thus the
the genealogy of the county is securely wound upon a wheel
within a wheel, so that the stranger coming here must be careful indeed what he says, if he has a grievance against any one
person, as he might be treading on the toes of half the community.

CHAPTER XXI.

PEN PICTURES.

WHEN one begins to look about him for items of interest connected with Talbot and its people, they crowd upon him like an avalanche that has to be stemmed and checked, or a book of modest size would grow into one that would dwarf the Bible in the number of its chapters. There is a Genesis to consider too of many a family, whose record would make most interesting reading, which cannot be dwelt upon in these pages. The citizens all have a reverence for the ancient tomes in their court house, and with reason, for there are strange records, wills, and documents within that old building, as may be understood when I say that in glancing over some of these works of ancient lore, dug out of the depths of vaults, I came upon records that would make rare reading.

The first county record shows that "court was held in Talbot county at the house of William Coureey, at Skipton, on a creek of the same name and a branch of the Wye, October 25th, 1662," just two hundred and thirty-eight years ago. I was also shown, through the courtesy of Mr. William Wilson of the County Clerk's office, one old book that tells all about the sale of the pirate Kidd's treasure, after the sea rover had been hanged in London for his crimes. This record, which has found its way into the vault of the Talbot court house, is a curious one, and put one of my famous "Pirate Heroes" upon the level of a sea thief.

From early boyhood I was charmed with Captain Kidd, also spelled 'Kyd', from having read the romance of my father, entitled, "Captain Kyd, the Wizard of the Sea." That novel had an enormous sale half a century ago, founded upon the romance in American history. I could not but admire Kidd, the pirate, for his daring, and regret that he painfully departed this life at the end of a rope, as he certainly did.

In later years, when I had begun to inflict a long-suffering, reading public with my own romances, "founded upon facts," I too ran to pirates and land robbers, with the result that a publisher ordered me to write a novel of Captain Kidd, and follow it as my father had done, with another of "*Lafitte* the Pirate of the Gulf." I obeyed for pecuniary reasons, and because I considered myself "up in pirates." Though the books sold well, old timers who drew comparisons, frankly told me, I had fallen from grace in more ways than one in attempting to follow in my father's foot steps. At any rate, in the Talbot court house, I found the real story of the taking off of Captain Kidd. It reads as follows, without any sentimentality, but in cold, plain facts and is learned from the ancient record.

"Addenda to the third volume of the state at large, beginning with fourth year of the reign of Queen Anne, and continued to the end of the last session of Parliament April 1st, 1788." Then follows: "And be it recorded under authority that it shall, and may be, lawful for her Majesty, if she pleases, to dispose as a charity to the Royal Hospital at Greenwich, the sum of 6470 pounds and three shilling, which has been paid into the exchequer, on or about the one and thirtieth day of January 1704, by Richard Crawley, being of goods and perquisite taken on the ship with *William Kidd, the notorious pirate,* who was executed in London several years since." The italics are mine, for piracy was too common in those days to require distinguishing reference; but there is the record of how the captain of the innocent name, had been "hanged in London," and that his booty, taken with him, after his captors and the officials had doubtless had their pick at it, amounted to over thirty-two thousand dollars. It was a large sum in those days, but the pirates of to-day, afloat and ashore, could discount Captain Kidd in the amounts of their booty. A certain charm lingers around every spot with which a romance is connected, just as a morbid curiosity is felt by many to behold the place, where some dark tragedy has happened. It is a sentiment that clings to the people of Talbot, this desire to see the *local* of a romance, and learn more about it and the actors therein, rather than curiosity, for they have been born and bred in an historic atmosphere, and all about them are scenes that appeal to their interest in the mystery and romance of the past.

With no home in Talbot is there a prettier romance linked than with that of "Plimhimmon," the estate then owned by Captain John Coward, the commander of the good clipper ship "Integrity." The captain was a blunt old sailor, but honest and true; he was a planter as well, his estate of "Plimhimmon," later owned by the Tilghmans, and now by Mr. W. H Myers, of Oxford, and in good repair to-day, being a fine old home, where he dwelt at ease with his family, when his vessel lay in port. The "Integrity" lay in the Thames river, off London, one morning in the year 1751, when the plot of this true story begun, and which was woven into a novel by Miss Sedgwick, the author of of "Redwood." Aboard the "Integrity" came a youth who begged the captain to take him on the voyage to America as a cabin boy. The handsome face, slender form, and refined appearance of the youth caused the captain to hesitate, but he yielded to entreaties, and the good ship sailed with the boy on board. Passing Gravesend, the cabin boy looked longingly shoreward, waved his handkerchief, and seemed to be bidding farewell to some loved one. When the ship had passed Gravesend, he turned very white, then burst into tears, and won the sympathy of all on board. From that moment, he seemed to be utterly wretched, though he strove hard to attend to his duties. Across the broad Atlantic, "the Integrity" sailed in safety passed into the Chesapeake, and was nearing Oxford, when the cabin boy went to Captain Coward, and confessed that he had deceived him, telling him that he had left home for reasons not to be told, and that *he* was a girl. The captain was intensely angry at having been deceived, but told the girl he would take her to his home with him. This he did, and his wife and his daughters received her kindly, yet with suspicion that all was not as it should be with the girl, especially as she refused to give her real name, telling them to call her "Perdito." Under a cloud, as it were, the girl's life was not a happy one, and she longed to escape, yet at first found no means of doing so. One day, her story being known, she met a handsome young sailor who had been anxious to make the acquaintance of the beautiful girl. To him she told her story, but not a word as to why she had left her home, or her name, only that she wished to return to England. He promised to aid her, and being second mate of the ship "Hazard," said that he could smuggle her on board and keep her hidden, until they got out into the Atlantic. The name of the mate was Stewart Dean, a good name for a hero, by the way, it is so romantic, and he was a dashing, handsome fellow, it is said, the very one to catch the eye of a lovely maiden in her teens, or out of them, for that matter. Stewart Dean made his arrangements, prepared his hiding place, went ashore alone in a boat at night, to the point of land near "Plimhimmon Mansion," formed by the Avon and Town creeks, Oxford. There, under an apple tree, where there was an arbor, Perdito was waiting, and entering the boat, was rowed aboard the "Hazard," and gotten into her hiding place without being seen by any one, for, as the ship was to sail at dawn, the captain and men were ashore in Oxford, taking a few glasses of grog to the safety of the voyage. Just before the sailing of the vessel, Captain Coward came aboard, reported that the girl had left his home, and that he was responsible for her safe return to England, she having come out with him. She had been seen in a boat with a sailor coming toward the "Hazard." The ship was searched, and Stewart Dean aided Captain Coward in his attempt to find the girl, but all in vain, and the vessel sailed.

Once well out into the Atlantic, Stewart Dean went to the captain, and told him the whole story, how the unhappy girl had wished to return to England, and he had determined to help her, but had kept his own secret, not wishing to get him, the captain, into trouble. The captain was naturally angry, but the girl was brought from her hiding place, and questioned. She refused to give her name, but said she only wished to return to England, that Stewart Dean had treated her nobly, and begged the captain not to carry out his threat, and send her back, should he meet a vessel returning to Oxford. The captain promised to take her to London, and later the amazement of the first mate and crew at finding a beautiful young girl on board was great As a punishment for what he had done, the captain reduced Stewart Dean from second mate to ordinary seaman, but the brave, young fellow did his work before the mass as faithfully as he had on the quarterdeck.

Arriving in the Thames with the aid of a couple of sailors, for the crew to a man were his friends, Stewart Dean rowed the girl ashore, and took her to the corner of two streets in London as she asked him to do, she telling him she knew her way from

KNIGHTS AND MAIDS OF HONOR—CORDOVA TOURNAMENT.

THE SUMMER GIRL ARRIVES BY EXPRESS.

there. There they parted, the girl giving him a ring and asking him to wear it in remembrance of her, but not a word more
did she tell him about herself, and she was still a mystery to
him. Returning aboard ship, he was further punished by not
being allowed ashore while in port. On the return voyage, the
"Hazard" was caught in a hurricane, the first mate was swept
overboard, the captain was injured severely, and Stewart Dean
was called to command the ship. That he saved the vessel, all
knew ; he carried her safely into port, but neither the captain
nor the men would tell in Oxford how he had kidnapped
Perdito.

Years passed by, and Stewart Dean commanded his own ship,
a handsome brig built in Oxford for him, and which he had
named the "Perdito." Soon after her first voyage, the "Perdito" was armed and manned by a large crew, for the war of
the Revolution had broken out, and Stewart Dean had turned
his fleet craft into an American privateer. The young captain
was not long in making a name for himself, for his prizes were
many, until one day he fell in with an English brig-of-war,
much his superior in guns and men. It was in West Indian
waters, and the port of Antigua was not far distant. At once
a battle between the brigs was begun, and after a most desperate
encounter, the Englishman struck his colors, as his vessel was
hulled and sinking. Going on board, Captain Dean was told
that the wife, mother and son of the Governor of Antigua were
on board, and asked what was to be done with them. "I shall
sail for port under a flag of truce and return them in safety, as
your vessel cannot be saved, and Americans do not war against
women and children," was the reply. Overhearing the response,
the wife of the Governor came out of her stateroom, and Captain
Dean found himself face to face with the mysterious girl whom
he had aided to escape, and desperately loved ever since. The
recognition was mutual, and the name of his vessel, her ring on
his finger, told the story he had never breathed to her when she
was under his care. Then he met the Governor's mother, Lady
Stanford, and Perdito's little son, who bore the christian name
of Stewart Dean.

That night on the deck of the brig, Stewart Dean heard Perdito's story. It had been a love affair with a young American
then in London, and they were to elope to America on the "In-

tegrity," he to board her at Gravesend.   But he had not been
there, the "Integrity" had not landed, and so she went on to
America alone and broken hearted.   When she returned to London, she found her father willing to forgive her, if she would
marry Lord Stanford, a man of fifty.   She did so, and some
years after, he was sent out as Governor to Antigua.   A few
months before, he had died, and she was returning to England
with the Governor's mother and her child, when the sea-fight
had occurred.   Back to port Captain Dean took his passengers,
and then set sail once more to win new laurels.   The war ended,
and soon after he visited London, and again he met Perdito, the
widow of Lord Stanford, and a quiet wedding followed.   Tradition says that Captain Dean brought his wife and her son to
Talbot, and that his home was on Broad Creek Neck, in the old
homestead where Editor George Haddaway of the *Easton
Ledger* was born, also that young Stanford, when he reached his
majority, returned to England to assume his title and estate ;
but that the story of Perdito is true throughout.   Just what
became of the hero and heroine is not known, while there are
some who assert that their descendants are now to be found
in Talbot.

 INDING so much tradition, legend and anecdote to write of, when every "oldest citizen" is a perambulating fund of information, where every family has its fireside tales of long ago, it is hard to sift the wheat from the chaff, to select the best to relate. To jot down all would make my book a biographical Encyclopædia, instead of the humble story of a remarkable country's history and people. One recalls events of importance more vividly in a community where life has gone only a half century in the even tenor of its way, than if there had been constant happenings of more than the average in importance.

Thus the Revolutionary war was "the event" in Talbot's career, for it made a free people of royal slaves, caused a new nation to spring into existence in a day, which in a hundred years has become the greatest of the nations of the earth. The war of 1800, though but a ripple with France that soon blew over, was another "event" in Talbot's career, and there are citizens here to-day who wonder why the debt to their ancestors, their inheritance known as the French Spoliation Claim, still remains unpaid by this rich American government, which long ago had more than equivalent for the claims, and yet "refuses to pay" through its Representatives in Congress. The war of 1804 with Tripoli was another stirring event in Talbot, through its worldwide shipping interests ; and again the trouble with the mother country, England, in 1812 sent a thrill along the Chesapeake shores. In that three years struggle, Maryland took a most important part, as history reveals. Then followed the Mexican war of 1846 to 1848, and Talbot's sons again went to battle under the stars and stripes. Next came the greatest strife of modern times, the civil war, in which the men of Talbot were equally divided, as the "Hick's Post, G. A. R." and "Winder Camp U. C. Veterans," in Easton, now give evidence. The coming of prominent persons into a community is an event to be jotted down, and it is to be recorded that Kosciusco recruited most of his soldiers here and in other counties of the Eastern Shore. Then Lafayette was "mighty near" coming here ; only, for some reasons, his plan miscarried, and he lost the chance of his life, and doubtless regretted it to his dying day.

A visitor to Talbot after the civil war, was Jefferson Davis, the "Chief of the Lost Cause," and indisputably one of America's greatest statesmen. Mr. Davis visited Colonel Edward Lloyd, of "Wye House," after his retirement from public life. His record had been made as a soldier at Buena Vista and on other battle fields in Mexico, as Secretary of War from Mississippi and as President of the Confederacy, truly a man of remarkable destiny. The Eastern Shore of Maryland, far, far beyond the limits of Talbot, came to see him, to grasp his hand for what he had been, and was,—the one time leader of the lost-cause. To-day he sleeps in a grave in Hollywood Cemetery, Richmond, Va., his lonely mound marked with a tiny rosebush, but his memory engraved in the hearts of the people of Dixie. Other great men have come to Talbot, and it is said of Bayard Taylor, who visited all of the Eastern Shore by rail, steamer and carriage, that he spoke of it as one of the most charming spots of all he had seen in his travels the world over. It was Bayard Taylor who named the Atlantic shore at Ocean City the "Velvet Beach." Charles Wilson Peale, the world renowned portrait painter, came to Talbot, and many of his paintings are today found among the old families of the county, notably, one of George Washington, the original of a portrait, from which many copies have been made, in the possession of Colonel Oswald Tilghman, of Easton. Colonel Tilghman has others from the same famous brush. Talbot can boast of its own artists, sculptors, writers, soldiers, sailors and statesmen ; some of whom, having won fame, are contented to rest from their labors here in the home of their youth, while awaiting the final call to join the great majority.

Of Talbot, and other counties of the Eastern Shore, many pretty romances have been written, while now and then one finds a libel, and that in fact, not a few falsehoods have been

written and told of this county. One book in particular, I may
make mention of here, as its writer wields a pen that had done
excellent work, and made him a name among men of letters. I
refer to the story of "The Entailed Hat," by George Alfred
Townsend, writing under the *nom-de-plume* of "Gath." "The
Entailed Hat," deals with slavery days in Maryland and is vici-
ous in tone, and unworthy its distinguished author. Mr. Townsend has too brilliant a mind to rake over the ashes of the by-
gone, for plot and character, to reopen old sores, and thrust his
pen, dagger like, into the dead, and misrepresent the society
and people of the time of which he writes. There is enough
that is good in men to make entertaining reading without delving into the bad ; and what there is of evil one had better let be
interred with their bones, for while living, if they offend, the
mailed hand of the law is able to punish.

A story of pleasing romance is of Miss Sarah Covington, the
daughter of a prosperous and prominent Friend, whose record
was among the first, of a fair Quakeress "marrying out of the
meeting." She was first seen on horse-back by two brothers,
the Lloyds, on her way to church, riding behind her father, a
custom in those days. The Lloyd brothers were not together
at the time they met her, but each was enraptured with her
beauty, a case of love at first sight with both. Each brother
went to the Meeting House, the old structure that is still standing, and was surprised to see the other there. The meeting
over, they mounted their horses and rode separate ways to
the home of the beautiful Quakeress, for, knowing her father,
they were determined to become acquainted with the object of
their admiration. To their amazement, they met at the outer
gate. Each felt the purpose of the other, and one suggested
that they compare notes, and agreed that the one who had seen
her first should have the field to win or lose. Each frankly
named when and where he had first beheld her, and the van-
quished wished his brother success, turned his horse, and with
a sigh, rode homeward. The victor made his visit, met Miss
Covington, became more in love than ever, and, in time, won
her heart, and she became his wife.

Thereis another pretty romance of a love affair in those early
days, among the old families, for Henry Nicols, a poor youth,
met and loved Sarah Hollyday, the lovely daughter of the

wealthy owner of the fine plantation of "Darley." He was loved
by the maiden, but being poor his suit was displeasing to her
father, in spite of a noble nature and honest life that won for
him the sobriquet of "Sterling Harry." Disappointed in the
love of his life, Henry Nicols went to England to seek his fortune, and obtained it sooner than he had hoped for, inheriting
a kinsman's rich estate. Returning to Talbot, he again offered
his heart and hand, the latter now full of riches, to Sarah
Hollyday; but again came disappointment, for though the
father's consent was now given, the plucky maiden refused,
saying "if she could not marry the man she loved when poor,
she would not marry him because he had found a fortune." They then went their separate ways through life until at last he married. His wife lived ten years, and left him a
widower. For eighteen years, he remained single, but his
heart still turned to Sarah Hollyday, who at last, on her *sixtieth
birth-day* became his wife.

There is a tradition of "Plaindealing" of how Susan Robins of
"Peach Blossom," married Thomas Chamberlaine, and was taken
to his lovely home on the shore of "Plaindealing" creek to dwell.
Soon after their marriage, the husband died, and for seven
years, his inconsolable widow sat at a window in her room gazing out upon the grave of her husband in the adjacent family
burying ground. Rumor has it that at night she had a lantern
placed upon his grave, that her eyes might still rest upon the
sacred spot. Though for seven years thus inconsolable, the
sequel is that one day she saw her handsome cousin, Robert
Lloyd Nicols, ride before her window. Their eyes met, the long
sorrow ended then and there, and the beautiful widow soon
after married the young man, who had ridden between her and
the grave over which she had so long held vigil. Thus go the
old stories told in Talbot.

An incident of considerable interest of the war of 1812, in the
Chesapeake and Talbot, happened to the family of Mr. Thomas
H. Dawson and others, who were passengers on the packet
"Messenger," bound for Baltimore. Notwithstanding the perils
of navigating the bay, on account of the British cruisers, the
packet vessels would run the gauntlet to and from Baltimore
from Eastern Shore points. Captain Clement Vickers commanded the "Messenger," sailing between Easton Point and

Baltimore, and he frequently ran the blockade with his swift vessel. But one morning in a light breeze, on her return trip to Talbot, the "Messenger" was captured off Poplar Island, by Lieut. Pearson, and a crew of men in a barge from the British man of-War "Dragon," a seventy-four gun ship. An attempt was made by General Benson to ransom the "Messenger," and get the release of her passengers, but it was only in part successful. The British commander, though willing to set the ladies and children free, wished to exchange the men, man for man, for British subjects; he also said as the "Messenger" was such a beautiful model, and so elegantly fitted up, she was to be presented to the Prince Regent as a yacht. The following is a list of the prisoners taken from the "Messenger:" Mrs. Edith Dawson and two children, Miss Harriet W. Day, Miss Susan McGlaughlin, Miss Isabella Prince, Miss Elizabeth Frazier, Mrs. Brown, Dr. Traverse, James Cockayne, Joseph Spencer, Robert Spencer, Samuel Holmes, Harry L. Clarke, William Bromwell and two negroes, Ned and Kitty. Before these passengers were released, the ladies and gentlemen were invited to participate in a fete given by the officers of the "Dragon." To Mrs. Dawson, Captain Barrie of the "Dragon" was particularly kind, and at the feast, finding one of her children had been given a pewter spoon, ordered a silver spoon from his own locker, and presented it to the little girl as a souvenir of their capture. This spoon is now an heirloom in the family directly descended from Mrs. T. H. Dawson, a Quakeress, and the little girl to whom it was given, was the grandmother of the present generation of Jenkins, in Easton.

Dr. Charles Lowndes, of "Sunny Side," has in his possession some old and interesting papers, among which are legal documents going back considerably over two hundred years. One of these bears the bold signature of Charles Calvert, its purport showing the bestowal of certain land in Talbot to Francis Brooks, bearing date at London the second day of July, in the year of our Lord, one thousand six hundred and forty-third. It is signed by "Charles Calvert, Captain General and Chief Governor of our province of Maryland." This would indicate that deeds were given to land in Talbot, Maryland, as far back as 1643, which goes back still some score of years to the date of its execution in London, England, and St. Mary's, Maryland. An-

other of these old papers is a will, and reads : "In the name
of God Amen the fourteenth day of seventh month A D one
thousand seven hundred and one I Alexander Ray of Talbot
county in the Province of Maryland being sick of body but of
sound and perfect mind and memory praise be given to God
do make and ordain this my last Will and Testament in manner
following (that is to say) I first and principally commend my
soul into the hands of Almighty God my Maker hoping
through merit and death and the passion of Jesus Christ to receive pardon and remission of all my sins and to inherit ever-
lasting life and my body I commit unto the ground to be decent-
ly buried at the discretion of my friends and as touching all
such temporal estate as it hath pleased Almighty God to bestow upon me I give in form and manner following to wit."

The above was written by the maker of the will as the signature shows, and from his great anxiety to make his peace with
God, Mr. Alexander Ray was doubtless badly scared at the approach of death, and in such haste, that he did not place a
punctuation mark from the beginning to the end of his will.
To those interested in what he could not take with him, I will
add that he died possessed "of a goodly number of acres in
Talbot and considerable personal property."

THE HOTEL AVON, EASTON.

SPRING HILL CEMETERY, EASTON, LOOKING SOUTH.

CHAPTER XXIII

F the thousands who have heard of Fred Douglass, how few know more of his very remarkable career than the fact, that he escaped from slavery, and in a long life, made a name for himself that cannot be disputed? How far this success was owing to the white blood in his veins, (Fred Douglass was a quadroon,) and the great aid bestowed upon him by abolitionists, and others, from abolition sentiment, simply because he was "a fugitive slave," I need not dwell upon here, and yet, as he came from this part of the Eastern Shore of Maryland, I deem it but right to refer to him and his strange destiny, as one who may be set down as a foot-ball of fate.

Frederick Douglass was born in the district known as Tuckahoe. The exact date of his birth, he never knew any more than he did as to just who his father was. His own words on this subject in later years were: "Genealogical trees did not flourish among slaves. A person of some consequence among freemen, sometimes designated father, was literally abolished in slave law and slave practice. It was only occasionally that an exception was found to this system. As to the time of my birth, I am equally indistinct. Indeed, I seldom knew a slave who could tell exactly how old he was, for slave mothers knew nothing of the months of the year or the days of the month. There was no family record among them. They measured the ages of their children by spring-time, harvest-time, winter-time, and planting-time, and naturally, little by little, even these designations became obliterated. From certain events which subsequently occurred, however, I am led to believe that I was born about the year 1817."

One of the earliest recollections of the child who came into the world thus unheralded, unrecorded, unprotected by the ties

of family, was his separation from the old grandmother, who
had been permitted by his master and owner to nourish his
infancy. Arriving at the mansion of the "old master," whom
even at that early age he had learned to dread as some mysterious and ill-favored personage, his grandmother, weeping bitter-
ly all the time, pointed out to him a number of children somewhat older than himself, and assured him that they were his
brothers and sisters. This was indeed the case, that is to say,
the same mother had borne them. Heaven only could tell
who their fathers were. Brothers and sisters though they were
however, their presence stirred no pulse of affection in the slave
boy's heart. Housed, fed, and clothed as described, the boy
passed what he believes to have been about three years, and
then, when, according to his best recollection, he was about ten
years old, a happy change occurred in his situation. By the
orders of his master he was sent to Baltimore to live with a
relative of his owner's family. His new master, and particularly his mistress, proved to be very kind and warm-hearted people. The lady of the house was a religious woman in more
senses than that of church-going, and under her care the boy
of quick intelligence and really remarkable natural ability rapidly gained much useful information, and quickly developed
many qualities which, under other circumstances, would doubtless have lain dormant. It was in this new home that Frederick Douglass learned to read, so laying the foundation for
that better education which in the years afterward made him
a marked man, not only among his own people, but among the
citizens of this country.

Having gained this knowledge, his next desire was to learn
to write. He did so by a most ingenious process. Near his
master's house there was a ship-yard, to which he was allowed
to go during his hours of leisure, and in which he observed the
carpenters, after cutting and getting a plank or rail or piece
of timber ready for use, write on it the initials of the names of
those parts of the ship for which they were destined. For instance,
when a plank was ready for the starboard bow, it was marked
"S. B.," and so on for the different parts of the vessel. The
boy quickly saw for what purpose these letters were intended,
and learned to make them. Douglass remained in Baltimore
until his sixteenth year. Then, suddenly, because of the death

of his owner, he was sent to St. Michaels, on the Eastern
Shore. It was from St. Michaels that Frederick Douglass went
to "Wye House," the home of the present Colonel Edward Lloyd's
father Later he was employed in various duties, and was a hand
on board of a small vessel trading in the Chesapeake. This
gave him the chance he had been longing for, to make his escape. In those days negroes employed upon vessels were
obliged to have "papers" stating who and what they were.
Such a protection "paper," Frederick Douglass secured from a
negro sailor, a freeman, and when his vessel reached Baltimore,
he deserted, and with money he had saved up, took the train
for New York. His "paper" passed muster, and from that day
Frederick Douglass entered upon the career that made him the
most famous representative of his race, that is, allowing for
argument's sake, that he was a negro.

The exact connection which Frederick Douglass had with
John Brown is somewhat a mystery, though he did not join him
in his famous raid in Virginia. As letters to Brown were found
in the latter's possession, implicating Frederick Douglass, he cast
his eye to the windward to make his quick escape, gave up a
lecturing tour he was then filling in Philadelphia, and did as
absconding cashiers were wont to do, skipped into Canada, and
thence to England, thereby showing the wisdom that had al-
way enabled him to take care of himself. That he acted wisely,
the following "requisition" will show :

RICHMOND, VA., Nov. 13, 1850.

*To His Excellency James Buchanan, President of the United States,
and to the Honorable Postmaster-General of the United States.*

GENTLEMEN : I have information such as has caused me upon proper affidavits, to make requisition upon the Executive of Michigan
for the delivery of the person of Frederick Douglass, a negro man,
supposed now to be in Michigan, charged with murder, robbery,
and inciting servile insurrection in the State of Virginia. My agents
for the arrest and reclamation of the person so charged, are Benjamin M. Morris and William N. Kelly. The latter has the requisition,
and will wait on you to the end of obtaining nominal authority as
Post Office agents. They need be very secretive in this matter, and
some pretext of traveling through the dangerous section for the execution of the laws in this behalf, and some protection against ob-
trusive, unruly, or lawless violence. If it be proper so to do, will
the Postmaster-General be pleased to give Mr. Kelly for each of
these men a permit and authority to act as detectives for the Post

Office Department without pay, but to pass and repass without question, delay, or hindrance? Respectfully submitted by your obedient servant, HENRY A. WISE.

It is needless to say that the requisition did not "fetch" Fred Douglass. When the civil war broke out, he was one of the first to advocate employing negro troops by the United States Government, but he did not enlist himself. His late career is well known, so need not be commented on in these pages, though the few lines that follow, written by the facile pen of Dr. John William Palmer, in the Century Magazine, will doubtless be read with interest as descriptive of the visit in his old age of Frederick Douglass to the scene of his youth and slavery days.

In 1881 Frederick Douglass, being then marshal of the District of Columbia, was moved to revisit the scenes of his childhood and his thrall, and one day found himself on the porch of "Wye House," where he was received by the sons of Colonel Lloyd, their father being absent, with that courtesy which is extended to every stranger who finds his way thither. When he had made known the motive of his visit, he was conducted over the estate, from spot to spot that he remembered and described with all their childish associations ; here a spring, there a hedge, a lane, a field, a tree. He called them by their names, or recalled them by some simple incident, and all the glowing heart of the man seemed to go out to the place as he passed from ghost to ghost as in a dream. And then a strange thing happened ; standing mute and musing for a while, he said slowly and low, as one who talks in his sleep, "Over in them woods was whar me and Mars Dan useter trap rabbits." "Mars Dan" was the Governor's son. Was it the man's half-playful, half-pathetic sense of the grotesque incongruity of the situation ? Or was it glamour ?—all the tremendous significance of a phenomenal life compacted into the homely reflection and phrase of a barefoot "darky."

CHAPTER XXIV.

 HE environs of Easton are attractive in many ways, on account of the marine views, good roads, fine old homes, well tilled farms and other advantages : also dotting the landscape and shore, are a couple of dozens of towns, villages and hamlets that are naturally very important factors in the eyes of their separate inhabitants. Oxford, in point of age comes first in the Easton District and has already been described. Tunis Mills is a pretty village, situated upon both sides of a river—Leed's Creek, it is called—and boasts of being a port in direct communication with Baltimore by steamers, as well as the seat of a large lumber industry. Easton Point is a suburb of Easton, the landing-place of the Baltimore steamers and a considerable commercial centre and seaport. Kirkham is a hamlet, with the traditional store and blacksmith shop, and of enough importance to have a representative of "Uncle Sam" as postmaster, who in reality is a postmistress. In the St. Michaels district, we find Bellevue, situated upon the Tred Avon, with its postoffice, steamboat wharf and store. Both Bozman and Neavitt are postoffice hamlets, and do an extensive trade with the country surrounding them.

Royal Oak is an "old timer," the interesting story of whose name has already been told. The village has a postoffice, carriage factory, several good stores, a drug store and several churches, and a handsome school house, while it is proud it is a village with a history. In the neighborhood of Royal Oak, is "Solitude," the old home of the late Judge Ormond Hammond, a distinguished and much beloved citizen of Talbot. St. Michaels, on the Miles, is a peculiarly situated, but hospitable and pleasant town of over two thousand inhabitants. With its pretty homes and attractive stores, it is another claimant, not only for

honors of long ago, but for its progressiveness of to-day. It
lies on a neck of land, from a quarter of a mile to a mile in
width, the Miles or St. Michaels river, for it has been renamed,
upon one side, the Broad on the other. The latter is navigable
to the town, and forms a good harbor. Canoes are abundant in
those waters, which for boating, has no superior. Upon the
other hand, is the Miles, and an inlet from it forms a fine harbor, not only for the many fishing craft, but for the coasters and
yachts, while there is a good wharf and warehouse belonging to
the Baltimore steamboat line. It is a beautiful sight to see the
numerous vessels in harbor, and especially when the oyster fleets
are coming homeward in the evening These marine pictures
of fleets are not surpassed on any waters, and yet are very common to these shores, at Tilghman's Island, St. Michaels, Claiborne, Oxford, Cambridge, and Easton.

St. Michaels always was a place of considerable importance and is to-day, with its large oyster traffic, fisheries and
boat-building, for be it known, along with the several places
named above, there are shipyards, and in them are built the
fleet buckeye, the graceful canoe, and slippery dead-rise bateau.
At present St. Michaels depends principally on its oyster business, which is carried on extensively. There are about two
hundred of the finest and fleetest canoes in the world there, and
any good morning or evening, the sight on the river, would delight a yachtsman's eyes. There are also many schooners and
pungies which carry oysters to other markets. In the summer season, the town is always crowded with summer visitors
from the cities, and ample traveling facilities are supplied by
the Baltimore, Chesapeake and Atlantic Railroad. All the
principal streets of the town are paved, and the town is well
lighted, and the roads are very fine for bicycling or driving.

It is said that the Rev. James Clayland was performing
the duties of a clergyman of the Church of England there as
early as 1672, and that the church building was the nucleus
around which gathered the village. It is also claimed that the
earliest recorded mention of the town was an action to recover a
bet on a horse race, which took place in 1680 ; hence the church
building was built prior to that date. In very early times the
town was noted for its ship-building and in it were built many
of the famous Baltimore clippers, which were the ocean grey

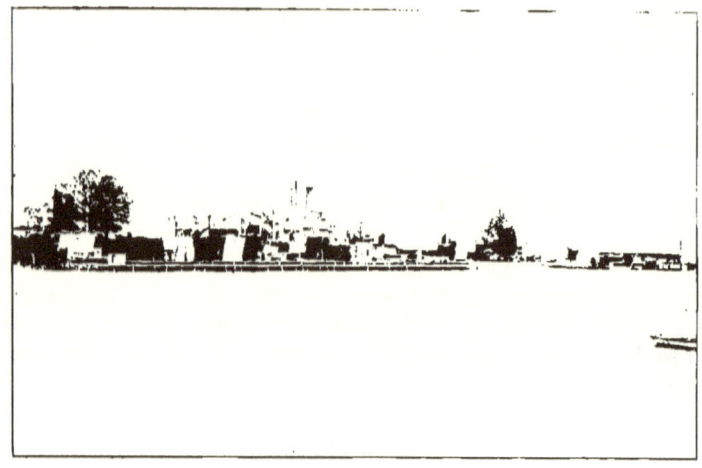

TUNIS MILLS HARBOR AND LUMBER MILL.

SCENE ON MRS. K. J. ROBINSON'S ESTATE ON THE AVON.

hounds of that day. In olden times, the Indians used to *portage* their canoes across the narrow neck of land from river to river, and the people of to-day do the same with their vessels, rather than take the trip around, more than fifty miles, though a more delightful trip than this same sail cannot be imagined.

There are two cannon, six-pounders, in Fort McHenry which belong to St Michaels, and which can be restored to the town, if the corporation or the people want them. Jacob Gibson, of Marengo and Sharp's Island gave these guns to the town in 1813, as a kind of peace offering to those whom his famous prank had offended. There is no one living now who remembers what occurred eighty five years ago; but there were only a few years since, those alive who could tell the circumstances of this incident in the war with Great Britain. Mr. Gibson owned Sharp's Island, then a farm of seven hundred acres, and on it he had slaves and live-stock and other property. When Admiral Warren's British cruisers came up the Chesapeake they raided Sharp's Island, as foragers for food, and took off cattle, sheep and hogs to the fleet. Mr. Gibson himself boarded the Admiral's flag-ship, where he was hospitably entertained, and succeeded in getting paid for the property taken, and a written protection for himself and island. Report exaggerated this diplomatic victory into something like treason, and in St. Michaels and elsewhere it was said that Mr. Gibson had sold out to the enemy.

The whole of the Bayside country was on the *qui vive*, expecting a British attack on St. Michaels. Mr. Gibson had meanwhile planned a scare for the "panicky" people. He came from Sharp's Island one day in his barge, rowed by his slaves, with a red bandanna at the mast head, and an empty rum barrel for a drum, to land on the San Domingo side of St. Michaels, on his way to Marengo. The people thought the British were coming. Women and children were sent up the country, and the militia got together on the banks of the creek to prevent if possible the landing of the marauders. When they saw they had been fooled by Mr. Gibson's untimely prank, they were incensed, and he was threatened with bodily harm. He was a man, however, whom it was impossible to frighten, and he was allowed to depart.

The two six-pounders he bought in Baltimore, and had them transported around the head of the bay. These two guns did good service on the 10th of August, 1813, when the British attacked St. Michaels on the Miles river side. After the war they were put in a disused market house on St. Mary's Square, and were only brought out to fire salutes on the twenty-second of February and the fourth of July.

When the market house was demolished, the cannon were sent to the armory in Easton, where they remained until June 9th, 1861, when they were seized by Col. Abel Smith, by order of General Banks, with all the other munitions of war, and taken to Fort McHenry, where they are to this day. These guns did not belong to the state, but to the town of St. Michaels. They ought to be restored. They have much to do with the history of that town, and should be in its keeping. There is another old cannon marking a boundary line on the farm of the Rev. Dr. W. M. Poisal, now of Easton. The history of this piece of ordnance I was unable to learn, but it has doubtless played its part in the attack made on the town by the British. Of late years, St. Michaels, Oxford, Royal Oak and other shore places are developing into summer resorts and are crowded with visitors. The people of to-day of St.Michaels are proud of their town and its history. They are hospitable, take life as it comes, and are prosperous.

It is in St. Michaels, it will be recalled, that Christ's Episcopal Church stands, right in the very town and surrounded by its dead, while the ancient Methodist Church also written about in these pages, had its story to tell of the long ago. There are other churches as well, and a public high school, which is an ornament to any place, for, outside learning to row a boat, sail and swim, the children are taught that education is the most important factor in these days of general learning.

Sharp's Island, though not a village, is an annex to Talbot county, and is now developing into a sanatorium. Once it was known as Bateman's Island, belonging to a kinsman of the well-known Bateman family, of Easton. This was many years ago. In olden times Sharp's Island was very large and imposing, and had its history ; but not founded on a rock, according to biblical injunctions, the storms and waves have gathered it in, until now it has not one half the acreage it had two hundred years ago. Improvements now in progress will check its destruction, and it will doubtless become an important place as a resort and sanatorium, being delightfully located in every respect.

The village of Trappe, I had almost written the word *town*, for it is a popular centre, is inland, a short distance back from the river. It has a landing for steamers on Trappe creek, and does a large business with Baltimore, in the grain and fruit season. Trappe might have gotten its name from its hospitality, for its people have a persuasive and kindly way of *entrapping* all who visit it, only that is not the way it did get its rather peculiar cognomen. Some how Trappe is like Rome, for it seems that all roads lead to Trappe, save the railroad. That it intends to have a railroad is an avowed fact, for Trappe station, on the Delaware and Chesapeake branch of the Pennsylvania, is four miles distant, and the railroad, freight, telegraph and express agent, all in one, thinks the station will get to be the centre of a mighty city. Others do not have his opinion, especially the people of Trappe itself. Trappe is also within reach of another river landing, Kirby's, on the Choptank, and Oxford and Easton are easy drives, so that it can hold its own with water-privileged towns, if it is located inland, and inland in Talbot does not get one far from tidal shores. Two hundred years ago, you see I am constantly looking backward a couple of centuries in this land of tradition and Legendary Lore, Trappe was almost the centre of the Talbot settlements. White Marsh was its church, Oxford was its port, and from tobacco and grain fields about it, its revenues were drawn. About Trappe there are some fine old homes, and though proud of its age, it keeps up with the times, has good stores, is prosperous and growing. It boasts of a handsome Episcopal Church and rectory, a fine M. E. Church, pretty residences and the best of schools, those for colored as well as white children. Talbot takes especial care that the negro has the best of education. One striking feature of Trappe, and which is often passed by unnoticed, is a grave in the centre of the pavement of one of its streets. The grave lies parallel with the walk, its head and foot stones are well preserved, though dating far back, but I could not learn how it was that this grave came there in the public thoroughfare.

Not far from Trappe lies the village, also inland, of Manasses, where there is a church, stores and school house, and where a good highway leads to a landing on the Choptank. The winding course of this river, whence it derives its name, Choptank, may be thus well illustrated :

Any one in Easton desiring a delightful afternoon and evening sail on the steamer, can drive to Dover bridge, four miles distant on the Choptank, take one of the several steamboats, sail around the river and land at Easton at nine o'clock the same night, having had a run of over seventy miles. At Dover is the drawbridge over which the people of Caroline county come to their metropolis---Easton. In making this delightful run, the steamers stop for an hour at a place, that many look upon as Easton's rival, the quaint, old-time, yet up-and-doing city of Cambridge.

Ivy-town is more attractive in name than in reality, being a village which is long-drawn-out along the highway. About Ivytown cluster, or rather cling, the colored race, and many of its people are well-to-do farmers on a small scale. There is another such village of colored citizens, Uniontown, across the Miles river, and rather picturesque than otherwise are its world wide styles of architecture. Both Ivytown and Uniontown have their churches and schools. The inhabitants of the latter town, I have been told, make the proud boast that not one of its citizens was ever in jail. Other towns might take particular notice of the above pleasing intelligence, and learn the same method of keeping out of "limbo."

CHAPTER XXV.

Home Sweet Home.

HILE a preceding chapter referred to a few of the towns of Talbot county, there are still others, villages generally, to bestow a word upon, that are more or less attractive features of the environs of Easton, the "Hub" about which they centre. To the people of the humblest hamlet, it must be borne in mind, clings a special love for their abiding place, for "Be it ever so humble, there is no place like home." The spot where human eyes first open to the light of day—is the one above all others that will be cherished.

It is the birth-place, there where the family gathered around the hearth stone; and callous must be the heart that does not hold fond recollections of it. Days of earliest childhood, of boyhood, are recalled; and those were pleasant days, fishing, sneaking off to go swimming when strictly forbidden to go near the water, until they learned to swim, trapping birds, going to school, "playing hooky," "sassin' the teacher," being kept in "just for nothin'," making eyes at another fellow's girl, taking a tonic of green birch-tea prescribed by the teacher, and in fact enjoying all the pleasures of childhood, bright with hope one moment, full of despair the next—such are the links that bind one in indissoluble bonds to memories of "Home, sweet home." In writing therefore of the environs of Easton, it will be well to refer to the pretty cross road villages as well as those of more pretentious growth. Windy Hill, Matthewstown, Lewistown, Montague, and Franklinville are all villages, some of them with histories worth remembering, and whose inhabitants are of the right sort. Cordova is a place of more than average importance, there being a post office, railroad, express and railroad station and having its churches, schools and cheery homes.

Chapel is a pretty place, and I know is important enough for the politicians to feel great anxiety as to "how Chapel goes" in election times. About it are pleasant homes, and its people are hospitable to a degree, but then hospitality is a failing, as it may almost be called, of this entire Eastern Shore.

Woodland is another railroad town, hence has ideas up to date. Longwood is a well located village with something of a preponderance of churches, but has a good store and schools, and a large circumference for trade. The Episcopal Chapel, rectory and cemetery make a very fine picture, having an "old English" look that is very attractive.

Wye Mills is located near the beautiful Wye river, and the new railroad from Queen Anne to Baltimore, via steamer connection at Queenstown, passes through it. The "Mills of the Gods" may grind slow, and the grist may be "exceeding fine," but Wye Mills grinds all right as regards speed and the proper size of the grist, and the people congratulate themselves upon the narrow escape their village made of not being in Talbot, for they are on the county line; but then Queen Anne is also a county to be proud of, and Wye Millites have a strong leaning that way.

Then comes Wye Landing, a hamlet, and Skipton, a postoffice, which claims the distinction of the first court held in Talbot, dating back two hundred and forty years. Skipton, therefore, has its history, and being on the direct line of a proposed railroad, the Easton Northern, it may yet become from its favorable location, the site of a flourishing town.

Dundee is a postoffice store near the boundary of the Wye House estate.

Claiborne is a delightfully situated place, being on the shores of Eastern Bay, an arm of the Chesapeake, with the Miles river in the rear. It is a new village with century old surroundings, and it claims distinction of being the terminus of the Chesapeake and Atlantic railroad, where connection is made with the steamboat from Baltimore, and Bay Ridge on the western shore. This railroad runs|through Easton and Salisbury, to Ocean City.

Tilghman's Point, the farm known as Rich Neck, will doubtless yet become a very popular resort, for it borders on Claiborne.

McDaniel is a village situated near Claiborne, and looks very pretty from the railroad, yet is more attractive, when one goes there and meets the people.

Wittman and Bozman are postoffice centres, in the midst of a flourishing community, while Sherwoodsville is the neck of land formed by the Chesapeake Bay and Harris' Creek, and on the line of the proposed railroad to Island City, commonly called Tilghman's Island. Along the shore about Sherwoodsville are some grand old homes and historic ground, for it was in these waters that Governor Claiborne figured in the first settlement of the Eastern Shore of Maryland.

Island City is a place of considerable importance in more ways than one. It is located on the point of a neck of land, with the broad Chesapeake in full view to the westward and Sharp's Island almost due south, Poplar Island bearing north west, and Harris' creek, Broad river and the magnificent Choptank to the eastward. It is cut off from the mainland by a bridged inlet that boats of a good size may pass through. Island City is visit ed by the Choptank and Avon steamers, and is considerable of a port and haven for the valuable fleets of the Chesapeake. Its oyster and fishing industry is large, and what its inhabitants don't know about boats and boat building, no one else need try to learn. Here are built the fleetest of canoes and buckeyes, deadrise skiffs, sloops and schooners, not only for trading craft but for sport as well. Tilghman's Island boats are crafts that can show a clean pair of heels to almost anything afloat driven by sail power. There are good stores in Island City, it is a thriving place, something of a summer resort, and its churches and schools are well attended, but the children are taught that the alphabet runs, B-O-A-T, and the good Christians there hope they will find just such a pleasant place beyond the grave. Island City is distant from Washington City forty-five miles via Bay Ridge, from Baltimore fifty-eight, from Easton thirty miles. It has a good harbor and ideal cruising waters. Suburbs of Island City on the shore are Tilghman and Fairbank, and thus we come to the mainland shore end of Talbot County, with its landscape and water views presenting on the map the appearance of a piece of lace work, yet in reality as substantial as the Rock of Gibraltar. There are three towns on the Baltimore, Chesapeake and Atlantic railroad that, as neighbors of Easton may be mentioned here—Preston, Salisbury and Berlin.

The nearest to Easton is Preston, near the Choptank, in Caroline county, a thriving little town, and very prettily located.

The people of Preston are energetic and refined, and keep well in touch with the times, while their town has sent forth men, who have made names for themselves known the world over.

Salisbury in Wicomico county is an old town, as years go, and yet it has the appearance of a new and booming place. It has a naturally beautiful site, lying in a fork of the Wicomico river, and grew from a landing, about which in 1782, by an act of the Maryland Assembly, authority was given to purchase fifteen acres of land to be laid out as a town under the name of Salisbury. Being in the very centre of the fruit belt, it naturally would prosper, but aside from its good situation, Salisbury has a most progressive and up-to-date class of citizens, who devote their energy and money without stint to making their town a delightful home that wins admiration abroad. All improvements there, water works, ice factories, gas, electric lights, telephone and public buildings are of a modern and substantial kind. Its streets and avenues are well paved, shelled, and kept in fine condition. The private residences of Salisbury are particularly attractive, its stores of the best, and its trade, import and export large. Many of Maryland's old families dwell in and around the town, and a number of fine farms are within easy drive. In addition to her two lines of railroad, Salisbury is reached by the Wicomico river steamboat line, and in summer particularly is an attractive resort.

Berlin lies in Worcester county, situated almost within sound of the Atlantic surf. The town is a railroad centre, and is new in appearance from the fact that it was visited by a most disastrous fire in 1895, which destroyed a large part of the business section, and many residences. The Eastern Shore is waking up, there are few of its one time dreamy old villages, that will not soon be within sound of the locomotive's shrill whistle, and where the railroad, the iron veins of the country, run, busy life follows as the daylight does the darkness.

Times have changed since the long ago, when malaria—then known as fever and ague—was prevalent in Talbot. Proper drainage, cultivation and sanitary methods have made this section as healthful and as free from disease as any other place on the Atlantic sea-board. It should be borne in mind that from reliable health statistics published by Dr. Chancellor of Baltimore, Royal Oak was found to be the centre of a circle of ten miles radius, which embraced the most healthful spot in the country, taking the death rate to the average thousand of population, which was found to be phenomenally small. In truth deaths are few and far between here, and recently a grave digger of Easton on being asked if times were not dull with him, replied, "Very, I have not buried *a living soul this month.*"

CHAPTER XXVI.

EGINNING with the present century, there have been men in Talbot, who have won fame in their separate walks in life, be it afloat, ashore, in statesmanship, literature, or in the church, or as military men. Such have added lustre to Talbot's escutcheon, and their names, if not all engraven on tablets of marble will be treasured in the hearts of the generations that follow. Admiral Franklin Buchanan was born in 1800 of distinguished parentage and entered the U. S. Navy as midshipman in 1815, on the frigate Java, under Commodore Oliver H. Perry. From first to last he distinguished himself in his nautical career, and was the first American officer to place his foot on Japanese soil. In 1855, he became a captain, and was the first commandant of the U. S. Naval Academy, which he established upon a successful foundation. In 1861, he was in command of the Washington navy yard, but resigned to go with the south, where his record won him fame throughout the world as the daring commander of the first iron clad—the Merrimac. His later career was a brilliant one, and after the war ended, he returned to "The Rest," his beautiful home in Talbot county, near Easton, on the shores of Miles river. In 1835, Admiral Buchanan married the third daughter of Governor Edward Lloyd of "Wye House." He died on May 11th, 1874, at "The Rest," in the seventy-fourth year of his age.

Governor Philip Francis Thomas was born in Easton in 1810; was educated at the Easton academy, studied law, admitted to the bar in 1831, elected to the legislature in 1838, congressional representative in 1839, elected Governor of Maryland in 1847, in 1850, comptroller of the treasury, collector of the port of Baltimore in 1853, in 1860 was appointed secretary of the treasury in the cabinet of President Buchanan. This he resigned and return.

ed to his home in Talbot during the war.   In 1868, he was made
U. S. Senator from Maryland, but was not allowed to take his
seat on the plea of disloyalty, so entered upon the practice of
law in Easton, and held important offices up to a short time before his death.

Judge H. H. Goldsborough is a native of Talbot, and descended from the old and honorable family of that name.   He was educated in Easton, and at St. John's College, Annapolis.   Admitted to the bar in 1841, was auditor of the court in 1848, and
held that office until 1861 ; he was chosen state senator, and
was a member of the legislature, of which he was president at
the breaking out of the war, whose influence did much to keep
Maryland in the Union.   When Easton was made the head
quarters of a military district, Mr. Goldsborough was appointed brigadier general of volunteers, and placed in command of
this point.   It was through Mr. Goldsborough that Maryland a-
bolished slavery before Mr. Lincoln's emancipation proclamation.

Dr. Solomon Martin Jenkins was one of Talbot's distinguished
physicians of his time.   Born in Easton in 1803, he went
through the public schools with honor to himself.   Determined
to receive a classical education, he entered Harvard university.
Deciding upon medicine as a profession, Dr. Jenkins devoted
himself to its study, and entered the University of Pennsylvania
from which well known institution he received his degree.   Returning to Easton he begun practice, and was known in a very
short while for his superior skill in medicine, and as a man of
brilliant talents.   In 1848, when only forty-five years of age, he
died, and great indeed was his loss to the community, where he
had won fame and popularity.

Hon. Samuel Hambleton was born in Easton in 1812, whose
father had been for many years a member of the legislature from Talbot county, and held other important state offices.
His grandfather was a captain in the Revolutionary army.   Hon.
Samuel Hambleton was educated at the Easton academy; was
admitted to the Talbot bar in 1833, elected to the House of Delegates, then state senator, was appointed colonel of calvary in 1845
by Governor Pratt, was president of the Chesapeake and Ohio
canal, and in 1870 was elected to Congress on the democratic
ticket, and reelected to the Forty Fourth Congress. In 1838 Col.
Hambleton married Miss Elizabeth Parrott of Talbot, and had

two children, a son and a daughter. The son served in the Confederate army during the civil war.

On May 30th, 1890, there passed away in Easton, Dr. Samuel A. Harrison, a man of distinction in more than one calling, a man whose loss was a great one to the community in which he dwelt, his profession and to the literary world. Dr. Harrison was the son of A. B. Harrison and Eleanor Spencer, and was born at "Clay's Hope," Talbot, in 1822. He was educated under a private tutor, and graduated at Dickinson College in 1840. Entering upon the study of medicine, he received his diploma from the University of Maryland, begun to practice in St. Michaels, then moved to St. Louis; but in 1854 returned to Talbot and became a planter, for he was a devoted lover of agriculture in all its branches. He declined the nomination for state senator, but accepted the appointment as president of the county School Board, for which by education, he was so well fitted, and proved himself a most efficient and untiring official. Returning to his agricultural pursuits, Dr. Harrison settled upon his fine estate, "Woodstock," on Miles river, and devoted himself to the management of his property, and to literature, in which he proved himself an author of superior ability. His literary taste ran mostly in preserving the traditions and annals of Talbot, where his scholarly mind found so much of interest in its history and people. He was an untiring worker with his pen, seeming to rejoice in all he did in a literary way, showing his superiority in all subjects pertaining to history, rhetoric, logic and philosophy. He was devoted to the improvement of Talbot, and was an earnest laborer to that end. Of broad and intellectual mind and of amiable disposition, he was a peer among his fellows and his aim in life was the betterment of mankind in every particular. He left to posterity a vast amount of literary work, in the field of Talbot's history, and his search for the truth was untiring. At the time of his death Dr. Harrison willed that his writings should go to the Maryland Historical Society, realizing their value to that institution; for it had been his intention to prepare a book of Talbot, and no one was better fitted for such a work than he. His widow, who was Miss Martha Denny of Talbot, and two daughters, Mrs. Horace Noble of Baltimore, and Mrs. Oswald Tilghman, survive him, the home of the latter being "Foxley Hall" in Easton.

James Lloyd Martin was an influential citizen of Talbot, and a distinguished member of the bar. The death of few of Talbot's sons created such a void in society and professional life, as did that of Mr. Martin. He came of highly respectable parentage, his father having been Edward Martin of Island Creek Neck, and a nephew of Governor Daniel Martin. Born in 1815 he was educated at the Easton Academy, studied law, and was admitted to the bar of Talbot in 1837, and elected in 1840 to the House of Delegates. He was an elector for Breckenridge and Lowe. He was also appointed Deputy Attorney General, States Attorney for Talbot in 1871, in all of which offices he served with honor. In 1864, he was made judge of the judicial district of Talbot and Caroline counties, and was prominent in the affairs of this state.

General Tench Tilghman was born at his estate of Plimhimmon in 1810; he was the son of Tench Tilghman, grandson of Col. Tench Tilghman of Washington's staff, and great-grandson of Matthew Tilghman of Revolutionary fame. A graduate of West Point, he was an officer in the Black Hawk war, but resigning his commission, he returned to his estate in Talbot and devoted himself to agriculture and building up this part of the country. He devoted much of his time, energies and means to bringing a railroad to Talbot, and was made president of the Maryland and Delaware railroad, which he originated. Devoted also to the cause of education, Gen. Tilghman did much to establish the Maryland Military Academy at Oxford in the forties, and through his instrumentality the new parish of Trinity at Oxford was established, and the foundation was laid of the present handsome stone church. General Tilghman married the daughter of Hon. John Leeds Kerr, and after her death he married a daughter of Robert Lloyd Tilghman of "Hope." He died in 1874.

One whose death was a great loss to Easton thirty years ago, was Dr. Edward Jenkins, a man whose popularity was unbounded with all classes of his fellow-citizens. Honored by all and highly esteemed in his profession, Dr. Jenkins was a man of learning, cultivation and much experience, for he had held for years the position of surgeon in the U. S. Navy, had traveled extensively, and arisen to eminence as a practitioner. Born in Talbot in 1816 and descending from a most worthy ancestry, Dr. Jenkins after receiving a fine education, determined to devote his life to medicine; with him its practice was a work of love and ambition as well as a profession. Dr. Jenkins died in 1865, and his descendants are living in Easton, his two sons, Edward and Thomas H. representing the drug firm of Dawson and Jenkins.

As the Right Rev. Henry Champlin Lay, D. D. has been so intimately connected with this county, it is well to make mention of him among Talbot's men of note. Born in Virginia in 1823, his father being a merchant of Richmond, he was educated at the University of Virginia. Graduated as master of arts, he became a private tutor, then studied for the Episcopal ministry at the Alexandria Theological Seminary, was ordained deacon, and removed to Alabama. Was ordained priest at Huntsville, Alabama, in 1848, and in 1857 Hobart College made him Doctor of Divinity. He was made missionary bishop of the southwest in 1859. He was in the south during the war, and did much to unite the divided church after the struggle ended. He was made bishop, and through his influence Easton was made a cathedral town. Bishop Lay was also a writer of much force, and his writings were of a popular character. He died in Easton universally beloved by all who knew him.

The late Ormond Hammond of "Solitude" comes of Scotch lineage, his family having been prominent in Scotland. His ancestors came to America several generations ago, and settled in Maryland, where they became large land-holders and were influential in the social and political life of their time. Judge Hammond, as he is better known, was born in 1825, was educated in Baltimore and Georgetown, intending to enter upon a professional life. Abandoning this intention, he begun a business career in Baltimore, but marrying, he removed to the beautiful home of "Solitude," where he lived for fifty years. He was prominent in the history of Talbot socially and politically, being a man of sterling character, noble nature, unbounded hospitality and of great popularity. Judge Hammond was a political leader in Talbot, and was honored by being sent to the state senate. He did much for Talbot's agricultural development, its schools and general advancement. The high office of judge of the Orphans' Court was a position he filled with honor to himself and his party, until appointed by President Cleveland a sub-treasurer of the United States, which position he held at the time of his death. Judge Hammond died in 1897, and left a void in Talbot hard to fill, for he was beloved by all who knew him. He left a large family of children, Mrs. Hammond having died some years ago, and "Solitude" is now the home of his daughters, his sons being in business in Baltimore. Judge Hammond's wife was Mary M. Cox, daughter of Rev. J. and Mary M. Cox, and a sister of Lieutenant Governor Cox of Maryland.

Gen. Lloyd Tilghman was born at Rich Neck, Talbot, and was educated at West Point. He served through the Mexican War, and joined the Confederate army within the first year of the war. At Fort Henry, February 6th, 1862, he held the fort until nearly half his gunners were killed or wounded. When Foote took the fort, he had as prisoners General Tilghman and staff, and sixty men. Gen. Tilghman remained prisoner a few months, and was exchanged. In the the fall of 1862, he joined the army of the west then in Mississippi, and was put in command of the first brigade, Loring's division. At the battle of Corinth he took a prominent part, and in all subsequent operations of that army under Van Dorn, and, afterwards Pemberton, he bore a conspicuous part up to the time of his death. General Tilghman was killed by a shell on the evening of the 16th of May, 1863, on the battlefield of Baker's creek, or Champion Hill, Mississippi. General Tilghman left Rich Neck when he was a young man, and went to Baltimore to live. His son visited Rich Neck hotel last July, being the first time he had ever been there. Rich Neck mansion was built by James Tilghman, the father of Lloyd Tilghman.

Colonel Thomas Hughlett, one of Talbot's most honored citizens, came from a long line of prominent ancestors, his father being William Hughlett, the owner of "Warwick Manor" in Dorchester county, a county by the way, that has given Maryland many distinguished sons. Colonel Hughlett was born May 5, 1826, at "Warwick Manor," received his earlier education from private tutors, and attended college at Princeton, after which he returned to Maryland and devoted himself to planting. Later he married a daughter of William Harrison of Dorchester county, and making his home in Easton, entered earnestly into the political and social life of Talbot. Elected to the responsible position of Clerk of the Court, he held it up to the time of his

RESIDENCE OF EDWIN SINCLAIR, OXFORD.

CITY VISITORS ENJOYING THE SALT BATH, IN THE MILES RIVER.

death, March 31st, 1896. Colonel Hughlett was a genial and courteous gentleman, popular with all, and his death was a great loss to the community in which he lived.

Commodore Charles Lowndes, U. S. N., is another of Talbot's sons in whom the state holds great pride, and his beautiful old home on the Miles river is today pointed out to strangers as one of the ancient manor houses of long ago. The house is now the property of Colonel Charles Chipley, who has done much to improve it, yet it still reserves its old time attractive features. Entering the navy at fifteen, Commodore Lowndes went to sea as a midshipman and learned his profession by the real hard knocks and *modus operandi* in vogue in those days, and which used to bring out all that there was in a man. He was sent on foreign cruises and won his way up to higher rank by downright worth, and a heroism to do and dare all he had to face in the line of duty. Appointed to the command of the sloop-of-war Germantown, twenty guns, he was ordered to Mexico during the war of 1846-1848, and later commanded the flagship "Hartford," as her captain, at the time that the great Farragut was in command, and the voyage was being made to the East Indies. Having been nearly a half century in the navy, Commodore Lowndes was promoted and retired in 1861, having married Miss Sarah Scott Lloyd, daughter of Governor Lloyd. He made his home at "The Anchorage," on Miles river, and took rest from his labors after a service well done. His ashes now lie in the family burying ground at Wye House.

One of the heroes of the "lost cause" who lost his life under the stars and bars of the south was General Charles S. Winder, a native of Talbot. Born in 1829, at the fine old home of "Knightly" a few miles from Easton, then the property of his family, Charles S. Winder, as are almost all Talbot-born boys, was a good sailor before he was in his teens ; and yet, raised on salt water as he was, he chose the life of a soldier rather than that of a naval officer. Educated in his earlier years in Talbot under a tutor's care, he later went to St. John's College, and afterwards received an appointment to West Point Military Academy, in 1846. He graduated there, with honors, in 1850, after a four years' course and became a lieutenant in the third artillery and captain in the ninth infantry. He was ordered to the frontier, where he saw hard service against the Indians, then

most troublesome in their warfare against the soldiers and settlers. Stationed in California, he was on a troop ship, that
was wrecked on the Pacific coast, and showed the hero, when
only the officers and a few of the men could be taken off in
the boats, by saying:

"I remain with my men to die with them."

Later he was rescued with his men, and just in time, by
the English vessel "Antarctic," taken to Liverpool, whither the
ship was bound, then returning to the United States, when he
was stationed at Fort Vancouver, Washington Territory. Of
just such a nature was General Winder, self-sacrificing, brave
and generous, that he won favor as he did praises. A Marylander, when the war came, he cast his lot with the South, resigning his commission in the United States army. He was
at once made a captain, and his ability and courage took him up
the grade of promotion rapidly, for early in 1862, he became a
brigadier general. He handled his command well, his brigade
forming one of Stonewall Jackson's division, and met his early
death at the battle of Cedar Mountain, August 9th, 1862, while
in the act of placing his artillery in a desperate duel that was
going on with the light guns. General Winder married Miss
Alice Lloyd of Wye House, in 1855, and his widow and son now
reside in Talbot. This ended his brilliant career, while yet a
very young man, but his memory is warmly cherished by all in
Talbot. When the camp of Confederate veterans was formed in
Easton a year ago, it was given the name of the "Charles S.
Winder Camp."

Thomas Chamberlaine Nicols was born in Easton, June 28th,
1834, and dates back through a long line of honorable ancestry.
The first of the family to settle in Talbot was the Rev. Henry
Nicols of St. Michaels parish, who came over from England
where he had graduated at Oxford university, as has been told
in a sketch of this really great and good man, whose strange
epitaph is also given. He lies buried within the St. Michaels
Churchyard with other rectors of the ancient parish. William
Nicols, the son of Rev. Henry Nicols and his wife, a Miss Elizabeth Rolle, married the daughter of Honorable Samuel Chamberlaine, whose wife was Henrietta Maria Lloyd. The subject of
this short memoir was related also by kindred ties and by mar-

riage to the Robinson, Goldsborough, and other historic families of Talbot. Graduated in Easton, Mr. Thomas C. Nicols went to Philadelphia, and early in life entered upon a business career with success. He then returned to Easton, and once more begun a mercantile life for himself with eminent success, for he built up in a few years the large hardware house so well and favorably known in Talbot, and now under the management of his son, Mr. Edward T. Nicols. Mr. T. C. Nicols married Miss Margaret Wroth, daughter of Dr. Peregrine Wroth, once president of Washington College, Md., and left a family of three, his daughters Mrs. H. M. Hardcastle and Miss Margaret Eugenia, and Edward T. Nicols, of Easton.

THE STRANGE STORY OF THE VILLA.

HE Miles river, for thus the St. Michaels has slipped its consonants, is one of those broad salt water streams, the home of the oyster, crab, terrapin, and wild ducks, that pierce the peninsula of the Eastern Shore of Maryland, until there is scarcely as much land as water. Near its upper course a tongue of land thrusts itself into the river, with a tasteful boat-house and pier, near which a yacht lies moored. Above the grove of trees, a square red tower, capped with white, indicates the site of "The Villa."

As with families, so it is with land. Some tracts undergo a quiet humdrum existence from century to century, while others are as full of affairs as a bailiff. This tongue of land, with its neighboring estate, is one that seems to be inextricably woven into the fate and fortunes of men. In 1661 occurred in Boston the memorable trial of Wenlock Christison, for the crime of being a Quaker, of which the quaint old volumes of Besse give so full a story. Having been exiled, he returned to Boston to protest against the murder of a fellow Quaker named Leddra, where he was seized by a mob, headed by the Rev. Seabury Cotton, club in hand. Christison had a robust tongue of his own, and after his trial was, with other Quakers, condemned to death by Governor Endicott. The day before the execution came the pardon of the King, and the prisoners were released, the Governor being obliged to satisfy himself with whipping two of the men through the streets.

Wenlock Christison then emigrated to Maryland, taking advantage of the religious toleration extended by the Calverts. Here, in 1661, he obtained a grant of land from Lord Baltimore, including this tongue on which "The Villa" stands. He became one of the substantial men of the colony, and took part in the House of Burgesses, of which he was a member.

A TALBOT TEACHERS' ASSOCIATION.

The descendants of the Christisons here dwelt in peace and prosperity, and in time the estate fell into the hands of Isaac Atkinson, who had married into the family of Christison, and their house of old English bricks remains in part upon the land until this day. After the Christisons had married, borne, and died, the family gradually dwindled away, and the estate passed into the hands of Richard France, the lottery king of Maryland. The state recognized and legalized the lottery business, and Richard France waxed rich and prosperous. He built a palace, (the word is used advisedly,) on Mount Vernon square, Baltimore, and bought an estate on the Eastern Shore. Here he built "The Villa," with its red tower overtopping the trees. In magnificence nothing in the vicinity rivalled it. There were winding walks and fountains, rich vases and marble statuary, glass houses and everything else that money could buy to complete a gentleman's country seat. It was the wonder of all the country roundabout.

So enviable was the prosperity of Richard France that a man named Broadbent set up an illicit lottery, known as the "Lottery Policy Company," which in time made such inroads into Richard France's business, that he was forced to admit Broadbent into partnership. Then Broadbent also waxed rich and prosperous, and built a superb place beyond the limits of Charles street, a place now owned by the Perrotts.

But the conscience of Maryland had become tender. In time the lottery license issued to Richard France was revoked. He then, with Broadbent, went to Delaware, which being a small state, he with great simplicity bought up the legislature. This was not in each case a private sale. One of the members also had a tender conscience. For him Richard France built a church, where his constituents worshipped for many a year.

Then Delaware in its turn became sensitive to the enormity of the lottery, and revoked the license of Richard France. Meanwhile Broadbent had been plundering the business with rapid hand. It became necessary to buy up other states. In this effort Richard France failed. Baffled and plundered, when the lottery king came to take stock of himself and his belongings, he found he was in debt everywhere and a ruined man. Going back to Delaware in the desperation of his affairs, his person was seized for debt, and he died there in prison, a pauper.

In the wreck "The Villa" was sold to Henry May, of Baltimore. This was before the civil war. In his hands the career
of the place was continued. It was still the finest place for
miles about, and again renewed the scenes of hospitality and of
luxury, which distinguished the old Maryland days. Then the
war broke out. With great shrewdness Henry May immediately invested his fortune in gold. His broker was a banker
named Carson in Baltimore. All went well until the surrender of General Lee, when gold declined, and swept Henry May
along with unfulfilled margins. But between him and ruin
stood the broker Carson. He, abandoned by May, went down
in the crash. In vain he called upon his client to protect him.
A suit was brought and, against the feelings and temper of the
community, it was won by Henry May. The broken Carson
never recovered, but died a few months after, literally of a
broken heart.

Henry May returned to Baltimore, but his old friends turned
their faces. An isolated, ostracized man, he returned to "The
Villa," and in a few months he, too, died, it is said, out of pure
chagrin. "The Villa" was then bought by a young man named
Randall, who, with his young wife, more than revived its old
reputation for luxurious hospitality. The fun was fast and furious, and with it slipped away the great fortune to which Randall had fallen heir. In a few years, utterly ruined, young
Randall was obliged to give up "The Villa," which was then
bought by Mr. Brady, of New York. Mr. Brady had none of
the qualifications for a country life. He was the owner of a
superb place, with its walks and fountains, its vases, its marble
gods and goddesses half clothed in foliage. That fact seemed to
content him.

After a time there came a rumor, told about mysteriously by
the negroes, of a yacht flitting about the river, and of a strange
man, bearded and old, seen by chance, but furtively keeping
out of the way. So isolated is "The Villa," the tongue of land
stretching out far into the water, and the gates as usual kept
locked, that there could be no better place for concealment. The
rumor spread further, and was confirmed in details by the
curious negroes. Then came the news of "Boss" Tweed's escape
from New York. Some people remembered that in the earlier
days of the occupant of "The Villa," he had been heard to say

he knew or had met "Boss" Tweed. So the rumor grew, and was
confirmed in the belief of the people of the neighborhood, that
the strange owner of "The Villa" had now his chance to return
the favors of his old friend, and possibly benefactor, and what
better place could a hunted old man find ? To complete the tale,
a party of officers descended upon the place, but whatever
might have been going on there, nobody was found by them.

But the story was believed, and contributed to the interest in
the place and its changing fortunes that every one feels. Without further knowledge than crystallized rumor affords, "The
Villa" is pointed out to the stranger as the place where Tweed
lay hid, when the newspapers believed him in Florida. The story
is plausible, because he could be so easily removed by yacht
down the Chesapeake and off to Cuba. It was here Tweed lay
concealed, and from here he was taken away by night by the
son of a prominent Democratic politician of Maryland, who was
once the political ally of the dethroned boss. The story is too
direct for doubt, since it is on the authority of one of the prin-
cipals of that midnight adventure, the young man himself, and
through unquestioned channels.

"The Villa" is still a show place with its past grandeur and
memories. In 1895 the property passed into the hands of Dr.
George F. Nickerson, who sold it to Mrs. Fleming, of Washington.   Under the management of Mr. H. H. Balch, of New
York, it is now the home of the Maryland Nautical Academy.

CHAPTER XXVIII

ES ; they's right many ducks yet ; but tain't like 't used to be, when you could walk down to bit of a blind before breakfast and knock over a dozen or so in an hour." The speaker, clad in store clothes for a visit to Baltimore, sat on the forward deck of a Chesapeake Bay steamer, the autumn sunlight falling warm upon his figure, the vessel's nose pointing nor' nor'west, her sides rolling gently through an arc of twenty degrees, the blue waters laughing on every side, and long, hissing swells in her wake. No other body of water in the United States, not even Long Island sound or the great lakes, has exactly the same sort of of local commerce that distinguishes Chesapeake Bay. There is a broad navigable stream opening into the bay at every few miles on either shore, many of them nameless on ordinary maps, but all of them bristling with public wharves, and each visited once, twice, or thrice a week by a steamboat trading with Baltimore. To make the voyage on one of these creek traders going well down toward the point of the peninsula is to see an absorbingly picturesque and interesting panorama of life in the lower bay, and to encounter the Eastern Shoreman in unstudied simplicity on his native soil.

The so-called creeks of the Chesapeake would be spoken of as rivers elsewhere, though many of them, especially on the Eastern Shore, are really estuaries, sometimes a mile wide at the entrance, and rapidly narrowing to swift streams of fresh water that intersect inland roads in every direction, and when especially high tides come, flood wide areas of lowland. A creek of this sort sometimes has a public wharf every mile of its navigable length. The wharves lie first on one bank and then on the other, and it is the business of the steamboat to make each

wharf in turn, kinking from one to the other, and sometimes
waiting patiently for water enough to navigate. Each wharf
has a freight shed, great or small, and on the landward side a
country store containing every article that a reasonable Eastern
Shoreman can desire. The storekeeper is also the wharf owner,
as he is oftentimes the local banker, postmaster, fire insurance
agent, and what not else. The arrival of the steamboat is the
event of the day. Half the neighborhood awaits her on the
wharf. Light carts drawn by a Chincoteague pony, a mule, or
a bullock and laden at the season with barrelled sweet potatoes
await the coming of the boat. Here and there a belated team-
ster is seen driving his mule through the rising tide toward the
wharf, while every sort of craft known to the region is either
tied up at the wharf or making all sail toward it from the
neighboring coves. As soon as the vessel is tied up, and the
gang plank is thrown out, a dozen deck hands, muscular strap-
ping negroes of demoniac energy, seize their small iron trucks
and wheel off at a run whatever can be wheeled. As soon as the
cargo is off, the negroes turn to with unrelenting energy and
load potatoes. Each truck follows close upon the heels of the
truckman in front, and there is a merry jingle of iron accompanied by a negro chorus. It is the business of every truckman to
know his own truck and keep out of every other man's way
without warning. The deckhand who cannot run his truck
within a quarter of an inch of another deckhand does not earn
his forty dollars a month, and is not likely to remain long in the
business. The deckhand who cannot carry out four empty
barrels at a trip is equally unsuited to the trade. The Eastern
Shore potato barrel is made at Baltimore of stout hardwood
staves, and has no head and no provision for putting in a head,
because potatoes are put into the barrel until they bulge out at
the top, and are then covered with burlap, secured under a
hoop.

You can learn more about sweet potatoes in a ten-minute talk
at an Eastern Shore wharf than in a whole volume of reading
matter. From September to May oysters and sweet potatoes
are the talk of the Eastern Shore. The latter sell at fifty cents
per barrel in the early autumn, and the prudent Eastern Shoreman always "banks" fifteen or twenty bushels in leaves and
sand to be sent to Baltimore in mid-winter when prices are up.

You hear at the wharf every sort of maxim as to the treatment of the sweet potato. "Never let the frost touch your vines while the potatoes are in the ground," is one motto; another is "don't let stored potatoes get within twenty-five degrees of freezing point."

Sometimes as the steamer, outward bound to the bay, leaves the wharf, a long, narrow, strongly built scow, manned by two or three negroes, is taken in tow. This is the boat of the pound fishermen. It is ordinarily driven by two long and enormously heavy oars, and is steered when in tow with one such oar, the steersman giving his whole strength to the business and the oar bending like a wand beneath the strain. The pound fishermen are a hardy and peculiar race, whose home is most of the time upon the waters of the bay. Few bodies of water teem with fish as does the Chesapeake, and a Chesapeake fishing shore sometimes rents at $1,500 a year. The pound fisherman pays no rent, for he sinks light piles in the bottom of the bay, and constructs a sort of trap, that shall fish for him while he sleeps. The pound is "fished" ordinarily at least once a day, and the great scows lie alongside, while the fish are drawn out. Every sort of creature that swims the Chesapeake is found in the pound net, and the sight revealed when the pound fisherman comes to a wharf with his catch is a comprehensive lesson in marine natural history. As the vessel moves up or down the creeks, especially at early morning, the passengers see here and there the wavering sail of a canoe as it puts out from the shelter of a cape fronting some small dwelling ashore. The canoe is to the Eastern Shore man what the buggy is to inlanders. It is his craft for all weathers and all journeys, and every sort of business. He goes to market, calls on his neighbors, and sails to church in his canoe. Before there were steamboats his ancestors went to Baltimore either in their canoes or in the canoe's big first cousin, the buckeye. Small pickaninnies manage the canoe with the ease of old sailors, and one commonly sees at the wharf half a dozen canoes, each with a little black boy for steersman, who does the work of an adult as he begs his father to buy ginger nuts at the store. The stranger unaccustomed to the prolific waters of the Chesapeake is astonished to see the waiting boy idly dipping his tongs into the water, and drawing up a dozen oysters at a time within six feet of the wharf.

Far down the bay features ashore and afloat become more strongly characteristic of the south. Tiny, ancient, round-topped windmills survive here and there, their shingles a century old, and their sails long since rotted away. The shores smile with green pastures, and everywhere there are signs of a new awakening, neat fences and fine new Queen Anne cottages with all the effects of unrestricted paint. Here and there a dignified old mansion of an earlier period shows against the sky, great chimneys that speak of ample fireplaces and the good cheer of a generation gone by. Some passenger always knows the landmarks and can point out this or that old plantation house and tell its story, usually one of failing fortunes and humbled pride, for the old slave holding aristocracy has given place to a new generation of men who cultivate oysters for the market, sell terrapin instead of eating them, and buy no acre of land that does not promise profit. The kindly climate smiles now upon a busier race than of old, and luxuries that were once a matter of course on the table of every planter now go to feed the gourmets of Baltimore, Washington, Philadelphia, and New York. Out in the bay the pound fishermen are busy, and in every cove the oystermen show waving tong handles. Here and there, perched high on piles half a mile from shore, is a little watch house guarding private oyster beds. Ducks and geese, singly, in pairs, and in bunches, as the phrase is for a small flock, are always in sight, swimming or on the wing, while gulls and ospreys are seeking their prey. About the mast flutters a butterfly, miles of salts water between him and his accustomed sweets. The menhaden steamers pass from time to time, and the dullest nostril scents the fertilizer factory, while it lies, deceptively beautiful, on the horizon.

When night comes and the hardy Long Island captain, almost made over into an Eastern Shoreman by thirty years upon the Chesapeake, is gazing seaward over the forward deck, where a silent negro paces on the lookout, the warm and lighted saloon takes on the cozy air of a floating home. The men sit about spinning long yarns of ducking thirty years ago, and of terrapin in the days when hungry northerns had not put up the price, while a young woman with no voice in particular sings popular airs to her own accompaniment on the piano, and now and then she slips out on deck to watch the moonlit panorama of the bay.

CHAPTER XXIX.

HE caption of this chapter has some
what of a business ring, and might
be interpreted by the reader of
practical turn of mind as savoring of
the busy mart of life. If he may the
better understand the writer's intention by such a construction of the
sketch that follows, it were well
for him to know that these "notes"
will be "presented" to debtor and
creditor alike, with the hope that
that they may "bear interest" sufficient to justify the record
of some early events in Easton's history. But "sentiment"
and not "settlement" is my theme, and for a time at least
may we indulge our fancies in the poet's dream :

> "How often have I paused on every charm—
> The sheltered cot, the cultivated farm,
> The never-failing brook, the busy mill,
> The decent church that topped the neighboring hill,
> The hawthorn bush, with seats beneath the shade,
> For talking age, and whispering lovers made."

Why—gentle reader--do you smile at this sentimental opening of a chapter that possesses the prosy name of "notes of interest ?" From your acquaintance with this Eastern Sho', do you
think that with the rustle of its pines and the croak of its frogs,
the soft voice of sentiment finds no congenial harmony ? Do
you not think that were the feeling of sentiment in Talbot
county suddenly congealed into visible form by some occult fall
of the metaphysical temperature that our Land of Legendary
Lore would be peopled with veritably living snow-men ? or has
your education been so neglected that you must admit you have
received but little instruction on this important point ? If this
be true and your sentimental germ is yet in embryonic state,
come place it in the atmosphere of fancy, where the warmth and
glow of musing memories may quicken it into the life of a full

blown imagination. Then can we harmoniously visit the temples
of the past, and enjoy the spirit of the long ago.

TALBOT COURT HOUSE.

"The hope of all who suffer,
The dread of all who wrong."

Easton was first known as Talbot Court House and was selected as the county seat as early as 1700. At one time in the early
days, Oxford was spoken of as a proper site for the court house
owing to its prominence as a business centre and its ready ac-
cessibility by water, but its present situation was later selected
from its central position and nearness to the headwaters of the
Avon, Miles and Choptank rivers. In those early days the court
house was a thing more in name than in deed, for the first session of court in Easton of which we read, was held in the old
tav ern, which by the part it was made to play, became in
fact the first court house. Talbot county was larger then than
it is today, and the need of a suitable building became early apparent. Necessary roads were built to Town Point, on the
Avon, to Miles river ferry, and to Dover, the deserted town on
the Choptank, whose memory alone survives in the name of
Dover street, Easton. Here a court house was built near the
river, but all that remains is the cemetery adjoining it. Insignificant a village as Easton was in those days, it lived to see its
rival become a ruin, its dead alone marking the spot of those
who had passed away with their hamlet. The villagers made
a strenuous effort to keep their court house, and legally authorized the building of a town with definite bounds, laying the
same off into regular streets. This appeal to the legislature
was successful, and in March, 1785, an act was passed to build a
town. A new court house was built some years after on the
site of the old one—completed in 1794—and at a cost of $15,000,
a good price in those days, and that the work was well done a
glance at the building today will show, for it stands as a monument of the last century. Further details of the Talbot court
are given in the following account by the late Dr. Samuel A.
Harrison :

Prior to 1682 the courts for this county were of an itinerant character, that is, they had no settled meeting place, and were held in different portions of the county, mostly at private houses. In 1680-1 the first court house in the county was erected on Skipton creek, a branch of Wye river, near the present site of Skipton, and there the courts continued to be held until 1707, at which time Queen Anne's county was formed, and the bounds of Talbot for the first time definitely and accurately established. This building at York, situated as it was in the north-western extremity of the newly formed county, was too inconveniently located, and gave rise to the necessity of its removal. At the last session of the court at York. a commission was appointed to "select a suitable place for holding the courts thereafter." This commission decided upon Oxford ; and on the nineteenth of August, 1707, court was held at Oxford, in the house of Daniel Sherwood, Sheriff. Oxford at that time was the most flourishing town in the county, and was accessible by water from all parts of the county. In 1709, a contract was entered into between the Justices and Daniel Sherwood and Colonel Nicholas Lowe for the erection of the building. This contract was never carried into effect.

A tract of land, designated in the act of Assembly that authorized the erection of the court house, "Armstrong's Old Field near Pitte his Bridge," and embracing two acres, as stated in the above order, was purchased for the sum of five thousand pounds of tobacco. It formed part of the original patent of Londonderry, the name being still perpetuated in the tract of land at present owned by the heirs of the late Admiral Febiger, United States Navy. "Pitte his bridge" is now known as the tan-yard bridge, and spans the stream near the northern boundary of the town, upon this tract, and on the site of the present court house was accordingly erected a brick building twenty by thirty feet ; and the cost was one hundred and fifty thousand pounds of tobacco. On the seventeenth of June, 1712, the first session of court was held in the building. A jail, pillory, stocks and whipping post were also erected shortly after, the jail being built in the northeast corner of the square.

This court house, completed in 1711, formed the germ of what is now Easton. During its erection the road leading to Easton Point, at one time called Town Point, was laid out ; also the road

VIEW OF "LLANDAFF," ESTATE OF JOHN M. ELLIOTT,

ANOTHER VIEW OF "LLANDAFF."

to Miles river. A tavern or "ordinary" was established for the accommodation of those who attended the sessions of the court ; small county stores were from time to time started ; and a few dwelling houses erected by the officers of the court, the village taking its name from the seat of justice, the one in question being for a long time called and known as Talbot Court House. Nor was it incorporated into a town for seventy-eight years after the erection of the building. It is not to be presumed, however, that the annals of the village of Talbot Court House were altogether simple and uneventful during this long period. Being the headquarters, as it were, of the entire county, the planters would assemble here on special occasions, for the mutual interchange of views on the social, political and religious topics of the day. No doubt a great crowd was gathered to witness the trial of that French pirate, who was charged with the murder of the captain and two boys sailing on a small boat captured by the pirate, who after the murder was apprehended in the streets of Norfolk, wearing the silver knee and shoe buckles of his victim, marked with the initials of their former owner, and who at the Talbot Court House was condemned to be hung in chains at a place that still retains the name of Bloody Point, on Kent Island. This, as well as other important trials, attracted at various times great gatherings. But one of the most important assemblages of the people at this old court house, prior to the incorporation of the town, was that held on the twenty-fifth of November, 1765. It will be remembered that this was the year of the passage by the British Parliament of the celebrated "Stamp Act," the precursor of those other oppressive measures, that finally resulted in an open rupture between the colonies and the mother country, and the establishment of the independence of the former. When the news of the passage of this act reached the colonies, it was received everywhere with indignation, and especially in Maryland was this the case. Here in Talbot the court, which met early in November, refused to hold its regular session, and adjourned to the first Tuesday in March, thereby refusing to comply with the act, which required that all papers used by the court should have the obnoxious stamp affixed.

OLD EASTON HOTELS.

"Near yonder thorn, that lifts its head on high,
Where once the sign-post caught the passing eye,
Low lies that house where nut-brown draughts inspired,
Where gray-beard mirth and smiling toil retired,
Where village statesmen talked with looks profound,
And news much older than their ale went round."

Wherever there is a court house, there must be a tavern, a place where "accommodations may be had for man and beast." So it was with Easton, and I can say there is little connected with the early history of the town, that is not in some way associated with the first tavern. By a strange coincidence the first landlord in Easton was a woman. Her name was Elizabeth Winkles, and authorities differ as to whether "mine hostess" was an old maid or a widow. In either case she "knew how to keep a hotel," as the judge, lawyers and jury, not to speak of the others, were much pleased with "Elizabeth Winkles' table food."

With the passing away of the Tavern Court House, the name and fame of Elizabeth Winkles disappears, and another began to cater to the palates of the judges and lawyers, and all who sought shelter in Easton at the public house. Just who the landlord of the next tavern was, or where it was, is not known, but it is said to have been located just where the Odd Fellows' Hall now stands. At that time Easton boasted of a population of 428 whites and 212 blacks, 640 in all; but the tavern had the meeting of Court and the surrounding country, as now, to draw upon. Coming from England, as many of our people did in those days, the taverns were doubtless planned and constructed upon the English idea. One of the delights in London to-day is to drive out into its suburbs and enjoy a meal, or a night in one of those comfortable old inns that are so numerous there, and do not appear to have changed much in the past two centuries, from the accounts we have of them in "ye olden time."

Easton begun to have new life infused into it early in the present century, and many improvements were made, substantial buildings, yet to be seen, were erected of brick, though the tavern of that day was a frame structure, and is now the home of

Dr. E. R. Trippe. As it stands today, the Trippe dwelling, then with its neighbor, was the tavern, and shows the old fashioned comfort of that age, the rooms large, the fireplaces commodious and the air of good cheer in the past. The old Harrison Street market house was built, and doubtless the landlord of the tavern of that day was the best patron of the good things to be found there, for there has never been a time when public house or private has failed to keep up the Eastern Shore reputation for true hospitality and keeping the very best the land could afford.

The building now occupied by Mr. Harry Councell on Goldsborough Avenue is another of Easton's old taverns, and formerly stood on Washington Street, corner of Railroad Avenue, on the site of the present hardware store, and later moved to its present site. Bonifaces of that period have passed out of remembrance. It is, however, told of some of them, at certain times no liquors were allowed to be sold in them, a strange thing in those days of good cheer. We now come to a tavern in Easton which is still to be seen in a very substantial building—what is known as the Moreland Block to-day, yet still called by many the "Brick Hotel." This was to distinguish it from the old tavern, a frame building, which the far more pretentious one supplanted. That Easton wanted a good inn is proved by a look at the "Brick Hotel" to-day, eighty-nine years after it was built, just at the time of the breaking out of the second war with England. Just who the first landlord of the Brick Hotel was, there is no data at hand to find out, but we can imagine how proud he must have been of such a building, to be the presiding genius of a tavern at that time worthy of Baltimore, Philadelphia and even New York. It had a rival in another house, which, however, did not long remain such against the attractions of bed and board of the Brick Hotel, owned by Samuel Groome.

William T. Hardesty was the next proprietor of this popular hotel, grown out of all idea of longer being called a tavern, and Tobias Merrick followed him. Then came others to share the honors in a landlord partnership between Albertson and Norris, to be followed by C. W. Bennett, and last by the present proprietor of the Avon, Colonel James C. Norris, who can look far enough back into the past to have been educated in the old school of hospitable landlords, and is yet progressive enough to

keep up with mine hosts of this most go-ahead age. As good
as the old Brick Hotel had been, and having served its purpose
well, Easton outgrew it. This was realized by a number of its
citizens, who knew that Easton, must not be lacking in a suitable hotel. The outcome of this desire was the Hotel Avon.
It was completed in 1891, and located in one of the most desir-
able parts of the town, not only to accommodate transient but
regular guests. It cost over $40,000, exclusive of the land.
The first proprietor, Mr. Lechler, was soon succeeded by Colonel James C. Norris.

THE EARLY CHURCHES OF EASTON.

"What is a church?"—Let truth and reason speak :
They would reply—"The faithful, pure and meek,
From Christian folds, the once selected race,
Of all professions, and in every place."

The first church of which there is record in Easton was erected
by the Methodists on a lot on Goldsborough street in 1790. The
structure was of frame, and it stood in the midst of what was
then a burying ground. In 1829 a brick church was built by
the same congregation, to be succeeded in 1856 by their present
house of worship. The second church in Easton was on Harrison street. It was built by the Protestant Episcopal congregation in 1803, the court house being their place of worship prior
to their building a church of their own, which is still standing
in good condition. It is now owned and used by the Baptists,
who purchased it in 1897. The Episcopalians were the first
congregation in Easton, however, though they had no church
here. The cornerstone of the present picturesque and handsome
stone edifice, with its rectory, was begun in 1840, and completed
in 1843, at a cost of over ten thousand dollars. The bell of
Christ Church was presented by Mr. G. A. Mackey in 1856, and
was the first one in Easton to call the good people to their
prayers. In 1868 the Eastern Shore of Maryland was made a
a separate diocese, a bishop was sent here, and at a later period
the second Episcopal church, the Cathedral, a unique and hand-

some stone edifice, was erected, and Easton was made the "Cathedral Town."

In 1828 the Methodist Protestant Church was organized in Easton, and having but a few members to start with, held services in the dwelling now the residence of Dr. Edward R. Trippe. Later they worshipped in what was known as the "Old Bank," and later the present building was erected, and has since been greatly improved. After the war three other religious denominations established themselves in Easton, the Roman Catholics in 1866, building a neat frame structure on Railroad Avenue with rectory attached, while the Southern Methodists first erected a brick church in 1876, and later the handsome one on the corner of Harrison street and Railroad Avenue. There is another church, or as its members more modestly call it, meeting house, which, though not within the limits of Easton, may be so classed, for it is just beyond the suburbs. This is what is better known as the old William Penn church, the Friends' meeting house, already described in these pages.

TALBOT'S NEWSPAPERS.

"Turn to the press—its teeming sheets survey—
Big with the wonders of each passing day,
Births, deaths and weddings, forgeries, fires and wrecks,
Harangues and hailstones, brawls and broken necks."

The newspapers of a town are the mirrors in which society sees itself as others do, and in this age of haste become as necessary to our mental wants as food is to the body. The news of the day gives spice to the breakfast. Of Talbot's papers, it can be said with truth, that though county papers, they have city airs. The *Gazette* was the first paper established in Easton, its first issue appearing in the year 1817. It is still a prosperous sheet, of eight well filled pages, but like good wine it improves with age, and stands today one of the substantial weeklies published in Maryland. The *Gazette* from its foundation was the advocate of free schools and free education, and while it has always been firm in its political opinions, has accorded to others the free exercise of their own judgment. During the war it sustained the side of the Government with energy and spirit, and now advocates the principles of the Republican party. In the last few years the *Gazette* has made rapid strides in progress, and has established in connection with it an extensive steam book printing and jobwork annex. The paper is owned by Mr. Wilson M. Tylor, editor.

The Easton *Star* has known the ups and downs of life in their full sense. Though really older than the *Gazette* by some years, it yet cannot be called the oldest paper as it has been suspended three times, and Phœnix like, sprung into life again out of its ashes. It is the old democratic paper of the county. It was established as a Jeffersonian democratic paper, in the year 1800, by Mr. Perine Smith. In 1833, after the death of Mr. Smith, it was suspended. In 1841 it was revived. In 1846 it was bought by Colonel H. E. Bateman. In 1849 he sold it. In 1855, Mr. Robson purchased Mr. Rowlenson's interest in the paper, and was the exclusive editor for thirty-two years. In May, 1865 it was suspended by the military power, and its editor banished to Richmond, Virginia, for adhering to, and persistently defending what he conscientiously believed to be constitutional principles. In September, 1865, after the war, Mr. Robson revived the paper, and it at once entered actively in the work of abolishing the proscription laws enacted during the war, in abrogating the constitution of 1854, and in giving the people of Maryland a liberal constitution. The *Star* throughout its existence has been consistently democratic, and is still advocating democratic principles. The present proprietor is Mr. S. E. Whitman, managing editor, who bought the paper in 1896 and combined with it the *Democrat* which had been founded in 1886.

The Easton *Ledger* was founded in 1874, by Mr. Julius A. Johnson, who was an able editor, and a practical printer of large experience, and his constant aim was to make the *Ledger* a first class newspaper in every respect. He succeeded in making it one of the brightest and most popular county papers in the state. In the beginning of 1881, Mr. G. E. Haddaway purchased the *Ledger*, and has fully kept it up to the standard of its former excellence.

The St. Michaels *Comet* is another paper that looks well into the past. It was established on a firm foundation, and under its different editorial pilots has been a bright and newsy sheet.

The *Comet* is now under the editorial management of W. D. J. Morris, a well-known democrat.

The Trappe *Times* is a newcomer in an old town, but it is under an able management and on the highway to success. It is a Republican paper, and Mr. Percival Mullikin is the editor.

SCHOOLS, BANKS AND SECRET SOCIETIES.

"Beside yon straggling fence that skirts the way,
With blossomed furze unprofitably gay,
There, in his noisy mansion, skilled to rule,
The village master taught his little school ;
A man severe he was, and stern to view,
I knew him well, and every truant knew,
Well had the boding tremblers learned to trace
The day's disasters in his morning face."

The Easton High School looms up grandly as an educational centre, of which, along with its annex, the primary school, the citizens are justly proud. It would be a credit to any large city. It is well located, and a commodious, handsome structure, well arranged, while in each department there are outward signs of the ablest management. This may also be said of the primary school, though for beauty of architecture it is not exactly a success. What is arrived at in the Easton High School is to give its graduates a thorough education in all that is taught in the separate grades, and this means that a pupil goes forth equipped to begin the struggle of life.

The Easton High School was built in the year 1894. This handsome building occupies the site of the old Easton academy, which was erected in 1800 ; and after ninty-three years of service, was deemed unsafe by the School Commissioners, and was torn down and the handsome structure which now stands in its place was erected at the cost of eighteen thousand dollars. The building is of brick, and has two stories and a basement, cloak rooms, studio, and a library. There is accommodation for four hundred scholars. The building is heated by steam and has large and airy recitation rooms. The front of the building is finely finished in marble, with dates of the erection of the old building, and also of the new building carved on marble plates placed on either side of the front door. There are six teachers, and about two hundred pupils in the school, which are divided into the fifth, sixth, seventh, eighth, ninth and tenth grades. The fifth and sixth comprise the grammar, and the other grades the high school. The common branches of studies are taught, and in addition to these the classics and sciences, also an excellent course in drawing and manual training.

As the schools stamp a place of residence, so do the banks and stores make a decided impress on a town or a city. Easton has two banks, the Easton National and the Farmers and Merchants, both in successful operation. Besides these there is a savings bank and a building and loan association. The lumber mills, brick and tile works, carriage shops, fertilizer manufactories, boat-shops, laundry, shirt factory, canning establishments, and oyster packing houses are all important enterprises, and reflect creditably the improvement and advancement the town has made. The fair gounds, with the substantial buildings, erected for the purpose of stimulating a just competition on all products of factory or farm, are worthy of note, and it may be said, deserves its place in the structure of the body of enterprises. The grounds are well laid out and suitably adapted to its uses.

Secret societies are likewise in evidence in Easton. Both Masons and Odd Fellows have handsome houses, which are among the finest buildings in the town. In addition there are many fraternal orders with lodges in Easton, the Knights of Pythias, Heptasophs, American Fraternal Insurance Union, Red Men, Ancient Order of United Workmen. Easton has excellent stores, dry-goods, millinery, hardware and groceries, and its market abounds in all those delicacies for which the Eastern Shore has a just reputation.

But the complement of a dainty dish is domestic "darky."

THE EASTERN SHORE NEGRO.

"We may live without poetry, music and art;
We may live without conscience, and live without heart,
We may live without friends, we may live without books,
But civilized man cannot live without cooks."

VIEWS IN CORDOVA.

RESIDENCE OF J. M. AYERS, CORDOVA.

The negro is an inseparable factor of the life on the Eastern Shore, and no history of our people would be complete without recognition of the unconscious influence he has exerted on life, manners and language of the people whom he serves. The traditional negro of slavery days is now seldom seen—such change has his character undergone as the result of his freedom. There is much doubt whether the change, though confessedly an improvement in abstract knowledge, has succeeded in enhancing his worth as citizen, or bread-winner. The negro's nature is childish and dependent, worthy when guided, useless when unsupported. He does not possess the power of self-preservation, and so will succumb to the law of the "survival of the fittest." Little has the white man to fear from his weaker brother, and the situation demands his pity and his care more than it does his apprehension. The pure blooded negro is weak enough, but the half-breed has no longevity on which to depend for the perpetuation of his race. Our present problem is to see that the negro's best days have not gone, for ahead of him there is a struggle for existence under which he labors unequally. None but those who have lived with him can duly estimate his capabilities and his worth. To measure him by the standard of the white is to stretch his nature beyond the pale of his possibilities, and to do this would be an unconscious extinction of the race from mistaken humanitarian principles. If the anthropologists have correctly placed him, he was made to be a "hewer of wood, and a drawer of water," to subsist by the work of his hands, to serve his higher brothers and so fulfill his appointed destiny. Let us not seek to ruin him, but help him faithfully to do his part in the great design. Negroes exist in the realm of imagination, and are unable to survive the consuming strain of reason. The negro is tender-hearted but neglectful, appreciative but improvident, faithful according to his standard of morality, and dependent from the fact that he is made to live a civilized life on a barbaric structure. Easton's colored population as a whole are sober, honest and industrious, though there are too many men and boys, who appear to love idleness rather than work, and to sit about upon boxes awaiting the millennium.

Among the negroes who have gone from here, I have found the same love of the old land, that is in the hearts of the natives. They talk of old Talbot, and hope some day to come back. In this connection it may be said that the first cotton ever planted in America was here in Talbot. It was planted on the Goldsborough plantation on "Peach Blossom Creek," within sight of the original home, which is still standing, a relic, between the handsome homes of "Llandaff" and the "Beeches."

THE CANOE AND BUCKEYE.

"Give me of your bark, O birch tree !
Of your yellow bark, O birch tree !
Growing by the rushing river,
Tall and stately in the valley !
I a light canoe will build me,
Build a swift Cheemaun for sailing,
That shall float upon the river,
Like a yellow leaf in Autumn,
Like a yellow water-lily."

While dwelling upon these random notes of Easton and Talbot, of people and affairs, it must not be forgotten that in their borders are built some remarkable vessels, as the Chesapeake "canoe" and "buckeye." The latter vessel is upon the same lines, in a measure, as the former, light draught, sharp stem, narrow beam, and with about the same rigging. They are built to *go*, and nothing can equal them in speed the world over. Being open, save a small deck forward, and carrying no ballast, the canoe is a craft that only an expert can manage. The Eastern Shore is full of just such experts, and a canoe "cranky as the devil" apparently, will yet, in proper hands, ride out a gale, and carry sail when large vessels are hunting harbor. The negroes from the shores of the Chesapeake, handle these craft superbly, and many of the masting vessels have negro sailors upon them, and good seamen they are. The canoe—the negro calls it "kunnah"—is rigged with fore and main masts, upon which are spread leg-of-mutton sails, a short bow-sprit and a jib. The masts can be quickly unstopped, thrown overboard in a gale, if need be, and then, with her log hull and a good oarsman, it becomes as safe as a life boat. It is amusing to see the crack yachtsmen bring their cat-rigs and sloops to race, and watch these canoes drop them out of sight, slipping along like marine ghosts. The buckeye—also spoken of as bugeye—is a splendid style of craft, being staunch in wild weather, good carriers, swift sailors on any wind, and trim as yachts.

CHAPTER XXX.

HE largest tributary that feeds the Chesapeake bay from the Eastern Shore is the Choptank river, whose winding course and Indian name have been elsewhere mentioned in these pages. Rising as it does in Kent county, Delaware, this river traverses Caroline county, and forms the eastern and southern boundaries of Talbot, its small creeks and bayous ramifying on both sides through the adjoining land, and affording a varied and extensive coast line in almost every conceivable direction. Tracts of land are thus encircled by these winding streams, which form not only natural boundaries between estates, but are as well means of communication and thoroughfares for trade.

The Choptank river with its numerous tributaries has been not inappropriately named "Talbot's Meat House," so abundantly does it supply our people with its delicious products of fish, oysters and crabs. Along its tidal shores lies land of unsurpassed fertility, which, coupled with the advantage of water situations, has attracted men of means and culture to settle here and develop its resources. The southern end of Talbot, known as Trappe district, is almost a peninsula, being surrounded by the Choptank and Avon rivers whose headwaters are within less than three miles of each other. This district is broken up into "necks," or divisions of land separated by inundating creeks, which radiate from the centre and empty into the encircling rivers. These "necks" are rarely so wide that more than one road is ever necessary to traverse them, from which road, lanes lead to the various houses, which are usually on a point or rise of land overlooking the water. The land is generally flat, occasionally gently rolling, light in character and well adapted to

the culture of wheat and corn. The names of these "necks"
have been derived from some prominent landowner, some geographical feature, or some fancied resemblance to an association
with some shire of similar name in England, whence the first
settlers came. This is seen from the following list of names:
Oxford Neck, Island Creek, Little Neck, Ferry Neck, Bolingbroke, Bambury and Landing Neck.

To obtain a comprehensive view of some of these interesting
old Maryland homes, one might imagine a sail along the shores
of these bounding rivers, with brief stops at the various homesteads, and a ramble through the houses and gardens, and chat
with their owners, whereby he could enjoy the life itself, as
lived by those old landed proprietors. During his call, he
would find the genial host and hostess, proud perhaps in the
dignity of some sixty summers, and cultivated to the extent
that learned leisure could afford, or perhaps hale and hearty
with a genial roughness that bespeaks a nature "rich in the milk
of human kindness," their sons and daughters of culture and
beauty, each in turn lending their attentions to that entertain-
ment that lacks exertion, yet produces a pleasurable ease; the
ever-ready attendant that serves refreshment, and an invitation
to "come again," that would create a desire certain of gratifica-
tion. Some such picture of the home-life with further imagi-
native details, might be added and found to be more or less true
at each of these old homes.

Starting from Trippe's Creek, and confining ourselves to the
southern shore, one is attracted by the handsome home of
"Harley," owned by Mr. Preston B. Spring, formerly of New
York. This estate was once a part of the "Belleville" tract,
previously referred to as the home of the Bozmans. The house
which stands in a grove, is of modern architecture, and has all the
interior appointments of a country gentleman's home. The
grounds are tastefully laid out, and are arranged for tennis and
golf. The house overlooks the water, which adds much to the
beauty of the place and enjoyment of the owner.

Further to the west is passed the former home of Rev. T.
Bayne, familiarly known as Parson Bayne, at one time rector of
White Marsh parish, and then the comfortable home of Nicholas
Goldsborough comes in view. "Otwell," as it was named, is
almost a peninsula, and is still owned by the heirs of Colonel

Goldsborough, who is already mentioned among the noted and worthy men of Talbot. The house overlooks the Tred Avon river, from whose waters at this point the best flavored oysters are found.

The adjoining farms of "Plimhimmon," the home of Lieutenant Tench Tilghman, and "Bonfield," the home of the Chamberlaines have already been described, yet are passed in rounding the point of land, upon which Oxford is situated. Towards the south is "Bachelor's Point," the lovely home of the late Mrs. Emerson commanding a water view on three sides.

Here one enters the placid waters of Island creek, so named from the small island which lies in its mouth, which is dotted on both sides with comfortable homes surrounded by goodly acres. On the left bank, ascending the river, may be seen "Evergreen" where lived Dr. W. G. G. Willson, a surgeon in the United States Navy, and later a prominent physician of Easton. It is now owned by Mr. McKenny Willis, who lives on the adjoining farm. Proceeding up the creek, one finds the beautiful spot of "Judith's Garden," long known as the Ben Bowdle farm, and now owned by Mr. Ritter.

The land in this section of Oxford Neck is particularly fertile, and so conveniently situated that grain may be taken directly from the field to the boats that anchor within a hundred yards or less of the shore. The ease with which farm products may be taken to market by the water courses is a unique and highly advantageous feature of Talbot county.

On the opposite bank in Island Creek Neck may be mentioned "Milan," the old home of the late Alexander Barnet, and those of Mr. John Caulk, and Mr. Anthony Ross. "Walnut Grove," one of the oldest homes in the county, was owned by the Hon. Nicholas Martin, inherited by his daughter, Mrs. Rebecca Matthews, and now owned by Mr. G. M. Jenkins, of Trappe, which tract of land also includes the farms of Mr. Robert Bartlett and the late James Chamberlaine. Other homes on Island Creek are those of Mr. E. W. Hopkins, Mr. Caulk Kemp, Mr. George Graham, and "Clora Dorsey," the home of Mr. Nicholas Willis.

Here there is a point of land known as "Clora's Point," for a long time the landing where passengers and freight for Baltimore boarded the steamer. The point derived its name from the

BAPTIST CHURCH AT CORDOVA.

SKIPTON SCHOOL HOUSE.

"HAMPDEN," ISLAND CREEK, OLDEST BRICK HOUSE IN TALBOT.
See page 212.

owner of the "Hier-Dyer-Lloyd" tract of land. The tract was taken up in the early days by a Spaniard named Clora Adora, and its northeast boundary ran from the "Crosiadore" on the Choptank to the headwaters of the Tred Avon. A commission appointed by the court to determine the line, marked it with stones which embraced portions of Oxford, Island Creek and Little Necks. The river at this point has a wide sweep and presents a beautiful sheet of water, and little is one's surprise that the Indians who lived along its shores, and were reared n full view of its heaving bosom and within sound of its rushing tide, had learned to regard it even in their barbaric way, as their very own, and a part of their great hunting grounds. Along this curving beach may be picked up Indian arrow heads of exquisite workmanship, hatchets and implements of hunting and warfare. Some years ago there appeared an Indian in the village of Trappe, with signs of having traveled a long distance. He was destitute of money and clothes, and was physically in a wretched condition, but made an attempt at gaining a livelihood by making bows and arrows, for which purpose the only implement he used was a long butcher's knife. He was unable to speak English or to understand anything that was said to him. The villagers supplied his wants and would have given him work, but after wandering several days around the shores of the Choptank, he disappeard as suddenly as he had come. From his careful search, and an evident familiarity with the region, it is believed he was a member of the trib of Susquehannas, who formerly roamed the Chesapeake shores, in search of the graves or relics of his ancestors.

> "Lo ! the poor Indian,—whose untutored mind,
> Sees God in clouds, or hears him in the wind ;
> His soul proud science never taught to stray,
> Far as the solar walk or milky way ;
> Yet simple nature to his hope has given,
> Behind the cloud-topped hill, a humbler heaven."

This same sentiment was possessed by the mistress of "Wilderness" on the Choptank, Mrs. John W. Martin. By her energy and benevolence, she was instrumental in doing much to assist the Indians in the western reservations, and annually large boxes of gifts and useful presents of all kinds were sent by her to the various tribes. This intercourse was the means of bringing

two Indians on a visit to "Wilderness" years after, one a chief
and the other an Episcopal clergyman, who had been in Washington on business connected with their people.   It is pathetic
to hear the accounts of their resentful feelings in regard to all
this lovely country, which "might have been" theirs, and, of
how toward evening they would sit down near the bank for
hours, smoking their pipes, and looking with longing hearts over
the great waters of beautiful Choptank. This grand old home
of "Wilderness" was built in 1816 by Colonel Daniel Martin,
then a colonel of cavalry in the state militia, and here he
brought his bride. The house during its construction was su-
pervised by him, and so careful was he that neither haste nor
imperfect work should mar the solidity of his home, that the
floors were allowed to season a twelve-month beyond use, and
all such cautions were duly observed. The bricks were made
and burt upon the farm, and the lime was made of shells taken
from the river, and mixed with *sharp* sand found on the beach,
for the mortar, that today is impenetrable and solid. The house
stands in a grove of magnificent poplars, lindens, willows, oaks
and sycamores. One oak planted by the present proprietor,
now shades a circle sixty feet in diameter. The site is on an elevation, and from the observatory on the house one may obtain
a view of the broad water unequalled in beauty the world over.
In these waters, during the early days of this century, the British gunboats were often seen and feared by the owners of "Wilderness" and "Clora's Point." These fears were never realized,
however, as the English found a warmer welcome at "Castle
Haven," the haunted home of the tory, Noel.

"Wilderness" was the home of Colonel Martin until he was
made Governor of Maryland in 1828, and again in 1830, when
during his term of office he resided in Annapolis. The parents
of Governor Martin were celebrated people in their day. His
mother, known as "Madame" Oldham, owned much land in Talbot county, and was distinguished by having the only coach
and four for miles around. The father was a sea-captain, Captain Thomas Martin, and led the adventurous and successful career attributed in those days to men of a sea-faring life. It is
told that when he returned to his home, he would bring sufficient coin to cover the large dining room table over with Spanish dollars a foot deep. Dr. John Martin, descended from an

Englishman of that name, married Miss Elizabeth Bond of Philadelphia, daughter of Dr. Thomas Bond, one of the founders of the University of Pennsylvania, whose grandson, Mr. John W. Martin, is the present proprietor. Leading in a north westerly direction from "Wilderness" is Dividing Creek or Trappe River, bounded on both sides by fine and fertile farms. On the Island Creek Neck side, now owned by James M. Leonard is the unpretentious yet dignified home of "Hampden," long the abode of a prominent branch of the Martin family, and of late years owned by Mr. John S. Martin, now deceased. "Hampden" was in the possession of the Martin family from 1660 until 1866. The house was the first brick building in Talbot county, made of bricks brought from England by the first Thomas Martin in 1663. This farm was his home place which he named "Hampden," and was inherited by three other Thomas Martins, and later by Joseph Martin, and Thomas the father of John S. Martin, whose descendants are still prominent citizens of Maryland.

On the opposite shore is seen "Compton," the former home of Governor Stevens, of Maryland, who filled the gubernatorial office from 1822-1825, and whose house was long the rendezvous for men of letters and the local celebrities. Adjoining this farm is "Boston," owned by the late W. B. Martin, brother to Mr. John W. Martin, of "Wilderness." His family now occupies the home place, well known for its hospitality. It is situated in a beautiful grove of trees, extending to the water, and on its lawn are cultivated exquisite roses and chrysanthemums of more than ordinary beauty.

South of "Boston" on a tongue of land running out boldly into the Choptank is "Howell's Point." This land was originally granted to the Dickinsons by proprietary enactment, and embraced the land as far as Reed's Creek. In the division of the land, "Crosiadore" the home place, always went to the eldest son, and "Howells's Point" to the minor heirs. In this way John Dickinson who married the daughter of Howell Powell, possessed it, while Samuel the eldest in name for several generations obtained "Crosiadore." This lovely old home is situated on Dickinsons's Bay, formed by a widening of the river at this point, and protected by two large islands, which bound it on the river side.

Here lived the eldest sons of the Dickinson family for many generations. The first house was remodeled into a beautiful modern country home, was built of English bricks, and in English style. The wainscoted walls and winding staircases spoke of the age in which they were built, then regarded as the most costly and elegant finish for a gentleman's home. The whole appearance and air of the place gives one the impression of refinement and hospitality, while the resourceful country and the beautiful river afford "Crosiadore" a situation and advantage that make a the spot an ideal one for a home. On the walls today hang tapestries spun and embroidered by the ladies of that house, and in several instances the subjects of the pictures were romances in the lives of members of the family. On the lawn are grand old trees, which have stood guard these many years and have been the silent witnesses to many a gathering of old and young. Alike to wedding marches and funeral dirges have their soughing winds played soft accompaniments; and now in turn they, too, are in the "seer and yellow leaf," yet still replete with memories dear to those who read. "Crosiadore" is a corruption of the French "croix d' or" meaning "cross of gold," derived perhaps from some heraldic design of the ancestors who were engaged in the Crusades.

In this old home was born in 1732, John Dickinson, Governor of Pennsylvania, and founder of Dickinson college, Carlisle. He was the second son of Samuel Dickinson, the grandson of the first proprietor of the estate, and of Mary Cadwalader, his second wife, sister of Dr. Thomas Cadwalader of Philadelphia. In 1740 Samuel Dickinson moved to Kent county, Delaware. Another scion of this house was the Dickinson, who fought and was killed in a duel with President Andrew Jackson. The cause of difference was a trivial one, but according to the code of those days, honor had to be satisfied by resort to arms. At the first fire Dickinson wounded his opponent, but Jackson reserving his fire, advanced, shot and killed Dickinson instantly. His body was brought to Talbot, and he was buried in the adjoining county of Caroline.

A beautiful shore line extends from Reed's Creek to Bolingbroke Creek, along which extends the fertile farms of Mr. E. W. Kirby, the heirs of the late Alexander Bowdle, and Mr. James Dawson. The home of the latter kown as Cambridge or

Harris' Ferry, is directly opposite Cambridge, where in olden
days, the mail that was brought by stage down the peninsula,
was ferried across the river to be continued down the "shore."

At this point the Choptank makes its great bend, turning almost through an arc of ninety degrees to the north-east, and
making the southernmost extremity of Talbot county, known as
"Chancellor's Point." The land from Bolingbrooke Creek
northward to Bambury neck is bounded by a bold shore, in
some places quite high for this flat section of the country.
Through the energies and means of Col. Wm. Hughlett, father
of the late Col. Thomas Hughlett of Easton, this section of Talbot
was largely developed. Col. Hughlett was a merchant of Greensboro, where he amassed a large fortune. Coming to Talbot he
bought up large tracts of land in Bolingbroke neck, which he
left to his son, William R. Hughlett, and legacies to his other
sons. Thomas Hughlett built the beautiful home of "Ingleside," which name is suggestive of the warmth and hospitality,
that was dispensed around that fireside. Several times has it
changed owners, and is now in possession of Mr. James Dawson.
William R. Hughlett built "Jamaica Point," a fine old brick
house with ample lawn and shade. This he settled upon his
son Thomas, and then built "Retreat," which he sold to Mr.
Hannigan, of Baltimore. A short distance away he built the
"Home," and after living there seven years, he gave it in trust
to his son Richard's wife and children. Buying "Ingleside"
from his brother Thomas, he resided here until he sold it to Mr.
Franz Scheppers, of Philadelphia, when he built his last house
on "Chancellor's Point," where he died. Besides these places
two other houses on the Hughlett property were built by his
sons, John and William. First "Cherry Grove" on the Choptank, now owned by the heirs of Mr. Benjamin Outram, of England, and "Belmont," in Bolingbroke neck, since purchased
by Mr. Alfred Kemp, who married the Colonel's only daughter,
widow of Mr. George Naylor. "Hilton" the home of Miss Irene
Orndorff, on this same tract was built by Mr. Frederick Baggs,
sold to William Hughlett, Jr., and then to Mrs. Ariette Orndorff. All of these places possess superb locations on the broad
salt water, and fortunes have been expended in developing and
maintaining them. Each owner in turn has indulged his ex-
travagant fancies in the possibilities of landscape beauties. All

that art and money and taste could do, has been spent on these
homes, some still in their pristine glory, while others have only
the marks of their departed greatness. Before the civil war in
the days of slavery, the fun was fast and furious. Hospitality
was dispensed with lavish hand, and the charms of social intercourse were of that nature that to be once enjoyed was never to
be forgotten. It was as much as a stranger's life was worth, to
use a strong expression, to run the gauntlet of the successive
entertainments with which his visit would be honored He
usually survived however, and never failed to repeat his visit to
the land that flowed with "milk and honey." Soon after the
war the "Retreat" was bought by Colonel Bradford, who changed its name to "Allonby," which reached its greatest glory
while in possession of Mr. John Riker of New York. This
gentleman beautified the place in every way that was possible,
laying out a beautiful park and lake, and adorned the lawn with
flowers and shrubbery of the choicest varieties. The natural
situation with these artificial adornments produced in the place
one of the handsomest homes in the county. At Mr. Riker's
death, the property passed into the hands of Mr. Bayliss, of
Baltimore. Along this same Choptank farther to the north, are
many pretty homes, and that of Colonel J. Percy McKnett is delightfully situated ; beyond him is the old estate, "Lloyd's Landing," the former home of Robert Lloyd.

On the adjoining farm is Talbot's health resort and old campmeeting grounds, known for many, many years as Lloyd's
Springs. Traversing the land, which here is undulating, is a
deep ravine, through whose valley runs a little stream, the
outlet of an abundant and constantly flowing spring of delicious-
ly cool chalybeate water. Surrounding the spring for a wide
area is a handsome grove of beeches, under whose spreading
branches, generations for years past have trod the mazy dance,

> "When the merry bells ring round
> And the jocund rebecks sound
> To many a youth, and many a maid
> Dancing in the chequered shade."

Upon the trunks of those smooth bark beeches, that still stand
as libraries in the wood, may be read the names of hundreds of
the happy youths, who from sentimental fancy have carved
their own with their sweetheart's names upon those monarchs

of the forest, that stand like ghosts revealing the merry hearts that have gathered in their midst. Upon one hillside is the famous wild grape-vine, so long serving its term as a natural swing for the boys and girls. The fountain of Arethusa or the Idæan groves were no more cherished by the rustic nymphs and fawns than were these natural beauties by the natives of this Eastern Shore, who though far removed they may be from its genial presence, still softly sigh—"this is my own my native land."

CHAPTER XXXI

THE HUMOROUS SIDE OF THE NEGRO.

ERE it not for the fact that the colored race figures so prominently in this section, this chapter would scarcely have a place in this book. But the jottings of interest would not be complete without giving a few pages to the readers, who perchance might not have been acquainted with this strange people of misfortune and calumny, who, without their volition, are forced to stand side by side in comparison with the most enlightened people of the world. The colored man of America is gradually emerging from the tunnel of darkness into which he by nature found himself and may yet prove master of the situation—who knows?

Between the bays of Delaware and Chesapeake he is typical in all that pertains to the race. He has been kept in the even tenor of his natural instincts, unadorned with much "book larnin'" and filled from the cradle with the lore of his kinfolks. This class forms a large part of the population of the peninsula, and taking them as a body, they are by far the happiest people ever created, and collectively speaking, much more so before the civil war than at present. The education they have been receiving, say most competent authority, has tended to unfit them for their calling in life. It is no trouble in riding along the road to distinguish a negro of anti-bellum days by the manner in which he speaks, always being thoroughly polite. Indeed, every one of sufficient age to remember the negro forty years ago will say that then he stood much closer to the white people by means of his simplicity and childish manner, than at present. It is a well known fact that no white child raised in those old times who had the opportunity, could be kept from the kitchen or the negro quarters, for the reason that what was seen and heard was so primitive in its nature that it was thoroughly entertaining to the children. Who is it old enough that cannot remember when he sat attentively and listened to the ghost stories and miraculous experiences of these people until he was afraid to retire at night?

To the present day, to such a person it is a pleasure to get a quiet moment with some of the old people and hear their stories. Not long since in conversation one was telling of his religious ideas. He said he thought people ought to pray to the one they served, and exemplified it in the following story :

When a lad of about seventeen years there came a rain one afternoon, after which his master permitted him to go chestnut hunting. At this he was very much pleased, so in great haste he sought the woods and soon found a tree loaded with nuts. Being strong and athletic he at once proceeded to climb the tree, and met with such success that he did not notice the approach of night. Suddenly the darkness came upon him and he thought how far he was from home, in a large and dense wood filled with "varmints" and "ghost-ies." In his hurry to get down the tree his foot slipped, owing to the smoothness of the bark, and it being also damp from the rain, which caused him to hug the tree tightly, though he could not stop himself until he struck a close fork. Here he found himself in a straddling position and completely wedged by the momentum of the slide. This fact, together with the fast closing in of the night, very much terrified him. He instinctively began to pray vociferously for deliverance, using all the strength he had to extricate himself, but to no avail. Suddenly he said the idea dawned upon him that he had thus far in life served the devil, whom he had seen fit to call "Rock," and had no business asking the Lord for favors. So he immediately swore at "Rock" to take him from his perilous position, and again making a strong effort, he removed himself from the crotch of the tree, and was perfectly satisfied with the business promptness of his deliverer.

One spicy old character known in slavery days was "Billy." He seemed then almost antediluvian but lived many years after the emancipation. Having been "brung up" by a family of good christian people by the name of Jump, "Billy" adopted the name of William Henry Jump. His knowledge of letters was so limited that he merely remembered the names of a few,

"WYE HOUSE," HOME OF COLONEL EDWARD LLOYD.

and it had been so long that he imagined he had forgotten far more than most people knew. Whenever "Billy" was asked if he knew so-and-so, would invariably answer that he "uster but had forgotten it."

"Did you know the dictionary by heart?" a wag asked one day.

"Awh yes, sah, I uster say it backards, I knewed it so well, but I'se done gone disremembered it now."

"Did you ever know geography and grammar?"

"Yes, done knowed dat, too, long ago, but hit's 'scaped my dismembrance."

"How about mathematics, can you figure?"

"Figger? figger? land sakes, boss, I could figger all roun' de corn crib and keep tally wid de cob."

"Can you write?"

"Not now, sah, but I uster."

"Let's hear you spell, "Billy." Spell 'tobacco.'"

"B-a-t, 'bacco."

"Spell 'possum.'"

"P-o-s, possum."

"Spell your name."

"W-i-l, Willum—R-a-n-d, Henry,—J-a-m-p—Jump, William H. Jump."

And the old darky pronounced his name in full after spelling, with that gusto which gave him all the satisfaction that the fullest quaff from a Pierian could have given a Solomon.

Another character on seeing the incandescent lights in Easton for the first time, was curious to know "what kind of ile do dey burn in dem 'lection lights?"

Some years since a preacher who came to Talbot, and styled himself a leccalite minister, attracted wide attention among his fellows by his deep and incomprehensible learning. He preached until he was hoarse, rolled up his sleeves stamped the pulpit, smote the Bible with his clenched fist and thundered eloquence into his audience until he reached the climax he worked so hard to obtain. This was a due appreciation of his learning and power recognized by ejaculations all over the room and unto the farther corners, such as:

"Listen to him, sista'; brudda, hear him talk!"

"Mm-mm, now he's preachin', " etc.

And when the entire audience would be responding audibly with all the commendatory expressions they could lay tongue to, the preacher would mop his brow and ask for a hymn.

These performances became so noted that whenever certain young white fellows wanted to be entertained they would station themselves upon the outside of the low frame edifice and listen. On one occasion a reporter accompanied them and took the following stenographic account, the accuracy of which is not questioned, and recorded here as fact : Gesticulating wildly as described, the preacher began on the favorite theme of magnifying the greatness of Jehovah.

"De Lawd made de heabens and de yearf, and de sea, an' all dat transmographies the atmosphere."

"Listen to'im, listen to'im."

"But what yo' know about what dat means? You don't know, 'cause yo' hain't been lucified. I's been 'structed in de mafematies, an' I knows."

"Yes, yo' do—'deed yo' do."

"Ef a strain of cayers could run a million yeahs, wid steam up, dey would not reach de circumboundary lines of dis yearft, an' yet de ole moon climbs dem hills every night and slides down de odder side jest as easy as a black snake 'mong de reeds, an' de moon doan quire no steam."

"Dat's a fac, brudda', dat's a fac."

"Dis yearf is bigger'n dat, an' I might as well tell yo', if you doan know how big et is. Hit is twenty-five million miles in diameter, an' eight fousand miles across de beam."

"Hear dat will yo', hear dat, honey? Lord bless us !"

And thus the discourse continued, but after some weeks of an ineffectual effort to subsist by his deep learning and eloquence, the preacher left the county, and abandoned the hope of building up a new congregation in Easton.

The church, campmeeting or protracted meeting is where the colored rustic is at his best, and at such times his superstitions are boundless. Much singing and shouting, however, will suffice to keep old "Sattin" at bay. If his feet itch in church service, "Sattin" is tickling him; if he sleeps in church, "Sattin" is soothing him ; if he yawn, "Sattin" will jump in his mouth.

Brother Gardner's Lime Kiln Club could not have much exaggerated some of the characters well known among the colored people of this section to day—though it is said with regret that the old type is fast passing away to give place to the modern-schooled negro.

One old specimen of Hammondtown—a suburb of Easton, a "darkey befo' de wah" and raised in Richmond, was lead into argument relative to the Bible. He said that the preacher told his congregation that the Bible said for man not to do labor on Sunday. The gentleman, desiring to draw him out as much as possible, said that the Bible said no such thing—that the word 'Sunday' could not be found in it. The old colored man would not give up, but insisted the preacher was right until the gentleman told him to go to the preacher and have him to show the passage of scripture and if it were found, the gentleman would support the family of the colored man in question, one whole year. This proposition was gladly acceeded to, and the conversation came to an end   The next day the old man from Hammondtown was sought and inquiry made as to his success with the preacher, and he reported the case about as follows:

"Boss, dat preacher said dat sartin, sho! but I got feared to ax him to splanify, so I said to my boy after supper las' night, 'hea, sot yo'self dar by that table and take dat Bible an' read twell you comes to de place where de Lawd disrebukes working on Sunday,' an' dat boy read an' read untwell he *don eread clean through d' book* an' it took him to mos' 'leven o'clock and he say dey ain't no such place in de Bible. So I guess, boss, yo' is about right an' when dat preacher axes fo' increase of salary, I, as one of de elders will extortion him."

A well-known gentleman in the lower part of Talbot relates the following:

On one occasion an old and reliable "darky" appeared on the scene very early one morning and I said to him, "Why are you out so early this morning?" "why," said he, "do you call this early? I have been up for the last four hours. I bought a jug of whisky, late yesterday, and my desire this morning for a drink made me wake up that soon, but I heard that if one commenced drinking in the morning before the roosters crowed, he would be sure to get drunk before night, and not wishing to get drunk, I waited to hear the chickens crow. I waited, and waited and waited, and still no crowing, so I proceeded to light a lantern, and went to the chicken house to see if they were dead, or had been stolen, and found them all quiet on their roosts. I had no time piece and my desire for the drink was strong. I then began stirring around among them hoping to start them to crowing but to no avail. I then concluded I would just have to wait, so I returned to the house and waited, and after a long time the crowing commenced, and also the drinking. So you see if the chickens had been up with me I would have been here four hours ago.''

These illustrations are upon the humorous side of the "natural negro"—but there are other views of character which protray oftentimes the deepest sentiment—lofty feeling—purest motive—and pathetic endurance.

BATHING IN THE PEACH BLOSSOM.

ON THE HURRICANE DECK DOWN THE CHOPTANK.

CHAPTER XXXII.

EMORY points vividly to the days of American history when General La Fayette made his second visit to this country. The recognition which Talbot gave to that event has been recorded in the public prints of that day ; and as late as the nineteenth day of October, 1898, the school children of Talbot county contributed a large sum of money toward the erection of the La Fayette monument to be unveiled at the Paris Exposition in 1900, and appropriate exercises were recommended throughout the public schools to commemorate the day as "La Fayette Day." From the files of the Easton *Gazette* of September eleventh, 1824, the following account is taken :

PROPOSED CONVENTION

OF

The People of Talbot County, to welcome

GENERAL LA FAYETTE upon his arrival in the United States.

The inhabitants of the county from their own knowledge, or from history, or by tradition, are well acquainted with the essential assistance rendered to this country by General La Fayette in the achievement of its independence and in the establishment of its liberties, and must be presumed to be always willing to acknowledge their gratitude to him for the share of these blessings which they enjoy. But as it will be scarcely practicable for them to wait upon the General, on his arrival in Baltimore, to express their sentiments in *person*, and it might be a subject of extreme regret if so suitable an occasion of forwarding their congratulations should be omitted ;

It is therefore proposed that a meeting of the people of Talbot county be held at the court house, in Easton, on Saturday
the eighteenth day of September instant, at twelve o'clock, for
the purpose of enabling them to express their sense of his services
and virtues, to declare their satisfaction at his arrival in the
United States, and to greet him with that cordial welcome which
his association with Washington during the Revolution, his continued love of liberty, and his attachment to the institutions of
our country, so justly entitle him to receive.   The people are
respectfully and earnestly invited to attend accordingly.

THE WISH OF MANY CITIZENS.

Talbot county, September 6, 1824.

The suggestions contained in this communication seemed to
meet with the approbation of the people, and accordingly on the
twenty-first of September a large public meeting assembled, of
which we have the following account in the *Gazette* of October
twenty-third, 1824.

LA FAYETTE CONVENTION.

The citizens of Talbot county, Eastern shore of Maryland, assembled in the town of Easton on Tuesday, the twenty-first day
of September, 1824, at twelve o'clock to express their feelings
on the arrival of General La Fayette in America.

Major Gueral Benson was called to chair, and Tench Tilghman chosen Secretary.   The chairman stated the object of the
assemblage after which Robert H. Goldsborough, Esq., rose, and
addressed the convention in a feeling and eloquent appeal, por-
traying the prominent acts of the life of General La Fayette,
and closed by submitting the following resolution :

That a committee of——persons be appointed to consult, and
to present to the meeting for their approbation a respectful and
becoming salutation of General La Fayette, and an expression of
their sentiments and fellings upon his arrival in these United
States.

This resolution was immediately adopted ; the blank filed
with the number seven, and the following gentlemen, to wit : Governor Stevens, the Honorable Edward Lloyd, Nicholas Hammond,
Esq., Thomas J. Bullit, Esq., Colonel Daniel Martin, Robert H.

Goldsborough, Esq., and John Leeds Kerr, Esq., were selected by the chair to carry its provisions into effect.   The
committee retired, and the meeting adjourned until three o'clock
P. M., to receive their report.

At three P. M. the meeting reassembled, and the committee
reported the following address and resolutions, which were
unanimously adopted :

*The expression of the feelings and sentiments of the citizens of Tal-
bot to General La Fayette upon his arrival in America, presented
by a deputation appointed for the especial purpose composed of
Major General Benson, Robert H. Goldsborough, Esq., and the
Hon. Edward Lloyd.*

The Freemen of Talbot county, on the Eastern Shore of Maryland participating in the universal joy, that is diffused throughout this country at the arrival of General La Fayette upon the
shores of the United States, welcome him as the tried friend of
the illustrious founder of the Republic, their beloved Washington, and as one of the boldest adventurers in the achievement
of American Independence.

*They hail him as the noble and disinterested friend of liberty and
of mankind.*

Gratitude is a sentiment, that belongs to generous hearts, and
it becomes Freemen to cherish and express it.   The homage of
respect is due to merit, but the adulation of servility has no
abode with us.

The remembrance of great actions is sweet, the pleasure of
expressing that recollection to the hero, who has performed
them, is the pride of the free and the duty of the virtuous.

Therefore *Resolved*—That we fully participate in the universal joy that is felt by all classes of our fellow countrymen at the
long desired arrival of General La Fayette—

Resolved—That we receive him as the guest of the nation and
as a citizen of Maryland—as one of those illustrious and generous benefactors, to whom we are indebted, under Providence,
for the enjoyment of national independence, and equal liberty
and rights.

Resolved—That the arrival of General La Fayette in our
country has infused into us a more lively recollection of a period

and of the scenes, that ought never to be forgotten ; because it was a time of magnanimous struggle in the best of causes ; and a sacrifice of brave men and of honest patriots for the freedom and prosperity of that country, which we now inhabit and enjoy.

Resolved—That a deputation of three citizens be appointed to wait upon General La Fayette in the name of the freemen of Talbot, to present him with these expression of their sentiments towards him, and to say to him, that although as a plain, frugal country people, we have not the means of adding splendour to his progress nor of furnishing luxurious banquets to entertain him, yet we have hearts faithful to love him, and ingenuousness to bear exulting testimony to his great worth—that his name and his glory are familiar to us and to our children, and that he will live as he ought to do, in the affections of Americans to the latest ages, and hold a merited station in the foreground of American history—That so dear has he ever been to the American people, they have marked and admired his course, in his native country, since he left us ; and if he, as one of the fathers of the French Constitution of '89, was, with other friends of public liberty and popular rights, foiled in their noble and patriotic exertions by events which no human efforts control, they regard the grand attempt, as worthy of a man who had signalized himself in aiding in the achievement of American Independence with better fortune and with a happier fate.

Resolved—That it is our sincere wish, that General La Fayette would call his family to him from France and spend the remainder of his years in our country, that the remnant of his life he might enjoy with us a portion of that happiness, which has been so disinterestedly and eminently instrumental in procuring for our country, and that our fellow countrymen might have an opportunity of testifying to him more calmly their gratitude, their veneration, and their love.

The convention selected Major General Benson, Robert H. Goldsborough, Esq., and the Hon. Edward Lloyd, the deputation, to wait on General La Fayette on his arrival in Baltimore, and present to him the Address, Resolutions, and congratulations of the freemen of Talbot. The following resolution was also submitted and adopted :

Resolved—That the trustees of the steam boat company be requested to present to the La Fayette deputation the freedom of the *Maryland* to and from Baltimore for this occasion.

P. BENSON, Chairman.

Attest,   TENCH TILGHMAN, Secretary.

There is no doubt that this address and these resolutions were from the eloquent pen of the Hon. Robert H. Goldsborough. They were presented, by the committee appointed for the purpose, to General La Fayette during his sojourn in the city of Baltimore. At the time of the presentation he gave a verbal reply, and promised to furnish the committee an answer in writing, but as no record is made of any such in the public prints of the day, it is presumable, amidst the multiplicity of similar demands, it was wholly forgotten.

The people of the county having been dissappointed in their first attempt to prevail upon General La Fayette to visit Talbot, another effort was made, by offering what was thought to be a pleasant inducement for him to come. The Maryland Agricultural Society was then in full vigor of its usefulness. Under its auspices cattle shows were held upon the eastern and western shores. In the year 1822 the first of these bucolic festivals or fetes for the Eastern Shore was held at Easton, and in 1824 it was proposed to hold the second, or the fifth counting those held on the Western Shore. The Agricultural Society at one of its meetings in Easton elected General La Fayette, who had always professed great partiality for rural pursuits, an honorary member, and a committee, consisting of Governor Samuel Stevens, Robert H. Goldsborough, Esq., and General Perry Benson, was appointed to express to that distinguished gentleman the pleasure experienced by the society in having his name enrolled among its membership, also to tender an invitation to him and his suite to attend the cattle show to be held in Easton on the eighteenth day of November, 1824. To this invitation and the notification of his election the General returned this reply, from the seat of Mr. Jefferson, where he was the honored guest :

MONTICELLO, November 12, 1824.

Gentlemen :

"The honor I have received on being made a member of the Maryland Agricultural Society is highly valued by me, and I most sin-

cerely lament the impossibility I am under to attend the exhibition
on the Eastern Shore. My utmost expectation is to be able to
arrive in time for the last day of the second exhibition near Baltimore, an object upon which I am now writing to a friend in that
city. The date of your letter will itself offer an apology, as I am engaged after this visit to stop a few days at Montpelier, Mr. Madison's
seat, to dine at Orange Court House, to visit Fredericksburg, and
be one or two days in Washington city. These particulars I take
the liberty to lay before you, as an excuse, which I hope will be acceptable, as well as the expression of my grateful and affectionate
respect.   LA FAYETTE."
  P. BENSON, ESQ.,
        EASTON, TALBOT COUNTY,
              Eastern Shore Maryland.

It is a matter of interesting reminiscence that those premiums, which were in the form of pieces of silver plate, that
were awarded at this cattle show as well as those awarded at
the cattle show upon the western shore, had this inscription following after the recipient's name : "From the Agricultural
Society by the hands of La Fayette."—Some of these premiums
still exist in the country, and are estimated beyond their in-
trinsic value on account of the pleasing associations connecting
them with our great national benefactor.

Although the large body of our people were debarred from
the privilege of seeing General La Fayette, and of expressing
to him in person their admiration of his character, and their
gratitude for his services, large numbers visited the city of
Baltimore during his stay, and made up a portion of the throng
that saluted him in his progress through the streets of the joy-
ous city. The steamer Maryland then new, under the command
of Captain Clement Vickers, and the various sailing packets,
were employed in conveying those citizens who were anxious to
gratify a laudable curiosity, and indulge a pleasing sentiment,
to and from the city, and many took their children with them,
that they might have it to say in after years, their eyes had
rested on the unselfish benefactor of their country, and that
they might witness with what acclaim freemen could reward
this champion of civil liberty throughout the world.

CHAPTER XXXIII

OCAL annals of Talbot county have suffered greatly because there are so few memoirs of events that preceded the Revolutionary war. Newspapers, those repositories so invaluable to the local historian had not begun to be published within the bounds of Talbot, and the court and church records that have been presented are meagre in mention or details of any local occurrences caused by the struggle for independence.

There is one record in the keeping of the clerk of the court, dated 1765 to 1768 which gives account of the action taken by the county court, on Tuesday, November first, 1765, on the famous "Stamp Act," passed by the British Parliament, which imposed a stamp tax on all legal documents, newspapers, pamphlets, etc. The county court "finding it impossible at this time to comply with the said act, adjourned the court until the first Tuesday in March seventeen hundred and sixty-six," and took "into consideration the mischievous consequences that might arise from proceeding to do business in the manner prescribed by the above mentioned act of Parliament, and as it would be highly penal to do anything contrary to the directions of the act, would not open nor hold any court."

Public sentiment in the county was clearly expressed which may account for the phrase "mischievous consequences" used above. The court was unwilling to place itself between two fires, popular indignation and legal penalties, so it wisely refused to hold court at all by adjourning.

An old periodical known as "*Carey's Museum*" of July, 1788, contains an account of the indignation meeting held at Talbot Court House (now Easton) when an effigy of a stamp informer was hung from a gibbet in front of the court house door. The intense feeling of the time is clearly seen in the following account :

"RESOLUTIONS OF THE FREEMEN OF TALBOT COUNTY,"

"MARYLAND,"

"*November*, 25, 1765,"

"The Freemen of Talbot County assembled at the Court House of said county, do in the most solemn manner declare to the world :

I.   "That they bear faith and true allegiance to his Majesty, King George III.

II.   "That they are most affectionately and zealously attached to his person and family ; and are fully determined, to the utmost of their power, to maintain and suport his crown and dignity and the succession as by law established ; and do with the greatest cheerfulness submit to his government according to the known and just principles of "British Constitution ; and do unanimously resolve :

I.   "That under the Royal Charter granted to this Province, they and their ancestors have long enjoyed, and they think themselves entitled to enjoy all the rights of British subjects.

II.   "That they consider the trial by jury, and the privilege of being taxed only with their consent, given by their legal representatives in assembly, as the principle foundation, and the main source of all their liberties.

III.   "That by the Act of Parliament lately passed, for raising stamp duties in America, should it take place, both of these invaluable privileges enjoyed in their full extent, by their fellow subjects in Great Britain, would be torn from them ; and that therefore the same is, in their opinion, unconstitutional invasive of their just rights, and tending to excite disaffection in the breast of every American subject.

IV.   "That they will at the risk of their lives and fortunes endeavor by all lawful ways and means, to preserve and transmit to their posterity their rights and liberties, in as full and ample a manner as they received the same from their ancestors ; and will not by any act of theirs countenance or encourage the execution or effect of the said Stamp Act.

V.   "That they will detest, abhor and hold in the utmost contempt, all and every person or persons who shall meanly accept of any employment or office relating to the Stamp Act ; or shall take any shelter or advantage under the same ; and all and every stamp-pimp, informer or favorer of the said Act ; and that they will have no commuication with any such persons, except it be to upbraid them with their baseness.

"And in testimony of this their fixed and unalterable resolution, they have this day erected a gibbet, twenty feet high, before the

RUINS OF OLD WHITE MARSH CHURCH.

A STREET SCENE IN OXFORD.

Photographs by J. E. Dodson, Baltimore.

court house door, and hung in chains thereon the effigy of a stamp informer, there to remain *in terrorem*, till the Stamp Act shall be re pealed."

His Excellency, Horatio Sharpe was the next to the last Proprietary Governor of Maryland, and after serving for sixteen years was succeeded by Robert Eden, Esq.

Before the time of the removal of Governor Sharpe, those political questions which were at the foundation of the revolt of the colonies against England were in agitation among the people of this state, and although our historians give no intimation that such was the fact, it is not improbable that he was, at heart, in sympathy with that spirit of independence which was then appearing, notwithstanding he, in his public declarations, maintained the proprietary rights, and defended the royal pretensions. The following address gives countenance to this surmise, for it is hardly probable that the justices of Talbot county, who were men from the people, would have spoken to him and of him in so complimentry and affectionate a tone, had they not been assured of Governor Sharpe's secret sympathy with their own opinions and aspirations. But this is inferential only. The "Worshipful Commisioners and Justices of the Peace" whose names are signed to the letter, have almost all representatives in a near or remote degree of relationship in the country, to this day.

To Horatio Sharpe, Esq., late Governor of Maryland.—Sir :—The Right Honorable, the Lord Proprietary of this Province, having been pleased to appoint his Excellency, Robert Eden, Esq , a near relation of his Lordship, to succeed you in this Government—permit us, sir, on taking leave of you as our Governor, gratefully to acknowledge the mildness and equity of your administration, and the benefits and happiness which have flowed from it to the people of this Province.

Ever since you have presided over us, we have observed, with pleasure, your steady care to have the laws duly executed, and justice impartially administered and that a desire to promote the good of this Province hath been the ruling motive of all your ac tions. Such motives and such action worthy of those that are appointed to rule, must render your memory dear to a grateful people

Your public vitues impressed us with esteem and reverence for the magistrate, whilst your social virtues inspired us with the warmest affection for the man, and must now give you the heart-felt pleasure

of being followed into your retirement by the prayers and blessings
of a people you made happy. But virtue like yours will not be
suffered to remain long sequestered from the world, and happy will
that favored people be, over whom his Majesty shall hereafter appoint you to preside.

RISDON BOZMAN,

JOHN GOLDSBOROUGH,

ROBERT GOLDSBOROGH,

EDWIN OLDHAM,

JAMES DICKINSON,

JONATHAN NICOLS,

WILLIAM MARTIN.

THE REPLY OF GOVERNOR SHARPE.

To Risdon Bozman, Esq., Chief Justice of Talbot County.—The
very polite and affectionate address I have received from the
justices of Talbot county, since the arrival of the worthy gentleman,
appointed to succeed me in the government of this Province, demands my grateful acknowledgements, which, sir, I desire the favor
of you to present to them. As it was the heighth of my ambition to
discharge the trust reposed in me by the Lord Preprietary, to the
satisfaction of his Lordship, and the good of the people over whom
I have the honour to preside, the assurances that have been given
me that my endeavors were not unsuccessful, make me quite happy.
In whatever state I may pass the remainder of my life, my sincere
wishes for the prosperity of Maryland will never cease, and nothing
can afford me greater satisfaction than to know it flourishes more under the administration of my successor than it did during mine, or
in any former period. I am, Sir,

Your most obed't, humble servant,

HORATIO SHARPE.

ANNAPOLIS, June 24, 1769.

Of the political annals of the county none stand out more
clearly in the memory of the older citizens than the great Whig
meeting of 1840, during the campaign of log cabins, coon skins
and hard cider, which was an epoch in the history of Easton. It
was held on the grounds of which Spring Hill cemetery now forms
a part, this with the adjoining land comprising quite a field.
Large shade trees were taken from the woods and planted out
over the grounds in great numbers. Invitations were extended
to most of the leading Whig orators and statesmen of the day;
Clay had a special committee to wait on him in Washington and
insist upon his attendance. The old chieftain informed the com-

mittee that his public duties might preclude his attendance in person, but if he did not come, he would send in his place "a man who could beat the world upon the stump—'Old Crit,' of Kentucky," and him he did send. Our people were charmed with the homely looking and plainly dressed old Kentuckian, and roused to the highest enthusiasm by his burning words of eloquence and power. One of the most sumptuous dinners ever seen on such an occasion was prepared. Mr. Kerr had a dinner for the orators, to which the old Kentuckian was invited ; but after his speech he went up and surveyed the dinner table, spread with all the Eastern Shore luxuries. He looked at it for some time in silence, and then said : ''I have never seen anything like this, even in old Kentuck—the land of barbecues and stump speakers. The people too, like my people,—I must dine right here !'' Graves, of Kentucky, was present and spoke at the meeting ; Reverdy Johnson, George R. Richardson, and many others. The enthusiasm was kept up until late at night. Nine steamboats from Baltimore and elsewhere aided in bringing the multitude. The fine "cool spring" in the meadow adjoining suplied water for the thousands. In the evening the speakers' stand broke down whilst Mr. Graves was speaking ; fortunately on one was was hurt. The numbers present were variously estimated at between fifteen and twenty thousand. The Whig avalanche over the country that year is well known, resulting in the election of General Harrison to the Presidency.

Easton has a remarkable relic in the shape of the first market house ever built in the twon. It is located on Harrison street, near Goldsborough street, and is one and a half stories high, built of brick. It was erected in 1790 and was used as a market until 1801, when a subscription having been made by the citizens, a new one was erected on Washington street near the site of the present market. In 1813 it was destroyed by fire, another building was erected and used until 1869, when another, more modern and commodous, was erected with town hall above. This was also destroyed by fire in 1878, which was replaced immediately by the present handsome building, an illustration of which appears in this volume.

The most ancient and the most honorable of the charitable organizations in Easton is that of the Masons. It is probable

that a lodge existed in this town as far back as 1764.   Here in
1781, was instituted the Grand Lodge of Maryland in the old
Court House, and for six years continued to hold its sessions in
that building, since which time this Lodge has met in Baltimore.   In 1802, St. Thomas Lodge, No. 37, was charted, secured
the old market building on Harrison street, and held its meetings in the "loft."   This place continued to be used by the
several lodges for Masonic purposes until 1857.   St. Thomas
Lodge went down in 1806, and Masonry was not revived in
Easton until 1823, at which time Lodge No. 76, was first
organized and adopted the name Coats' Lodge, in honor of the
Grand Master of Maryland, and an Eastonian by adoption.
This lodge also went down, and in 1855, on the twelveth of May,
in the room on Harrison street was instituted the present lodge.
It likewise assumed the name of Coats, No. 102.   In 1860, when
the building on the southeast corner of Washington and
Dover streets was erected, Coats' Lodge furnished a proportion-
ate part of building fund, and thereby secured far more
comfortable quarters in the third story of the building; here
this lodge continued to meet until the erection of the hand
some Temple on Washington street in 1880, where the order
now meets.

That beneficial organization which has remained intact the
greatest length of time in Easton, and which at present contains the largest membership and represents the greatest wealth,
is Miller Lodge, I. O. O. F.   It was instituted in 1833, with
forty-three charter members.   The original meeting place
of the lodges was a building known as "Washington Hall"
that stood on Washington street, nearly opposite the Point road.
In 1839 a building standing on the corner of Washington street
and Market space, originally intended for a hotel but never
completed, was procured.   Here the third story was fitted up
for the purposes of the order, and in 1853 meetings were first
heldhere.   On Sunday, the 4th of March, 1855, another terrible conflagration laid this property and that in its immediate
neighborhood in ruins, the burning shingles being carried to
other portions of the town and destroying several houses.   Miller
Lodge replaced the burnt building with an excellent structure in
the following year, when in 1878, on the morning of October
first, this property was destroyed by the fire which swept the

entire length of Market space, taking in its course the Market
House and Town Hall. With characteristic energy the members of the order immediately proceeded to erect another building, which was dedicated September 25th, 1879. This last
building claims to be the handsomest structure on the Eastern Shore, and is undoubtly the handsomest Odd Fellows' Hall
in the State of Maryland.

The great speculation fever which swept the country from
1835 to 1840, and brought about the terrible collapse in 1837,
had its victims here. It attacked the people of Talbot through
the medium of the silk worm. The food of this insect is the
species of mulberry, technically known as *Morus Multicaulis*. In
1838, the desire to invest money in the purchase of the "sets"
of this plant seized nearly every one who could raise even a few
dollars, while some morgaged their farms for this purpose.
Thus many thousand dollars were spent, and every available spot
used for setting out the plants. Farmers planted down their
fields, and citizens of the town filled up their gardens, every-
body expected to be rich in a very short time. At the end of
the first year the prospect had increased in value five hundred
per cent.; but the next year the *Morus Multicaulis* buble burst,
and only those who were lucky enough to unload after the first
year, by selling out, were the ones who made by the operation ;
all others lost, some, as much as ten thousand dollars, and became utterly ruined. There were a few persons who saw the
irrationality of a universal and unlimited growth of the food of
the silk worm, while no attempts were made to propagate the
worm itself, so these persons established a cocoonery at Mulberry Hill, near the town, and here efforts were made to utilize
the vast amount of foliage which the mulberry plantations were
producing. But the enterprise was swamped in the general de-
luge which soon followed.

 GLANCE at the educational advantages given to Talbot from its earliest days may prove interesting and serve to show that this county has always been abreast of the times in matters pertaining to learning, both for mental discipline and manual dexterity, for the latter was always included as a special course by "indenture" before the boy was considered competent to battle with the problem of life. The system of today deviates from, as well as improves upon the old methods, but the training of the whole child, body and mind, which includes manual dexterity, is the foundation of our present system. It is also interesting to note among things recent, that Talbot is the first county in the state to introduce manual training and industrial work in her public school system, and the example set, no doubt will be rapidly followed by other counties.

Our early records, almost from the organization of the county, indicate the presence of school teachers among us. The first school master of whom we have any record was one John Stevens. It is to be regretted that the only information which we gain of him is that in 1680 he was presented by the grand jury of the county for being drunk on the Sabbath day at the house of John Aldridge, for which he was fined one hundred pounds of tobacco. In 1691 we learn of one Thomas Wallis, who seems to have lived in Miles River Neck, and had his goods and chattels seized for debt by William Hemsley in 1689. Henry Adcock "being a man, well skilled in the art of teaching good letters," kept school in Miles river (this may have been intended for Miles creek in Trappe district) sued William Warrilowe, in 1693 for the amount of his tuition fee of four hundred pounds

OLD FRIENDS' MEETING HOUSE NEAR EASTON

of tobacco for teaching and instructing "his son William Warrilowe, Jr., in good letters and manners for and during the term
of one year." Henry Adcock was not only cast in his suit, but
had to pay two hundred and forty-two pounds of tobacco for his
"false clamour" against William Warrilowe. The names of
many other early Talbot teachers could be given if necessary. In
the year 1723 a law was passed by the General Assembly of the
state for the establishment of one free school in every county,
provision having been made by preceding assemblies for raising
a fund for the purpose. In conformity with this law, the board
of visitors for Talbot county, therein named, the Rev. Henry
Nicols, Colonel Matthew Tilghman Ward, Robert Ungle, Esq.,
Mr. Robert Goldsborough, Mr. William Clayton, Mr. John Oldham and Mr. Thomas Bozman, purchased in the year 1727, for
the use of this school, one hundred acres of land, being a part
of Tilghman's Fortune and lying between St. Michaels and
Third Haven rivers, and upon Betty's cove.

Here a school-house was built, and a public school was kept
for many years, in which was educated as many charity pupils
as the master should designate   This school was upon the land
formerly owned by Joseph Price's heirs, upon the left of the
road to St Michaels, in which parish it was located.   But there
is a notice of the existence of a public school in St. Peter's as
early as 1724, in a report made by the Rev. Daniel Maynadier,
to the Bishop of London, of the condition of his parish.   This
school may have been organized under the law of 1723-4.

The Rev. Thomas Bacon purchased of David Robinson several
parcels of land, adjoining each other, "for the use and benefit
of a charity school intended to be set up and supported in the
parish of St. Peter's * * for the maintenance and education of
orphans and other children." This school occupied what is
now part of the alms house.

From these and other instances that might be adduced if
necessary, it is very clear that schools and school houses were
common and that a plain education, from the first, was within
the reach of almost every one. But there are evidences also, of
a desire upon the part of the more wealthy of the county, even
at an early day, that their children should have a better education than could be afforded by the schools of the county. Thus
Michael Howard, a distinguished lawyer of Talbot, provides in

his will, proven in 1737, that his nephew Michael William Howard should be sent to Westminster school and then to King's College, Cambridge, England.

William Harper provides by his will of 1739 that the tutor of his son Samuel Clayland Harper, shall be paid double what he was paid for the tuition of other children. Mr. Harper's judgment was better than his orthography, for he says "at the age of fifteen years his son shall be bound out to some emenent calling, if his capacity suits, such as a lawyer, phicition or merchant, &c., &c.; but if his jennus is not fit for such, let him be bound to some handy craft trade, as his jennus shall best suit him, regard being had to the person's exemplary life and conversation, to whom he is bound." To the credit of Mr. Harper be it remembered that he directed, in case his son should die before he should arrive at the age of twenty that one half of his whole fortune with his books should go to the support of the Talbot county public school, others, no doubt followed this example of encouragement.

The very earliest memoranda that are extant indicate that schools of a higher order, and taught by men of thorough training were patronized in Talbot, a proof of the appreciation of something more than the mere *principia* of learning. On the whole, it may be said with truth, there did not exist that general or even common illiterateness in Talbot which has been attributed by annalists and historians to our forefathers; and the stories of many people of condition that they could not sign their names, are not founded on fact, at least there is not as much truth in them as there should be in an assertion that is made with such persistent repetition, and so little qualification.

Mr. Chandler, of the university of Cambrige (England) opened a school in Easton on the first Monday in July of 1792. His curriculum was extensive, embracing "most of the useful and ornamental branches of education"—grammar, writing, arithmetic, geography, the Latin, Greek and French languages, logic, natural and moral philosphy and English composition, and declamation. Mr. Chandler, believed in long as well as hard study, for his hours of attendance were in summer, from six to eight o'clock A. M., and from nine o'clock A. M., to twelve o'clock M., and from two to five o'clock P. M. ; in winter, the early morning session was pretermitted. Mr. Chandler, was succeeded the next year by the Rev. Owen Magrath, a graduate of the University of Dublin, Ireland.

But extensive as was the course of Mr. Chandler, it was surpassed by that of Mr. B. M. Ward, who in 1792, had already been teaching six years at the Trappe. His course of instruction comprised the following : "Reading, writing, English grammar, (he omitted the Latin, Greek and French languages) vulgar and decimal arithmetic, and accomptship, instrumental and logarithmetical arithmetic, and algebra, geometry, trigonometry, mensuration, applied to a variety of mechanical branches, architecture according to the five orders, gauging, surveying, geography, navigation, the use of the celestial and terrestial globes, exhibited in a number of useful problems, astronomy, both absolute and comparative, &c., &c.; and the practical uses of the instruments appropriate to each branch, the whole taught according to the newest and most approved system at six pounds (or sixteen dollars) per annum." Certainly he offered his intellectual wares at very low figure. But Mr. Ward's course in its turn, was surpassed by that of Michael Ryan, who in 1798, opened a school "at Wye, near Mr. John Thomas." This gentleman, Mr. Ward, was in 1793 employed by Mr. Magrath in his school in Easton, as an assistant in the English branches. The school established by Mr. Chandler, and subsequently taught by Mr. Magrath was the germ of the Easton Academy. After the re-election of Mr. Magrath, in 1795, to a professorship in St. John's College, which institution he had previously left to take charge of the school in Easton, a plan for the foundation of an institution, was "submitted to the consideration of the friends of learning and liberty in our neighborhood." The plan seems to have proven acceptable, and June 13th of that year a "Grammar School" under the care of the Rev. Joseph Jackson, was inaugurated.

A long and able address from the board of visitors of this school, recommended it to the favorable notice of the people of the county. In this address written in all probability by the Rev. Dr. Bowie, it is very sensibly said : The advantages of a virtuous education and its influence on men, manners and society, are so obvious, * * * and its importance so universally acknowledged, that endeavors are less requisite to prove its utility

than to establish the means of its accomplishment.'' This was
the direct initiative of what grew to be the Easton academy, a
school which survived down to the time of the establishment in
1866, of a high school, under the general school law.   The act
incorporating this school was passed in 1799, the legislature
having at its previous session in 1798 passed act, appropriating
eight hundred dollars to an academy to be established in Talbot county, of which John Edmondson, Nicholas Hammond,
Samuel Chamberlaine, Thomas J. Bullitt, William Hayward,
Ennalls Martin and Stephen Theodore Johnson, were the trustees.   To the direct and indirect influence of this school much
of the literary culture of the county in subsequent years may be
traced.

CHAPTER XXXV.

 T no time in the history of Talbot has the idea of dependency been uppermost. The principle of independence has been fostered and encouraged from the earlest. While it has always been necessary to depend upon other places for those necessities which could not be provided at home, yet it was ever conceded that Talbot could raise or manufacture a sufficient surplus of one thing or another to give the balance of trade in her favor. This has been so persistently followed, that the county stands to-day one of the, wealthiest of this section of the tide water counties.

The county of Talbot has been from the date of its planting, and must ever continue to be almost exclusively agricultural in its pursuits. Manufactures and commerce have always been of subordinate importance, and from the absence of water power and mineral deposits, and from its peninsular situation, with no large area of tributary country, these industries are not likely ever to acquire any predominance. Mining is wholly unknown to us, unless the lifting the fossil shell deposits, to be utilized in fertilizing our lands, be considered a kind of mining. Even our fisheries, until within a comparatively recent date, when the oyster beds of our bays and estuaries became a source of wealth, were insignificant and were confined to the supply of a merely local or very limited demand. Early agriculture, like that of the state at large, was restricted almost exclusively to the raising of tobacco. That plant was our staple. It actually made our medium of exchange, our currency. Debts were paid, taxes collected, church rates assessed in tobacco. No more grain was produced other than what was requisite to supply the wants of the colony, and as there was rarely a surplus, there were often periods of actual distress for want of bread. Maize was the principal cereal product that was reared, and hence it was called *par ex-cellence corn*. The bread made from it was that which was in common use, flour from wheat being the luxury of the rich. The culture of tobacco continued up to the time of the Revolution, when as great a change was effected in our industry as in our politics.

In 1775 there were six warehouses in Talbot county for the storage and inspection of tobacco, namely, at Oxford, Kingston, Head of Wye, Parson's Point, Bruffs' Landing, on Miles and Sherwood's Landing on Broad Creek. These which not very long after this date were discontinued by order of the court were each under the care of a sworn inspector, whose certificate of the quality and quantity stored with him passed from hand to hand, as a kind of currency. Ships from the English ports, London, Liverpool and Bristol, visited our county annually, bringing such supplies as were needed by the settlers, and going out freighted almost exclusively with tobacco in the cask. Advertisements of the time of sailing of the these ships, their rate of freight, and their place of receiving cargo, were made by posting notices in public places, mostly at the court house and the parish churches, these being the places of greatest resort, and the towns being insignificant. It was the custom for the large planters to ship their tobacco direct to their agents in England, but the smaller farmers disposed of their crops to the factors of English houses settled at several points within the county. When the war of Independence broke out, already had the culture of this plant begun to be superceded by that of wheat, for a growing trade with the English and Spanish West Indies, had caused a demand for flour; and besides our farmers had discovered that their lands were undergoing a rapid impoverishment from a too persistent planting of an exhausted crop, while they themselves were often reduced to great distress by relying upon a single article liable to extraordinary fluctuations of price.

The coming on of the war of the Revolution, hastened the change in our agriculture, which had already begun as early as the middle of that century.

The cutting off of our export trade with the mother country in tobacco, and the demand of food for the armies, drove or invited the farmers to the production of grain; so that much the

greater part of our arable land was withdrawn from the cultivation of the Maryland staple, and devoted to food products.
Owners of land forbade their tenants from raising tobacco, or
they allowed it under special contract. Thus Robert Lloyd
Nicols in 1797 advertised for rent his immense farm, "Plaindealing, of between two and three thousand acres, and stated as
an inducement to those disposed to undertake its cultivation
that "the privilege of making tobacco would be granted." By
1796 the production of the staple had so far ceased that the tobacco warehouses were abolished by the Levy court: at least
that at Kingston of which James Dudley was inspector, and
which, apparently, was the last to be kept in use, was in this
year discontinued; and this gentleman advertised that "all persons having any tobacco remaining in said house are requested
to take the same away immediately, as I shall not hold myself
answerable for the same after the 10th of June next." Richardson's warehouse in Caroline had been abolished in 1793. There
has not been a hogshead of tobacco raised in Talbot county
for over seventy-five years.

Baltimore had become the principal market for all our farm
products. In a card of Thomas Cooper of August 30th, 1793,
accusing Captain Charles Sherwood with settling with him for
his wheat at a less price than it was sold for in the city, we not
only have an intimation that produce was sold by the commanders
of the vessels, but we also have the price of wheat in December
1792, namely, eight shillings three pence, or estimating our
Maryland currency, at 7s. 6d. to the dollar, a bushel of wheat
sold for one dollar and ten cents, which, considering the relative value of money at the two periods, would now be regarded
as a very remunerative price. Clover seed seems to have been
introduced somewhere about 1792, and timothy a little earlier.
The former was recommended in a pamphlet on the "Rotation
of Crops."

The following curious advertisement may be found in the
Herald of December 18th, 1792, and will not only serve to indicate that this crop was cultivated at the time, but it will also
illustrate the character of the eccentric gentleman whose name
is affixed. * * * "A man who can come well recomended as a
teacher of small children in an English school will meet with
good encouragement by applying to the subscriber—who has a

negro woman to hire, and clover seed for sale.   Jacob Gibson, Miles river, Talbot county, December 12th, 1792.''

The application of machinery to threshing dates back in this county to 1803, although the portable machines which are now in common use are of a comparatively recent introduction.   In the year just mentioned Samuel Yarnell and Robert Moore advertised that ''Hoxie's Patent Treshing (or ginning) machine, is now in full operation and may be seen at Samuel Yarnell's farm near Easton. * * *   We may mention that it will with three hands and a horse separate one hundred bushels of grain from the straw in one day.''   This differed immensely from these steam threshers of the present day.

In the early years of our county, and up to time of the Revolutionary war, our larger planters shipped their own tobacco direct to England, and received in return by the same ship those luxuries and comforts which could not be procured within the colony.   These larger planters were also merchants, and supplied to their poorer neighbors what they needed of foreign wares.   But there were agents of English houses, who also were merchants and kept supplies of goods for the consumption of the colonists, receiving tobacco in payment.   All this foreign *commerce* was interrupted by the war of Independence ; and after its close, owing to the discontinuance, in a great measure of the culture of tobacco, and also to the growing importance of the city of Baltimore as a center of trade, there was but a very partial revival of the direct intercourse with the mother country. Our agricultural products, passed through the hands of commission merchants, just as they do now, and our foreign supplies were obtained mostly through the importing houses of Philadelphia and Baltimore. Nevertheless, even as late as 1802, and perhaps later, merchandise was imported by the larger merchants of the county. Thus, an advertisement of John Petty in 1792 states that his goods were imported from London by the ''William,'' Captain Bolton ; one of Peter & Samuel Sharp in 1793, speaking of nails as coming to them direct from London, by the ship ''Cincinnatus,'' and one of Samuel Harrison, of St. Michaels, in 1802, sets forth that he expected a general assortment of goods in the spring direct from London. All these seem to indicate that at these several dates the merchants of Talbot

MARKET HOUSE AND TOWN HALL, EASTON.

WINTER SCENE ON NEW OXFORD ROAD.

Photographs by J. E. Dodson, Baltimore.

continued to import their wares, without the interposition of the foreign traders of the large cities.

About the time here referred to, in 1791, there was an advertisement of certain transportation agents, who obligated themselves to carry passengers and freight from Philadelphia to Easton. There was a line of packets from the city to New Castle, on the Delaware. Thence across the peninsula, to the Head of Elk, now Elkton, travelers and freight were transported by stages and wagons. From Head of Elk they were carried by packet, via Annapolis, to Easton Point. By this route passengers paid a fare of one pound one shilling, and heavy freight was charged two shillings sixpence per hundred—rates really lower, dollar for dollar, than is charged by the railroad or steamboats at the present time. Of course all travel and carriage on water was by sailing vessels, steamboats having been first used upon the Hudson in 1807, while they did not make their appearance in our waters until 1817, when the steamer "Surprise" first came up St. Michaels river, commanded by Captain Jonathan Spencer.

Captain Samuel Thomas, who commanded the schooner "Betsy," in 1794 had accommodations for ladies, such as all the packets of the time were provided with. Passenger fare was placed at seven shillings and sixpence, or just one dollar, if the traveler found his own provisions, or if he was found, the charge was one shilling ten pence half penny, or twenty-five cents per meal. Of course there were packets long before any of those that have been mentioned.

The manufacturing interests of Talbot have been always limited. Except in one line of business, nothing more has ever been attempted than to supply the local wants of certain articles of prime necessity. Upon every plantation domestic manufacture of certain fabrics for clothing and household purposes, was carried on from the very beginning. The whir of the spinning wheel, and the banging of the hand-loom were heard all over the county for many years in her history, and up to the time, within the recollection of some now living, when the employment, of machinery in large factories superceded the home-made clothes with the finer products of the power looms. It was the policy of the mother country to discourage manufacturing industries in the colonies, and consequently nothing was made in America, but the commonest and most necessary articles. But the general assembly of the Province offered bounties for the encouragement of this branch of social economy, and there are many records in the clerk's office of awards which were made after a competitive examination of home-made fabrics. It is a curious fact that the Quakers refused to accept the conntry's pay for making cloth, and they made this a matter of conscience and discipline.

After our independence was achieved, a great impulse was given to this branch of industry, and our country in some small measure shared in the impulse. Still our manufactures were of a rude description, and, with the single exception just now to be mentioned, were confined to articles, that with difficulty could be brought from a distance, or such as required small capital, little skill, and simple machinery for their fabrication. That branch of manufacturing which was of first importance, which from our necessities dated of course from a very early period in our country's history, was ship building. At one time, and that time within the dates to which these articles are limited, there were ship yards upon every deep creek within our limits.

On the first of May, 1792, Matthias Bordley advertises as being for sale, a vessel, then upon the stocks, upon St. Michaels river, and ready to be launched. Another advertisement in the same paper calls for a master ship-wright capable of superintending the building of a vessel of about eighty tons. Other intimations of the active prosecution of ship building might be given but it is not necessary. The Harrisons, the Haddaways and the Spencers, at or near St. Michaels had ship yards, at which large sea going vessels were constructed. St. Michaels indeed seems to have been a centre for this industrial interest.

The fine white oak and pine timber of the stiff lands of the bay side, favored naval construction, and the early division of the landed estates in that region diminished the slave population and attracted or retained a population, a very considerable proportion of whom were intelligent ship-wrights. The town of St. Michaels itself owes its origin, after the parish church from which it derives it name, to a settlement of ship builders.

After ship-building the manufacturing interest next to importance in Talbot was tanning. Leather is an article of the

first importance, and in its preparation no expensive appa-
ratus is required, nor large capital. It may be made in one
place as well as another, where hides and bark can be obtained.
Both were to be had within our county. As a consequence we
find that there were tan yards at a very early day in many locations. Thus Samuel Stevens advertises for sale his tan yard
near Easton in 1792, and Corse & Atkinson were conducting a
yard for the business of tanning and currying within half a mile
of the same town in 1793. This tan yard probably gave name
to the bridge just below Easton on the road to Oxford.
Joseph Martin, in 1804 carried on the business of tanning at
Trappe. There was also a tannery at Hole-in-the-Wall. At a
meeting of the tanners and curriers at Easton and its vicinity
on the 27th of August 1794, to establish rules and regulations
to govern them in their business, William Rose, Israel Corse,
William Atkinson. Christopher Nice and James Richardson were
present, and signed their names to an agreement respecting the
prices for tanning hides. It would appear from this agreement
that it was common for the planters to furnish the hides, and
pay for their conversion into leather. This leather was subsequently manufactured upon the farms into shoes for the household, the whites as well as the blacks. The custom of employing a shoemaker to make the shoes for the family from leather
furnished by the head of the family, continued down to a late
date. There is now no tan yard within the county.

The manufacturing interest next in importance in the county
was hatting. The earliest advertisement of any one following
this calling in Talbot was that of John Martin Needles, who in
the *Herald* of September 13th. 1791, gave public notice that he
had taken the shop formerly occupied by Daniel Carnon, on
Washington street, Easton, opposite Troth's tavern, and was
prepared with proper materials and acquaintance with his business to accomodate his patrons. The advertisement of mechanics in this trade frequently and continually appear after
this date, but it is unnecessary to refer to any of them. This
branch of mechanical industry is no longer pursued. Our hat-
ters now are only sellers of hats manufactured elsewhere. The
last hat that was ever made in Easton and Talbot, (except the
coarse straw hats platted and sewed by the negroes) was made

by the hands of Stephen P. Layton, for Thomas Beaston, in the year 1844.

The two following advertisements are introduced, the one as evincing an attempt to introduce a branch of business to which our county seems to have some adaptation; the other for its curious interest to antiquarians. It is not necessary to say to a citizen of Talbot that now we buy all our pottery from the city, that our dentists extract all our teeth, and that our barbers draw no other blood than with their dull razors.

"*Eastern Shore Earthenware Manufactory.* The subscriber begs leave to inform the public that he has commenced the pottery business in Easton, near the head of Washington street, where he intends keeping a constant supply of all kinds of Earthenware, equal (if not superior) to any in the state. Our terms are equally low as those of Baltimore. He has burnt one kiln, which he will dispose of wholesale or retail. County store keepers will find it much to their advantage to purchase of him, as they will avoid the expense of freight and risk of breakage. Samuel Sharpless, Easton, Maryland, tenth of eleventh month, 1803."

The following advertisement of April 15th, 1794, is curious as evincing the survival of the old custom of allowing barbers to perform some of the operations of minor surgery. "Jacob Alborn, Hair dresser, Bleeder and Tooth-drawer, respectfully informs his customers that he carries on his business in the house where Mr. Wickersham formerly lived, &c. By their most obedient and humble servant, J. Alborn, *A true Republican.*" The assertion of his political sentiments to us of this day, is rather equivocal. It is probable the barber was a Federalist, although the opposite party bore the name of Republican.

It would be useless to go through the whole list of mechanical trades, such as blacksmithing, silversmithing, carpentering, tailoring, saddle and harness making, shoe making, cabinet and carriage making. Each was represented. John Fonerden was a blacksmith in 1792, William Skinner a silversmith 1790, Cornelius West, the builder of the court house, was a carpenter in 1793 and before, James Ewing was a tailor and habit maker in 1795, Samuel Stevens, a saddler in 1798, Samuel Sherwood was a shoe maker, Henry Bowdle a cabinet maker, Henry Elliott, a coach maker, all in 1794. From the same source we obtain a knowledge of the lawyers, doctors, clergymen and teachers. But there is no longer space for details of this kind. Sufficient has been said to indicate the condition of our industrial interests during the period when the Maryland *Herald* was printed.

HAVING carried the reader through the early days and scenes of Talbot county, related its romances and legends, told of its noted sons and daughters, and in fact all that pertains to this land of promise, it is but fitting to conclude this compilation with a description of the Talbot of today. Located in the centre of the peninsula, known as the "Eastern Shore of Maryland" almost surrounded by two great arms—estuaries—of the Chesapeake bay and the bay itself, is Talbot county. Pierced in every part by navigable waters that abound with fish, oysters, crabs, terrapin and wild fowl in their season. It has water fronts on the Chesapeake bay, Choptank, Tred Avon, Miles and Wye rivers, which furnish transportation facilities to every farm, and make a landing near every estate, for sailing crafts—there being no farm more than four and a half miles from navigable water. The land is high and slightly rolling, gently sloping towards the bay. Nature has provided for this section one of the best systems of drainage in the world ; the several rivers and their tributaries pervade every part and perform the same functions here that hundreds of thousands of dollars spent in tilling has not done in other localities.

The natural fertility of the soil is of the most productive kind —it produces bountifully the staple products, wheat, corn, oats and hay, and is adapted to the cultivation of vegetables, fruits and berries. The land is susceptible to improvement, is easily worked and yields immediate results when properly cultivated.

The climate is luxuriant and healthful, being in latitude 38° and 39° N., and longitude 1° E., from Washington, the national capitol, and 76° W. from Greenwich, with a mean annual temperature of 55° and 60° ; on the same isothermal line as many of the favorite health and pleasure resorts, in Italy and France, with additional advantages derived on account of the

"FOXLEY HALL," RESIDENCE OF COL. OSWALD TILGHMAN, EASTON.

close proximity to the Gulf stream, which flows within ninety miles of this place, and of the Atlantic ocean which dashes its mighty billows on the sand capped shores only fifty miles away. These climatic advantages render this particular locality comparatively free from pulmonary diseases, and contagious diseases are rare in this vicinity. Such is a general outline of Talbot county, Maryland.

The county has an area of two hundred and eighty-five square miles. The population, according to the census of 1890, is nineteen thousand, seven hundred and thirty-six; twelve thousand, two hundred and forty-eight, are white and seven thousand, four hundred and eighty-eight are colored. Most of the latter class are farm hands and servants, never having shown any inclination to learn trades or professions, but being content in those occupations for which they are best adapted.

The county's business is conducted on a cash basis, and is most satisfactorily administered by a board of commissioners composed of three members, who are elected every four years. Nearly every Christian denomination is represented by a congregation with handsome edifices in which to worship.

Public highways are kept in excellent condition the year around, and being aided by natural drainage the roads are inexpensive and easily kept in repair. Many of the roads are laid with oyster shells, which pulverizing under the wheels of vehicles and the hoofs of horses, form a bed of unsurpassed smoothness and solidity. These roads pass through charming scenery at the heads of ravines, inlets and bays. The road leading from Easton to Tilghman's Island is thirty miles in length, and has no rise of more than twelve feet in height. Each side of this beautiful drive is dotted with houses, villages and towns within close proximity.

Excellent roads and beautiful drives are incentives for lovers of the equine species to own good horses, and in this particular industry, the raising of good horses, Talbot county is fast becoming a strong competitor with Lexington, Kentucky, many thousand dollars being invested in blooded stock, and the progeny of some of the most famous horses in the country are stabled here. Cattle, sheep and swine, thrive in this locality, indeed considerable money is invested in the higher grades of cattle and sheep, much attention is paid to raising of these animals.

Factories are much needed here, though the county is not entirely void of these enterprises : it has many flouring mills, for the manufacture of the highest grade of flour made from wheat raised in the surrounding country. As a matter of fact, the Eastern Shore wheat commands higher prices than any shipped to the Baltimore market ; several canning establishments are in operation, packing tomatoes, vegetables and peaches. Oyster canneries are established at the watering towns, and furnish employment for hundreds of men. Brick yards utilize the clay that abounds in nearly every section a few feet below the surface.

Three distinct lines of railroad pass through the county, furnishing easy and quick communication with New York, Philadelphia, Baltimore and Washington. Telegraphic and mail facilities are convenient, while steamboats and sailing crafts play upon every river affording excellent water transportation.

Unlike most comparatively level countries, the climate of Talbot county is most beneficial for the health of mankind. With its salubrious breezes, comparatively even temperature and freedom from the great storms and intense heat and cold of other sections, it becomes as an earthly paradise to less favored portions of the country. While on the parallel of the Ohio river, the temperature is more like that of Western Tennessee, but not subject to that dread curse, "yellow fever." The mercury in the Fahrenheit thermometer rarely ever falls to zero in the winter, and seldom reaches ninety-five above zero in the hottest weather of summer. And at no time in summer, even the hottest, can the observer fail to see a breeze stirring the leaves of the trees, fresh from the ocean or bay. Another advantage is that the nights are cool, thus giving opportunity for refreshing sleep and rest. Snow storms are, as a usual thing, very light, and seldom does the snow lie more than a day or two. High winds never prevail, and such a thing as a cyclone is unknown to this section. Rains are well distributed through the season, and seldom is there anything like a drought.

The climate of this section has justly been compared to that of the most popular health resorts of France and Italy in Europe, and is always admired and praised by those who have had the pleasure of enjoying its many beneficial advantages. Acclimation is easy, and very few would perceive the change

TRIPPE'S CREEK, P. B. SPRING'S ESTATE IN THE DISTANCE.

CADETS AT WORK IN SHIP YARD MARYLAND NAUTICAL ACADEMY.

so far as ill effects are concerned, while many who have come
here suffering from constitutional disease have been benefited
at once. Salubrious, temperate and free from terrible storms and
with refreshing breezes in summer and mild winters, this climate is unsurpassed, and it is believed unsurpassable anywhere
on this continent.

The schools of Talbot county are par excellent and have been
often looked upon as criterions by other counties of Maryland,
and by other states in the Union. The examiner, Prof. Alexander Chaplain, has been connected with the schools of the
county for more than forty years, and has been holding the
office of Examiner for more than thirty years, and it is to his indefatigable energy and advanced ideas that the schools of the
county are what they are. The school buildings are modern
and comfortable, heated and ventilated upon scientific principles and number fifty-one white schools and nineteen colored
schools. This includes the Easton High and Manual Training
School to which pupils are admitted from all sections of the
county without extra charge, and also the high schools of St.
Michaels, Trappe, Cordova and Oxford. Seventy-one white
theachers preside over 2,875 white pupils, and twenty-four colored teachers have under their charge 1,729 colored pupils who,
grade for grade, have the same uniform instruction that white
children have, including free books.

A colored Manual Traning and Industrial school is being
started, and manu-mental instruction is being included in the
curriculum throughout the county.

The salaries to teachers aggregated in 1897-98 $28,000 but
will go considerably beyond that figure in the succeeding year.
One unique feature connected with the public schools and which
is not to be seen at the present time outside of this county, is
the savings bank system by which each pupil becomes a de-
positor of savings with the teacher, and whose account is carefully kept by the cashier of the bank, the treasurer of the school
funds, who pays interest to the pupil, thus encouraging thrift
and economy. The schools are under the supervision of a board
composed of three members. At present these are M. B. Nichols,
President ; Dr. R. A. Dodson, and John F. Mullikin associates.

THE END.

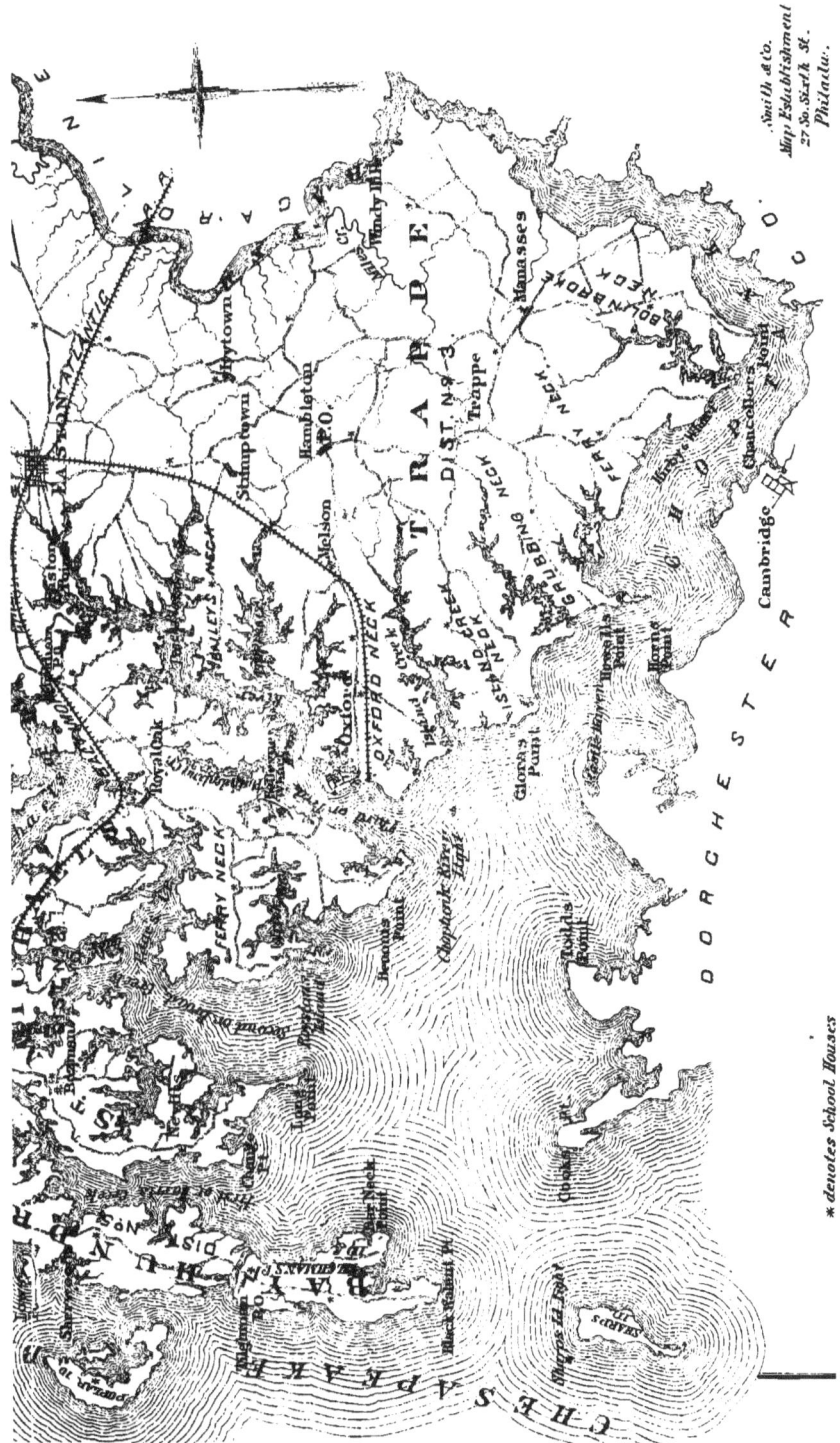

* denotes School Houses

Smith & Co.
Map Establishment
27 So. Sixth St.
Philada.

BIOGRAPHICAL.*

ADAMS.—The Right Rev. William Forbes Adams, D. D., D. C. L., Bishop of Easton, the Cathedral town of the Eastern Shore, is a man who stands high in the Episcopate of America, whose leaders are men of mark. Bishop Adams comes of fine old Irish family. His parternal ancestor settled in Ireland some little time after 1669. He fought under William of Orange at the battle of the Boyne. His maternal ancestors are Scotch— and indeed his grandmother upon the father's side was also Scotch. Bishop Adams was born January 2nd, 1833 in Enniskillen, but his father, a man of means, came to America in 1841, when the subject of this sketch was in his eighth year, and settled in Kentucky. In Kentucky, the middle youth of William Forbes Adams was passed, and having been educated for a professional career, he was prepared for Yale college, but prevented by business reverses befalling his father, from attending, he at once went to work, entering for a while, upon a mercantile career, which being distasteful to him, he completed his classical course under a private tutor, began the study of law, and after three years was admitted to the bar in the state of Mississippi.

A particular friend of Mr. Adams was Rev. George W. Sill of Pass Christian, Miss. ; through his influence he was led to feel that for him there was a still higher aim in life, and his thoughts were turned toward the ministry. Yielding to the new-born purpose to become a clergyman of the Episcopal Church, Mr. Adams moved to Clarksville, Tenn., entered upon the study to fit him for his new calling, with heart and soul in his work, and became a candidate for Holy Orders, under Bishop Otey, in 1857. After completing his studies, he returned to Mississippi, and on St. John the Evangelist's Day, 1859, was made a Deacon in the Church of St.

*[The character sketches which follow are not intended as an exhaustive list of persons who are alone worthy a place in this book. The compilation is made from such data or personal contact which could be obtained. A general notice was given in public print for several weeks for persons to send sketches of themselves or others, and the author as well as publisher wishes it distinctly understood that no lines were drawn in the selection of names. They fully recognize the list could be increased many fold and at the same time thank all who have assisted in giving them what is herein published —for to that extent the book will be made more and more valuable as time advances.]

Andrew, in Jackson, Miss., then under the charge of the Rev.
William Cruse Crane, a man of revered memory, and so well and
favorably known upon the Eastern Shore of Maryland, whose
many friends still honor his memory and recall him with affectionate regard.   Mr. Adams was ordained a Priest by the Rt.
Rev. William Mercer Green, D. D., Bishop of Mississippi, than
whom no more saintly man ever lived, and whose whole life in
the Episcopate was a benediction ; his memory will long live in
the hearts of Mississippians independent of creed or calling.

In 1860, Mr. Adams was given charge of St. Paul's, Wood-
ville, Miss., and the dream of years had been realized.   He was
in charge there during the civil war, and within the sound of
the guns of Port Hudson during the long and desperate struggle
of fifty-two days.   During the war, the Rev. Mr. Adams was
elected to the chaplaincy of a Mississippi regiment but the
Colonel of the regiment being one of his parishoners, and whose
family were also, objected to his leaving, and prevented notification of it.   His services were rendered to our sick and
wounded in the hospitals as far as his time and ability permitted.
Called to a wider field, he went to New Orleans as rector of St.
Peter's ; in five months he was called to St. Paul's in the same
city and was pastor of that church when elected to the Episcopal
office ; in 1874 his consecration followed, by Bishops Green,
Beckwith and J. P. B. Wilmer in January 17th , 1875. The
degree of D. C. L. was conferred upon him by the University
of the South, in recognition of his worth.

Sent to the territory comprising New Mexico and Arizona, Bishop Adams, whose health was already impaired by his self-sacrificing services during the yellow fever epidemic in Shreveport,
La., broke down when exposed to the long and severe journeys
he had to undergo in his new field, and compelled his resignation, after heroic efforts to discharge his arduous duties proved
of no avail.   In 1877 the House of Bishops, feeling that his life
would be the sacrifice, relieved him of his charge, and after re-
cuperating his health, he resumed pastoral work, becoming rector of the Church of the Holy Trinity in Vicksburg, Miss.

He was in 1887 still in charge of the Church of the Holy Trinity, when he was elected to the Diocese of Easton, the duties of
which he entered upon in 1887, and a position he has since held
with acceptance and great success, for his whole life is in his

work, and the Eastern Shore is fortunate in having just such a man to fill the high position he holds.

Bishop Adams is an unassuming man, gentle in demeanor, ever courteous, is not one to believe that to be a good christian one's face must be cast in a mould which a smile would shatter, but is full of cheery stories, amusing anecdotes and is a good raconteur. He is liberal in his views, most tolerant of the views of others, a good speaker, energetic, quick in action and possesses great ability in his calling, while he is an ardent reader of almost every class of literature. In 1858 Bishop Adams married his cousin, Miss McCallen, the daughter of the Rev. William McCallen, an Episcopal clergyman, and an A. M. of Trinity College, Dublin.

ADKINS.—William Hughlett Adkins, a prominent Talbot lawyer, was born on the family homestead near Easton in 1862, his father being Dr. J. L. Adkins, a distinguished United States Army surgeon and after his resignation a physician of this county. The Adkins home is a fine mansion situated upon the Tred Avon river and is surrounded by several hundreds of acres in the highest state of cultivation. William Hughlett Adkins was educated in early life under private tutors and later graduated with honors at Johns Hopkins University, Baltimore, receiving the degree of A. B. He studied law at the University of Maryland Law School, received his degree of B. L. in 1883, and after practicing his profession for awhile in Baltimore, came to Talbot at the death of his father to look after the large estates here. Mr. Adkins, in addition to having a large practice, is interested in a number of enterprises in Easton, where he ranks high in his profession and holds important positions, being a director and counsel of the Easton National Bank, director and counsel for Water Works Company, Ice Company and Hotel Avon Company, also attorney for the B. C. & A. Railway Company, and W. P. B. and L. Association, and other corporations. In 1891 Mr. Adkins married Miss Mary Hand Dawson, daughter of one of Easton's influential business men.

Rev Franklin B. Adkins, brother to the above named, was born near Easton, September 26th 1856, received a liberal education and graduated at Shenandoah Valley Acdemy, Winchester, Virginia, after which he studied Latin, Greek, Hebrew and Literature at the Johns Hopkin's University. In 1882 he graduated at the Berkley Divinity School and was ordered

Deacon, by Bishop Lay, at Christ Church, Easton, and later was ordained priest in the Church of God, by the same Prelate. Mr. Adkins has filled many prominent positions and holds high rank in many benevolent and christian orders. He married the eldest daughter of Rt. Rev. Wm. F. Adams. As an index to the christian character of the man, the following quotation is taken from a private letter of his to a friend : "As an humble instrument in the hands of my Eternal Maker, with an absolute and adoring faith in the fatherhood of God and an enduring hope and love for the brotherhood of man, in the unity and fellowship of Christ Jesus, my Lord, I am in humble submission striving to labour to build up that Temple not made with hands— eternal in the heavens."

BALDWIN.—The Rev. Leonidas Bradley Baldwin, Rector of Christ Church, St. Peter's Parish, Easton, is one who is becoming thoroughly identified with Talbot. A man of scholarly attainments, pleasing address and social disposition, he is popular in and out of his church and interested in the affairs of the people. He can look back over a long line of ancestry who dwelt in Connecticut, and the subject of this sketch was born in New Haven in 1834, his being the seventh generation of Baldwins that claimed that city as their birthplace. The Rev. Mr. Baldwin received his education at Trinity College, and studied theology at the Berkely Divinity School, being ordained Deacon in 1863 and Priest in 1864, St. Mark's at New Britain, Conn., being his first charge, then St. Mark's, Boston, next moving to Keene, N. H., after which he sought a more congenial climate and was called to Christ Church, Easton. In 1863 Mr. Baldwin married Miss Annie M. Willard, of Middletown, Conn. Mr. Baldwin is a logical speaker in the pulpit, devoted to his ministerial duties and works hard in the interest of the church and those connected with it.

BARBER.—The Honorable Isaac Ambrose Barber, member of Congress, was born in Salem, New Jersey, on January 26th, 1852, and after a good education in the excellent schools of the society of Friends of which sect he is a member, as have been his people for generations before him, he selected the profession of medicine as the one seemingly best suited to his taste. He chose the Homeopathic school, and a hard and devoted student, graduated when just of age, and finally selected Easton as the best place for him to locate, a growing town among a refined, enlightened and progressive people. In a short while, by his energy Dr. Barber built a practice which increased as time went on, when circumstances led him into other business he became largely interested in milling. Living in the midst of an unsurpassed wheat country, the milling business was profitable, and the work so much to his taste that he gave up medicine after years of practice, and devoted his attention wholly to this business. Dr. Barber was sent to the Maryland legislature, and filled other important political offices. Elected President of the Farmers and Merchants National Bank of Easton, Dr. Barber was recognized for his full worth in the business enterprises of town and county. He married Miss Nellie Collison, of Easton, a grand-daughter of the late Judge Perry W. Stewart, a prominent citizen of Talbot. Dr. Barber is a calm, forcible speaker, having clear cut reasons for what he says, and saying it tersely and well. He uses few metaphors, deals in no useless words, is not flowery in diction, but lucid in argument and convincing. Chosen by his party as a Congressional candidate, he was elected to a seat in the House, which he has filled to the satisfaction of his constituents.

BARTLETT.—Hon. John C. Bartlett is Chief Judge of the Orphans' Court and holds a high place in the esteem of his fellow-citizens. He was born on the "Bloomfield" estate, 1839, and comes from honored ancestry on both his paternal and maternal side. Judge Bartlett represents the fifth generation of his name in Talbot. Educated at Milton academy, he returned to Talbot and entered into the milling business in connection with farming, and in both made a success. In 1895, he was elected Chief Judge of the Orphans' Court, having previously been an associate on the bench. Judge Bartlett belongs to the Society of Friends, and is a man of sterling worth, commanding the esteem of all who know him.

BENSON.—Captain James Benson, who was also a physician, was living at Benson's Enlargement, near St. Michaels, about 1674. He had four sons and four daughters. A son, Perry, was the father of James, who was the father of General Perry Benson. Samuel Perry Benson rose to the grade of Brigadier

General, commissioned in 1807, and in 1814 was commissioned as Major General. Nicholas Benson, another son of the settler, had a son also named Perry who died in 1814. This Perry had a son named James, who had five sons and three daughters. One of his sons, Perry, was the father of Gustavus Keihl Benson ; another son of this James Benson was Charles, who was the father of the late James Benson. Mr. O. H. Benson is in business in St. Michaels.

BATEMAN.—Wilfred Bateman is a representative man of Maryland, rather than to say of his town and county, for he is known all over the state, and is universally popular. Mr. Bateman belongs to an old and respected Maryland family, is a man of genial nature, a *bon vivant*, liberal, progressive and socially and politically a favorite. Born in 1859, his father being Col. Henry E. Bateman of Easton, Wilfred Bateman was reared in Talbot and while in his teens, became a school teacher, later attending a military school in Virginia. Returning to Easton, Mr. Bateman studied law, was admitted to the bar in 1881, and has made a success in his profession. He was appointed Clerk of the Talbot Court, is a Mason, an Odd Fellow, an officer of the Chesapeake Bay Yacht Club, is attorney for several large Easton enterprises, and his friends may be written down as legion.

CAULK.—The Caulk family of Talbot county goes back to Lord Baltimore's time, so that James H. Caulk has a long line of Maryland ancestry. A farmer by occupation, Mr. Caulk lives in Bay Hundred District, and has attained prosperity. Born in 1844, Mr. Caulk has passed his life in agricultural pursuits, at the same time interesting himself in all that would advance his neighborhood and county.

CARRINGTON.—Mr. Charles S. Carrington is a young lawyer of Easton whose ability places him in the front ranks of the Talbot county bar, noted for its legal lights. He dates his ancestry, maternal and paternal, back to 1632 on one side, and 1680 on the other, but in Massachusetts and Connecticut, not in Maryland. One of his grandfathers was a major in the Revolutionary army, and another an officer in the war of 1812. Mr. Carrington's father, D. N. Carrington, was born in Georgia in 1836, and the family moved to Talbot in 1874, and purchasing the fine old home of "Oaklands," on the Peach Blossom, and one of the ancient mansions with a history, having been built about 1750, and upon the site of an old homestead that still dates back a hundred years.

Charles S. Carrington was born in 1860 ; was educated in Brooklyn and Columbia College ; studied law in Easton, and admitted to the bar, entered later into partnership with Hon. Charles H. Gibson, then Senator from Maryland. The Carrington family are Daniel N., an officer on a steamer in the South American trade, Charles S., Walter, Robert and Mabel.

CHAMBERLAINE.—Dr. J. E. M. Chamberlaine may be called a "gentleman of the old school." Dignified yet genial, courtly in manner, he bears his age well, inheriting a splendid physique and iron constitution from a long line of ancestry, noted for their physical make up and strength of character. Dr. Chamberlaine is the fifth of his race in America, his first ancestor in this county having come here prior to the year 1700 and become largely interested in shipping and mercantile pursuits, settling at Oxford until latter he established himself, in a fine home on the "Plaindealing," a part of the mansion still remaining and already referred to in a previous chapter of this book. For generations before, from the year 1000, the Chamberlaines had been prominent in English life, having two homes there, the main seat being "Saughall" in Cheshire. In Talbot, the Chamberlaines also had two homesteads "Plaindealing Manor," and "Bonfield," both imposing mansions built on a hill thrown up by slave labor, and now in possession of Dr. Chamberlaine. In 1700 the first of the Chamberlaine family in America had built on what is now Trippe Creek, a fine fleet vessel, paying for her in so much tobacco from the plantation of "Plaindealing." The vessel was named the "Elizabeth" and had twenty-four guns and a crew of ninety-six men, for those were the days when the black flag floated on every sea. The "Elizabeth" made many successful voyages from Oxford to London and other foreign ports. Dr. Chamberlaine was born at his father's homestead at Clora's Point, Talbot, in 1826, was educated at Cambridge, studied medicine and graduated in the Maryland University at Baltimore, when he came to Easton and entered upon the practice of his profession in which he made a

distinguished record. He has been twice married, his first wife
having been Miss Elizabeth D. Hayward, and his present wife
was Miss E. Catherine Earle, a grand-daughter of Judge Thomas
I. Bullitt, a distinguished man of his day. The Easton home of
Dr. Chamberlaine is a substantial brick mansion built in the
last century, and its walls are adorned with ancient family portraits, while many valuable souvenirs of the long ago, are also
to be found there.   Dr. Chamberlaine retired from practice
some years ago. From a village he has seen Easton grow into
the handsome place it is today.

CHIPLEY.—Col. Charles A. Chipley of the historic old mansion "The Anchorage," has become identified with Talbot and
its people from having made his home in their midst.   Looking
about him for a home in which to spend the late years of his
life, Col. Chipley wisely selected Talbot county, combining as it
did refined society, beautiful land and water scenery.   When
Col. Chipley made up his mind, after a most extensive search
for the right kind of a home, he acted promptly and purchased
"The Anchorage on the Miles," and at once set to work to improve it, and make it more comfortable in every way, though
still leaving the old style of architecture undisturbed.   The result was that at a large outlay, he has one of the handsomest
homes in Maryland ; and with his family about him, greatly enjoys his summer days of rest in his beautiful retreat, while his
hospitality is unbounded.   A member of the Chesapeake Bay
Yacht Club, Colonel Chipley was the donor of an elegant racing
prize, known as the "Anchorage Cup" and takes great interest
in all yachting matters, as he does in all else to the advancement and pleasure of Talbot.   Colonel Chipley is the General
Freight Agent of the Pennsylvania Railroad Company, with
headquarters in Philadelphia, and his energy, and determined-
to-get-there manner of taking hold of his work, earned him his
high position.   A man of fine executive ability and a good man-
ager, he has done much to add to the success of the great road
he is connected with, and to which he devotes so much of his
indomitable energy.   A Virginian by birth, born in 1836 in
Alexandria, he attended the public schools, then learned the
machinist's trade, and in 1854, entered the navy, a training
that he says greatly benefited him for the life he entered upon.

In 1869 he entered the employ of the Baltimore and Ohio Railroad Company, and 1881 accepted the general agency of the Union Line of the Pennsylvania Railroad, and thus went onward to his present position. A man of generous fortune, Colonel Chipley is charitable and generous hearted, and is glad to add to the happiness of those about him. In 1859 he married Miss De Camp, of Washington, D. C., and they have three children living, Mrs. W. A. Sproull, of Ridley Park, Pa., Charles Chipley, Jr., and Miss Sarah M. Chipley. The great grandfather of Colonel Chipley came from England and settled in Maryland, so he can claim descent from Marylanders as well Virginians.

CHAPLAIN.—Professor Alexander Chaplain is a gentleman known to every child in Talbot county who is old enough to have been cut loose from his mother's apron-strings to learn his A B C. as they are taught in the public schools. For one holding the position he does, Professor Chaplain is not unfavorably known, for he is popular with all classes of scholars, the boys as well as the girls. He is a man who has served longer in the harness as School Examiner than any other person in the State who holds a like responsible position, for he can count thirty years of hard labor in the scholastic field. Thorough in his work, knowing what his duties are and doing them fearlessly, versed in the old and new methods, keeping up with the times in all branches taught in the schools, from the old style to the occult sciences, Professor Chaplain is a man of scholarly attainments and progressiveness, and quick to seize upon the very best there is in modern instruction.

COBURN.—Captain Thomas H. Coburn, the commander of Hick's Post G. A. R., No. 24, was born in Baltimore in 1830 though his family came over with Lord Baltimore and took up a patent of land in Talbot. The tract was known as "King's Grant"; consisted of 1,700 acres, and the village of of Trappe now occupies a part of it. Educated in Baltimore, Mr. Coburn moved to Cambridge, Dorchester county, and began business for himself, proving successul in his enterprises, but enlisted in the Union Army, September 1861, in the first Eastern Shore regiment and was made first Lieutenant, Company A.

Later he was made aide to General H. H. Goldsborough, and
after serving in that capacity for some time, was placed in command of the drafted camp at Easton. Having been promoted,
he was ordered to Cambridge as deputy provost marshall, and
so served until the close of the war. Removing to Easton after
the war, he entered into business. He has been Junior and
Senior Vice Commander of G. A. R. for Maryland, for three
years was Deputy United States Marshal, and for thirteen years
has been Commander of Hick's Post Easton, and is now a Justice
of the Peace, and member of fraternal societies.

DOUGLASS.—Dr. Eugene Douglass, of Talbot county is a
credit to his profession, and a short time ago removed from his
home in Oxford to a wider field of usefulness in Baltimore,
where he is now building up a large practice. Dr. Douglass
has the advantage of being a surgeon and pharmacist as well as
a physician, a great aid indeed to one who practices medicine.
He is another of Talbot's adopted sons, born in Preston in
1860, and is a descendant of an old and respected family of that
county. Educated at the Preston Academy, he graduated at
the Maryland College of Pharmacy, studied medicine meanwhile and received his degree from Maryland University School
of Medicine. He was assistant resident physician at the University Hospital, and then went to Oxford and entered upon the
practice of medicine, soon making his influence felt. He is devoted to his practice, and a man who makes many friends, as a
practitioner and socially.

DIXON.—Mr. Robert B. Dixon's fore-fathers settled in Talbot
county in 1670, and he dwells today upon land just taken up by
them, though the vast tract then taken up by the Dixons has been
sold off in part. Near the present home of Mr. Dixon, "North
Bend," the first Friend's meeting house in Talbot county was
built, as has been referred to in the chapter on the ancient
churches of this county. It was known as "Betty's Cove Meeting
House," and unmarked graves of the dead of two centuries ago
alone designate the spot. The Dixons of that day, and the
Bartletts as well as many other names of the families of Friends
in Talbot, were prominent then in the agricultural and social
life. Coming down through the genesis of the Dixons, we find
that each one who bore the name was noted for thrift, perma-

nance, steadfast faith in their religion and honesty of purpose.
Mr. Dixon is the son of James Dixon and Mary Ann Bartlett,
and was born on the family homestead in Talbot county, August 22d, 1834, and is an energetic, well preserved man of sixty-
five today.   His father was a thorough man of affairs and the
leading business man of his time in Easton, universally respected and beloved.   He was prominent in all progressive business
enterprises in Talbot county, held high positions of trust, was
hospitable, generous, liberal in his views and so educated his
sons that they imbibed his ideas of business and felt the full
imprint of his thorough training, a training which has brought
each one of his sons William T , Isaac and Robert Bartlett
Dixon into the front rank of the most successful of Maryland's
business men, for no men stand higher in the public esteem than
they, and Talbot county is proud of such sons.   Educated in
Easton and at the Westtown Boarding School, in Pennsylvania.
Mr. Dixon then entered upon the life of a farmer upon the home
where he now resides, but in 1859 he also connected himself
with mercantile affairs, engaging in the coal and lumber business.   Later he entered into other business enterprises in Easton, and today is President of the Easton National Bank, of
the Nickerson Fertilizer Company, Treasurer of the Easton Ice
Company, the Easton Water Company, and of the Building and
Loan Association, and is a director in numerous other corporations.   Mr. Dixon married 1861, Miss Amos, daughter of William Lee Amos, of Harford county, and they have two sons,
James and William, and four daughters, the first named son,
James, being connected with his father in business in Easton.
Mr. Dixon has always been prominent in Talbot's enterprises,
and his influence has been felt in politics as well, though he is
not partisan, yet a staunch Republican.   He has represented
his county in the House of Delegates, and believing that the
office should seek the man was the candidate of his party for
other honored positions, being named as the successor of Hon.
Charles H. Gibson for United States Senator, but made no personal effort to secure the honor.   A man of pleasing address,
courteous to all, Mr. Dixon pursues the even tenor of his way
socially and publicly, as one of Talbot's most prominent influential and honored citizens.

DODSON.—Thomas Dodson was born near St. Michaels in
the early part of the eighteenth century.   He had a son who
was the father of Captain William Dodson, born in 1786, who
commanded one of the barges under Commodore Barney during the war of 1812.   He also was in command of the fort at
Parrot's Point, when the British attacked the town of St.
Michaels.   Captain William Dodson married Amelia Brown,
and they had a son, named William, another son Captain
Robert A. Dodson.   He left quite a large and very prominent
family.   Dr. Robert A. Dodson served through the civil war as
surgeon.   Dr. C. Marion Dodson moved to Baltimore.   Hon.
H. Clay Dodson is now State Senator.   Amelia Dodson married
Rev. D. C. Ridgaway, a very prominent Methodist minister.
Hester Dodson married Mr. J. W. Grandy and moved to Norfolk, Virginia.   Hon. Henry Clay Dodson, a resident of St.
Michaels, is a leader of the Republican party in his locality,
while he has been elected to many offices of honor and trust.   A
member of the General Assembly for three terms, he is now a
State Senator.   He was born in 1840, in the old home that has
belonged to their family for generations.   Mr. Dodson attended
school in St. Michaels, and when quite young began a business
career in a drug store in Easton, later he entered into journal-
ism, was postmaster of St. Michaels and then entered the
Assembly.

EVEREST.—Mr. Everest came of Scotch and England parentage, descending, on his maternal side from the well-known
Crawford family of Scotland and from Sir John Cole on his
father's side.   He was born October 22d, 1810, before the breaking out of the last war in England, and is a Marylander by
birth.   Educated in the local schools where he lived, he begun
to study for the ministry of the Methodist Protestant Church,
and was admitted to the Conference in 1833.   In those days the
position of clergyman was by no means a sinecure office, for
souls were to be ministered to, conversions made, sermons
preached, the dead to be buried, marriages performed and all
in parishes far apart, so that it kept a man constantly on the go
by night and day.   Ministers were few in numbers then, charges
far apart, the roads often such only in name, and a saddle horse
was frequently the only means of communication, while the pay

was a trifle, so that the clergyman's lot was not a happy one save in the thought of duty nobly done. Such was Mr. Everest's early life work, and if ever man had the gratifying thought that his life work had been nobly done, he certainly has. He occupied many of the most important charges, spared not himself in his labors, and was honored by being made President of the Conference in 1855, an exalted position he held for some years with great credit to himself, for always conservative, gentle, courteous, yet a good reader of human nature, he planned well and his appointments were good and just. In 1834 Mr. Everest married Mrs. Charlotte Worthington Hammond, who had one son, a son who rose to distinction and held many offices of trust and importance—I refer to the late Hon. Ormond Hamond, of Talbot. After a service of over thirty years in the ministry, Mr. Everest purchased a home on Miles river and settled there, moving later after the death of his wife, to "Solitude," the beautiful home of his stepson, Judge Hammond, of whose family he has since been an honored member. Tall, erect, active, bearing his eighty-six years well indeed, Mr. Everest is as courtly as a Chesterfield, and his whole life has been that of a true christian gentleman. [Deceased since this was written.]

EARLE—The subject of this sketch, Dr. John Charles Earle, is a man full of years and honors, one who can look back over a life well spent. Dr. Earle's ancestry dates back a couple of centuries in Maryland, and many of the name have won distinction. Dr. Earle was born in 1824, his father being Hon. Richard Tilghman Earle, Chief Judge of the second judicial district of Maryland. His birth place was "Medford" the family home in Queen Anne county. His earlier years, as a student, were passed in the Centreville academy and private schools, and he graduated at the Newark, Delaware College in 1839. Taking up the study of medicine from a love of the profession, he studied under Dr. James Bordley, in Centerville, and graduated at the University of Maryland in 1845, when he was appointed resident physician at what is now the University Hospital. Then he returned to Centerville and entered into a partnership with his old preceptor, Dr. Bordley, and for many years practiced in Queen Anne's county, where he was known far and wide as a skilled physician. Removing to Talbot, he expected to retire from active practice, but found it was impossible for he was at once sought after and for over thirty years, has been a prominent and energetic physician in the county. Having for half a century been a devoted practitioner, he has now retired to rest from his arduous labors, devoting his leisure to agriculture, a pursuit of which he has ever been fond, and lives at his fine old home in the suburbs of Easton. In 1848 Dr. Earle married Miss Clara E. Goldsborough, daughter of the late Colonel Nicholas Goldsborough, of "Otwell," on the Avon.

GRIFFITH.—John S. Griffith is one of Easton's energetic and up-to-date business men, and one who believes in being in touch with the times. He is a liberal conservative and has worked his way to his present position by his own energy and determination. His family came from Wales, several generations back. John S. Griffith was born in 1852, in Delaware, a little state that has turned out a great many big men. He was educated in Easton, became a clerk, and, from that start, begun the success he has made of himself as a business man.

GOLDSBOROUGH.—Colonel F. Carroll Goldsborough is of ancient lineage, and his name is well known in Maryland as one that dates from the first settlement of the shores of the Chesapeake. A typical Maryland country gentleman, Colonel Goldsborough is a planter, dwelling at his beautiful home of "Ellenborough" on the Peachblossom, a branch of Avon river, where he lives in the real old time southern style. Colonel Goldsborough can look back over the many generations of honored ancestry, and claim descent from men distinguished in Maryland history. He was born on the family estate, "Llandaff," near Easton, and brought up on the homeplace under a private tutor, and was educated at the University of Virginia, graduating in 1869. Colonel Goldsborough has traveled in Europe, and over much of this country, and has devoted a great deal of his time to the improvement of his large estate and the raising of blooded cattle and sheep. He has held important positions in the county and state, and received his title from serving on the staff of Governor Hamilton. In 1885, Colonel Goldsborough married his cousin, Miss Mary Hill Goldsborough.

GIBSON.—Hon. Charles Hopper Gibson of "Ratcliffe Manor," Talbot county, is a citizen whose fame has gone far beyond the confines of his state, which he has most ably and acceptably represented in the House and United States Senate. Senator Gibson, as he is still called, traces his ancestry far back in the history of Maryland, and several of his name served in t he Revolution and the war of 1812. Born in Queen Anne's county, he was educated at the Centreville Academy, Archer School and Washington College. He studied law and was admitted to the bar in 1864, commencing practice in Easton with Colonel Samuel Hambleton, and at once began to make his mark as a lawyer. He was appointed in 1869 Commissioner in Chancery, and auditor in 1870, but resigned to accept appointment of State's Attorney for Talbot, an unexpired term, but was elected for four years to the same office, and re-elected in 1875, but declined a fourth term. He was elected to the forty-ninth, fiftieth and fifty-first Congress, serving with marked credit to himself and the good of his party—the Democratic. Mr. Gibson was appointed to the United States Senate to fill unexpired term of Senator E. F. Wilson, and was elected for the full term ending March 1897. Senator Gibson is a man of commanding and striking appearance, and one who has not been spoiled by the high honors he has won.

HAMBLETON.—Samuel N. Hambleton, then living at St. Michaels, was presented with a medal by Congress for his services in the battle with Comodore Perry on Lake Erie, and named his farm "Perry Cabin," in honor of the victory. "Don't give up the ship" is said to have been originated by him. One of the earliest settlers in the vicinity of St. Michaels was William Hambleton who emigrated here from Scotland about 1659. His residence was at Martingham near St. Michaels. In 1663, he was High Sheriff of Talbot county, the second of that title. In 1668, he was appointed one of the Worshipful Justices of the Peace and Commissioner of Talbot. The Colonel Samuel N. and John S. Hambleton were descendants of William Hambleton.

HADDAWAY.—Captain W. H. Haddaway has been both a soldier and a sailor, but is now a leading business man in Oxford. Born in 1844 on the family homestead, he was a farmer until the breaking out of the civil war, when he entered the Union army and served with credit to himself, until his honorable discharge, when he returned to Talbot and became a sailor. Until 1879 he followed the water, becoming Captain of a vessel, and then entered upon a commercial life in Oxford, where he is now a prosperous business man.

HOLDEN.—Major Hiram L. Holden, of "Gilnock Hall" on the Peachblossom, is a new resident of Talbot county. His home, though built in the old colonial mansion style of architecture, is a new one, for he said he did not think it just right to erect a cottage class of building upon an historical site. Born in Steuben county, New York, long enough ago to enter the army at the breaking out of the civil war, he entered the service for which he had had some training, having gone to Kansas after receiving a thorough education. There he lived through the troublesome time that agitated that country in what was known as the "Free State War. At the breaking out of the civil war, Mr. Holden was on a visit to Williamsport, Pa., and from there enlisted in the eleventh Pennsylvania regiment and went with it to the front. Serving until the time of his enlistment expired, Major Holden returned to Williamsport, and soon after married Miss Armstrong, a daughter of Judge Armstrong, of the Supreme Court of the State and whose brother, Judge Armstrong, of Philadelphia, is one of Pennsylvania's prominent citizens. Removing to Colorado, Major Holden entered into the banking business, and was largely interested in mining. Later his business interests called him to Chicago, where he spent some years. Major Holden has passed much time abroad, traveling in foreign lands, and it is to the credit of Talbot county that when he came here on a visit some years ago, its beautiful scenery, restful and general surroundings determined him to make this his home. The result of his determination is his handsome home of "Gilnock Hall" beautifully situated upon an eminence of the Peachblossom, and commanding extensive views of the surrounding country, and as well, a refined and hospitable home.

HARDCASTLE.—General E. L. F. Hardcastle was born 1824, his father being a merchant of Denton, Maryland, where he was much esteemed. The Hardcastles are of English descent, settling in Maryland in 1748. The eldest son of the one who founded the family in America was Thomas, the builder of "Castle Hall," the handsome old homestead in Caroline county. Educated at home, the subject of this memoir was sent to West Point in 1842, graduating in 1846 with distiction. He was commissioned Second Lieutenant in the corps of Topographical Engineers, United States Army. In his class at West Point were Generals McClellan, Foster, Reno, Couch, Stonewall Jackson, Sturgis, Stoneman, Oakes, Maney, Palmer, Wilcox, Jones, Gardiner, Maxey and Pickett. truly a galaxy of distinguished officers to come from one class. The Mexican war breaking out, Lieutenant Hardcastle was ordered to the staff of General Winfield Scott, and participated with conspicuous gallantry at Vera Cruz, Cerro Gordo, Perote, Puebla. Churubusco, Molina del Rey, and City of Mexico, being thrice promoted by brevet for services in the field. After the war the duty assigned to Captain Hardcastle was to survey the surroundings of the City of Mexico at the request of the Mexican government, which later made acknowledgments of his able services rendered. Later he was ordered to astronomical duty on the Mexican Boundry Commission, and then went to Washington to complete maps and reports of his surveys in Mexico. 1854 he was appointed Secretary of the light house board, and he had under his supervision the preparations of plans for the new light house among which was Minot's Ledge light on the coast of Mass. Resigning his commission in the army, having married Miss Sarah D. Hughlett, daughter of Colonel William Hughlett of Talbot county, Captain Hardcastle entered upon the life of a planter. He took no part in the civil war, yet made himself useful in many ways to the people of Talbot. In 1867 he became President of the Maryland and Delaware Railroad, and he brought it out of its financial troubles and placed it upon a firm foundation. He became also a director in the Easton National Bank ; was elected to the House of Delegates ; was the author of the Militia law, and was appointed 1874 General of State troops. Again elected to the Legislature he made himself a most useful member, and was the author of the elevator bill. He is a Democrat, a man of much influence, and has two large estates in Talbot, while his home is in Easton.

HARDCASTLE.—Dr. Edward M. Hardcastle comes from the adjoining county of Caroline, a county that has sent many a good man forth to win fame and fortune. Dr. Hardcastle was born in the homestead of "Castle Hall" in 1819, but today is a remarkably well preserved man for his years, and still keeps up his practice. He received his education at the schools in Caroline and was sent to Lancaster, Pa., to finish off, after which he came to Talbot to teach school in 1841, and at the same time read medicine. He attended the Jefferson College of Philadelphia, and graduated as an M. D. in 1844, when he settled in Trappe, Talbot county, to practice his profession. After a long and successful practice in Trappe, Dr. Hardcastle removed to Easton where he now resides. He was for long years a Vestryman of the old White Marsh Church, has been School Commissioner sixteen years and is a man skilled in his profession, and one who is esteemed by all who know him, for his life has commanded the respected of his fellow citizens.

HARDCASTLE.—Edward M. Hardcastle, Jr., was born December 10th, 1867, at Trappe, Talbot county, attended the public schools of the county until 1882, when he went to St. John's College. After completing the entire college course, graduated as valedictorian in 1886 with the degree of Bachelor of Arts. The following year was spent as assistant teacher in the Easton High School. Deciding upon a medical education, he attended lectures at the University of Maryland, was resident student of Maryland University Hospital, graduated fourth in a class of 112, and was awarded, after competitive examination, the Tiffany surgical prize. Post-graduate courses were taken at hospitals in Philadelphia under private instructions. He Settled in Abington, Va., in 1891, and was for a time acting instructor of French and German at Martha Washington College for girls. He married Miss Nannie Lloyd Meiere, granddaughter of Admiral Franklin Buchanan, the Confederate hero. Mrs. Hardcastle died in 1893, after which Dr Hardcastle came to Easton and accepted a position as assistant teacher in the high school, of which he soon after became principal, in which arduous and responsible chair, he won golden opinions for himself. In addition to his severe labors, Dr. Hardcastle entered upon the study of divinity and has been ordained deacon in the Episcopal Church. He is a man of fine mind, a hard student, has read much and traveled extensively, while his courteous and genial manners with all make him universally popular. In 1897 Dr. Hardcastle resigned as principal of the Easton High; and Maunual Training School, and after a year's work at the Nautical Academy, accepted a position on the staff of Rev. Dr. W. R. Huntington, of Grace Church Parish, New York City.

HOOPER.—Leander R. Hooper is an example of what business intelligence and push will accomplish. Born in Baltimore city, June, 28, 1857, he moved to Denton, Caroline county, where he spent his boyhood. In 1877 he came to Easton at the request of Thompson & Kersey, who at that time were the largest retail dry goods merchants in this section. Mr. Hooper was soon promoted to the desk of book keeper in this firm, and filled the requirements of the position until the firm went out of business, nine years afterwards. Mr. Hooper then associated himself with Hubbard & Brother, manufacturers of fertilizers, and remained with that concern for eleven years, when he opened an office for the sale of fertilizers, with several branches, such as brokerage in canned goods, insurance, etc. He is now recognized as one of the substantial business men of the town, and his advice is frequently called for by fraternal orders and in the religious circles with which he is associated. In December, 1886 Mr. Hooper married Miss S. Gertrude Mathell, of Easton. They have one child, a daughter of ten years.

HOLLYDAY.—Henry Hollyday was born June 29th, 1836. His father, Henry Hollyday, of "Readbourn," son of James and Susan Hollyday, (a Miss Tilghman,) married Miss A. M. Hollyday, daughter of Henry and Nancy Hollyday, of "Ratcliffe," Talbot county. After spending a few years at a country school near "Readbouru," Henry Hollyday was sent to "Ratcliffe" to attend the old Easton academy in 1847. In 1848 he went to St. James College, Maryland. In 1852 he entered upon a mercantile life. Going to Philadelphia first in the drug business, and then the importing—silk and fancy dry goods—remaining in it till 1861 Being southern in all his tastes, habits, and connections, he found it best to leave the "Quaker City," so accordingly on the morning of April 20th, 1861, the day after the memorable riot in Baltimore, he left for his Maryland home, and entered

the store of McKenney & Co., Centerville, Maryland, and in
March 1862 became one of the firm. In September 1862, having
fully determined not to join the Union forces or furnish a sub-
stitute, he went south enlisting in Company "A," Captain
W. H. Murray, Second Baltimore Infantry, C. S. A., Colonel
Herbert, commanding. It is as well to state that a draft was
made in Maryland about the time Mr. Hollyday left, and ten
days after joining the Confederate ranks, he was informed that
he had been drafted into the Union army. The record of the
Second Maryland Battallion of infantry cannot be given here,
suffice to say, it saw very active and severe duty. The first muster roll of Company "A" called one hundred and thirty-five
men, and only thirteen of this number surrendered at Appomatox. Mr. Hollyday participated in the battles known as the
second Winchester, Gettysburg, second Cold Harbor, Hatchers
Run and others, beside numerous skirmishes. Under terms of
parole given at Appomatox, he returned to his Maryland home,
"Readbourn," coming back on the second day of April, 1865,
exactly four years from the day he left Philadelphia. A few
months rest at home, a rest necessary to enable him to regain
full health, found him again actively at work. His father dying
in September 1865, his brother Richard and himself took charge
of the estate, In 1869 he moved to "Ratcliffe," Talbot county,
to manage the farm and the fall of that year again entered mercantile life. In 1869 he married Miss Sally H. Hughlett,
daughter of Colonel Thomas Hughlett. In 1871, he gave up
mercantile life for farming. He moved to "St. Aubin" near
Easton, where he has since lived and reared his large family.
He held the position of secretary to the Workingmen's Permanent Building and Loan Association of Talbot county, when
it was first organized, but resigned in March 1875 to enter the
Easton National Bank of Maryland, filling, at various times,
most of the positions in that bank, being at this date assistant
cashier. The five children by Mr. Hollyday's first wife are:
Henry, now Deputy Clerk of Talbot county Court, Hughlett,
in business in New York City, Fannie Harrison, art instruct-
ress in Baltimore city public schools, Susan, who lives at home,
and Sally who died in infancy. Mr. Hollyday's second wife
was Miss M. M. Chilton, of Baltimore county, Maryland. The

children of this marriage are Ann Maxwell, who died at nine years of age. Margaretta Robins, Frank and Rosalie.

HIGGINS.—Martin M. Higgins was born in Talbot county in 1844. His father was Josiah Higgins, of Trappe. He received his education in the public schools under the tuition of various teachers, and among his teachers was the Hon. Jonathan Willis, later Congressmen from Delaware, and, for a time, he attended the private school of Wiliam H. Brown, now an eminent lawyer in Philadelphia. At the age of sixteen, Mr. Higgins entered the store of the late Montgomery Lloyd, and later moved to Oxford, but in 1863, he moved to Easton and entered business, but gave it up to take the position of enrollment clerk under Captain Andrew Stafford, then Provost Marshal for the district. After leaving his office he immediately re-entered business. In 1867 he accepted a position as special assistant to the Clerk of the County Commissioners and continued there until he embarked in mercantile life on his own account, and made a most successful business man. In 1887 he moved into his present office and became an Insurance and General Business Agent. He was one of those active in the formation of Talbot County Fair Association, being one|of the incorporators, and was elected secrtary and treasurer. In 1885 he was nominated on the Republican ticket for the House of Delegates, but was defeated as was the entire Republican ticket. In 1887, he was again nominated, and elected. In 1891 Mr. Higgins was a candidate for Clerk of the Circuit Court but was defeated by Colonel Thomas Hughlett. He was a member and chairman of the Republican State Central Committee for Talbot county, but declined a re-election in 1894. He represented his congressional district as a delegate to the National Republican Convention, at Minneapolis in 1892. He received the unanimous Republican vote and was chosen Chief Clerk of the House of Delegates at the session of 1896. He served for years as secretary of Miller Lodge, No 18, I. O. O. F., the richest lodge in Maryland, and for over fourteen years as treasurer of the same body. He is treasurer of Tred Avon Lodge, Knights of Honor, and other orders, and also manager of the Easton‚Town Hall Company. He was married in 1867 but lost his wife in 1896. Mr. Higgins was chosen secretary of the present Senate without any suggestion or effort on his part. Mr. Higgins is decidedly a progressive man and wields much influence in both business affairs and politics. He has been identified with all the improvements and matters of public interest and welfare in Easton and the county.

JENKINS.—I refer to the well-known drug store under the firm name of Dawson & Jenkins, but with Messrs. Edward and Thomas H. Jenkins as proprietors. Just think of the sales of drugs, to say nothing of castor oil, sold in that store in the present century, going away back to the days when calomel, jalap, quinine, rhubarb and herbs were the cures for almost every ill that flesh is heir to, or was in those days, for now it is fashionable to have many diseases then unknown. The present Jenkins generation can look far beyond their ancient store to their ancestry, going back to centuries in good old American stock. On their maternal side they are descended from a prominent family of the Society of Friends, Miss Elizabeth Dawson who married Dr. Edward Jenkins. There are interesting historical incidents also connected with their family of the Revolutionary war and 1812, already referred to in these pages. The family settled in Talbot county before 1700, and the first firm in the old building spoken of was Dawson & Thomas, latter changing to Dawson & Brother, and then to Dawson & Jenkins, the present name of the firm. Both Edward and Thos. H. Jenkins are well and favorably known in Talbot county, where they were born, and Edward now lives in the old home in Easton. They were educated in Easton, and may be said to have been brought up in the drug business, while they have been hard students in pharmacy. The Jenkins family of today consists of Edward, Thomas H., Mrs. Valk, of Baltimore, Mrs. Edith D. Gillingham, and Miss Mary Jenkins. In 1892, Mr. Thomas H. Jenkins married Miss Elizabeth Causey, of Delaware, and they have two children, Elizabeth and Frances Hunter.

JOHNSON.—Dr. Julius A. Johnson is a prominent physician, and citizen of Talbot county living at his handsome country home on the banks of the Miles river. Dr. Johnson was born in Easton July 15th, 1849, his father being Julius A. Johnson, of Talbot county. Educated in the public schools of Talbot county, and at Baltimore, Dr. Johnson studied medicine at the

the University of Maryland in 1871, entering at once upon the practice of his profession in his native town   In 1880 he married Miss Elizabeth T. Lowndes, youngest daughter of the late Commodore Charles Lowndes, United States Navy.

KEMP.—John H. C. Kemp, of distinguished ancestry, is a man who has followed the sea as well as the life of an agriculturalist.   He was born at the family homestead in Bay Hundred in 1844, and with the beautiful Chesapeake before him, he longed to become a sailor, so when still in his teens, shipped on a coasting vessel to work his way up to the quarter deck.   In time his ambitious hopes were realized, and he became master of a ship ; but soon after, gave up the life of a sailor to become a farmer, in which work he has also been successful.   He lives in Trappe district, has a handsome home, is lavish in his hospitality and is regarded as one of the leading men of his community.

LLOYD.—Colonel Edward Lloyd of "Wye House" was born in 1825, and is a direct descendant of Edward Lloyd, the first of his name who came to this country in 1640.   He inherited the large estate of many thousand acres he now dwells upon and his home is typical of the old time mansions built in those early days by the wealthy landholders.   His family has furnished a large number of sons, who have held distinguished offices in the state.   Colonel Lloyd was educated under the care of the celebrated Rev. Dr. Muhlenberg, at College Point, Long Island, entered Princeton and graduated 1844 ; returning home he was elected to the Maryland House of Delegates, and though just out of his teens, made a fine record. He entered the army in the war with Mexico, and was on the staff of General Tench Tilghman ; promoted to capatin, then to major.   After the war was over he returned to House of Delegates.   He owned large tracts of land and many slaves both in Maryland and Mississippi, and was a man of wealth, but at the breaking out of the civil war, siding with the south, he lost the greater part of his large fortune.   A democrat, he was elected in 1873 to the State Senate, and on his second term, became its president, no one voting against him.   Colonel Lloyd has been an extensive traveller, is a man of superior learning, and a splendid type of a gentleman of the old school.   He married in 1851, a lady of great beauty and accomplishments, Miss Mary Howard, the grand daughter of General John Eager Howard, and upon her maternal side, the grand-daughter of Francis Scott Key, the author of the "Star Spangled Banner." Their home is one of the greatest attractions of Talbot, and noted for the hospitality of its host and hostess, and their children.

LOWNDES.—Dr. Charles Lowndes, of the fine estate of "Sunnyside," on Miles river, followed in the career of his father, the Commodore, in part, as he entered the United States Navy. Born in 1832 in Talbot, he was educated partly at the academy at Oxford, then St. Timothy's Hall near Baltimore, St. John's College, Annapolis, and finished by graduating with honors at Princeton University in 1853, having just become of age. Determined upon a professional career, he began the study of medicine in Baltimore, attended the University of Maryland and later Jefferson Medical College in Philadelphia. Appointed to the Navy as assistant surgeon, Dr. Lowndes went on voyages to foreign lands and saw much of the world and its people, but resigned in 1861 at the breaking out of the war, and began the practice of medicine in Baltimore. Dr. Lowndes married Miss Catherine M. Tilghman, of Talbot, and resides at his home of "Sunnyside," which is indeed a veritable haven of rest and is near the former family country seat, "The Anchorage." A younger brother of Dr. Lowndes is Lloyd Lowndes, who is now occupying the position of Secretary of the Board of Fisheries at Annapolis, to which he was appointed by his distinguished kinsman, Governor Lloyd Lowndes of Maryland.

LOWE.—Colonel James Marion Lowe was born in 1837, near McDanieltown, educated in the schools of the town, and at the military academy at Oxford. He taught in the schools of Bay Hundred, and for many years, was devoted to this occupation and to farming. His father died in 1863, leaving a large estate comprising a thousand acres of land, twenty slaves, many vessels and other valuable property, the care and management of which devolved upon this son. In 1875, he married Dorcas Elizabeth, eldest daughter of W. Seoquick McDaniel and Anna (Wrightson) McDaniel. Losing their only child, Marion, the parents traveled for some years and then settled in St. Michaels, where he has taken an active part in politics, as a democrat. Was twice school commissioner, twice clerk to the Maryland

Senate, twice a member of the Legislature, and was the first
Colonel named on the staff of Governor Hamilton. The Colonel's
father, William Webb Lowe was born in 1804, at Lowe farm,
on Tred Avon. In 1829, he married Mary Wrightson, and located on his farm near McDanieltown, where he conducted
many large enterprises with success. In his day, he was one of
the most popular and influential men in the county. As a democrat he was twice elected to the legislature, and once sheriff,
afterward declining further honors. His ancestor, John Henry
Lowe, related to Colonel Vincent Lowe, whose sister Jane, as
the widow of, Hon. Henry Sewall, married Lord Baltimore,
came from Derbyshire, England, in 1700, married Mary Bartlett, daughter of Thomas and Mary Bartlett, of Yorkshire,
England, and settled on his farm on the Chesapeake Bay. The
Lowes still own the, homestead, with its quaint old dwelling
thereon. In 1701, John Lowe, Robert Clark and William
Worrilow, founded the Quaker meeting house at McDanieltown.
Colonel Lowe's great-grand parents, Ensign James Lowe and
Colonel William Webb Haddaway served in the war of 1776.
The earliest ancestor of Mrs. Lowe was Laughlin McDaniel,
who married Mary Lowe, and died in 1732. John Mc-
Daniel, March 30th, 1777, married Mary Morsell, daughter of
James and Elizabeth Seoquick Morsell, of Calvert county,
Maryland. Her sister Dorcas Seoquick, who married Joshua
Johnson, was the mother of Governor Thomas Johnson and
Louisa Catherine Johnson, a very beautiful and accomplished
lady, who on July 26th 1797, in London married John Quincy
Adams, afterward President of the United States.

MAYNARD --Henry Maynard was baptized at a spring when
he was six or seven years old, by Robert Strawbridge at Harris
Creek, Frederick county, in 1762. It is claimed that here Mr.
Strawbridge, two years later, built the log chapel said to have
been the first Methodist meeting house in Maryland, and even
in America. A son of Henry Maynard, Capt. Foster Maynard,
one of the old defenders of Fort McHenry in 1814, purchased a
farm near St. Michaels and moved there. His daughter Elizabeth married Rev. T. J. Thompson, D. D. They had ten children, among whom are Rev. Henry S. Thompson of the Wilmington Conference, and Mrs. Lillie Gracey, wife of Samuel

Gracey, United States Consul to Torchon, China. Mrs. John
W. Dean, of St. Michaels, is a grand-daughter of Capt. Foster
Maynard. Her father was the late Stephen Denny, who died in
1875, aged ninety-two. Mr. John W. Dean is now the trustee
of the M. E. Church, justice of the peace, town commissioner
and holds other positions of trust.

MERRICK.—Mr. William S. Merrick is one of Trappe's influential men, and he has made a success in agricultural pursuits.
For a number of years he was journal clerk of the House of Delegates, and later of the Maryland Senate. Born in 1851, Mr.
Merrick passed his boyhood upon a farm near Trappe, was educated in the public schools, and became a teacher, at the same
time devoting himself to the study of law. Later he entered
upon a mercantile life, opening a drug store in Trappe, and has
been a most successful business man.

MULLIKIN.—Col. Mullikin is a man with a double record—
military and political. If in New York, his name would imply
that he was a late comer from the Emerald Isle, but here in Talbot the Mullikins have been a power in the land for over two
centuries, for the Colonel owns the farm his first American ancestor received under Lord Baltimore in 1662.

James Clayland Mullikin was born fifty-seven years ago in
Talbot, was educated in Baltimore; liked studying so well he
became a teacher, but heard the call to arms at the breaking out
of the civil war and recruited the only company Talbot raised
for the Northern army, yet modestly made other men the senior
officers over him. As a soldier Lieut. Mullikin made a gallant
record for himself and was promoted and appointed to the staff.
Here he rapidly advanced in promotion for distinguished services on the field, until he attained the rank of lieutenant-colonel and was placed in command of the Eleventh Maryland regiment, serving in numerous battles and conspicuously at Gettysburg, so aptly named the "high tide of the Confederacy."
The title of "Colonel" was fought for and won, and not bestowed upon him "by courtesy." After the war Colonel Mullikin returned to Talbot and once more became a teacher, at the
same time studying law under General Joseph B. Seth. Entering upon his new profession of law, he quickly gained a lucrative practice. An ardent Republican, he took a leading position

in his party, a leadership he has held through all the ups and downs of political life in Maryland. He is an untiring worker, yet unselfish in his demands and willing to yield to others for the party's good. He has been candidate for Clerk of the Circuit Court Presidential elector, candidate for Comptroller, and candiatde for the House of Representatives, has been chairman of the Republican State Committee, and his name was twice brought before the Legislature for United States Senator. He was appointed postmaster of Easton by President Harrison and made a good record as such. In the late war Colonel Mullikin was appointed in the Commissary Department with the rank of Major and has jurisdiction over the department of Havana. In 1865 he married Miss Emily E. Mullikin, of Trappe, and they have one son, Clayland Mullikin, who, following in the footsteps of his father politically, is a republican, a rising young lawyer, and was elected State's Attorney for Talbot, the only republican ever chosen to that office, and he has filled the position with much credit to himself and the good of the county.

NICHOLS.—M. B. Nichols feels a just pride in having made the success he has in life through his indomitable will, pluck and energy. The family of Mr. Nichols came to America in 1852 from county Mayo, Ireland, and settled in Maryland, and two years later, in 1854, M. B. Nichols was born. Educated in the public schools up to the age of fourteen, Mr. Nichols became a clerk, and from his entrance upon a business career began to prosper, being well fitted for a mercantile life. In 1876, he entered into business for himself, and his ability, perseverance and probity as a merchant won for him success and the respect of the community. Continuing to prosper, Mr. Nichols has become one of the leading merchants of the peninsula, and his store in Easton has a decidedly metropolitan appearance, while it is conducted upon the strictest business principles. Keeping up with the times in his purchases, seeking the best markets in which to buy, wholly up to date in business methods, Mr. Nichols has attained what he determined to accomplish at the outset of his life. In addition to his mercantile life, Mr. Nichols is also largely interested in farming and other enterprises, while in the affairs of his town, county and state, he greatly interests himself. He is a man of liberal views, charitable in all schemes for the good of the community, and is president of the Board of School Commissioners for Talbot, a distinguished honor, as he differs politically with the other commissioners.   He has gained an enviable reputation among his fellow-citizens.   In 1878 Mr. Nichols married Miss Kate F. Roberts, daughter of Judge W. D. Roberts of the Orphans' Court, and a sister of Colonel Edward Roberts, a gallant Confederate soldier and now a United States Government officer.

NICKERSON.—Mr. Charles C. Nickerson is a son of W. P. Nickerson, of Delaware.   He was born in 1854.   He was educated in Oxford and moved to Easton where he has shown himself to be a most progressive and representative citizen, being connected with many of the largest business enterprises in Talbot county.   In 1892 Mr. Nickerson established a phosphate factory in Easton, and incorporating it into a stock company has made it one of the largest enterprises of its kind in the state.   Mr. Nickerson married in 1885 Miss Lillian R. Moreland, of Westminster, Maryland, and owns one of the finest houses in Easton.

NORRIS.—Adjutant Owen Norris, the executive officer of the Charles S. Winder Camp of United Confederate Veterans of Easton, was born in 1845, hence was a very young man when he entered the Southern army in the civil war.   Mr. Norris can trace his ancestry in Maryland back to the earliest settlement, when his family came to this country and found a home in St. Mary's parish.   The family are descended from Sir John Norris, Rear Admiral in the English navy, and from whom the American branch trace their direct descent.   Entering the Confederate army in 1862, in Trimble's brigade as commissary sergeant, Mr. Norris served to the close of the war, having seen the hardest of campaigning and been engaged in many battles.   He was promoted to the signal corps and was signal officer under General Early, while he was twice wounded, once severely at the second battle of Manassas and slightly at Winchester.   In the war of 1898 he served as first lieutenant of Company F, First Maryland regiment.

In 1874 Mr. Norris married Miss Margaret Tilghman Owen, whose mother was a niece of Commodore Lowndes, one of Talbot's naval heroes.   He has a handsome home, "Coverdale," on the Miles river, and about it linger many memories of the olden time.

NORRIS.—Col. James C. Norris, the proprietor of the Hotel Avon of Easton, is a typical southern landlord, and one who is as popular as he is widely known. Colonel Norris has had a great deal of experience in hotel life, and he runs his home on business principles. He comes of a family that has descended through half a dozen generations in Talbot, and the Colonel was born in the old homestead in 1835, received his education in the public schools, entered upon a mercantile life in Easton, and became proprietor of the old Brick Hotel in 1865. In 1891 he became the landlord of the Hotel Avon, and his ability and energy, added to his genial nature, have built up for this famous hostlery a reputation that places it at the head of all hotels upon the peninsula. The Colonel was on the staff of Governor Jackson, and thus gained his title. He has been twice married, his first wife, *nee* Kirby, dying in 1872, his second wife was Miss Helen M. Dodson, Associated with Colonel Norris at the Avon is his son, William K. Norris, who, in his father, has a very thorough teacher of what is necessary to make a first-class hotel man.

POWELL.—Judge Edward A. Powell comes of a good old stock of the Society of Friends, and looks back some generations in Talbot county ancestry. He was born in 1851, and by some mischance failed to bear the name Howell Powell that so many of his grandfathers had borne with honor before him, and a name that so often appears in the old records of the Society of Friends in Talbot county. Judge Powell is an associate Justice of the Orphans Court, and has held other important offices of trust, while he is also both farmer and merchant, having a large mercantile business in Trappe. A man of sterling character, modest in demeanor, he is also social, hospitable and charitable and well deserves the esteem of his fellow citizens.

PASCAULT.—Colonel Louis C. Pascault was the progenitor of the family of that name in America, he having come over with Lafayette and fought bravely in the war of the Revolution. Colonel Louis C. Pascault's son of the same name, was the father of Alexis A. Pascault, of Talbot, who was born in 1822, and was reared a farmer. Alexis A. was an influential citizen and held many important trusts. In 1848 he married his cousin, Miss Maria E. Goldsborough, daughter of Hon. Henry Goldsborough, of Talbot county and who is closely connected with many of the most distinguished families of the state. They have two sons, Alexis G. and Henry G., the former interested in both business and farming, the latter clerk to the Register of Wills. Alexis A. Pascault died June 22d 1898.

POISAL.—The Reverend William McKendree Poisal was born and educated in Berkeley county, West Virginia. He is the son of Sebastian J. Poisal, deceased, who was a brother of the late Rev. John Poisal, D. D. Mr. Poisal entered the ministry of the Methodist Protestant Church when but twenty years of age, joining the Maryland Conference in 1861. His first assignment to pastoral work was in Talbot county, and after three years, he was again appointed to the same charge. In that year he married Miss Laura V. Covey, daughter of the late Edward and Susan Edmonston Covey, then residing on the fine "Sherwood" property, skirting the beautiful Miles river. Some years latter Mr. Poisal retired from itinerant work and resided in St. Michaels, where for many years he published the St. Michael's *Comet*, making a most able editor, while he also was identified with other business interests in the county. In 1888 Mr. Poisal resumed active relations with his Conference and has since been pastor, in the order named, of St. Michaels, Alexandria, Virginia, Oxford and Easton, Maryland, thus showing that most of his years, since reaching his majority, have been spent in Talbot county. Mr. Poisal is a well-read man, a classical scholar and hard student, not only of theology, but of political and social life, while his views on all subjects are liberal and unprejudiced, for he does not allow himself to be controlled by narrow confines. He is a man of courteous address, a speaker of force and his influence is felt far beyond the bounds of his own church, in fact, he does a vast deal of good without ostentation, is charitable without show.

RICH.—A clergyman recently called to the Cathedral is a man with a record to be proud of, and who will, no doubt, make his mark here, as he has elsewhere. Born in Baltimore, something over fifty years ago, the Rev. Edward R. Rich is the son of Dr. Arthur Rich, Sr., a prominent physician of Cambridge and later a practitioner in Baltimore for many years. Before he was out of his teens, Mr. Rich entered the Confederate army, going South and enlisting in the First Maryland cavalry, a command that saw hard service and won great distinction fighting for the "Bonnie Blue Flag." Serving through the war with conspicuous gallentry, Mr. Rich was twice wounded, and twice taken prisoner. Mr. Rich's reminiscences of the war are many and of very great interest, and he is a good *reconteur* of the scenes through which he passed, the life he lead as a "Man in Gray" in strange contrast to that he now leads as a soldier of the Cross. But this very life in the army taught Mr. Rich to know men as they are and the better fitted him for this high calling he later entered upon as a clergyman. When the war ended Mr. Rich became a theological student, to enter the Episcopal ministry, and was first ordained in Baltimore, in St. Paul's Church, by the Right Reverend Bishop Whittingham. Going to the South, he was later ordained to the Priesthood by the Right Reverend Bishop Atkinson in St James' Church, Wilmington, North Carolina Called to Raleigh, the Church of the Good Shepherd was built under the direction of Mr. Rich, who was for twelve years its rector. The church is now the Cathedral Church of the Diocese of North Carolina. For five years Mr. Rich was a member of the Standing Committee of the Diocese. Going to Orbisonia, Pennsylvnia, Mr. Rich was for six years rector of the church there, and later called to Greensboro, Maryland, he remained there for five years, resigning his latter charge to accept a call to the Cathedral at Easton. During the pastorship of his last two charges Mr. Rich built a rectory at each place, and left both parishes free from debt. Mr. Rich was warmly welcomed to Easton, not only by his church, but also by his old Confederate comrades here, for he has already been made a member of Charles S. Winder Camp of Confederate Veterans. A man of deep learning, Mr. Rich is a fine pulpit orator and forceful speaker, while he is genial in manner and altogether a man of the people.

REISLER.—Professor Edward Reisler was born in Maryland in 1851. In his infancy his parents, Thomas J. and Margaret Reisler, removed to Frederick county, where his boyhood was spent. He was educated in the public schools, Liberty

Academy, and Western Maryland College, receiving from the last named institution the degree of Master of Arts. After teaching in the public schools of Frederick and Carroll counties three years, he reopened the old Liberty Academy, where he conducted a successful school for years. In 1880 he was appointed Principal of St. Michaels High School, in Talbot county, which position he held four years, but in 1884 he resigned his position at St. Michaels, and removed to Union Bridge, where he established a private school, known as the Union Bridge Elementary and High School. In 1886 he began the publication of the *Carroll News*, a weekly newspaper, in Union Bridge, and he made as good an editor as he had been a teacher, for the *News* was a very bright paper. During the publication of the newspaper, he was engaged also in teaching, most of the time in the high school, and for two years was a Professor in the Western Maryland College. In 1897, Mr. Reisler was appointed principal of Easton High and Manual Training School, and subsequently removed his family to Easton.

REDDIE.—The parents of William Reddie came from Kinglassie Fifeshire, Scotland, and in 1851, and settled in Talbot county, where the subject of this sketch was born in 1856. He was educated at the Trappe High School, and then became a teacher. Entering politics he was elected Sheriff of Talbot county, after which he became a farmer; was appointed Clerk of the Board of County Commissioners. Mr. Reddie was appointed by the Governor a supervisor of elections in 1896 and 1897, and is now interested in business in Easton. The oldest brother of Mr. Reddie entered the Confederate army, Company E., Second Maryland Battallian and was killed in his seventeenth year at Gettysburg. Another brother is a large manufacturer.

ROBERTS.—Captain Edward Roberts was born in Maryland in 1842, and was educated in Baltimore. He joined the first regiment at Harper's Ferry, April 1861, and was in all the engagements in which this command participated, when the First Maryland Regiment was disbanded after the seven days fight, he joined an independent Alabama command, "Kit Freeman's," and served until the end of the war and was paroled at Greensboro, North Carolina, May 1865. He was commissioned captain

by the state of Alabama, in November 1865, and aided the
authorities in establishing law and order in Tuscaloosa county.
Captain Roberts located in Easton in 1867, and engaged in con-
tracting and building, as a member of the firm of W. D. Roberts
& Sons. He was twice commissioned captain of the Maryland
National Guard, was chief of Easton Fire Department for
twenty-five years, and commissioner for a long term. He resigned from the guard service, to accept a position of United States
Inspector of Public Buildings. To this position he was appointed June 1st, 1893, by Secretary of Treasury, Hon. John G. Carlisle. Captain Roberts married Miss Cornelia P. Gannon, of
Talbot county, and they have three children, Lulu C., Edward
W. and George Richard Roberts. A man of striking appearance, Captain Roberts is a whole-souled gentleman, universally
popular in Talbot county and one whose career has been an
honored and brilliant one, deserving of the success he has
won.

SPENCER.—James S. Spencer's family settled on the farm
about half a mile from St. Michaels, now owned by Mr. John E.
Marshall, as early as 1670. James S. Spencer the second married Ann, a daughter of Dr. James Benson. He came into the
Province prior to 1674.

SHANNAHAN.—Mr. William E. Shannahan is another
Marylander with Irish ancestry that have been completely lost
in the generations of Americans from which he is descended,
for the name of Shannahan dates far back on the records of
Talbot, and those who hear it have reason to feel a pride in
their family. The subject of this sketch is one of Easton's fore-
most citizens, and a business man that is progressive in the extreme, for his handsome establishment is the largest of its kind
on the peninsula, in fact there are few such stores to be found
out of the large cities. Of this prosperous and substantial firm,
Mr. William E. Shannahan is the president. Mr. Shannahan
is fully aware of all that Easton is capable of, and he is of the
kind that builds up the business of a town, and does all he can
for its general advancement. He has a handsome home in Easton
and stands among the solid men of the town.

STEVENS.—Dr. James A. Stevens is a Talbot countian, and
he feels very sure that he has selected wisely and well in making

his home here, for he lives at Oxford, where he has a large and
lucrative practice. Born in Nova Scotia in 1852, he went as
a young man to Halifax, and then to Boston to finish the study
of medicine, and graduated at the Jefferson Medical College, of
Philadelphia. Connecting himself with a hospital, Dr. Stevens
gained much experience in surgery as well as in medicine, after
which he removed to Florida, and begun to practice there.
Having married in 1880, he moved some years later to Oxford,
Talbot county. He is a member of the Maryland Medical Association. A man of scholarly mind, of a generous nature, sympathetic in his practice, Dr. Stevens has won many friends. He
is connected with the Masonic order of Easton, is a member of
the Chesapeake Bay Yacht Club, and enjoys his leisure among
his books and men of liberal ideas on all important questions of
the day. Dr. Stevens merits the regard in which he is held by
those about him.

STEWART.—Major William Eccleston Stewart, a leading
lawyer of Easton, descended from ancestors who were among
the first settlers of Maryland. Born in 1839, he was educated
at Dickinson College and University of Virginia. He studied
law and was admitted to the bar in 1860. He moved to Arkansas and became a planter, but entered the Confederate army, was
twice captured, three times promoted, and commanded a regiment in the terrible siege of Port Hudson, where he greatly
distinguished himself. Having lost his Arkansas property, he
begun the practice of law in Baltimore and soon after was sent
to the legislature. He moved to Easton in 1876, having married
in 1872 Miss Margaret Douglass Wallack, of Washington,
D. C. Major Stewart has been District Attorney for Talbot
county, and is known as a fine lawyer and a telling speaker
throughout the state. He is a democrat of "purest ray" and is
as devoted to politics as he is to his profession.

SEWALL.—The Hon. Henry Sewall emigrated from England
to St. Mary's county, Maryland, in 1660. He settled near the
mouth of the Patuxent, on land originally the dwelling place
of the Mattapanient Indians. He was a Privy Councillor, and
his mansion during Lord Charles Baltimore's rule was the
government house of the Province. His wife was Jane Lowe,
who after his death married Lord Charles Baltimore. Bene-

dict, the son of the fifth baron was the father of Nelly, who married Mr. Custis. Major Nicholas Sewall was deputy Governor in 1689. He married Susannah, daughter of Hon. William Burgess, who was also a deputy Governor, a Justice of the High Provincial Court, and Privy Councillor. Secretary creek, on Choptank river, was named after Secretary Sewall. A member of the family is Arthur Sewell, the recent nominee for Vice-President of the United States, for the Sewalls and Sewells are of the same stock. The Sewells came to Talbot in 1709, with the Ralle's family. Mark Sewell, of Talbot county, died in 1724, leaving three sons and three daughters. A little later, Tuesday July 12th, 1757, in St. Michaels Parish records, we see that Clement Sewell is taxed three hundred pounds of tobacco for being a bachelor, and still later, January 1st, 1780, Mark Sewell and Basil Sewell were contributors to that church. In 1768 a member of the Ralle's family came on from England and rode from Philadelphia to Ralle Range, near St. Michaels, on horseback. Riding up to the northeast window, he stepped in and handed a copy of the English registry to Mr. Ralle, and in it he pointed out the English branches of the Ralle and Sewell families, and they are underscored with a pen. This old book is still in the possession of the family, and the underscored names are Denny Ralle, of the House of Commons, and Sir Thomas Sewell, Knight, Privy Councillor and Master of the Rolls of England and also representative for Winchelsea in 1768. On November 2d, 1773, Mark Sewell bought from Richard Mansfield the Third, the farm near St. Michaels, called "Belfast," and he, his wife and children moved there. He was in 1777 during the Revolutionary war a member of the Broad Creek Company, Thirty-eighth Battalion, and his sword is still in the possession of one of his descendants. His son James Sewell married Elizabeth Mason. He was in command of pickets at Ashcroft Point when the British attacked St. Michaels, August 10th, 1813. He fired the first shot, thus attracting the attention of the men in the fort at Parrott's Point. His son Jeremiah Sewell married Harriett Matilda Porter, and they were the parents of William E., Charles W., Thomas H., Mary A., Walter M., and Lewis. Thomas Henry Sewell is at present in the stationery and printing business in St. Michaels. He is president of the Epworth League, a trustee of the Metho-

RESIDENCE OF LEANDER R. HOOPER, EASTON.

MANSION HOUSE ON "ALLONBY" ESTATE.

dist Episcopal Church and a director of the St. Michaels Savings Bank. Historical articles written by him have been placed on file by the Maryland Historical Society, and he is one of the progressive and prominent citizens of the fine old town of St. Michaels.

THOMPSON.—Captain Hedge Thompson has a double title, for he is also entitled to the rank of Commodore, as he holds that position in the Cheaspeake Bay Yacht Club. He was for years in command of the oyster navy, and is a devoted yachts-man, a farmer as well, owning the handsome estate of "The Forrest," in Longwoods, Talbot county. His estate comprises over seven hundred acres, the residence is an old-fashioned homestead where the latch string always hangs on the outside. Born in 1834 of English ancestry, the grandfather of Commo-dore Thompson was an officer in the Continental army, so he justly claims to be an American of a number of generations. After receiving his education, he entered upon a mercantile life; but when he had prospered sufficiently to have a goodly bank account, he invested it in the home he now occupies, a model farm of Talbot. A genial gentleman, fond of the pleas-ures of life, Commodore Thompson is a man who is progressive, liberal and follows the golden rule about as closely as it is pos-sible to do, and of this all who fully know him are aware.

TURNER.—Hon. J. Frank Turner is a man whose energy and ability none will doubt, while he is also one of courage and indomitable will to successfully accomplish all that he under-takes. Mr. Turner is as well a man of ambitions, and where he has met with defeat he accepts it with a resignation that is most praiseworthy. Born in Talbot county in 1844, his father dying when he was an infant, while his mother, a Miss Mary Clark, also passed away before her son had entered his teens. Work-ing on the farm, Mr. Turner also attended the county school until he was eighteen, when he entered the office of Register of Wills, in which he soon made his ability felt. Later he was appointed recorder in the office of the Clerk of Court, and thus entered upon a political career, he being a "dyed-in-the-wool" democrat. In 1867 he was made chief clerk and deputy. In 1873 he was elected Clerk of the Court of Talbot. Mr. Turner has since held other important offices and made a record for himself. He is a man of genial address, popular with those who differ with him in politics, a forceful speaker and a most able general in a political campaign. In 1871, Mr. Turner married Miss Sallie Powell Hopkins, of Talbot county. He lives near Easton and has a most comfortable home.

TULL.—Hon. Levin H. Tull, of Oxford, was born in Talbot county, and with the waters of the Chesapeake before his gaze, he was not long in entering upon the life of a sailor. From sailing the Chesapeake and its tributaries as a boy and young man, Captain Tull entered upon the broader field of marine experience of a "life on the ocean wave," becoming a mate on board of a foreign bound vessel, later, as captain, visiting many lands and meeting with wondrous adventures afloat and ashore. Captain Tull has known what it is to be shipwrecked, and yet he followed the sea until he was nearing the half century mark in years. Then he entered upon a successful career as a boat builder, and modeled and constructed the fleet buckeye yacht "Flossie," which has carried off the honors in many races in northern waters. Though not having had the advantage of a college education, Captain Tull is yet a man of general learning, a great reader and considerable of a philosopher. He lives at Oxford, within a few feet of the Avon, and has a flower garden which he cares for with almost pathetic devotion, for he loves flowers and plants as though they were human beings. Captain Tull is well informed upon the political and economic affairs of the country, believes that the sun rises and sets in Talbot county, and his wanderings have given him the opportunity for comparisons. A republican in politics, he has served in the Maryland Legislature, representing Talbot county.

THOMPSON.—Few men have had a record through a long life that stands without reproach, and yet Walter H. Thompson is one upon whose escutcheon probity, honorable dealing and a temperate career are brightly engraven. He was born away back in 1823, and yet today carries his many years like a school boy, while his genial nature renders him a favorite with all. His father came from Dublin while in his teens, so grew up with the country of his adoption and prospered, married and died, leaving a wife and children, the subject of this sketch being one. After completing his education, Walter

H. Thompson entered upon a business career in Easton as a merchant. Since that time he has been intimately connected with the business affairs of Easton, and is really an essential member of the community, respected by all who know his sterling worth of character. He is an officer of a number of Easton's best enterprises, the Building and Loan, Maryland Improvement Company, Avon Hotel Company, Spring Hill Cemetery Association and others. A benevolent man, a Mason, and Odd Fellow, a leader in the Methodist Church, and is recognized as one of Easton's most influential citizens.

THOMAS.—General Richard Thomas is enjoying the twilight of his life honored by all who know him, and his long career as one of Easton's prominent citizens has won for him the confidence of the community. General Thomas is one of the few remaining links that connect the far bygone with present, for he was born in 1815, and has a long vista of years to look back over, being nearly four score and ten. He was born in Wye Neck, where two of his paternal grandfathers were also born, his grandfather having been an officer in the continental army, while his father served in the war of 1812. Educated in private schools and the Centerville academy, he entered upon a mercantile life in Easton, and having married in 1837, he was appointed a book-keeper in the now Easton National Bank in 1846, and in 1849 was made cashier, a position he has held ever since. During the administration of Governor P. F. Thomas, of Maryland, General Thomas was appointed Colonel of the Fourth Maryland Regiment, and later Governor Hicks made him a Brigadier General. From first to last he has been one of Easton's most progressive citizens, and he has well earned the high regard in which he is held today.

THARP.—Among the many bright lawyers of the Talbot bar, may be mentioned Mr. Alfred L. Tharp, a gentleman and a scholar. Mr. Tharp may be said to have many claims to Americanism, for his family dates its coming to America in 1662, settling in Delaware, in which state those of his name have risen to distinction, his uncle, William Tharp, having been thrice Governor of Delaware, a position also held by another kinsman of the subject of this sketch. Mr. Tharp's claim upon Talbot county is a double one, he having been born in Easton in May,

1855, in the same home in which he now dwells, and married
here in 1337, his wife, *nee* Emily Goldsborough, being a native
of the county, and a daughter of James N. Goldsborough, of
"Woodstock." Educated at the Easton public schools, Mr.
Tharp later went to St. John's College, Annapolis, graduating
in the class of 1874. He also read law at St. John's, continuing
its study upon his return home and was admitted to the bar in
1879. Nominated as State's Attorney by his party, the Republican, he was defeated by a few votes. He is examiner in
chancery, and holds several other offices of trust. A member of
the Chesapeake Bay Yacht Club, Mr. Tharp is genial, hospitable and has many friends.

TILGHMAN.—Colonel Oswald Tilghman, the son of General
Tench Tilghman, has also become a prominent citizen of Talbot
county. He entered the Confederate army in 1861, and made
a gallant record as a commander of a battery in the memorable
siege of Port Hudson, and was the only officer in his battery of
four who survived this siege. His battery in March, 1863, destroyed the steam frigate Mississippi. of which Admiral Dewey
was then the executive officer. Col. Tilghman was for a long
time a prisoner at Johnson's Island, Ohio. Col. Tilghman was
also an officer on the staff of his kinsman, General Lloyd Tilghman, of whom a short sketch is given, he having been also a
Talbot county man. Having been exchanged, Colonel Tilghman
again served the south in the field, and at the close of the war
returned to his home in Talbot. Some years ago, Colonel Tilghman married Miss Belle Harrison, daughter of the late Dr. Samuel Harrison, a wealthy and distinguished citizen of Talbot
county, a prominent physician and a man of letters, for as a lit-
terateur, Dr. Harrison was also well known. The residence of
Colonel Tilghman is the fine old home of "Foxley Hall" in Easton, and a place with a history, one reminiscence being that the
Charles Dickinson who was killed in his celebrated duel with
Andrew Jackson was born in this mansion. To the Harrison
estate also belongs the old home of "Wenlock Christison the
Quaker," and the most famous Friend of his times, save Fox
and Penn. Colonel Tilghman is a prominent member of the
Cincinnati and other Revolutionary organizations. He is well
known beyond his state lines ; has held prominent positions, and

his record in the Senate of Maryland was as creditable as was
his record when a Confederate soldier. Socially inclined, his
home is a most hospitable one, and his influence has been felt
and shown in many ways toward building up Talbot, and Easton, for it was due to his efforts that the State Bureau of Immi-
gration was established in 1886, and he has brought to the
county many influential and worthy people.

TRIPPE.—For a Talbot countian not to know Dr. Edward R.
Trippe, of Easton, would be to write himself down unknown,
for far and wide his fame has spread, not only as a physician and
surgeon, but as a gentleman to the manner born. Dr. "Ed," as
his particular friends call him, is as fond of a fine horse as he
is of his gun, and of the latter as he is of a yacht, and that is
saying a great deal. He is an enthusiastic yachtsman, and
dearly loves a tramp after game, large and small, while there is
no better shot in this county than he is, with shot gun, rifle or
revolver. Believing in the motto, "Dum vivimus vivamus,"
Dr. Trippe enjoys life in spite of his very extensive practice and
loves to have those about him do the same. He is hospitable, liberal and fond of playing the host to his many friends, a
pleasure in which his wife is ever glad to share, for their home
is ever open to extend a warm welcome. Born in 1840, in an
old mansion that has upon it the date 1760, Dr. Trippe traces
his ancestry to England in the time of King Henry V., as the
name was then changed from Howard to Trippe. The
family settled in Maryland in 1663, Captain Henry Trippe
having been the progenitor. Trippe's Creek, a branch of the
Avon, is named after the family. The family of Trippes may
be said to be noted for the many distinguished men it has produced. The boyhood of Dr. Trippe was passed upon the old
homestead farm, and he was given a good education, graduating at Bushington College. In 1862 he graduated in medicine
from the Maryland University, and begun his practice in Talbot
county, and his skill and devotion to his calling have brought
him to the head of his profession. Dr. Trippe is a prominent
Mason, and an enthusiast on Masonry. He is Rear Commodore
of the Chesapeake Bay Yacht Club, a member of many fraterni-
ties, of a generous, sympathetic nature and one who is glad to
say that he is still a student in medicine, and cannot learn too
much of his profession. In 1864 Dr. Trippe married Miss

Melusina E. Swartze, of Maryland, and a lady in every way fitted to be the mistress of a charming home circle.

WAGGAMAN.—The Waggaman family figured conspicuously in the history of the Eastern Shore of Maryland more than one hundred and fifty years ago. We read in the records of the court that Captain Ephraim Waggaman was commissioned as Sheriff of Worcester county in 1752. His brother, Captain Henry Waggaman, was elected as delegate from Somerset county for four successive terms   In fact from 1752 to 1794 members of the family represented the counties of Worcester, Dorchester and Somerset, Mr. Henry Waggaman having been appointed as one of the delegates from the state of Maryland to accept the Constitution of the United States. The Waggamans intermarried with the families of Woolford and Ennalls, and the old home at Monie still stands and is now used as the county almshouse. The family subsequently removed to Fairview in the vicinity of Cambridge. The sons of Henry Waggaman were George A. Waggaman, who settled in Louisiana and after filling various high positions in the state of his adoption was elected to the United States Senate in 1831; Dr. Henry Waggaman, of Dorchester county, and Thomas Ennalls Waggaman, who married Martha Jefferson Tyler, a sister of the President. Of the three sons of this marriage Major George G. Waggaman, of the United States army, and Purser Floyd Waggaman died without issue. John H. Waggaman the elder lived to an advanced age in Washington, of which his four sons are now residents.   Mr. Thomas E. Waggaman is widely known as a capitalist, a patron of art and a public spirited and benevolent citizen.   Dr. Samuel Waggaman after serving with Mosby's Rangers devoted himself to the healing art in its various branches and is one of the founders of the National College of Pharmacy. Mr. Henry Pierpont Waggaman is extensively interested in the development of the most beautiful suburban districts around the Capital. John Floyd Waggaman, besides his wide business interests in Washington and other cities, has invested largely in the Eastern Shore of Maryland. Though the owner of a beautiful home in the Capital, where he and his charming wife dispense princely hospitality, he purchased some years ago a portion of the old Duvall property on South River, near Annapolis, and erected a shooting lodge which is the scene of many festive gatherings. He is also the chief property holder of Ocean City, Maryland, which owes its great development of late years almost principally to his energy and liberality. The wizard wand of wealth and enterprise has transformed the once sleepy stretch of "Sinepuxent Beach" into a fashionable resort, alive with modern activities. Crowded hotels, cafes and beautiful Queen Anne cottages line the wave-washed shores, while its increasing tide of summer visitors attests the far-seeing judgment which first recognized its restful and health-giving charm that makes Ocean City an idyllic spot for a midsummer holiday.

WRIGHTSON.—Hon. Frank G. Wrightson was a prominent citizen of Bay Hundred until his election to the important office of Clerk of Court of Talbot county brought him to Easton to live. He represented Talbot county for one term in the House of Delegates, and has been an acknowledged leader in the Democratic party of the state, and has held important positions of trust and influence. The family of Mr. Wrightson is a very old one, going back in Maryland two hundred and fifty years, and his paternal ancestors have been men of distinction. His father, William L. Wrightson, was born on Clay Neck farm in 1813, died only a short time ago, revered by all who knew him. He was noted as a man of remarkable memory, and was called the "Historian of Talbot" from the fact that he knew the county's history so well. Frank G. Wrightson was born in 1850, was brought up on his father's farm, educated at home and at Calvert College, and then became a devoted agriculturist, connecting himself with the lumber business in Virginia. In 1877 Mr. Wrightson married Miss Annie R. Dawson, and they have a handsome home and a charming family circle in Easton. A man of courteous address, Mr. Wrightson enjoys great popularity, is a member of the Chesapeake Bay Yacht Club ; tells a story, and a good one, too, with the wit and mannerism of a veritable of Mark Twain ; is on the Democratic side of the political fence, and believes in the motto "While we journey through life let us live by the way." Mr. Wrightson has as his assistants in his office Mr. Henry Hollyday, Jr., deputy clerk, and Mr. William Wilson, both gentlemen in every way fitted for the important positions they hold and who know the old records as well as the new.

WILLIS.—Hon James H. Willis is a native of Talbot county, as were his father and grandfather before him, the former, Philemon Willis, having been Sheriff of the county in the first years of the present century. The father of Mr. James Willis married in 1839 Miss Mary Stewart, whose father, James Stewart, owned at that time nearly half the town of Oxford, and Mr. Willis says he can remember when it was cultivated in wheat and corn. Though Oxford was a most important and thriving seaport with large foreign trade over two hundred years ago, Mr. Willis recollects when it was almost a deserted village, half a century ago, with only eleven houses in it. Born in Oxford Neck in 1840, Mr. Willis was educated in the county schools and the Oxford Military Academy, became a teacher, then a farmer and soon after married Miss Virginia Harris, descendant of a Delaware family of Revolutionary fame. Mr. Willis has been twice married, his present wife having been a Miss Parsons, of Salisbury. For many years Mr. Willis has held great political influence in his state, and he has done much for the advancement and building up of Oxford and the surrounding country. His Southern sentiments got him into trouble and the jail during the civil war, a remembrance he recalls by no means unpleasantly, as he very narrowly missed wearing the Confederate gray as a soldier of Dixie. A genial gentleman, hospitable and progressive, Mr. Willis is today one of Talbot's staunch citizens, one ever ready to lend a hand for the good of the county and its people.

HARDCASTLE.—Aaron Bascom Hardcastle was born in Denton, Caroline county, Maryland, in 1836. After the death of his father in 1843, he lived with an uncle in St. Louis, where he was a pupil at the University of St. Louis. He was then sent to school at Alexandria, Va., to Benjamin Hallowell, by his brother, General E. L. F. Hardcastle, then living in Washington, who obtained for him an appointment from President Pierce as Lieutenant of Company B, Sixth United States Infantry. This company was then stationed at Fort Laramie in Wyoming, and there Lieutenant Hardcastle reported for duty, and received his first military training. His regiment was ordered to Salt Lake to take part in the exposition, thence proceeding to California, where it was stationed at Humbolt Bay. Promoted to

First Lieutenancy, he was ordered to Fort Yuma, thence to San Diego, where he was in command of the fort, until the return of Major Lewis Armistead, then captain of the company. When the civil war broke out, he with Major Armistead resigned his commission in the United States Army, and joining General Albert Sidney Johnston, who had also resigned, he came overland on horseback to Texas via El Paso and San Antonio. Reporting at Richmond, was commissioned as First Lieutenant in the Confederate States army and was ordered to report to General A. S. Johnston at Columbus, Ky. He was assigned to duty as mustering officer, reporting to Governor Harris of Tennessee. After mustering in a brigade of Tennessee troops, he proceeded to Mississippi on the same duty. Was then commissioned as Major of the Third Mississippi Battalion. He organized into a battalion of seven companies at Jackson, Mississippi. The legislature of Mississippi passed a special appropriation for their equipment. They reported for duty at Bowling Green, Kentucky, where General Johnston had command of the army. He engaged in the battle of Shiloh, after which he was placed in command of a regiment, his battalion being increased by addition of three companies from the Seventh Alabama. He commanded Marmaduke's brigade for a short time in front of Corinth, Mississippi. On the route to Kentucky he was disabled by having his right leg badly fractured by a kick from a horse while in camp. When on crutches he served as commandant of different posts, in Tennessee, Georgia and Mississippi. He returned to his regiment at Missionary Ridge and was in that battle and on the retreats to Atlanta under General Joe Johnston. He was then taken sick and when convalescent was ordered to command at Tuscaloosa, Alabama. He had for a command as garrison a corps of cadets at the Military University of Alabama and three companies of state troops and convalescents. They were attacked after midnight by a brigade under command of Gen. Croxton en route to Selma. He was captured while leading his line of battle to defend the bridge which was guarded by state companies who had all been surrounded without their knowledge in the darkness of the night. He was paroled through the persistence of his wife's colored maid Margaret, who saw General Croxton in his behalf the next day. Selma was then occupied by the Federals, and finally came the announcement of the surrender at Appomattox. He married Miss Hatch of Mississippi and lived in Aberdeen until 1876, then came back to Maryland, bringing his family. They lived at Sherwood's Mill, Talbot county, about ten years. He moved to Trappe in 1886, having lived near Easton since 1892. He entered the Easton National Bank in 1889, where he is now employed as personal book-keeper.

HUGHES.—Jesse Hughes was born in Vienna, Dorchester county, Maryland. His father was Captain Levi Hughes, who followed the water and owned packets for freighting grain, &c. His mother was Theresa Elliott, of Kent Island. Jesse Hughes was left an orphan at seven years of age, without means of support, his father having met with reverses. At this age he was apprenticed to William Wilcox, of Baltimore, to learn shoemaking. Soon after arriving at his majority he entered into partnership with Columbus Elliott and carried on quite a large business in Easton. Differing in politics, the firm disolved shortly after the war began. Jesse Hughes continued business on his own account, working ten or a dozen journeymen as well as carrying a large stock of ready made boots and shoes. He was appointed Justice of the Peace by Governor Henry Lloyd and held the office at the time of his death, December 29th, 1892, in the sixty-ninth year of his age. With the exception of two or three years in the eighties, spent in Salisbury, his entire business life was spent in Easton. He left a widow, who was Miss Georgeanna Councell, three sons and one daughter, Miss Georgie Belle Hughes. Charles H. Hughes, son of Jesse Hughes, was educated at the schools in Easton. Spent eighteen months in Dawson & Brother's drug store. Appointed runner in the Easton National Bank of Maryland, February 23d, 1870, now holding position of teller in the same bank. Married Oct. 8th, 1885, Mary Etta Boyd Burnett, daughter of Samuel and Sarah Reese Burnett, of Baltimore. Albert A. Hughes, son of Jesse Hughes, was educated at the schools in Easton. Learned the carpentering business with M. P. Flowers, afterwards formed a partnership with W. H. Withgott and opened shops for repairing of machinery, &c. He is now in the employ of the Gas and Electric Light Company. Walter C. Hughes, son of Jesse Hughes, was educated at the schools in Easton, entered the drug store of R. J. Trippe, afterwards succeding him in business, and is thus engaged at the present time.

HENRY.—John Campbell Henry was born December 20th, 1844, at Vienna, Dorchester county, and came to Easton in 1862 and engaged with Levin H. Campbell as a drug clerk. His father, Dr. J. W. Henry, practiced medicine in Vienna. In 1869 Mr. Henry went into partnership with Mr. Campbell, under the firm name of Campbell & Henry, and at Mr. Campbell's death Mr. Henry took the late Dr. Henry T. Goldsborough into partnership with him. At Dr. Goldsborough's death Mr. Henry associated with him his brother, Charles S. Henry, and the partnership continued up to 1893, and in 1896 he sold his drug business to Dr. T. A. Councell. When Alexis A. Pascault's term as Town Commissioner expired in 1887, Mr. Henry was elected to succeed him, and has since been reelected three times. By reason of his long service he was elected president of the board some years ago, to succeed Col. Edward Roberts, who resigned to accept the position of Building Inspector. Mr. Henry is descended from a long line of illustrious ancestors. His great-grandfather was John Henry, who was Colonial Governor of Maryland in 1797 and was afterwards United States Senator. The honorable Daniel M. Henry, of Cambridge, who represented the First District in Congress, is his uncle, and the late I. Nevitt Steele, of Baltimore, was his great-uncle. The Hon. Winder Laird Henry, of Cambridge, ex-Congressman, is his cousin. Mr. Henry married in 1879 the daughter of the late Colonel Thomas Hughlett. They have one child, a son Hugh-lett.

VIEWS AT ATLANTIC HOTEL, OCEAN CITY.

INDEX.

INDEX

A CITY BY THE SEA.

LTHOUGH in the main a story of Talbot on the Eastern Shore, I may be pardoned for having been tempted to dwell upon other localities of this beautiful land, and thus need offer no excuse for venturing upon our attractive Atlantic shore within easy ride by rail of Easton, and becoming so well known now as a resort in Maryland that can boast of the finest ocean beach from Maine to Florida. I refer to Ocean City, Maryland, than which no beach is more delightfully or conveniently situated especially for the citizens of Richmond, Washington, Baltimore, Wilmington and Philadelphia, not to speak of the towns and villages of the Eastern Shore, of which it can almost be claimed to be a suburb.

A visit to Ocean City adds a year to one's life for every month passed there. Its breezes are balmy, yet invigorating, its climate perfect and its situation all that could be desired, for with the Atlantic before it, it has Sinepuxent Bay behind it, and lies on a narrow strip of land, averaging a thousand feet in width and several miles in length. It is located just as Seabright and Moumouth Beach, N. J., are, only it has finer natural advantages for man to build upon. Sinepuxent Bay is fifty miles in length, from half a mile to several miles in width, and is not very deep, while the Government having cut an inlet through near the Delaware State line, it has a steady flow tide from the ocean. For still water salt bathing, boating and yachting it is unsurpassed. The fishing is excellent, crabs, perch, blue, rock and many other varieties of fish abound in the waters, with the ocean in front for deep water fishing.

Those who visit Ocean City wonder how it is that the beach is not swept over by the Atlantic in its fury, but the solution is

plain when understood. Off the beach a mile or more is a
long and shallow bar, averaging from six to a dozen feet in depth,
and beyond this still further is another bar, and these serve as
a breakwater to the huge and violent inrolling seas of the Atlantic. By them their force and fury is broken, so that when the
surf reaches the beach, even in a storm, it has lost seven-tenths
of its power, and thus Ocean City is safe, where Cape May,
Atlantic City, Asbury Park, Ocean Grove, Long Branch, Seabright, Rockaway, Coney Island and other ocean beaches get
the full force in a high tide and tempest, and ruin and immense
pecuniary damage results to them. Off Ocean City the Gulf
Stream flows nearer to the coast than elsewhere above Cape
Hatteras, and this tempers the water, making the bathing all
that could be desired. The water in use at Ocean City is from
deep artesian wells and hence the very best.

As to the beach proper of Ocean City, it is an ideal one.
There is something in the quality of the sand that has gained
for it the name of "Velvet Beach," and from no less a personage than the late Bayard Taylor, who had seen the beaches of
the world, and gave the palm to this one. The slope is gradual,
giving ample space for timid bathers, and it is a most safe and
delightful bathing beach.

Of the improvements at Ocean City a great deal can be said.
There are many private cottages spread out along the beach for
about a mile and a-half, interspersed with large, well equipped
hotels. The side streets--those running from the sea to the bay
—are also well built up with cottages and family hotels. The
boardwalk is lighted at night with electricity and lined with
rustic seats and benches, and the hotels and cottages, with their
music and gaiety, make it an ideal promenade.

Of the larger hotels the Atlantic takes the palm, and justly,
too. It is equipped with all that a modern hotel should be, and
its service and cuisine are of that character which has done
much to make old Maryland famous. It has, in conjunction
with its large, three-storied piazza, a dancing pavilion and an
auditorium hall, where most of the State and district political
conventions and other meetings are held.

Mr. John F. Waggaman, one of Washington City's popular,
well-known and progressive men—and it takes a progressive
man to make a mark in the United States Capital--is the back-
bone of Ocean City, and realizing all that it can be made, is de-

termined to bring it to the front, sparing neither money, time nor trouble. The plans are drawn for Ocean City's future, and Mr. Waggaman has interested with him men who appreciate that this Maryland beach is destined to be the seaside Mecca of hundreds of thousands. An iron pier is projected and also a trolley line to run the entire length of the beach.

To reach Ocean City from Baltimore, Washington and the South and the Southwest, one must go via the Baltimore, Chesapeake and Atlantic Railway. This road is under a good management, ready and willing to do all that can be done for the interests and quick transportation of its patrons. It has a steamboat leaving Baltimore twice a day during the summer to connect with trains at Claiborne, in far-famed and beautiful Talbot County, and thence passes through the pretty villages of St. Michaels and Royal Oak, the flourishing city of Easton, the very centre of Maryland's old-time wealth, old families and refinement, with its wonderful historic associations, and on across the Choptank into other counties of the Peninsula, and finally across the Sinepuxent Bay, dotted with numerous sailing yachts, canoes, etc., into Ocean City.

Many eminent men have expressed themselves as more than delighted with the place, among them Rear Admiral Jouett, who said: "Ocean City has the finest beach on the Atlantic seaboard and the best air in the world."

Dr. C. W. Chancellor, of Baltimore, said : "Too much cannot be said in praise of the beach. The State Board of Health reports that the Eastern Shore of Maryland is the healthiest portion of the Atlantic coast from Maine to Florida."

Alexander Grant, United States General Postoffice, thinks that, without any of the objectionable features which detract from many of the larger resorts, it affords all the facilities and attractions sought for.

Hon. J. C. Clements, Inter-State Commerce Commission: "We have found the place beautiful and particularly beneficial to children. The bathing is delightful."

Hon. J. H. Bromwell, of Ohio, speaks this high praise: "Has a fine surf, and a beautiful bay for fishing and boating."

Hon. J. C. S. Blackburn, former United States Senator from Kentucky: "I am in love with the place."

Beriah Wilkins, Washington *Post:* "Have visited every beach on the Atlantic coast, but none can compare with it."

A Landmark,

JOHN E. MULLAN,   HENRY F. RIEGER.

We Carry the Largest Stock Of Marble and Granite Monuments and Tombstones in City.

A view of our Yards situated at 505, 507, 509 North Paca Street, Baltimore, Md.

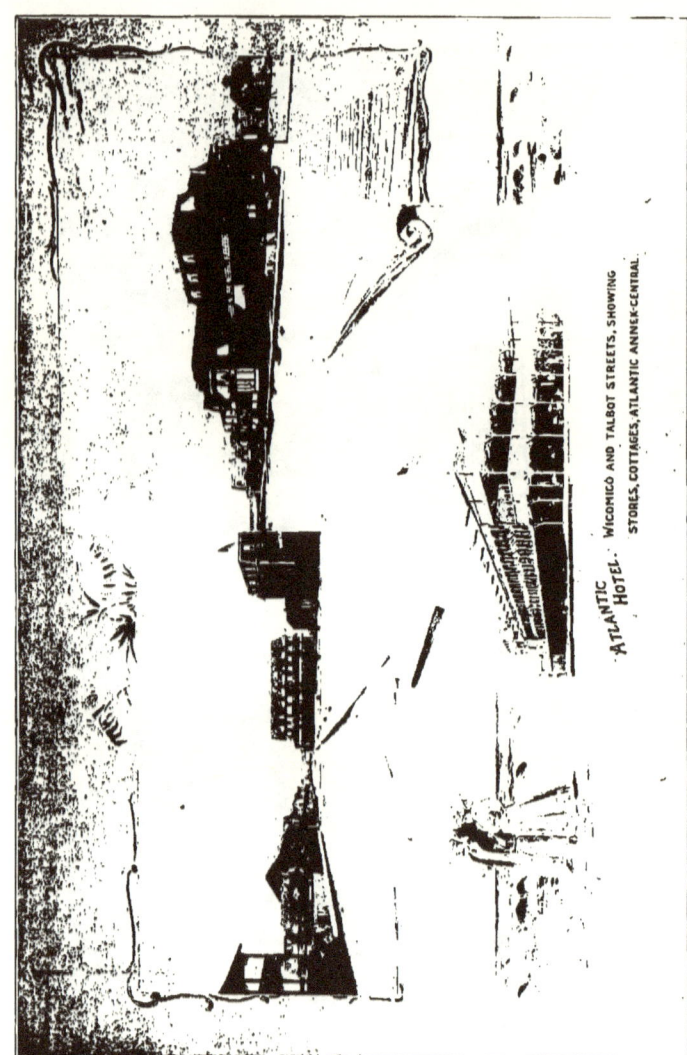

ATLANTIC HOTEL. WICOMICO AND TALBOT STREETS, SHOWING
STORES, COTTAGES, ATLANTIC ANNEX-CENTRAL.

VIEWS AT OCEAN CITY, MARYLAND.

Guarantee Building

and Loan Association,

# of Baltimore, Md.   9 St. Paul Street.

Offers Definite Contracts.
Limited Payments.
Guaranteed Settlements.
Guaranteed Dividends.
Purely Mutual.   ...   Stock Self-Sustaining.
Assured Fixed Income.   No Fines.
No Admission Fee.   No Withdrawal Fees.
No Extra Assessments.
All Officers and Employes
    Handling Funds Bonded in
Guarantee Companies.

Absolutely Safe and Equitable.
All Contracts Guaranteed.   Its Strength is
Absolutely Incontestable.

A PERFECT INVESTMENT

In the Full Paid certificates of the Guarantee Building and Load Association of Baltimore City, Md., investors find one of the highest class investments that has ever been placed before the public. An investment that combines the cardinal principles of safety, convenience and profit ; an investment that has stood the test of time, and stands to-day exactly where it stood in the begining. An investment that proved to be an investment when ninety per cent of other so called investments were transformed into whirlpools of loss and destruction.